BEYOND
THE GREAT WATER

The Story of John Jacob Astor's Determination to Defeat British Fur Trade Interests in the Untamed Wilderness of the Pacific Coast

BY FREDERICK KURI

Copyright ©2014 by Frederick Kuri

Cover Design by Davies Associates, Inc.
Interior Design by Pamela Morrell

ISBN: 978-0-9862641-0-8

All rights reserved. No part of this book may be reproduced in any form or by any electronic or mechanical means without permission, in writing, from Dragon Tree Books.

Published by

1620 SW 5th Avenue
Pompano Beach, Florida 33060
(954)788-4775
editors@editingforauthors.com
dragontreebooks.com

To a proud heritage of lasting memory

NINA MARIA GANAHL and JOHN NORCOM CARSON
EUPHROSYNE HENAINE and ES-HIYAH KURI

FARLEY MARKS O'BRIEN
man of letters
liberal, humane
bearer of the torch

and

AN INHABITED WILDERNESS THAT IS NO MORE
PEOPLE OF COURAGE WHO HAD THEIR DAY

"...whosoever commands the trade of the world commands the riches of the world, and consequently the world itself."

—*Sir Walter Raleigh*

Contents

Acknowledgments ix
Historical Note xi
Author's Note xvii

Prologue 1

Part I: New York City, 1810 43

Part II: The *Tonquin* 97

Part III: Fort Astoria 159

Epilogue 301

ACKNOWLEDGMENTS

To have delved over many years into rich repositories of rare books and manuscripts is an uncommon privilege. Extensive collections on their own, however, might be confusing at best and overwhelming but for the efforts and expertise of librarians and the fine, selfless work of unfailingly dedicated and helpful staffs—the backbone of their institutions. To both go my unending admiration and gratitude.

I wish here to record special recognition to:

Huntington Library
San Marino, California

Baker Library
Harvard University
Cambridge, Massachusetts

Bancroft Library
University Of California
Berkeley, California

without access to whose holdings this dramatic probe of history could not have been realized.

And with particular regard for the memory of Josette Bryson who, with energy and appreciation, translated dialogue into French.

Historical Note

At the close of the Revolutionary War, with the final evacuation of the British Army from New York on November 25, 1783, territorial authority of the thirteen colonies extended west to the Mississippi River, north to the Great Lakes, the precise boundary with British Canada to be determined at a later date, and to the south as far as the Spanish territories of East and West Florida, which included portions of today's states of Alabama, Mississippi, Louisiana, and all of Florida.

> *The Indian tribes residing within the limits of the U.S. have for a considerable time been growing more & more uneasy at the constant diminution of the territory they occupy, altho' effected by their own voluntary sales: and the policy has long been gaining strength with them of refusing absolutely all further sale on any conditions....In order peaceably to counteract this policy of theirs, and to provide an extension of territory which the rapid increase of our numbers will call for, two measures are deemed expedient. First, to encourage them to abandon hunting, to apply to the raising of stock, to agriculture...and thereby prove to themselves that less land & labour will maintain them in this, better than in their former mode of living. The extensive forests necessary in the hunting life, will then become useless....Secondly to multiply trading houses among them, & place within their reach those things which will contribute more to their domestic comfort than the possession of extensive, but uncultivated wilds. Experience & reflection will develop to them the wisdom of exchanging what they can spare & we want, for what we can spare and they want. In leading them thus to agriculture...& civilization, in bringing together their & our settlements, & in preparing them ultimately to participate*

in the benefits of our government, I trust and believe we are acting for their greatest good....

—*THOMAS JEFFERSON*
Confidential Message to Congress
18 January 1803

In the 1762 Treaty of Fontainebleau, concluded secretly, France ceded the Isle of Orleans and the vast and undeveloped land west of the Mississippi River ("Louisiana") to Spain. This was accomplished for two reasons: to compensate Spain for the expected loss of the Floridas (Spain had sided with France against Great Britain in the French and Indian War which France was now losing) and, in their unending rivalry, France was determined to prevent future British acquisition of the land west of the Mississippi. The following year the Treaty of Paris, signed by Great Britain, France and Spain, formally ending the French and Indian War, also ended French control over Canada and its territory and settlements east of the Mississippi River. France was effectively expelled from the continent of North America. As anticipated, Spain ceded East and West Florida to Great Britain while the government of New Orleans and Louisiana west of the Mississippi River remained in Spanish hands. By the Treaty of Paris of September 3, 1783, Great Britain formally acknowledged the independence of the United States and returned the Floridas to Spain.

Years later, when Napoleon found himself in desperate need of cash to support his ongoing European wars, the unexplored lands draining the Missouri and Mississippi rivers were ceded back to France by the Spanish Government in order to be transferred to the fledgling United States in exchange for a cash payment.

Early in 1803, while negotiations proceeded for ownership of the territory, Congress, in response to a private message from President Jefferson, gave sanction to exploring the interior of the continent of North America (still garrisoned by the Spanish) bordering on the Missouri and Columbia rivers. The object was to extend the flagging commerce of the United States. Meriwether Lewis, President Jefferson's private secretary, was commissioned Captain of the 1st Regiment of Infantry to lead what was estimated would be a two-year expedition.

The commerce which may be carried on with the people inhabiting the line you will pursue, renders a knolege of those people important. You will therefore endeavor to make yourself acquainted...with the names of the nations & their numbers; the extent & limits of their possessions; their relations with other tribes of nations; their language, traditions, monuments; their ordinary occupations in agriculture, fishing, hunting, war, arts & the implements for these; their food, clothing and domestic accomodations; the diseases prevalent among them, & the remedies they use; moral & physical circumstances which distinguish them from the tribes we know; peculiarities in their laws, customs & dispositions; and articles of commerce they may need or furnish, & to what extent....

In all your intercourse with the natives, treat them in the most friendly & conciliatory manner which their own conduct will admit; allay all jealousies as to the object of your journey, satisfy them of it's innocence, make them acquainted with the position, extent, character, peaceable & commercial dispositions of the U.S., of our wish to be neighborly, friendly & useful to them, & of our dispositions to a commercial intercourse with them; confer with them on the points most convenient as mutual emporiums, and the articles of most desireable interchange for them & us. If a few of their influential chiefs, within practicable distance, wish to visit us, arrange such a visit with them, and furnish them with authority to call on our officers, on their entering the U.S. to have them conveyed to this place at the public expence. If any of them should wish to have some of their young people brought up with us, & taught such arts as may be useful to them, we will receive, instruct & take care of them.... Carry with you some matter of the kinepox; inform those of them with whom you may be, of it's efficacy as a preservative from the smallpox; & instruct & encourage them in the use of it. This may be especially done wherever you winter....

—*THOMAS JEFFERSON*
Instructions to Captain Meriwether Lewis esq.
Washington, 20 June 1803

On July 14, 1803 a treaty from Paris was received at Washington ceding Louisiana according to the bounds to which France had a right. The price was $11,250,000 plus the payment of certain French debts to U.S. citizens which, in addition, would amount to between one and four million dollars.

> *Being now...sovereigns of the country, without however any diminution of the Indian rights of occupancy we are authorised to propose to them in direct terms the institution of commerce with them. It will now be proper you should inform those through whose country you will pass, or whom you may meet, that their late fathers the Spaniards have agreed to withdraw all their troops from all the waters & country of the Missisipi & Missouri, that they have surrendered to us all their subjects Spanish & French settled there, and all their posts & lands: that henceforward we become their fathers and friends, and that we shall endeavor that they shall have no cause to lament the change: that we have sent you to enquire into the nature of the country & the nations inhabiting it, to know at what places and times we must establish stores of goods among them, to exchange for their peltries: that as soon as you return with the necessary information we shall prepare supplies of goods and persons to carry them and make the proper establishments: that in the mean time, the same traders who reside among or visit them, and who now are a part of us, will continue to supply them as usual: that we shall endeavor to become acquainted with them as soon as possible, and that they will find in us faithful friends and protectors....*
>
> —THOMAS JEFFERSON
> Letter to Meriwether Lewis, Fort Mandan
> Washington, 22 January 1804

> *My children. By late arrangements with France & Spain, we now take their place as your neighbors, friends and fathers: and we hope you will have no cause to regret the change. It is so long since our forefathers came from beyond the great water, that we have lost the memory of it, and seem to have grown out of this land, as you have done. Never more will you have occasion to change your fathers. We are all now of one family, born in the same land, & bound to live as brothers....Our dwellings indeed are very far apart; but not too far to carry on commerce & useful intercourse. You have furs and peltries which we want, and we have clothes and other useful things which you want. Let us employ ourselves*

HISTORICAL NOTE

then in mutually accomodating each other. To begin this on our part it was necessary to know what nations inhabited the great country called Louisiana, which embraces all the waters of the Missisipi and Missouri, what number of peltries they could furnish, what quantities & kinds of merchandize they would require, where would be the deposits most convenient for them, and to make an exact map of all those waters. For this purpose I sent a beloved man, Capt. Lewis, one of my own household to learn something of the people with whom we are now united, to let you know we were your friends, to invite you to come and see us, and to tell us how we can be useful to you....

We propose to do in your country only what we are desirous you should do in ours....On your return tell your people that I take them all by the hand; that I become their father hereafter, that they shall know our nation only as friends and benefactors; that we have no views upon them but to carry on a commerce useful to them and us; to keep them in peace with their neighbors, that their children may multiply, may grow up & live to a good old age, and their women no longer fear the tomahawk of any enemy.

My children. These are my words. Carry them to your nation. Keep them in your memories, and our friendship in your hearts. And may the Great Spirit look down upon us, & cover us with the mantle of his love.

—THOMAS JEFFERSON
Speech to Chief White Hairs and select
warriors and children of the Osage nation
Washington, 16 July 1804

St. Louis September 23rd 1806.

Sir,

It is with pleasure that I announce to you the safe arrival of myself and party at 12 OClk. today at this place with our papers and baggage. In obedience to your orders we have penitrated the Continent of North America to the Pacific Ocean, and sufficiently explored the interior of the country to affirm with confidence that we have discoverd the most practicable rout which dose exist across the continent by means of the navigable branches of the Missouri and Columbia Rivers....making the total distance from the confluence of the Missouri and Mississippi to the discharge of the Columbia into the Pacific Ocean 3555 miles....

The Missouri and all it's branches from the Chyenne upwards abound more in beaver and Common Otter, than any other streams on earth, particularly that proportion of them lying within the Rocky Mountains. The furs of all this immence tract of country including such as may be collected on the upper portion of the...Red river and the Assinniboin with the immence country watered by the Columbia, may be conveyed to the mouth of the Columbia by the 1st of August in each year and from thence be shiped to, and arrive in Canton earlier than the furs at present shiped from Montreal annually arrive in London. The British N. West Company of Canada were they permitted by the United States might also convey their furs collected in the Athabaske, on the Saskashawan, and South and West of Lake Winnipic by that rout within the period before mentioned. Thus the productions of nine tenths of the most valuable fur country of America could be conveyed by the rout proposed to the East Indies....

—CAPTAIN MERIWETHER LEWIS
Letter to Thomas Jefferson
President of the United States

An American enterprise soon formed to take advantage of the closer China route. The Pacific Fur Company of John Jacob Astor moved aggressively to dominate the trade in furs of the new Louisiana Territory.

Author's Note

Jacques Marquette, who descended the Mississippi River through unexplored regions of the New World in 1673, relates in his journal that a nation of savages, the Illinois, bought firearms from Indians who traded directly with the French and then went to the south and west to capture Pawnee who were sold at a high price as slaves to other Indian nations. We learn, too, the significance of the Dutch and English trader to a comparatively stable though trade-dependent Iroquois league. In 1649 during the dead of winter, one thousand Mohawk and Seneca warriors, part of the Five Nation Iroquois League, armed with but a few dozen muskets received in trade, crossed 600 miles of snow-bound wilderness to strike fear in the hearts and completely devastate the prosperous, twenty thousand-strong Huron confederacy. The Huron controlled a trade to the north and west which was fertile in peltry at a time when the Mohawk River and neighboring Iroquois valleys were depleted of beaver. The Huron would not divert a portion of their rich trade to share the abundance, leaving the weaker though desperate Five Nations with little to exchange for the blankets and axes, the powder and ball and traps needed to kill game for food, or for any of the items on which they had become dependent for their very existence.

The influence on this continent of that venerable institution, the trading post, is everywhere remarkable. The trader was a pathfinder for his civilization, and the effect of his presence on aboriginal culture, either in its elevating or destructive influences, was final. His nation's commerce and manufactures, offered in ready trade for furs, caused fierce rivalries among tribes with a long-standing tradition of stability. For the indigenous people grown strong on the land an irreversible dependence would in time develop: exacting self-sufficiency, dictated in the rituals and ancient practices of tribal custom, would soon be forgotten and forever replaced by demand for the traders' goods. Thus simply began the transformation of a proud heritage, when the forces driving an expanding, industrialized nation encountered resource rich, Stone Age people rooted in the land. Warfare among neighboring tribes would then become more than a private, social enterprise. Inter-tribal warfare would be necessary for survival.

In the 17th century, the movement of European commerce into the wilderness continent of America through a vast network of natural waterways was motivated by the value of the fur trade. But movement by today's standards was slow, and in the interior, to the west of the Mississippi River, native American nations remained essentially untouched, in some instances for an additional two centuries. By 1810, the time of our story, the presence of the horse (stolen initially for food or escaped from Spanish missionary settlements in the Southwest at least three-quarters of a century before) has altered the living patterns of the more active of these tribes. The endurance and speed of the horse was soon realized and caused division among the sedentary agricultural peoples of the Great Plains: whole nations, or groups split off from existing nations, have become nomadic hunters who follow the buffalo for their source of food and shelter and who can invade great distances into a neighbor's territory for trade, theft, the hunt for food, or for reprisal. Except in the Southwestern desert areas and among some coastal tribes, little evidence of European civilization is yet to be found but the occasional red-handled London scalping knife or swatch of common scarlet cloth or glitter of enameled glass beads.

There is, however, a natural system of inter-tribal commerce: baskets and woolen blankets and corn and horses from the Southwest, salmon oil and strong hunting bows of horn and wood and straight-grained Port Orford cedar spears from the Pacific Northwest, sea shells prized as jewelry and horses from Spanish California reaching the plains tribes; horses stolen by the Assiniboine from the Mandan, the finest of buffalo robes and dressed skins, flints and red stone clay for pipes from the Northern Plains, ornamented buckskin shirts and feather bonnets from the Crow traded to the Coeur d'Alene to the west or the Cheyenne to the south, eventually reaching the Spokane or the Apache. This trade will, of course, be influenced by the presence among the border tribes of the advancing civilization's goods: a broken iron file or an old copper kettle will have significant value to an inland aborigine who once becomes aware of the utility of such an implement. Muskets with powder and ball were particularly prized. The Iroquois and later the Sioux tried to prevent their western neighbors from acquiring this deadly instrument of power.

Our story is of the men who established the first American settlement on the Pacific Coast. They were out to make their fortunes and that of their bold, visionary patron, the businessman John Jacob Astor. Yet many of the brigade would never know the fate of their remote outpost, for the promised land they entered was an inhabited wilderness of elemental force that swept some aside as though they had never existed. The survivors, led by seasoned outdoorsmen, required the skill and endurance of their combined experience to maintain the small trading outpost. And in so doing, those few men not only stimulated the local tribes toward that fatal dependence on European goods that would eventually spell the death of American aboriginal culture, but the tiny settlement helped assure America's claim over that of England for the Oregon.

While names, places and principal events were in most cases largely as described, a good part of the detail of this true story can only be realized through some effort of the imagination and is therefore subjectively drawn. Our task is to penetrate the obscure, extraordinary frontier of 1810 and grasp the challenges faced by our European and Native American forebears. To the extent we are able to enter their experience, we honor them.

PROLOGUE

Chapter One

An old, weather-worn slate grave marker with an inscription, barely legible of the year 1639, stood upright in the early spring grass of Trinity churchyard, New York City. Nearby, an elderly stonecutter chipped away at a plain headstone. His breath steaming in the frosty air, neatly shaven, ruddy cheeks bulged on one side from a wad of tobacco tucked against his teeth. Rough, swollen hands guided the mallet and chisel with skill as he completed the top line of the headstone: MARCH 25TH 1848. Without seeming to break rhythm, he removed a plug of tobacco from his pocket, cut off an end which he tucked into his other cheek, spit heartily, rummaged through his leather bag for a larger chisel and resumed chipping.

A second slate inscribed WILLIAM BRADFORD, 1752, rested in the uncrowded churchyard near an elaborate monument to Alexander Hamilton dated 1804. Bare peach trees stood out here and there against a light powdering of snow that remained on shaded ground from the night before. Past a high wrought iron fence that separated the churchyard and fashionable Church Walk, pedestrians ambled along this most prestigious promenade of the city.

The distinctive spire of Trinity Church overlooked the handsome trade buildings and active noonday traffic of Broadway. Horse-drawn wagons and carriages followed the cobbled avenue and entered congested Wall

Street where busy tradesmen moved hurriedly and vendors with wooden carts crowded the roadway as they hawked clams, hot spiced gingerbread, oysters, buns, hot corn or fish. In the distance, at the bottom of Wall Street, the massive standing rigging of three- and four-masted clipper ships tied together spread along the East River, rising well above the rooftops. With a growing population of over 450,000 people, New York City had become the busiest commercial port of the United States.

Across the boulevard a grey-haired but erect gentleman of sixty-two years departed 40 Broadway, a well-proportioned trade building marked *Pierre Chouteau, Jr., and Company, Fur Merchants*. Gabriel Franchère was oblivious to the confusion of street noise and traffic as he put on a fine beaver hat and pair of leather gloves and made his way along the thoroughfare to the corner of Wall Street, crossed the busy avenue and proceeded directly to a newspaper vendor.

The vendor, a little man wearing woolen gloves with the fingertips cut off, recognized Franchère and reached up from a tiny iron brazier with tea kettle on top to offer a *New-York Daily Tribune* dated Thursday Morning, March 30, 1848. "Sure an' there'll be no herring in the tide this day, sir," he greeted Franchère with a familiar nod, "not as the likes o' winter'll blow under spring skies."

Franchère acknowledged without speaking, placed two copper pennies on the cart, and turned away. After a few steps he paused, opened the paper and located a particular article on the second page. He was momentarily riveted, then folded the paper, walked down Wall Street and entered a private tavern.

Suddenly all was still except for the regular tick-tock of a tall grandfather clock which stood inside the entrance to a dignified dining room. Franchère handed his cloak, hat, and gloves to a black attendant and, carrying the folded paper, was escorted by a meticulous maître d'hôtel to a reserved table at one side of the quiet, wainscoted room. A log fire burned nearby. Without need for ordering, Franchère was served a first course of soup from a silver tureen by an elderly black waiter. The rhythmic beat of the pendulum, flickering firelight, and mellow Westminster chimes at a quarter past the hour were all that intruded on this solitary figure.

Franchère's place was cleared and the next course carefully set before him. He buttered a triangular-shaped, neatly trimmed piece of toast and spread on some pâté de foie gras from a garnished serving dish. As he began to eat, he turned to the newspaper.

On the second page, he located the article he had begun on the street titled, *JOHN JACOB ASTOR*, and went down to the third paragraph.

> *The young German adventurer made America his home; his talents and perseverance brought him immense wealth; he is said to have accumulated twenty-five millions of dollars. The richest man in America has died....*

While Franchère was reading, the waiter placed a portable wooden secretary on the table and held out a small silver salver with a neatly folded paper on it. Franchère looked up questioningly. "The gentleman is in the lounge, Mr Franchère."

Franchère set the newspaper aside and glanced at the slip of paper. "He is with the *New-York Herald*, sir. He would like to speak with you."

Franchère seemed puzzled but opened the small inkwell and with an ivory-handled pen from the top of the secretary wrote <u>1 PM</u> on the paper and underlined it. He set the pen and paper on the secretary and nodded to the waiter. "One o'clock, sir. As you wish."

Again he turned to the familiar article.

> *...John Jacob Astor was determined to destroy British commercial dominance of the fur trade in America. It was in 1810, in partner-ship with British traders from Montreal, that he formed the Pacific Fur Company.*

He set the paper aside as the main course was prepared before him. A fat rainbow trout was skillfully filleted by the waiter over the hot coals of a copper brazier and then served on a napkin garnished with fried parsley and trimmed half-lemons. Small covered salvers were then offered with Franchère's choice of vegetables.

Although he ate, Franchère was preoccupied and did not hear the chime at 12:30. He was in the grip of a haunting memory....

Chapter Two

The season is midsummer beside the broad St. Lawrence River where a sparkling blue current drains the densely forested landscape. Rich meadowland on the north shore, partially-cultivated, encloses a sprawling, active settlement of low timbered dwellings flanked by chimneys. Individual corrals, barns and outbuildings are interconnected with a network of wagon ruts and footpaths. A wall of strong posts made of the best wood separates the ploughed field from the forest.

Six men on a sandy stretch of the river's bank near a makeshift pier are in the final stages of loading a thirty-five-foot birchbark canoe. Nineteen year old Jean Baptiste Belleau and Antoine Belleau, seventeen, brothers, are aboard. Louis Bruslé who is twenty, and Joseph Nadeau, eighteen, are passing to them ninety-pound packs of supplies and gear from the beach. Seventeen year old Michel Laframboise stands to one side talking with Alexander McKay, leader of the party. McKay's fifty-eight years, silvery hair and even temper do not detract from an obvious native power. He holds a wide-brimmed, soft felt hat in one hand, and at the small of his back a tomahawk hangs inconspicuously from his belt. He speaks with a definite Scottish brogue. Laframboise is short and plucky, dislikes tobacco, and prides himself on being clean-shaven.

The canoemen each wear a long-bladed skinning knife. Their language is French and their command of English fluent so far as the fur trade is concerned. But in a life of endless toil they neither read nor write. They are, however, quick to sing and dance.

From the riverbank, horses can be seen inside the corrals. Dogs, chickens, and swine have the run of the place, and there is the occasional bark or yelp in protest of a seemingly peaceful afternoon. A few cattle graze the meadowland where it extends beyond the cultivated field. Here and there an oil lantern is lit and casts a faint glow through a doorway or the open shutters of a small window. The end of daylight is nearing as the setting sun touches the treetops of the thickly wooded horizon.

On the riverbank beside a rough stone hedge that separates a part of the settlement clearing from the cultivated field, a Frenchman and his teenage son are caulking a two-man birchbark canoe. The man goes to an iron pot of tree resin that is smoking over a low fire, carefully dips a homemade wooden ladle and returns to the canoe.

A bearded Frenchman with his two young sons, surrounded by a scattering of cut firewood, sharpens a splitting axe at a grindstone with the aid of his smallest boy. With both hands, the child turns the crank that makes the stone move and reacts to the shower of sparks and the sound of the iron blade against the stone. Father helps maintain a steady cranking motion by singing a song in French which marks the rhythm of the crank as it goes round and round. The bigger boy in the meantime drags split logs from the bulky stump of a chopping block to a nearby pile. Rows of firewood fill the space beneath the eaves of their bark-covered cabin.

A few yards from the river, an old Frenchman directs his grandson in the preparation of a hunting screen. The boy works with a knife which appears large in his hand. Green boughs and young trees are interwoven: the leaves are removed from one side of the barrier that the hunter will be able to approach close to game he seeks, to observe and to shoot.

Behind them, propped on the ground in front of a log dwelling in a handwoven basket where a goat is being milked, a dark-skinned baby is fascinated with the SQUIRT-SQUIRT-SQUIRT sound of the milk entering the shallow pan. A tall and youthful Ojibwa with hair well combed and oiled kneels beside the goat. Her abode, also covered with tree bark, is at the edge of the settlement near the forest where no barrier of posts has been constructed. McKay and the canoemen are some twenty-five yards away at the riverbank.

Three cows driven from the meadow by Ignace Roy Lapensée and Basile Roy Lapensée, both eighteen, move slowly toward a nearby corral and barn for the evening's milking. Ignace prods them with a long stick and Basile rests a Kentucky rifle on his shoulder where a powder horn and bullet pouch hang. The cows pass by a Huron and continue indifferently toward the barn. As they follow the muddy, well-trodden footpath, the boys urge them on with *"Allez-y!* (Go on!) *Allez-y!"*

The stout, elderly Huron, beside a rack of drying strips of meat, prepares a skin using a knife to remove pieces of fat from a wet and soft hide she has previously soaked in brine and staked out with the skin up, that it might dry smooth. The good London broadcloth she wears indicates her husband's prosperity. She is a strong woman with well-defined facial features and a wealth of long, shining hair.

Behind the Huron, a skinny, fair-skinned Lapensée girl in her early teens gathers coarse muslin clothing. Quick and sure in her movements, she grabs the simple garments from the pegs along the west wall of her dwelling, gives a firm shake and throws them onto her arm. Although young and appearing frail, her expression is one of concentration. Neither amusement nor consideration for herself enters her thought. She simply must keep moving to get through the work she faces each day.

Inside a corral, Olivier Roy Lapensée, nineteen, tall and thin but strong, finishes shoeing a horse. At the gate, twenty-four year old Gabriel Franchère unhitches a mule from a wooden plow and turns it into the corral with the horses.

Franchère is a clerk by training which, in his ability to read and write, sets him apart from the others of the settlement. A man of simple and correct habits, he is active and intelligent, kind-hearted with a strong faith in the Roman Catholic religion. As he pushes the plow to a nearby shed, Olivier calls out, *"As-tu fini?"* (Did you finish?)

Without looking up, Franchère removes the harness and answers, *"Bien entendu."* (Of course.)

Olivier gestures, *"C'est l'heure de départ.* (It's the hour to leave.) *Allons-y!"* (Come on!) He then turns toward the barn and shouts at his brothers, "Ignace Roy! Basile Roy! *Filons!"* (Let's go!)

As Franchère puts the plow inside the lean-to shed by the corral, Olivier shouts again, *"Filons! Filons!"* Franchère places the leather harness and bridle on a wooden peg under cover, takes up his Kentucky rifle which is slung from his shoulder while plowing. He crosses to a rain barrel next to the largest house of the settlement with upper and lower floors made of split stakes. The walls of his home are of squared timbers fitted one over the other, the chinks stopped with moss to prevent moisture and outside air from entering.

His mother, a stout, energetic and warm-hearted woman, is in the kitchen, built as a shed with a chimney, beside the main building. *"Monsieur McKay et les voyageurs sont arrivés.* (Mr McKay and the *voyageurs* are here.) *J'ai tout prêt pour toi, Gabriel.* (I have everything ready for you, Gabriel.) *Dépêche toi!* (Hurry up!) *Les hommes t'attendent."* (The men are waiting.)

"Oui, Maman." (Yes, Mother.) Franchère gives his sunburned arms and face a quick dousing in the rain barrel. He rubs the water from his face with his wet hands and looks toward the barn. Ignace and Basile are leaving and he motions to them and shouts, *"Filons!"* The brothers wave acknowledgement before they turn toward their roughly hewn log house.

Franchère sits against the wall and pulls off one of his high boots. He is not wearing socks and he stretches his leg and wriggles the bare toes in relief before slipping on a moccasin.

From the corral there is an unexpected low whinny sound. Franchère glances up to see the horses and mule tightly grouped in alarm against the railing farthest from the river. He leaps to his feet and instinctively reaches for his flintlock as he surveys the settlement in the direction of the river. Seventy-five yards away the river is quiet. McKay and the men at the canoe are going about their business without interruption. To the right, at the first dwelling the goat that was being milked kicks frantically as it tries to escape the short tether. The Ojibwa has abandoned the goat and pail and picked up her child. Beyond the goat a full-sized wolf is moving slowly, indecisively toward the settlement clearing from the forest. At the edge of the clearing the huge canine stops. *"Sacré enfant de Grace!"* (Holy Christ!) Franchère mutters to himself. The animal seems disoriented and hesitant, and Franchère immediately realizes that for a wolf to approach the settlement alone during daylight, it has to be sick, probably with rabies.

He raises his rifle silently and drops to one knee. There is the nervous whinny of the horses as he measures the distance with his eye and levels the flintlock. The wolf is again moving toward the goat.

Franchère cocks his piece deliberately and pulls the trigger. There is a POP with a sharp SNAP sound.

Sacré imbécile!" (Damned fool!) Franchère blurts out in exasperation at the misfire.

The wolf lunges suddenly but ineffectively at the goat. The goat rams the sick beast, deflecting its attack though it is knocked down by the larger, heavier animal. The wolf is panting and sluggish as it scrambles in the dirt, confused and clumsy in its movement.

The Ojibwa, not taking her eyes from the huge canine, inches toward the corner of her dwelling where she will be out of sight of the diseased animal.

The wolf sees her movement and begins to stalk. With head near the ground, it approaches slowly. There is a menacing growl. The woman in the shadow of the log hut continues to move backward. But the wolf is distracted by the goat which is again on its feet, jerking back and forth to escape the tether. The wild canine bares its teeth at the goat while the Ojibwa continues slowly backward. Instinctively she knows that to move quickly will bring on attack the sooner.

Sluggish and uncertain, the wolf turns from the goat, sees the movement of the woman and child and once again, with head low to the ground, begins to stalk. There is a deep-throated rumble as it approaches.

A blood-chilling "Ayeee-Ay!" suddenly cleaves the air from the direction of the river. The wolf turns toward the cry of attack. McKay is not ten yards away, hat in hand, running at breakneck speed toward the wolf. Laframboise and Nadeau are close behind. The wolf turns and leaps at McKay, who deliberately baits the wolf with his hat. The treacherous jaws close on the harmless felt and in that split second McKay springs past the flaying forelegs, pulls his tomahawk from behind and buries it in the spine of the diseased beast.

Laframboise and Nadeau at a full run fling their knives. Before it falls from McKay's fatal blow, two knives sink deeply into the poisoned flesh. The wolf is dead before it hits the ground.

The lifeless canine shudders on the ground as Bruslé approaches at a run, knife in hand. Nearly insane with fright, the goat thrashes at the end of its tether. Bruslé sheathes his knife and goes over to calm it.

"Poor devil," McKay comments quietly as he regards the wolf.

The Ojibwa approaches McKay and stops beside the dead wolf. *"O-be-mah-tuh-se-win e-nug-gah-mo-toan."* (He sings a death song.)

McKay scans the quiet forest where the wolf appeared. She continues, *"Ke-be-pe-mish-kaw-wa.* (Thou came by water.) *Neen-keen-waw-bo-min."* (I saw thee.) McKay turns to her as she continues, *"Ah-bin.* (Stay.) *Ke-ke-wee-sin."* (Thou must eat.)

McKay gestures in response, *"Kaw.* (No.) *Tah-mah-jah-men nees-sah-je-wun.* (We shall go across the river.) *Tah-mah-jah-men…"* (We shall go…) He points to the west. *"Duk-wawb."* (Far away.)

He turns as Franchère approaches excitedly with his rifle. The woman leaves them and enters her log house.

"I saw him, *Monsieur* McKay, but," he gestures to the sky, "a flash in the pan, *monsieur!"* He faces McKay, embarrassed and humiliated.

"No harm done, lad." His eyes are alert to every nuance of Franchère's expression. He continues in a quiet, paternal way. "'Tis a good feeling of a dark night in strange territory to see a pair of them yellow eyes staring at the fire, waiting for the remains of supper. You know then that no one is sneaking about. Aye! But I'll speak to the men." Nadeau and Bruslé drag the huge canine, as heavy as a man, away by the hind legs. "When they travel in packs, more than one could be crazed with the fever."

Laframboise hands McKay the tomahawk which he rubs with dirt to remove the blood. McKay unconsciously replaces it in his belt as he scans the settlement. There is excited conversation as Laframboise recounts the incident to residents who have gathered nearby.

McKay turns to Franchère. "Now where are the rest of our lads? We must cross the river this evening if we are to be at New York harbor by Monday next." With a glint of expectation in his eye, "The ship *Tonquin* awaits us, lad! Aye, Mr Astor expects us no later. Find those three Lapensée brothers."

Franchère throws his rifle onto his shoulder and eagerly sets off. "Franchère!" McKay takes a step toward him, then stops, searching for the right words. "Mind you, lad, where we're going won't be Grand Portage or the Athabasca. The Oregon's new territory." He hesitates. "The savages can be a might tricky until you've proven your strength. Aye, there could be trouble." He continues with feeling. "Have a word with your fine parents, if you understand my meaning. 'Twill be a long time at best before your eyes embrace them again."

Franchère is taken aback as he acknowledges to himself that he is actually leaving home. *"Oui, monsieur,"* (Yes, sir) he replies quietly and walks off. He turns toward the Lapensée house and shouts with an apprehensive edge, "Basile Roy! Ignace Roy! Olivier Roy! *Filons!* (Let's go!) *Filons!*"

The sun is behind the trees as a crowd of relatives and friends of those departing gather along the riverfront in the vicinity of the loaded canoe. A number of Indian women who have borne children are wives to some of the Frenchmen.

Laframboise is now on the beach tossing the remaining bedrolls and flintlocks to Bruslé in the canoe. Bruslé passes items back to Nadeau and the Belleau brothers who stow them.

The Lapensée brothers are listening to their sharp-tongued mother, a warm, affectionate woman who is old before her time from overwork. The five Lapensèe sisters, from youth to the eldest who earlier was taking in the dry clothing, are with them. They adore their brothers.

McKay stands a few yards from the canoe having a word with one of the older trappers of the settlement.

Gabriel and his father, grey-haired, soft-spoken but firm, walk together from their house toward the riverbank. The older man holds his son's arm and carries his bedroll as they talk privately.

"*Travaille dur pour Monsieur McKay, Gabriel.* (You must work hard for Mr McKay, Gabriel.) *Il t'offre une excellente occasion.* (He is giving you a wonderful opportunity.) *Tu l'as bien méritée, mon fils.* (You deserve it, my son.)

"*Quand tu arriveras à destination sur la côte du Pacifique, quand tu seras seul et que la famille te manquera, tu devras regarder chaque soir la lune se lever.* (When you have reached your destination on the Pacific Coast and you are alone and miss your family, look up at the moon as it rises each night.)

"*Je la regarderai aussi à ce moment-là et je penserai à toi.*" (I will be looking at it then and thinking of you.)

Suddenly overcome with intense and unexpected feeling, Franchère turns from his father and gazes back toward the familiar settlement for what he begins to realize might be the last time. There is moisture in his eyes. His father grips both his shoulders. "*Et maintenant, tu dois partir!*" (And now you must go!) They embrace and kiss on both cheeks.

Laframboise's voice interrupts them. "*Dèpêche toi, Franchère!*" (Hurry up...)

Franchère struggles against the unexpected wave of emotion to bring his thoughts back to the task at hand and with a natural lightness of step approaches the riverfront.

Laframboise, who is about to toss a bundle to Bruslé, stops in mid-motion and eyes Franchère from head to foot in supposed derision as he walks toward the canoe with his bedroll and flintlock. "*Écartez-vous!* (Stand back!) *Écartez-vous!*" He turns to those standing nearby. Franchère's serious expression at the moment becomes a natural foil for his excited, exuberant mood.

In exaggerated alarm, Laframboise drops the bundle he is holding and raises his head in mock elegance of manner. "*Tu vas à New York habillé comme ça?* (You go to New York dressed this way?) *Tu te crois déjà américain, ma parole?*" (You think you are already an American?)

Franchère is confused.

"*Tu vas aller dans un bal de New York fagoté de cette manière?*" (You will dance this way in beautiful New York?) He points to Franchère's feet and kicks his heels with laughter.

Franchère glances down to see that he is wearing one moccasin and one boot. His eyes light up with youthful embarrassment as he pulls the missing moccasin from the bedroll and tosses the flintlock to Laframboise. He sits down on the spot to correct his oversight.

Madam Lapensée's shrill tone of complaint dominates her family which is gathered around her. Frightened with emotions beyond her control, she yields unconsciously to a dread premonition that she will never again see her boys. Not a calm individual or free from superstition, her sporadic gestures, intense upbraiding then quick caressing, express uncertainty and anguish at parting with her boys. The five pretty sisters all take their mother seriously.

She speaks rapidly and with heightened emotion, at first to all three boys. "*Vous faut-il aller si loin?* (Why must you go so far?) *La plupart des gens ne sauront pas votre nom de famille el n'auront pour vous aucune considération.* (There are many people there who do not know your family name, who will not respect you.)

"Ignace Roy, *mon enfant!*" (my baby!) Her eyes fill with tears as she hugs the youngest twin to herself. Then noticing Basile, the smaller of the two, she turns to him, her mood suddenly pleading.

"Basile Roy!" She holds her child at arms length, looking him straight in the eye. "*Le Pacifique!* (The Pacific!) *C'est une terre inconnue, vaste et dangereuse.* (It is an unknown land, big and dangerous.) *Tu ne seras pas en sûreté chez les américains.* (You are not safe with the Americans.) *Ton père dit qu'ils se méfient des sauvages.* (Your father says they do not trust Indians.) *Ils les comprennent mal!"* (They do not understand them.)

She turns sternly to Olivier, the oldest, her mood again changed. *"Prends soin de tes frères!"* (Take care of your brothers!) And to the twins in the same tone, *"Faites ce que vous dit votre frère!"* (Do what your brother tells you!) She bursts into tears. *"Prenez garde,* Olivier Roy, Basile Roy, Ignace Roy. (Be careful...) *Pas d'imprudences."* (Be careful.)

Two French trappers, home for the brief summer season, watch the departure. One of them comments, *"C'est une terre inconnue, l'Orégon, où personne n'est allé."* (Oregon is a strange land to go where no one has been before.)

His companion replies, *"Mais Monsieur McKay y est allé, il y a vu une quantité de castors."* (But Mr McKay has been there, and he has seen many beavers.)

The tall Ojibwa approaches McKay and offers him a heavy joint of smoked venison. *"Ke-me-nin maw-buh waw-waw-wash-gais.* (I give you this deer.) *Che-po-tah kwi-aun o-tah-ke-koonk.* (Here is venison to put in the kettle.) *Ne-waw-gaw-kwut-ne-ke oon-jin-nee-sah."* (I killed him with my tomahawk.)

McKay accepts the gift without reply, turns toward the canoe and shouts, "Michel! Here is our supper. You'll not have to hunt tonight, me lads!" He points to Bruslé in the canoe. "Louis! Fetch me that fresh buckskin we packed earlier!"

As Bruslé searches through the bundles, he tips the canoe dangerously. Laframboise, who is nearly thrown into the river, hollers out, *"De l'autre côté, espèce d'imbécile!"* (The other side, you jerk!)

"Bougre!" (Bugger!) Bruslé replies in frustration as he locates the rolled skin and tosses it to Laframboise.

McKay hands him the venison in exchange and turns to the woman, unties the thong holding the skin and unrolls it for her to see. *"Neen-ge puk-ko-nah.* (I took this skin from a deer.) *Keen-ke-ti-eme."* (It is mine. It belongs to thee.)

She is pleased and accepts the gift. *"Ke-soan-ge-ta-ha."* (Thou art strong hearted.)

McKay replies, *"Kaw-ween."* (No.) *"Een-da-nin-ne-ne-ew."* (I am but a man.)

She gives McKay a personal blessing. *"Pon-ne-mah was-saw-k'duk-wawb."* (Hereafter, thou seest far off.)

McKay is moved. *"Ah-neen-azhe-ne-kah-so-yun?"* (What is thy name?) *"Ta-ta-sis-koo-see-men."* (Flower-that-follows-the-sun.)

McKay searches her expression. For a brief moment they discover in each other's eyes an unexpected bond of mutual feeling. *"Uh, Ta-ta-sis-koo-see-men, pon-ne-mah, was-saw-n'duk-wawb."* (Yes, Flower-that-follows-the-sun, hereafter, I see far off.)

Almost at once the spell is broken. The handsome woman turns and walks up the bank. McKay steps back and follows her movement for a moment then speaks quietly but firmly to Laframboise. "Let's be off. We camp at La Prairie de la Madeleine tonight."

Laframboise runs jubilant with the venison the few yards to the canoe. *"Nous allons à New York!"* (We go to New York!)

"Nous allons en Orégon!" (We go to Oregon!) Bruslé admonishes.

Laframboise stops by the canoe and bursting with pride gestures to those close at hand as he speaks carefully but with obvious effort and heavy accent, "I am go dee coon-trae of dee Oré-gon en dee very-very West, close by dee Rock *Montagne*. I am been free trappare! I am make put-y-much dollare!"

The family and friends of the *voyageurs* and clerk have gathered now for the departure and, except for Madam Lapensée, all react to Laframboise' humor. She, still, is overwhelmed with her own sense of foreboding.

"Le Roi Georges ne règne pas sur l'Orégon!" (There is no King George in Oregon!) Laframboise continues.

"Qu'est-ce que cela fait?" (Well, so what?) *Il n'y a pas de roi en Amérique!"* (There's no king in America!) Bruslé is quick to reply.

Laframboise heaves the joint of venison to Bruslé and points to himself in triumph. "I am been trappare! I am been *américain!"*

Franchère as clerk is a passenger and sits on stowed gear in the bow of the canoe, facing the canoemen who consist of the eight *voyageurs* (including the three Lapensée brothers).

Laframboise is at the front to set the tempo for the paddles. Bruslé sits at the rear to steer the vessel. Each of the canoemen carries his own handmade paddle, and these have been decorated with streamers of scarlet cloth for this important journey to America.

McKay steps aboard the fully-loaded canoe and remains standing amidships as he says his final good-byes.

The families are clustered along the bank waving and calling a final *"Au revoir!"* (Until we meet again!) or *"Bonne chance!"* (Good luck!) as the canoe is released from the pier.

Madam Lapensée scolds frantically over the general din. *"N'oubliez pas les prières de votre mère, mes enfants!"* (Remember your mother's prayers, my children!)

Monsieur and *Madame* Franchère stand together on a conspicuous prominence.

The moment the strong current catches the canoe, Laframboise starts a song to St. Anne, the patron saint of *voyageurs*. Paddles strike the water in unison and the canoe is brought under immediate control as the men join in hearty and spontaneous voice while keeping perfect time to their familiar river ballad.

McKay sings heartily in French with the men and waves to the settlement before turning his attention to the broad river ahead.

Franchère does not sing as he waves to his parents and friends. Smoke can be seen rising from the distant settlement. The sun is now below the horizon and faces at the shoreline can no longer be distinguished. Franchère stops waving but stares with intense feeling at the fast-disappearing settlement. He is trying to grasp what it means to leave home, perhaps forever. The Westminster chimes of one o'clock suddenly intrude as the *voyageur* song and the river....

CHAPTER THREE

At the luncheon table where we left him earlier, the elderly Gabriel Franchère stared into an empty wine glass he was unconsciously fingering with the same concentration of feeling that overpowered him years earlier at his departure from home. With a hint of moisture in his eyes, he looked up to see a dish of flaming brandy being poured with care over a Crème Anglaise. The final BONG of one o'clock rang and he took up his napkin.

Alert to the waiter's presence, Franchère cleared his throat and fussed with the napkin as he struggled to regain equilibrium with the present. "*Deux cafés, s'il vous plaît.*"

"I beg your pardon, sir?" the waiter replied, taken aback.

Franchère stared at him a moment then replied in a French accent, "Sorry. My mind was… Coffee for two, and show in *Monsieur* Lanier."

"Coffee for two. Right away, sir."

Franchère remained pensive and hardly noticed the custard when he took a bite before pushing it aside. He rested one hand on the folded newspaper and tapped it, waiting, until he suddenly looked up and stood, pointing to the empty chair opposite him.

Charles Lanier, middle-aged, gangling, self-effacing, a disheveled appearance but with no apparent concern for appearances, approached the table.

"*Monsieur Charles Lanier?*" Franchère asked graciously. *Asseyes-vous, je vous en prie.*" (Please sit down.) He remained standing. "*Puis-je vous demander, qu'est-ce me vaut cette visite?*" (To what, may I ask, do I owe this visit?)

Lanier stood looking at Franchère, somewhat mortified. "Oh! You don't speak English, sir. But I thought you were a clerk for the company." Fumbling with his note pad in confusion, he blurted out, "Mr Astor, the Pacific Fur Company?"

"Ah, *Monsieur* Lanier!" Franchère intoned vigorously, covering his disappointment. "Of course. Sit down. Sit down, please!" He again pointed to the chair across from him. "From your name I assumed we could speak French together. It is a rare pleasure for me. Frenchmen come to this city and they seem in a great hurry to forget their native language, *qui est une belle langue.*" (which is a beautiful language.)

"But English *is* my native language, sir!" Lanier replied with some energy.

"Of course, *mon ami.* (my friend.) Of course. It is my mistake. I am, as you say, overeager."

A demitasse of black coffee was served to each and Franchère removed a cigar case from his pocket. "Will you join me?"

"No, sir. I haven't formed the habit."

An awkward pause followed while Franchère lit his cigar and took a sip of coffee. Lanier opened his note pad and searched for a pencil. Both men were conscious of an inadvertent impasse but neither was quite sure how to put the other at his ease.

"You know about my career, *Monsieur* Lanier," Franchère finally offered. "You are correct, I was a clerk in *Monsieur* Astor's employ."

"Astor is no longer with us, sir, and, well..." Lanier paused, groping for the point. "He left behind the biggest fortune this country ever saw, sir." He turned to his notes. "You were with him for twenty-four years. Is that correct?"

"Yes, quite correct."

"After twenty-four years, sir, you must've seen a thing or two. At times events turned against him. You could tell me..." Lanier hesitated, glancing at his notes, trying to focus, "...how he got so much money? About some of his investments?" He looked up. "How did he make that fortune?"

"To understand *Monsieur* Astor's success," Franchère replied, resting his hand on the newspaper, "you must keep one thing in mind. Money itself meant nothing to him."

"What are you saying? He had so much it didn't matter?"

"Ten millions, thirty millions. I don't think he knew or cared. What mattered, what was the singular challenge peculiar to himself, was to make profitable investments, to make *more* profitable investments than any other man. And he did just that. In fact, his dream was to unite all the untouched lands of this continent under a single fur trading company of his own, but Bonaparte sold that prime Louisiana wilderness to *Monsieur* Jefferson. Then war began with the British and his plans were overwhelmed by circumstances."

"Astor was ahead of his time," Lanier observed, animated, scribbling rapidly as a story began to take shape. "Now I've got it, sir! He wanted control of territory ahead of the British. He knew what he was doing. He formed the Pacific Fur Company." Lanier turned to Franchère. "But it failed. Why, sir? Was it Astor? The war of 1812?"

Franchère took a sip of coffee, added sugar to it, sipped again. He was pensive but precise as he drew on the cigar before continuing. "That, *mon ami*, you will have to decide for yourself. I will tell you what I understand of the enterprise. Perhaps we will learn something in a world where so very little can be known. In any event, I was there."

Franchère leaned back in his chair as he considered where to begin. "*Monsieur* Astor offered to the North West Company of Canada a partnership. They would share the new territory and agree not to interfere with each other's trade. Of course, the territory was not Astor's, but he believed both could gain if they would cooperate in opening the Oregon. The North West partners considered but did not accept. So in 1810 *Monsieur* Astor contracted with seven experienced fur traders from Montreal and one from St. Louis. They became his partners.

"Those eight men led two expeditions. One proceeded overland from St. Louis and the other went by sea with canoemen and supplies. They were to meet the following year in the rich valley of the Columbia River. It was a race against time to get to the Oregon ahead of the British and claim as much of the territory as we could hold. And because the territory was new, *monsieur*, we would work doubly hard for everything." Franchère paused as he considered. "We were pledged for five years, partners, clerks and canoemen, and all of us were determined. We would secure our fortunes. You see, furs meant to us what gold meant to the Spanish, and we were going to God's country. We would open a new land and get rich. Ah, but we were naive!"

Lanier eyed Franchère closely. There might be more to this deceptively gentle man than he had realized.

"You must understand, *Monsieur* Lanier, there has to be a certain…" he paused, "What can I say… a certain strength, a determination to push a man, even a young and strong man, into the unknown. The sensations one experiences in the wilderness are not what one feels in the solitude of parks and gardens. In such a sanctuary one can indulge a flattering notion of self-sufficiency. But inside the great bowel of nature we discover our humanity. Wilderness shows us at every step only how little we can sustain, how little we can perform.

"It was a more serious venture for each of us than we knew at the time. Not a gamble with money. It is far more when a man's life could be taken from him."

Lanier stopped writing with the realization that Franchère had experienced what he himself would never willingly attempt. He grew reflective and drifted into his own thoughts.

The waiter refilled Franchère's cup.

Breaking the silence, Franchère asked, "Will you have a cognac, *monsieur?*"

Lanier was startled from his momentary reverie. "No! No thank you. Never take a drink before supper," indicating his stomach. "It won't do, sir."

"You have come at a time when I welcome another man's interest." Franchère was now relaxed. "I will speak as the memories come to me. We shall, as you say, amble in their company. Yes, that would be a comfort."

"Exactly right, sir," Lanier answered though for the moment not so confident of himself or his story.

"It began for me thirty-eight years ago, in preparation for the voyage to the Pacific, when ten of us, Alexander McKay, one of the partners, eight *coureurs de bois*, Frenchmen, *voyageurs* who were both expert canoemen and trappers, and myself, the young clerk hired to keep records, write reports and correspondence, crossed the St. Lawrence River in a birchbark canoe and followed the rivers to New York. Along the way there were no canals or turnpikes, no cities like Rochester or Buffalo. And New York City was not the great emporium she is today."

Franchère sipped from the demitasse as he mused over his thoughts. "To appreciate *Monsieur* Astor's extraordinary determination, you must understand how insignificant were the American states in those days. British fur trading posts were active from Hudson's Bay to the Rocky Mountains, more than halfway across the continent. The major rivers of Canada had been explored to the sea by Hudson's Bay and North West Company men. The Americans, on the other hand, had added only four new states to the original thirteen. These United States formed but a small population centered on the Atlantic Coast."

Franchère drew on the cigar and set it in the ashtray. "While the British were mapping the entire area of Canada to the Arctic and Pacific Oceans, there were but three wagon-ways in the whole of the American states that crossed the mountains and penetrated to the interior, two in Pennsylvania and one through Virginia to Tennessee with a branch crossing the Cumberland Mountains into Kentucky."

The cigar smoke rose as Franchère continued. "You followed the rivers into the continent, and you moved back in time. Even after two centuries this land was untamed. Yes, *Monsieur* Lanier, the American continent was a very big wilderness, an inhabited wilderness, in eighteen hundred and ten...."

Chapter Four

With the first hour of light on a winter's morning, day is breaking over aboriginal America north of the Texas Panhandle and west of the Mississippi River. Tribal custom, by now of long experience, has led to self-sufficiency on the land. Beliefs are expressed in a highly spiritual relationship to life.

The Sangre de Cristo Mountains are home to a nearly naked Apache who overlooks the desert floor to the east and the lightest portion of a clouded sky. Far below, a clear ribbon of water reflects early dawn where the Pecos River snakes through scrub growth and canyon on its way to the Rio Grande and the sea. No bird's song greets the coming of day but the wind surrounds this lone individual on a bare ridge of the foothills. He holds a small, open basket from which he ceremoniously tosses pinch after pinch of precious cornmeal to the air with silent prayers (first in order, to the rising sun that has power to cure disease as well as to give light to the day with its rays, imploring its beneficence *as soon as you look on me*, and then to the many deities of his people). In a land where food is insufficient to support large gatherings, ritual thanksgiving is of a personal nature.

Nearby, in a sheltered clearing between two fires, a mature diamondback rattlesnake is tethered to a tough bit of root. Not far away, the Apache's son peels a stalk of green mescal and adds it to a couple of pieces he has gathered. The coiled snake nervously probes back and forth when the man returns to the clearing.

Immediately he kneels beside the boy and casts the mescal into the nearest fire. Without losing time, he removes a whole deer's liver and an arrow from a skin pouch which lies with his bow and impales the liver onto the flint arrowhead. The boy remains by the fire as the man approaches the coiled snake which menaces with a cat-like hiss and intense rattle. It is now fully active after being warmed by the fires. He thrusts the liver-baited shaft at the snake's jaws. The rattlesnake strikes the liver, imbuing the porous flesh with its poison.

The snake remains coiled and rattling furiously, unable to escape. Without fear the man thrusts the liver at the snake a second and third time. Again the snake strikes the liver.

Again and again he thrusts the liver at the exhausted reptile until it strikes a third time. He then releases the snake which disappears in the brush.

The man returns with the liver and carefully embeds the flint head of each of the five arrows he has made into the deer's liver and sets the whole aside. Arrowheads coated with rattlesnake poison will be useful later in the hunt.

He and the boy each pick out a roasted mescal stalk and eat the only food they are likely to have that day....

A patch of wild green maguey plants grow on a fertile plateau in the mountains above the Valley of the Black River. At one cabbage-like plant, the sharp end of a wedge-shaped stick is placed at its stalk and struck with a stone to sever the root. The stalk of the plant is incised three times with a sharp flint.

The first light of dawn of this windy and partially overcast morning reveals a plateau teeming with activity. Apache women of all ages are in the field gathering maguey and carrying their full baskets to the edge of the field where they dump the raw maguey into dark, shallow pits. Additional pits are alive with flames and there are several mounds of earth which mark the location of others that have been filled.

At a second maguey, the plant is cut from the ground in the same manner by rough, sun-dried hands and a pair of lines incised on its stalk. A lean, young Apache throws the plant into a burden basket of her own making which is suspended by a woven strap from her forehead.

The young woman dumps her load into one dark pit that is now full. Steam rises from the hissing of the green maguey on the red hot stones that cover the bottom. She returns to the field as others work rapidly to cover the fresh, steaming plants with a layer of green brush, dry leaves, and finally, a mound of dirt.

Elderly men gather large stones for the blazing pits and drop them into the fires.

As a mound is uncovered, women from the field sort the roasted maguey into piles according to the incised markings on the stalk of each plant.

In the uneven firelight stands a row of crude, low, grass and stick huts covered except for their tiny entranceways with worn deerskin. Amongst these temporary shelters a few old and thin horses graze.

Against the early dawn sky, with intruding wafts of smoke from the nearby fires, the silhouette of a bent figure of many years is poised at the edge of one of the dark mounds holding a small, familiar basket. From it she casts pinch after pinch of cornmeal to the wind, in rhythm with her prayers, as she silently gives thanks for the harvest and asks that the cooking, part of their perpetual quest for food, be successful and her people be in condition to receive its nourishment....

A dim orange-yellow glow and rising smoke from cooking fires inside the cliff dwelling of a Hopi village at the mouth of Keams Canyon become visible as the first light of dawn awakens the inhabitants. The sky is streaked with clouds and the wind blows on this cold and threatening morning.

Two girls, balancing large crocks on their heads, walk down the solitary cliff path toward the desert floor. Hopi men run down the same path and pass the girls on their way to a stream below. Boys follow the men and behind the boys, an old man carries a young child at a trot down the trail.

The men stop along the stream by a deep pool, break the ice that has formed at the edge with a stone, disrobe and plunge into the water. They submerge themselves, and immediately scramble out. As they put on their shirts, loincloths and headbands, the boys catch up with them and, likewise, quickly disrobe and plunge into the water.

They return along the well-worn trail back to the cliff path a half mile away as males eight to fifty years old run to the same pool. Cultivated fields with new growths of cotton, corn, and beans grow beyond the wash.

The two girls skillfully balance the large, full crocks on their heads as they walk upright from the creek where the men have filled and set them to be carried. At the base of the cliff path, the old man, who has submerged and dressed himself at a shallow part of the stream, now disrobes the young boy and splashes him with the icy water. The child reacts to the cold, and the old man reacts with affection as he quickly dresses the boy and carries him off at a trot up the trail.

Within the cliff dwelling, the refreshed men and boys, each now wrapped in a white cotton bed blanket, gather on the roofs and along the outside walls of their individual lodgings to silently await the sunrise. They lean against the outside walls and face the Eastern sky as each in his own time makes an offering of meal and prayer to the rising sun for good luck and long life....

The flicker of torchlight plays on a large and foreboding raven totem carved from a rooted tree trunk to overlook a broad beach. In the first light of morning the clouds appear still but the wind carries the sound of incoming surf. The collapsed remains of a partially stripped gray whale are visible as the rising tide washes around the brute carcass. Above the high watermark are the smoldering remains of two fires, and beside each, a cedar chest for rendering blubber.

The blackened but distinctive prow of a thirty-one-foot pine whaling canoe, which is elevated well above the sand by bulky logs, is lit by firelight. Parallel rows of small white shells ornament the sides below the gunwale. The sounds of burning and scraping are heard near the source of light amidships. An aborigine works a blazing torch of split cedar and a wedge-shaped chisel of bone to alternately burn and scrape the final pieces of crustacean growth from the canoe's bottom.

Along one side of the canoe a half dozen aboriginal men, captives of the Nootka people, with torches planted in the sand behind them, vigorously polish the blackened surface of the hull with woven grass mats. To one side of the canoe, the rope tender, also a captive who, like the others, was given a chance to live in exchange for work, sits between two fires attaching a large inflated hair sealskin float to a heavy woven line. Coiled in front of him on the ground is another line with two floats already attached.

From the dark forest behind the beach, an immense figure, Maquinna, a principal Nootka chief, emerges. His thick hair is tied at the top of his head and blows freely with the wind. He is barefooted and wears a heavy bearskin, with claws visible, that hangs to his ankles. Bracelets of bone cover his wrists. He carries an enormous harpoon, made of a three-inch cedar shaft fourteen feet long, and a line with two inflated sealskin floats.

Maquinna stops to survey the beach. By the indistinct light he senses more than sees what is going on. But as he approaches the firelight and men, his face indicates intense concentration. He stops before the rope tender.

Maquinna's ears are pierced above the lobe where tiny bone ornaments hang. His broad facial features, with narrow eyes, full mustache and goatee, do not seem those of a Native American east of the Rocky Mountains: he could be a half-breed Aleut-Chinaman. He silently inspects the work of his rope tender and boat crew. Without a word, he sets the harpoon and floats near the rope tender who willingly takes the end of the line. He returns to the forbidding darkness of the forest.

All is silence as Maquinna approaches a riverbank. He throws off his bearskin cape and, from a rope that binds a cedar-bark covering at his waist, he pulls a large mussel-shell knife, hacks four young sprigs of hemlock from the nearby growth and then faces to the east.

With eyes closed, Maquinna raises his empty hands toward the first light of dawn in prayer.

Maquinna enters the lodge of the spirit.
Who can remain longer than Maquinna?
Earth above, listen!
Gray whale under ground, hear!

Maquinna disrobes and plunges into the river for a ritual purification underwater. He remains submerged until his lungs will burst then returns to shore and takes up a piece of hemlock. Maquinna vigorously rubs his upper body until all the leaves are gone.

Once more he submerges as long as possible before returning to shore to vigorously rub his lower body. The third time Maquinna enters the water slowly.

Out of the ground comes Maquinna.
Oh Great Spirit that makes this river flow!

Again on shore, Maquinna rubs his body with the hemlock until blood flows freely and all the leaves are gone. The giant figure then disappears underwater.

> *Come ye up, come ye up, gray whale!*
> *Hear thy mouth, hear thy heart, gray whale!*
> *Pierce thy heart, cleanse thy blood!*
> *The loud-speaking thunder helps Maquinna!*

He returns to the shore to cleanse his body for the final time. By now Maquinna has heard the spirit of the whale he will kill that day. He enters the water a last time, heartbeat throbbing in his ears, in indomitable communion with the Great Spirit.

When Maquinna finally returns to the shore, blood is flowing freely from his nostrils. He goes directly to a nearby secret declivity in a hemlock tree and removes a piece of cedar bark containing a miniature raven totem. He turns to the east, points it high above his head, and prays silently.

> *Oh, Great Spirit,*
> *that makes the east wind come and flow over the ground.*
> *Oh, Thou, whose fire burns forever,*
> *command the whale-spirit which has spoken to Maquinna!*
> *The gray whale is Maquinna's!*

At the seaside, Maquinna lays the harpoon in the prow of his canoe with the point forward beyond the tip of the bow and the line with the sealskin floats attached and carefully coiled by the rope tender. He removes the miniature raven totem from its cedar wrapping and places it in a special groove of the prow.

The canoe moves swiftly through the surf with Maquinna at the bow facing the sea ahead. The seven crewmen, all captives, each with a pointed paddle carved of cedar, row with great strength in unison. The light of dawn reveals a choppy sea on this overcast, turbulent morning....

Along Clarks Fork of the Yellowstone River in the foothills of the Rocky Mountains, large fires at regular intervals reveal an extensive Apsaroke encampment. Snow has begun falling and the ground and heavily forested hillsides are turning white.

The first light of dawn tints the Eastern sky as a lone Apsaroke horseman gallops along the line toward a cluster of tepees around one of the fires near the riverbank. He carries a long coupstick with a single feather which he holds proudly upright from the stirrup. His horse's nostrils steam noticeably in the cold morning air. He slows his horse and shouts, *Hun-hun-heeeeee!* (Prepare to depart!) *Hun-hun-heeeeee!*

A solitary, bent figure, an old woman with a bulky load of branches on her back, emerges bare-handed from the forest. She passes by a couple of horses tethered with manes and backs becoming white in the fresh snowfall. While she unburdens herself and throws sticks onto the flames, the horseman continues down the line with his call to depart.

A group of young herdsmen bring some one hundred horses whose steaming backs are no longer white with snow by the encampment. Women from the tepees run among them throwing braided rawhide halters over the necks of their own pack animals. Other women are breaking camp, the sixteen to twenty buffalo hides of a tepee rattling down, leaving a skeleton of poles with a bundle of sleepy children on the ground. A woman pulls the skin from under two little ones who are still bedded down. She tosses each a strip of dry, smoked meat before gathering household stuff into leather sacks of her own making.

Eight mounted chiefs complete a conference with a dozen mounted warriors before riding quietly downriver a short distance to await the formation of the line. A bearing of authority dominates their presence and each carries a coupstick with feathers attached.

The warriors disperse, some riding ahead, others fanning out left and right. They seek the crests of the hills which form the valleys their people will travel that day in order to warn of any hostile party which might approach their territory.

The encampment is made ready for the day's journey. Lodge poles are bundled together and tied at the horses' sides forming travois onto which buffalo hides and leather packs are attached. A horse breaks away and gallops through the camp before the packs are secured, scattering the load and causing confusion among the women and children.

A woman ties a papoose into a baby carrier and straps it to her shoulders before she mounts a big, gentle horse pulling a loaded travois. Her young son attaches another horse to her travois. It is also pulling a travois packed with bundles of skins. The woman assists the boy onto her horse.

He sits in front of his mother as they join the line, trailed by camp dogs. Fires are left to burn out.

The village has formed a line and begun moving: the chiefs and the few old men of the tribe are at the front to set the pace and direction. Next, a band of several dozen warriors, each leading a war horse with lance and shield attached to its saddle (their strongest horses will thereby remain close at hand and fresh in case of an unexpected attack). Behind them, the column continues to form, family by family, each driving travois loaded with skins, and followed by camp dogs. Extra horses by the hundreds are herded at intervals along the line by young women who will quickly replace those animals injured or exhausted in the course of travel.

In the early light and falling snow the column extends miles in length as it slowly traverses the land, following the path of the river toward lower ground and the buffalo herd.

From high in the mountains the movement of the nomad tribe is reduced to a dark line that vanishes in the snowstorm of this pure mountain air but on the ground will endure through the long day until the refreshment of nightfall and the communal fire....

Seasons pass. With summer's dawn above the northern plains, the sharp silhouette of the Continental Divide streaks the eastern mauve sky in long shadows. Pink and red cloud formations mark the southeast. The darkness of night obscures the western panorama where lightning flashes through thunderclouds that rise above distant mountains. To the north, the sky grows purple with dawn. As the sun at last enters the landscape a fiery orange glow reveals rivulets of water forming on the edge of a high, snow-bound meadow. The slender spring seeps between moss-covered rocks into a sheltered pool reflecting bare mountain peaks and golden sky, spills over flat, polished granite and through cragged breaches into a steep, rock-bound creek. Tumbling water divides, plunging past granitic outcroppings into a wide stream which nourishes small herbs and healthy bracken glistening with the morning's first light. A dead leaf caught in the water's movement submerges before being swiftly carried to a quiet pond behind a beaver's dam. The surrounding glen is redolent with the yellow glow of the rising sun. Early light casts long shadows where cutthroat trout feed near the surface of a deep, rippled, wide fork that passes under fallen trees as it courses the forested valley.

A blue jay gathering seeds from the ground darts across to a tree branch, hops to the main trunk, pecks at it, stops, turns, listens motionless for a moment, then flies off across the river squawking loudly on this fine summer's morning.

Chapter Five

The thirty-five-foot birchbark canoe that left the St. Lawrence settlement with young Gabriel Franchère aboard is laboring midstream against the current of the mile-wide Richelieu River. The Frenchmen paddle in unison with powerful strokes of exhausting effort. Franchère sits amidships, watching the river intently. McKay at the bow directs the men past a large and dangerous sawyer.

The following day McKay and Franchère carry the empty canoe over their heads along a portage. The *voyageurs*, each carrying a ninety-pound pack with the help of a neck strap, amble along beside the river which has narrowed to six hundred yards and is full of rocks and white water. McKay walks in the lead, breathing heavily. "'Tis the passengers' lot to portage the canoe. Aye, lad! An unspoken rule of the forest!"

The next evening at sunset a joint of venison roasts beside the fire. The canoe is beached on a lush island of tall pines as the men smoke pipes and do personal chores in a leisurely fashion. Laframboise is carving a new paddle. Franchère makes a journal entry. "Tomorrow we enter Lake Champlain, lads," McKay comments as he cuts a piece of the roasting venison.

"Three days more to New York, *monsieur?*" Franchère asks.

"Four days, lad, if the weather holds."

The following afternoon near the lakeshore, the canoe passes a small, apparently deserted settlement. A hand-painted sign *SMAL-POX* is at the water's edge.

Sitting by the campfire after supper, Bruslé plays his guitar and sings *Savez-vous Danser La Polka?* The men join in with spirit as the two younger Lapensée brothers bounce up and polka around the fire to the amusement of all.

In the early morning hours, a raft larger than the canoe, with blankets for sails, and three boys rowing, moves with the current toward Canada. It is occupied by a boatman, his wife and another man, with one young daughter, chairs, kettles, pans, three or four dogs, barrels, crab net and fishing gear. As it approaches, the whole exhibits poverty and filth.

The raft comes abreast and the *voyageurs* stop paddling to drift alongside.

The boatman shouts, "On ye lookout for better times!"

McKay calls back, "Where then?"

"St. Jean's on the Richelieu!"

"Aye! God send you speed!"

The boatman points south. "'Tis ye fever. Ye devil's own work!"

McKay turns to the men. "The smallpox. Come, lads." He waves to the boatman as they pull away.

By midafternoon, the canoe and baggage fill a wagon pulled by oxen. McKay and the wagon master walk at the head of the team. The Frenchmen are strung out ahead and behind.

"Have you seen death in these parts from the fever?" McKay inquires as they stroll beside the oxen.

"Nay. Only sickness what folks call ye typhus." The wagon master considers the point. "Ye Lord's voice is filled with wrath."

"But you have God's providence in this land. 'Tis not poor like some."

The man grunts skeptically in reply. Too much talk is a nuisance.

They walk on and McKay finally asks, "Many hours to the river?"

"I'll have ye to ye river Hudson by sunset."

Before darkness settles over the landscape, camp is made and one of the men kindles the communal fire. Franchère and Bruslé each pluck a large wild turkey in preparation for roasting. The canoe rests upside down on the bank by a broad river. Nadeau and Laframboise are caulking the seams. A pot of tree resin smokes over a small fire. "Cover the seams well, lads," McKay cautions. "We've a long three days ahead."

Two days later all is tranquil as the canoe moves with the current midstream down a wide, apparently virgin river. Along both banks a broadleaf forest grows to the water's edge. McKay in his wide-brimmed felt hat paddles the lead position. As they approach a bend of the river the silence is suddenly broken by a piercing, shrill whistle.

The Frenchmen immediately stop paddling and stare downriver in stunned silence. The canoe begins to drift with the current. A second whistle blows.

The birchbark rocks violently as Laframboise and Olivier lunge for a flintlock. "Mind the canoe, lads!" McKay shouts. With considerable difficulty he maintains control.

Laframboise and Olivier inadvertently grab at opposite ends of the same weapon. The two yank at the gun, pulling themselves off balance and tipping the canoe dangerously. It begins to drift sideways. McKay turns to them. His tone is final. "Michel! Olivier! Do as you're bid!" They let go of the weapon and Laframboise faces McKay in amazement. The others begin paddling. The canoe responds and is quickly under control.

"That whistle has blown on this same river these three years past. Remember, this is America, lads." The whistle sounds again. McKay continues with irony, "Or one wee corner of her!"

Laframboise takes up his paddle. "*Oui*-yes, *monsieur*. I am *composé*." He glances to the sky, confiding respectfully to the Lord. "Pardon, *monsieur*. I am almost laugh. *Supposé* 'tis bad wind dat blow in *Amérique*, ha? *Eh bien!*" (All right!)

As they round the bend, an ungainly, noisy, smoke-belching sidewheeler approaches a rude wharf of logs. Paddle wheels churn laboriously while a tall black chimney throws out heavy smoke and sparks as though the hull were consumed with fire. A gaff-rigged spanker is being lowered. Again the shrill, penetrating whistle pierces the air. The sound is louder now and readily identified with the ship. She is quite unlike anything ever seen or heard by man before.

The Frenchmen are transfixed by the incongruous thing afloat, painted white, moving without sails, and causing such turbulence and smoke. As the whistle dies, Laframboise stares in disbelief. "*Oh là, là! C'est un beau bougre!*" (Oh! It's a pretty bugger!)

Franchère suddenly comes to his senses. "She burns, *monsieur*! *Bon sang!* (Good God!) We must help. We must help, *monsieur!*"

McKay responds to Franchère's alarm as he guides the canoe downstream. "Without the smoke she would not move, lad. I've made the journey on her from New York City to Albany City in little more than thirty hours. Aye, think of it! We would require three long days to paddle our empty canoe that 160 miles against the current."

In his concern, Franchère does not comprehend. "But she burns, *monsieur!* We must help…" The sound of the yet louder whistle drowns his voice.

The Frenchmen completely forget the movement of their own craft as they drift in the current toward this white monster with moving paddle wheels and belching black chimney. They watch as deck lines are made ready to throw to black men who await with wide-eyed anticipation and confused urgency. A mounted, overweight horseman appears to direct them. The name *CATSKILL*, hand written at the landing, identifies the place. Excitement and shouts and movement are everywhere as the community gathers for the ship's arrival. Young black children and young white children run helter-skelter.

The rhythmic sounds of steam engine and churning paddle wheels are cut by a sudden blast of the whistle. The Frenchmen, distracted by the boat's size and noise, are unaware that the canoe is approaching one of the paddle wheels. The whistle stops and is immediately followed by a second long blast which drowns McKay's voice, but there is energy in his expression and lip movement. "Heave to starboard, lads! Bring her about!"

From the deck near one splashing paddle wheel, the boat captain waves and shouts as the canoe is finally brought under control and avoids a collision. The sounds of this ungainly ship overwhelm all as she maneuvers toward the landing. *CLERMONT NEW-YORK* is written in black on the white deck cabin.

The *voyageurs* hold their position and glide with ease around the *Clermont* while inspecting it. Passengers on deck react to the uncommon sight of a fully loaded birchbark canoe with long-haired, dark-skinned, buckskin and red wool cap-bedecked crew which appears to them an unexpected and up-close look at savages.

McKay guides the canoe toward the wharf. "I fancy jacketed potatoes with our venison. Aye, and tonight, an extra tot of grog." With real excitement, he exclaims, "We'll be saying good-by to this grand country all too soon! There'll be no potatoes for purchase in the Oregon, lads. You can mark me words on that!"

A gangway is put in place and a farmer, roughly dressed, and a tall Indian, wearing scruffy white man's clothes and leading four black children tied in line with a heavy rope, disembark and join the excited crowd on the busy riverfront. Six black slaves immediately begin loading wood onto the *Clermont* under the direction of the mounted white man while two black deck hands carry bolts of cloth, barrels and coils of rope down the gangway onto the landing.

The Frenchmen remain with the canoe while McKay and Franchère walk into the riverfront crowd. McKay spots an old woman, rawboned and toothless, dressed in rough homespun and smoking a short-stemmed clay pipe, sitting under a tree watching the goings-on and crosses to her. "Good day to you, mistress. Can I purchase some potatoes about?"

With a glint in her eye, she glances at Franchère before sizing up McKay. Then, without answering, she taps the ash from her pipe and takes some tobacco from a leather pouch that hangs about her neck.

McKay speaks louder. "Some potatoes for tonight's supper! Would there be any for sale?"

Without acknowledging him, she rubs out the tobacco, loads her pipe, then responds matter-of-factly, "There be no potatoes in this valley, sonny. Can scarce harvest 'em fast enough for folks down New York way, which all grow rich an' potent by 'em!" She lights her pipe with a shower of sparks from a flint and steel. "Barrels o' pork an' linseed oil a-plenty from the mill be ye current commodity."

"Thank you, mistress," McKay replies but is quickly cut off.

"Only place would have a quantity o' potatoes is ye agitatin' contrivance o' city folk," she points to the *Clermont*, "there! Strange it is to see the great alteration it makes among ye Indians themselves. It turn to ye ruin o' many."

"Thank you kindly."

"No law can restrain them as be rich an' powerful!" She points at the canoe. "Why abide ye with ye Indians? They all be poor and beggarly in these parts."

McKay is amused. "But those are Frenchmen, mistress!"

"Frenchmen?"

"Aye. Fur trappers!"

"Why there be no traffic o' furs this time o' year!" She tamps her pipe with disgust. "But ye Frenchmen and ye Indians be all the same."

"Aye, mistress. And good day to you!" McKay heads across the crowded landing to the *Clermont*.

The old woman shouts after him, "Folks be all unworthy nowadays!"

Franchère listens out of courtesy while she speaks, but as he sets off to follow McKay, the tall Indian with the four black children in tow, who disembarked earlier, grabs his arm, stopping him. He points to the children. "Them damn good, Captain. You buy?"

"*Va te faire fiche!*" (Get lost!) Franchère reacts and pulls his arm free.

The Indian is a middle-aged layabout, a pathetic borderland savage, corrupted by the European's vices but unable to thrive in his culture. The four children are skinny, young, and frightened. "You give money!" the Indian insists, pointing at the children. "Work plenty damned fast, Captain. No eat much!"

Franchère is shaken. "*Mordieu!* (God's death!) But where is the mother?"

"No damn good," the Indian replies. "Me sell. No get much. You give money?"

"*Salaud!* (Bastard!) You should keep together with the mother!"

"No damn good. Indian win cards. No want nigger. Want money. You give money? Work plenty damn good."

"No money!" McKay's voice booms out as he returns for Franchère.

"You give rum?" the Indian responds, pointing to the children. "Plenty work."

"No rum!"

"No want damn nigger. No eat damn nigger flesh." The Indian wanders off pulling the children along.

McKay and Franchère board the *Clermont* and walk toward the stern. The steam engine and powerful connecting rods are now silent. Wood continues to be brought aboard and stowed near the large boiler by the barefooted, overheated black men.

As they reach the large boiler, a deck hand throws open the door and feeds four-foot split logs into the blazing fire. The furnace-like flames and the heat startle Franchère as does the hiss of the boiler's noisy safety valve.

"Good evening to the Captain!" McKay calls out and motions Franchère to wait for him. The grizzled, red-bearded Irish steamboat captain leans heavily on the rail, intent on the activities ashore as McKay approaches. "My apologies to the Captain." The captain continues to face ashore, ignoring McKay who stops by the rail. "I fear the men were a bit distracted by the *Clermont*. They've not seen her likes on the St. Lawrence."

The captain turns to McKay and measures him scornfully from head to foot. "The St. Lawrence is it now! By God, home o' the British Navy!"

McKay holds the captain firmly with his gaze. "You've an interest in the British Navy, Captain?"

The captain releases the rail as he draws himself to full height. "And ye would, sir," he replies, full of indignation, "if ye were captain of an American schooner!" He gestures down the river. "Used to do a bit o' coastin'. A fair old trade out there. But let a British lieutenant board ye, man, and ye might as well surrender the entire ship's crew. Impress the seamen as they like! Damn their almighty souls! No respect for the American flag!"

"Aye," McKay replies. "A flag in the forest don't count for much these days. British against British. British against American. It's the brigade with the full packs that gets the best return in Montreal."

The captain takes a step toward McKay. "Lookin' for a passage, are ye? As far as Albany City, two-fifty." He lowers his voice. "I can give ye sixteen cents for every fare-paying passenger ye put aboard. Fifty cents for a meal, and no smoking in the great cabin!"

His attention shifts suddenly to the black deck hand beside the boiler who is closing the furnace door. "Fill 'er up, blast ye!" he booms out. "I'll have yer ugly hide for me supper!"

"It isn't a passage I'm wanting," McKay replies. "I'm wanting to purchase some potatoes."

"Some..." He pauses, incredulous, eyeing McKay distrustfully. "What did ye say?"

"Potatoes, Captain. Good Irish potatoes for a Sunday supper."

The captain is suddenly indignant. "Ye'll not find the likes o' Irish potatoes in this land, sir!"

"The men have supped on nothing but wild turkey and venison."

"Irish potatoes." The captain's tone becomes mocking. "A buckskin kilt would be more likely in these parts. Waxin' a bit sentimental, are ye?"

"Five shillings for a half bushel," McKay offers.

"One dollar did ye say? And it's half a bushel ye'll be wantin'?"

"Aye. You can hardly tell what satisfaction a potato would give."

"Ye have coin?"

"Aye, Captain. English sterling."

"No potatoes," he replies flatly.

"Sterling is legal tender in these states."

"No potatoes for sale, sir!"

McKay is startled, but replies with dignity, "Right you are, Captain. And good day to you." He turns and motions to Franchère.

After a moment of brooding the captain calls out, "From Canada, did ye say?"

McKay turns back to him. "Aye. Traveling to New York harbor. A bit of luck with headwinds, and the lads will sleep there tomorrow. I grant you making a fuss over Sunday supper is, as you say, sentimental. Good day."

The captain motions McKay back while taking a couple of steps toward him. "Carryin' a bit o' grog for the men, are ye?"

"A bit of rum for the lads."

The captain lowers his voice. "Ye wouldn't have with ye a jug o' Scots whisky, me man?"

"Aye, Captain. But only a wee drop to satisfy me-self."

He steps up to McKay and cautiously removes a half-pint flask from his pocket.

"Mind ye, there's no drop o' spirit I'd sooner draw than a full and sweet Irish whiskey. But ye fill me flask, man, and ye can have all the American potatoes ye can carry!"

McKay turns around to Franchère and winks in triumph as he says sternly, "Fetch me jug, Franchère!"

The captain extends his hand to McKay. "Aye. Well done!"

"I thank you, Captain. And Mr Astor thanks you!"

Part I
New York City 1810

Chapter Six

A STILL AND DAMP FOG enshrouds the buildings of South Street and, opposite, the brigs and ships tied together along the East River wharves of Manhattan Island. Here and there a lantern's ethereal yellow glow interrupts the silent early morning light.

Across from the ships, a plain woman dressed in full skirt and bonnet approaches a water pump at one corner of the row of houses which serve as shops on the ground floor facing South Street. She hangs a wooden bucket beneath the spigot, pushes up her sleeves and with both arms and considerable effort works the large lever up and down. After a couple of strokes water begins to spurt.

Not far away a tradesman rolls a barrel out through the open door of his shop and stands it beside others that line the outside wall. As he turns to enter, a rooster darts out the door and past him into the quiet, cobbled street. The tradesman shouts, "Get ye back here, Michael!" and immediately gives chase.

Hitched to a solitary dray that is heavily loaded with hundredweight sacks of coal, an old and blind horse stands motionless beneath a bowsprit at the edge of a wharf crowded with sacks of grain, rows of barrels and boxes of different sizes. An untidy, fleshy boy, perhaps fourteen but big for his age, wearing a worn wool cap and jacket, sits idly atop the sacks of coal. A thin and grizzled coalmonger, well past middle age, also wearing a wool cap, approaches the dray from the wharf and calls out sternly, "Aye, Jack! Up with ye, now!"

The boy swings a sack of coal by the corners and lowers it to the shoulder of the coalmonger who soon returns from his delivery. He mounts and without touching the reins, the dray proceeds over the wet cobblestones with a steady CLOP-CLOP, CLOP-CLOP, CLOP-CLOP.

Aaron Slaight, a duffle over one shoulder and a small bag of tools under his arm, appears in the fog beside the water pump. Slaight is short, strong, dark-haired, with a ruddy glow to his full but firm cheeks and a good-natured twinkle in his eye. He hails the dray with a vigorous wave of his cap.

The dray comes to a stop near an ornate figurehead with the name *BETSEY* carved in the bulwark planking. Slaight crosses South Street. "Would 'ee know the ship *Tonquin*, me good man?"

"Aye, a vessel o' 290 ton. Hull o' red cedar and live oak. Double-flush decked. As fast a sailer as any sloop o' war o' the Navy." Slaight stares speechless. "'Tis me next stop but one," the coalmonger boasts with a touch of pride and motions Slaight aboard.

Again the horse begins its monotonous CLOP-CLOP, CLOP-CLOP and pulls the dray under endless bowsprits that extend from massive, black hulls holding the giant yardarms and spars, shrouds and stays which are barely visible in the stillness of the early morning fog.

"Oh dear, oh dear! Don't often see such a day," Slaight remarks. "'Tis proper mazed." The coalmonger stares ahead without comment. Slaight continues, "A brave ship, the *Tonquin*, I hear say."

"Why, man, a tidy ship, the *Tonquin!*" The coalmonger warms to the topic. "Built, coppered, rigged and launched by Adam and Noah Brown. Takes their coal regular. Real gentlemen they are."

"Aye?"

"Aye." He halts the dray. "Up with ye, Jack. A hundredweight!"

Slaight leaps off the dray and shoulders the heavy sack the boy hands down. The coalmonger confidently points the direction and walks with Slaight along the wharf. He is pleased with himself and is beginning to like Slaight.

Near a gangplank on the quiet wharf, the coalmonger points to other goods that await loading and Slaight drops the sack of coal. "I've not been to the Pacific," Slaight confesses, breathless.

"Are ye crazy, man?" the coalmonger responds eagerly, at once confidential.

"What's that?" Slaight is startled. "Don't know as I follow thy meanin'."

"Why, look about ye! How many bottoms d'ye know to be a-clearin' for the Pacific?"

Slaight is puzzled. "None other but the *Lydia* from Boston, an' she has 'er full complement o' crew."

"There's the point, man! 'Tis a wild land, the Pacific. For the likes o' them that be daft, I'd say!"

A sow followed by her piglets wanders along, snuffling for food as the two men return to the dray.

"Know o' the ship *Boston*, do ye?" the coalmonger asks significantly.

"Nay."

"Why, man, 'tis more than seven year since she sailed for the Pacific." They climb aboard the dray. "Nor came she back that year nor the next!" Again the dray begins moving through the fog without the coalmonger touching the reins. "Aye. Destroyed by savages, by damn! The whole crew but for the smith and the sailmaker!"

Slaight is wide-eyed. "Oh dear, oh dear! That's me trade, a sailmaker."

"The crew burned and scalped!" Warming to the topic, he turns to Slaight. "And eaten, too, if ye ask me!" Slaight takes it all in. "Look ye! Them that goes are such as whalers. Gloustermen. From the Vinyard. Wild billies, I tell ye! Them that have naught o' the fear o' God in 'em. Why, them that goes would look a savage in the eye!"

Slaight squirms uncomfortably. "Do 'ee know the master o' the ship *Tonquin* then?"

"Cap'n Thorn?" The old man considers. "His first ship, man. Likes his comfort, I can tell ye. Goes through a hundredweight o' coal a week. Aye. But ye'll be a-meetin' Cap'n Thorn soon enough." He points to the brig they are approaching. "That's the *Tonquin* ahead there!"

All is astir on deck as they approach. A derrick boom of the foremast juts out prominently and is being worked by members of the *Tonquin*'s crew. Coils of cordage and bolts of canvas are hoisted from the wharf below. Both forward and aft gangplanks are in use with men carrying supplies on board. The coalmonger and Slaight dismount from the dray.

"Look a' that," Slaight observes with surprise, "pierced for twenty-two gun!"

"On account o' savages, man. What did I tell ye?" He turns to the boy. "Up with ye, Jack! The rest o' this coal for the *Tonquin*, here. Up with ye, now!"

In the center of the main deck, occupying most of the space between the mainmast and the foremast, is the large raised square of the main cargo hatch. A derrick boom of the mainmast, worked by a crew of seamen, is lowering the head timbers of a schooner into the main hold.

J. C. Fox, twenty-two year old first mate, rawboned, a short but strong man, is directing the seamen on the fall of the mainmast derrick. Fox comes from a family of Massachusetts merchant seamen and is confident and easygoing with both men and officers, making no fuss over a job that might require his lending a hand.

He peers into the hold as the load of head timbers descends, motioning to the men on the fall, "Easy… easy…" He turns to the nearest seaman. "Don't you go wakin' the dead, Edward Ames. Easy now!"

Ames, a young and skinny seventeen year old on the end of the fall, five feet tall and appears very much a greenhorn, tightens his grip.

Fox motions to the men. "She's down. Tie her off!"

The large hatchway gives access to two decks, both crowded, dark, and uninviting, which are packed with kegs, barrels and crates, bales covered with canvas, bolts of cotton cloth, bars of iron. The lower hold is nearly full but for the space where the men are working.

William Mumford, tall second mate of Irish descent who at thirty-three has sailed the Northwest Coast of America, disconnects the fall from the load as a dejected crew of seven young Frenchmen stand idly by not comprehending what is expected of them. All wear new cotton duck trousers received on their arrival from the St. Lawrence with McKay and Franchère as passengers. Finally they have reached the long anticipated destination, beautiful New York City.

Mumford barks orders with increasing impatience as the Frenchmen are inefficient and uncertain in response. "Tie her to starboard. Over there, mate! As far forward as she will go. This space is for barrels of gunpowder, the last item to go aboard."

Fox points sharply as he watches the men in the hold. "Flush up the starboard hold, Mr Mumford!" He turns to the men on the fall. "They'll have the deck beams next. Give'r the long stroke, Edward Ames!"

The empty hook flies aloft, and Fox turns to another man in new trousers who is bent over a corner of the hatch with a tar bucket. "Look you here, young fellow," Fox remarks in a stern but even tone, "if you want to get on aboard this ship without trouble, put some elbow grease into that swab and tar the seam proper like." Michel Laframboise looks up, his face wet with perspiration and eyes expressing something between bewilderment and anger. Although he understands little of what is said to him, he says nothing and continues to coat the seam. "We can't have no skulkers aboard this ship."

Fox spots Aaron Slaight at the gangway as he steps aboard the *Tonquin* and immediately crosses toward him. Fox eyes the duffle suspiciously as Slaight approaches. "I'd speak with Captain Thorn, sir. Would 'ee be the mate, now?"

"Aye. But we can have no men without papers. Orders from Mr Astor."

Slaight draws himself up to full height, "I be no Englishman, sir!"

Fox responds patiently, "Aye. 'Tis all the same aboard the *Tonquin*. Have you the American citizenship papers or not?"

"Aye. Purchased 'em yesterday, I did, sir."

"Mr Fox!" Captain Thorn's voice booms out from the quarterdeck.

Fox waves to the captain. "Aye, Captain!" He turns to Slaight. "Provin' gunpowder at the moment."

"Mr Fox, we're ready!" Thorn barks, an edge of impatience in his voice.

"Aye, aye, Captain!"

Slaight hurries to keep up with Fox who strides toward the quarterdeck. "Never known such a thing," Slaight remarks. "Provin' gunpowder. Blow us all asunder!"

"Captain will have no restored powder aboard the *Tonquin*."

"An pierced for twenty-two gun!"

"She mounts only a battery o' ten. But the captain'll use 'em proper, mind." He points as he increases his pace. "Stand at the rail, forward o' the mizzen."

As they separate, Slaight comments to himself, "Cap'n better know what 'ees about!"

Jonathan Thorn, twenty-eight year old master of the ship *Tonquin*, waits at the port bulwark with Stephen Weeks who fills a small flask from an open half-barrel of fine grain musket powder. Nearby stands a ninety-pound full barrel of large grain cylinder powder.

Thorn, a bachelor, handsome and trim, a native of New York, is determined to be exact in this, his first command. His entire schooling has been in the service of the United States Navy, where emphasis on obedience and orderliness is fundamental. He has been trained to depend solely upon his own judgement to order his men's well-being.

Weeks, a native of New York and not yet twenty-five years old, is the ship's armorer. With a second small flask in hand, he crosses toward the center of the quarterdeck.

Fox approaches as Thorn shouts, "Stand by!" He turns to Weeks. "One dram, Mr Weeks." With full concentration on Weeks, "All clear, Mr Fox?"

"In just a moment." Fox crosses in front of Thorn.

Thorn lashes out, losing all patience. "Mr Fox!" He faces his mate suddenly angry and challenging. "We are waiting to blast, sir!"

Fox stops immediately and replies with respect but matter-of-factly, "The powder is uncovered, Captain. Before you blast, I'll throw a canvas over it."

Thorn turns pale as he sees the open barrels of lethal powder and realizes at once he could have blown up the ship. He is unexpectedly but completely checked by his mate. With forced steadiness to cover a sense of humiliation and resentment at being corrected, he replies, "Of course. Take your position opposite the mizzen when the powder is covered."

Fox is unruffled and with the powder covered goes over to the port bulwark before he calls out, "All clear, sir!"

"All clear, Mr Weeks. Prepare to fire!"

Weeks empties a thirty-grain flask (about a teaspoon) of large grain black powder into a compact pile against the vertical piece at the center of a heavy "L" shaped copper plate. With the second flask, he pours a thin line of fine grain powder along the seam to the edge of the plate. Weeks then crouches behind the vertical plate, lights a slow-match, and puts it into the end of a two-foot match-staff. "Ready to blast, sir!" He holds the slow-match a few inches from the thin line of powder.

Thorn gives the command, "Fire!"

The slow match touches the priming powder and ignition is instantaneous with a concussion that drowns Thorn's command before it is completed. There is a flash of flame that momentarily envelops the copper plate leaving a discharge of heavy white smoke which slowly rises and spreads.

Weeks examines the plate closely. "No beads o' foulness, sir. Looks a good job to me."

Thorn and Fox approach. "Any sparks, Mr Fox?"

"None, Captain. Clean and sharp as she should be."

Thorn turns to the cabin door, "That will do, Mr Weeks. Come with me, Mr Fox."

Chapter Seven

Tiny mullioned windows fill the stern wall of Thorn's cabin. A double lantern hangs from the low ceiling over a heavy, rimmed table and six captain's chairs. To one side, a small iron fireplace is alight with a coal fire and next to it stands a chart table with a lantern overhead and a locker.

Thorn crosses to the chart table to gather invoices. "Have a seat, Mr Fox."

Fox approaches the Captain's table and seeing a pile of papers at one end takes a chair near them. A small engraved portrait of a woman lies atop a stack of handwritten letters. He turns to Thorn. "Very handsome, sir. Your wife?"

Thorn is startled. He returns to the table at once. "My mother," he replies awkwardly and carries the picture and letters to a locker.

"Your mother wears her years well, sir," Fox comments, trying to relieve the tension.

"Those should have been put away." Thorn returns to the table, his hands empty though he seems uneasy. Something is on his mind. "I don't like to be called on deck unnecessarily, Mr Fox." He paces to the fireplace and back. "Yesterday. Those infernal Frenchmen. Dressed like savages. Acted as if they owned the *Tonquin* the way they came aboard and touched everything."

"I've issued clothing and put them to work, sir. They will learn their place."

Thorn turns again and walks to the fireplace, speaking with unwarranted intensity. "You cannot maintain order without discipline, Mr Fox." He picks up the poker and jabs at the burning coals to knock the dead ash through. He does not look at his mate. "I will have no insubordination aboard ship!"

Fox stares hard at this new captain but quickly hides his concern. He speaks tentatively, searching for a way to communicate. "Crew tends to be a bit relaxed aboard a merchantman, sir. But there will be no grumbling once they understand the ship's routine."

Thorn approaches the table and asserts sharply, "There will be discipline on my ship, Mr Fox!"

"Of course, Captain. As you say, sir."

Thorn again crosses to the chart table and returns to Fox with a pile of invoices. He sits. "You should have finished loading these by now." He reads from an invoice, "Blankets, barrels of tar, kegs of vinegar, hogsheads of molasses and tobacco, boxes of soap, two hundred sides of sole leather."

"Aye, Captain. All stowed."

Thorn continues with another invoice, "Northwest guns, Philadelphia muskets, a brass howitzer?"

"All stowed, sir."

Thorn is more incredulous with each item as he reads from another invoice. "Forty barrels beads, thirty-one bales scarlet cloth, two chests round ear boobs." He glances up. "Rubbish." He reads on, impatiently, "fifty-dozen red-handled London scalping knives, thirty-dozen iron tomahawks?"

"All stowed, Captain. Items for the Indian trade."

"Five thousand pounds Louisiana lead, twenty-five tubs Swedish steel, an extra blacksmith's forge?"

"Aye, sir, all stowed. The frame and fittings for the schooner our men will assemble on the Pacific are being loaded at this very time. Most of the chickens are aboard. The pigs will be delivered this morning, I understand." There is a sharp rap at the door.

Thorn gets up from the table irritably, invoices in hand, as the door opens and Mumford enters. "Beggin' your pardon, Captain. The coalmonger is waitin' to be paid, and there's a sailmaker who would speak with ye, sir."

"Send in the sailmaker. The coalmonger can wait." Thorn turns from the door as Mumford exits. Slaight enters with his duffle and stands silently behind Thorn.

"We will drop down the channel to anchor off the Battery this evening. Tomorrow we take on the gunpowder. I want it stowed promptly, Mr Fox."

"Aye, Captain."

Thorn walks to his chart table without noticing Slaight and sets aside the invoices.

"Send out notice this afternoon to the inns at Brooklyn Village for the passengers' chests to be put aboard. There are four partners, eleven clerks…" Thorn stops abruptly as he notices Slaight. "Your name and business, sir."

Slaight straightens up. "Aaron Slaight, sir, a sailmaker by trade, and I'm wantin' to know about the *Tonquin*'s voyage.

Thorn sits down. "The voyage will be of about eighteen-months duration, 'round Cape Horn to the mouth of the Columbia River, at forty-six degrees of north latitude, where we leave passengers with supplies for a trading post. We continue north to trade and hunt for skins along the coast. We stop at the Russian settlement at fifty-seven degrees of north latitude, and then sail to Canton to trade. From there, we take on a load of China goods, double the Horn and return to New York."

"About the trade 'ee mention, sir. I hear them savages can be a might o' trouble. In a manner o' speakin', sir, 'ave 'ee any concern?"

"Mr Astor, the owner of the *Tonquin*, is purchasing nine thousand pounds of large grain cylinder powder which we will carry aboard the *Tonquin* with canister and grapeshot. Most of the gunpowder is for the Russian trade, but we have use of it, if necessary. In addition, I have obtained from navy stores a number of rounds of spherical case-shot which I had occasion to fire with great effect against the Bashaw of Tripoli in the Barbary Wars. With only a gunboat, sir, I was able to unman their frigates. One sweep from a broadside and their rigging dropped to pieces." Slaight is wide-eyed as Thorn continues, gaining confidence as he speaks. "This is a new type of projectile the American Navy calls shrapnel-shell. It is particularly effective at close range." Thorn stands up. "If you think a pack of Godless savages can harm the *Tonquin* while I'm in command, sir, find yourself another ship!"

"I thank 'ee, Captain, for the assurance. That be only in a manner o' askin', sir. Might I know, Cap'n, what would 'ee be offerin' in pay?"

"Twelve dollars per month and a half percent of the trade in skins, if you know your trade, sir!"

Slaight is pleased. "Aye, that I do, Captain, that I do. The *Tonquin*'ll do us proper, sir."

"Report to Mr Mumford, the second mate. His crew is in the hold. We need all hands for loading today. At eight bells, report here to sign the ship's articles, and bring your papers."

"Excuse me, Captain, but the Frenchmen are working below with Mr Mumford. The crew on the foremast derrick is short."

Thorn gestures impatiently. "Report to Mr Anderson, the bo'sun, at the foremast derrick."

Thorn turns to Fox as Slaight leaves the cabin. "I have a final meeting with Mr Astor tomorrow morning when the gunpowder is delivered." He eyes Fox pointedly. "You will be in charge. We up-anchor with the turn of the tide. I will not be delayed, Mr Fox!"

Chapter Eight

THE MORNING IS CLEAR and sun-swept as two men on horseback approach a "Y" junction. Their pace is leisurely but pleasurable with frequent gestures from the rider who takes the lead, indicating conversation between them. The road cuts through an extensive forest of pine and hemlock with the nearby East River running parallel.

John Jacob Astor at forty-seven is somewhat corpulent, with a thick crop of dark hair and an aggressive quality of energy and single-mindedness that makes his presence felt. A man of business, strengthened by success, he speaks with conviction and with the habit of looking directly at men. In his dealings with individuals he is honest and unwavering but when confronted with tariffs, embargoes or commercial regulations of any sort, he is keenly alert to every possible gain by manipulation. Although he has lived in America for over twenty-six years and has been married most of the time into one of the old, well-established families of New York City, he speaks with a heavy German accent which he would be the first to acknowledge.

Astor reins in his horse at the junction and turns to Thorn. "What do you think! The skins in two places was punctured! *Mein Gott* (my God)! The animals was shot!" He turns in the saddle, animated. "Can you think the amount I lose on this beaver? Ach! It is enough to make me ill!" They continue at a walk. "The skin is for me the same as the man. For the good ones, we cannot pay too dear. But the indifferent ones, they are too dear at any price." He spurs his horse and flies into the woods on a double-rutted wagon road.

Thorn's cheeks are flushed and his eyes water as he spurs his horse to pull abreast. The two men canter through the woods, over a creek, around a fallen tree, and into a glen. The road again divides and Astor follows the narrow trail that leads deeper into the forest.

Suddenly a fence appears ahead where the dirt track curves to one side. Astor points to the fence ahead with anticipation as he spurs his horse off the trail and jumps the barrier.

Thorn follows and they rein in and walk their steaming horses. Astor is breathless as he speaks. "This is my Hurl Gate Estate. Thirteen acres on the East River."

They reach a stream and dismount. "I like in the early hours to ride around the city and check the lands. But I think this morning to sell some land, otherwise your countrymen run his coach and six through my property and think it is his own by possession!"

The two men lead their horses along the stream. "This property I buy for the family."

"A good place to be when the smallpox or yellow fever breaks out."

Astor stops to loosen the saddle girth. Thorn follows his example. "This is the backwoods," Astor comments and points ahead. "The house is less than one mile."

They resume walking. "Are you satisfied with the crew of the *Tonquin?*"

Thorn stares ahead as he speaks. "I regret I could not convince Midshipman Blake to come aboard as first officer. He is hoping for a commission."

Astor is surprised. "But Mr Fox has the experience as first officer! And he knows the wind and tides in the Southern Hemisphere."

Thorn does not yield. "I will learn soon enough if he is a good officer. He is a bit independent, sir."

Astor turns to Thorn, gesturing intently as he walks. "Of course! He is seaman! This man bring my ship from Calcutta in eighty-four days. The record time!" Mildly, but with energy, Astor continues. "This is not the military ship but the merchant ship. The stowage is important, and this Mr Fox understands. And he has doubled Cape Horn, which is advantage to you, I think!"

Thorn is stung by Astor's remark. "There will be no problem with navigation, sir."

Astor stops him, replying mechanically, "*Das ist gut* (that's good)! Now, Captain Thorn, we must give full attention to these Frenchmen. They do not know the life on the sea. Feed them the best you can. We need all these men for the trade on the Pacific. You buy the fresh food at the Sandwich Islands. And you pick out twenty or twenty-five natives. Strong men, young men, to make work for us at the new post. They can return after two years."

Astor faces Thorn. "While on the coast of the Pacific, if you should meet any accident, *Gott* forbid, that force you to put by in distress among the wild people." His eyes are riveted to Thorn's. "Do not permit them to come aboard. Not even near the ship. Ships have been taken and with their whole crews destroyed!"

Thorn goes momentarily rigid but covers his offense at Astor's lack of confidence in him. He responds in a measured, deliberate tone. "You need not worry about the *Tonquin*, sir. I am prepared for the savages."

Astor lectures this young man oblivious to his reaction. "On all occasion, you consult and advise with Mr McKay, someone of great knowledge of these people and good judgement." Astor looks away momentarily then turns back to Thorn. "We must always make the favorable impression with these wild people. Mr McKay understands this. Our fortune depends on them! But, do not rely too much on their friendly disposition."

Thorn knows his employer to be successful and stares at him out of deference but does not concentrate on what he says. Astor senses this and takes a step closer. "All accidents which happen arise from too much confidence in the Indians."

"There will be no trouble, sir," Thorn answers at once, covering anger at the suggestion that his authority might be wanting.

"Stay clear of the coast of California. It is not hospitable place, and rest assured the Spanish padres will shave you if they have the chance."

They resume walking along the creek as Astor continues. "Make every caution possible with the Russians. At New Archangel, do not do anything contrary to Governor Baranoff, or the least slip will be jumped at. He is difficult man, but he would trade with whoever can be depended on. They need the gunpowder according to my reports. That is why you take the large supply."

"Do you wish a contract for a future voyage?"

"*Ja, das ist gut!* But obtain some few samples of Siberian sable." They continue walking. "Look out for the brig *Lydia* of Boston under Captain Davis. Each year he kills the sea otter and the seals, in a single season more than seventy-four thousand skins."

"Boston captains think themselves lords of the sea."

"But they speculate with the rum and the gunpowder to the Indians. This is against the wish of the Russians. For this reason, I think we have prospect for the trade." He turns to Thorn. "I wish to supply both our settlement on the Columbia River and the Russian American Fur Company. We must control all the trade, Captain Thorn, to have the command of the market! You will buy skins which do not cost as much as six-pence. And they bring one hundred dollars in the China market!"

Astor stops walking. "Do not omit to write to me as often as you can." He has said all he has to say and turns away. It does not occur to him to inquire of his young captain if there is anything further he wishes to discuss. Astor's mood changes as he surveys the peaceful woods that surround them. "Look at the trees, Captain Thorn," he remarks paternally. "You will see no trees for many months. Compared with them, we live to little purpose, I think so."

Astor turns to his horse and tightens the saddle girth. "Mrs Astor would be flattered if you change your mind and join us for dinner. She plan the small gathering of friends to bring the luck to the partners."

Thorn mounts his horse. "Thank you, sir, but I must attend to the *Tonquin*. We sail at midnight with the turn of the tide." There is an unexpected glint of friendliness in Thorn's eye. "But I will celebrate with you when the *Tonquin* returns."

Astor settles himself in the saddle. "*Sehr gut*, Captain (very good…)." He gestures ahead with animation. "Come! This creek lead by Trinity Church to the Broad Way." Challenging his companion, "Captain Thorn, only one gate to jump!" They spur their horses.

Chapter Nine

That evening two great doors with massive strap hinges are opened inward by liveried male servants to a spacious room with a well-appointed table set for twenty-six people. A large stone fireplace is blazing and, at the far end of the room, a sideboard holds two charcoal braziers that warm bulky, silver tureens.

Astor, leading the guests, enters first with Mrs Francis James Jackson, young, unusually attractive wife of the British ambassador, dressed in high style, who speaks with a marked French accent. He confides to her as they stop at the table, "There is no secret to successful trade, madam. You have to know your Indian."

"But I understand the success you have, *monsieur*, is beyond everyone!"

Astor is pleased. "I once sold to a Mohawk for a bale of beaver worth forty pounds a flute worth one pound." He helps her to a chair beside his place at the head of the table. "He wanted the flute because I taught him to play. He became my agent."

Sarah Todd Astor, industrious, stern but intelligent, softly spoken, a plain woman of forty-eight years who carries herself with dignity but without elegance, escorts McKay. She takes his arm as they enter the large room. "Come, Mr McKay. We sit at the far end." She has a last look over the room's appointments as they walk along the formally set table with place cards to indicate seating.

"Very nice, indeed, madam," McKay comments as he openly admires the table. "In the Northern settlements, Mrs Astor, it has become a proverb that whoever would know what is good to eat must live with the Indians."

"I have heard the buffalo ribs are a favorite among people in the Far West, sir."

"Aye, madam, but that is everyday fare. The most succulent and incomparable for tenderness is, of course, unborn fawn."

Mrs Astor reacts with surprise. At the head of the table, opposite Astor, she takes her chair and McKay sits to her right.

McKay continues gently, playing to her reaction. "Ducks and geese in the shell, unborn seal pup, these are the greatest dainties that can be eaten." With a twinkle in his eye, he comments, "One must taste them to know."

Mrs Astor is taken aback. "Dear me. I'm sure I haven't, sir!"

Mayor DeWitt Clinton, escorts Mrs Clinton into the large room. Robert Fulton and Mrs Fulton accompany them. Mayor Clinton is complaining vigorously to Fulton. "We read daily, sir, about the appalling condition of the Navy."

"It is beyond comprehension that we should have only five frigates in good repair while the British command upwards of ninety ships in their squadron at Halifax."

"How can we protect American seamen from British impressment?"

His Excellency Francis James Jackson accompanies Chancellor Robert Livingston who at sixty-four is a slightly deaf, white-haired man of wealth and political shrewdness. In his deafness, the chancellor speaks a bit too loudly. "I see no signs of gratitude from Mr Perceval's government," Livingston comments pointedly, "for the United States permitting your people to continue operating trading posts in our territories north of the Ohio."

"I was not aware, Chancellor," Jackson replies, gracious but firm, "that your government's policy involved any particular liberality." A little past his prime at forty years, Jackson is polished and alert, fluent in German while speaking the King's English but is of rather severe dignity. The two men are well acquainted from treaty negotiations in Paris seven years before.

Astor joins them. "I can tell you something, gentlemen. Fully two-thirds of the skins trapped within these American states are taken north to Montreal by the British trader instead of to New York for the American merchant to make the decent profit!"

Elizabeth Sullivan, a gracious eighteen year old, inexperienced but eager and intelligent, and Mary Fairlie enter the dining room ahead of Henry Brevoort and the twenty-seven year old Washington Irving. The four have been friends from youth and are talking intently together.

"The children of liberated slaves receive free books and clothing," Elizabeth comments.

"But everything is so expensive these days," Irving replies.

"Yes. It costs fully fifteen dollars to provide for a single child for one year."

Dorothea Astor accompanies two of her father's Canadian partners, David Stuart who is prematurely grey at forty-five but preserves a mild, even disposition, and his nephew Robert, twenty years younger, active, determined, fiercely loyal to Astor, his Uncle David, and his native Scotland. Both are dressed in kilts of Royal Stuart tartan and speak with a Scots brogue.

David turns to Dorothea as they enter the dining room, "You see, mistress, there is no law among the trading partners save to fetch all the furs they can lay hands on, by whatever means. The Indians believe the trader to be the most powerful person of his nation."

Dorothea, at fifteen precocious and bursting with vitality, responds with indignation. "But how can the North West Company petition the Crown for control of Papa's territory?"

David is amused. "Because the Oregon is *not* your father's territory, mistress! The United States and Great Britain have signed a treaty that guarantees the territory to settlers of both countries." He looks at her significantly. "But one thing is certain. Parliament will grant the North West Company an exclusive charter for the fur trade in any areas of the Oregon they open."

"So that's why Papa is in such a temper!"

"Very likely, Miss Astor," Robert replies.

"All Papa talks about is the ship." She leans confidentially toward Robert, "And the British." She then turns to both of them, insistent. "But what if the British are already there and have claimed the land ahead of you?"

Robert responds matter-of-factly, "I suppose we can have no difficulty being off their side o' the river, Miss."

Captain Edmund Fanning, a confident, robust individual, enters the dining room and stops with Mrs Fanning, Mrs Livingston, and Duncan

McDougall, one of the new partners who, at forty-eight, is fleshy, old for his years and possesses a quick temper and touchy sense of pride.

"We dress the chief up," McDougall comments in a distinctive Scots brogue, "a fancy jacket with bright buttons, and stockings and cap. Makes for a good feeling, madam. Aye, helps 'em relax, in a manner o' speakin'. Encourages the trade."

Mrs Livingston is fascinated. "You have to be shrewd, Mr McDougall, to trade with savages." They approach the table and the couples separate to find their places. McDougall helps Mrs Livingston to a chair in front of her place card.

"In Albany the fashion is to seat couples opposite one another," she comments.

McDougall is bored but very polite. "Aye, indeed, madam." He bows slightly and moves to the other side of the table to find his place card.

James Fairlie, heavy set, of Philadelphia, and John Sullivan, of New York, prominent businessmen, stop near the table with Mrs Fairlie, Mrs Sullivan, and Martin Van Buren, a promising young attorney. Fairlie comments to Van Buren, "I hear said that on the river two Canadians are worth six Americans."

"So I've heard, recently. But I'll wager that in the forest one American hunter is the equal to three Canadians."

Astor is seated at the head of the table conversing with Mrs Jackson as the first course is served. "But, madam, Indian nature I have found to be human nature. The savage is a man. Courtesy, gentleness, and fairly good flute playing soothe him."

Liveried servants begin at each end of the table serving bowls of steaming soup. Mayor Clinton leans forward to a guest across from him. "Captain Fanning, sir, I have wondered for some time where you found that curious name to give your ship. *Tonquin*. An extraordinary name!"

Fanning is amused and pleased with the question. "Yes, sir, quite so! The name is, in fact, from a small but splendid Asian country."

As a bowl of soup is set before him, Fanning continues, "The northern half is called Ton-kin. It houses a gulf of the same name, one of the most temperate I have sailed."

Robert Fulton turns to him. "I know that name. It is near Siam."

"Correct, sir! It is an insignificant country called Viet-nam."

"Insignificant in size, but a fiercely independent people, I have read."

"Exactly, sir," Fanning replies in full agreement, "and I do admire them for it."

Irving comments with interest, "Independence would be a quality needed in a good sea captain, would it not, sir?"

"Absolutely so!" Fanning turns back to Clinton. "I named her *Tonquin* for that splendid gulf, before I set sail on her maiden voyage to China, but," he adds with emphasis, "you must realize, sir, she is Mr Astor's ship now."

"You've sailed to China, sir?" Mary Fairlie seems amazed. "But isn't there danger crossing the Pacific Ocean, such a large body of water?"

"Compared with river travel, miss," Fanning responds, "the sea is an easy and safe highway."

Slender bottles of hock are lifted from a large silver tub of broken ice, expertly wrapped in white linen, and taken to the table.

"Our connection with the Pacific Coast is indicated by the hand of nature," Astor says intently to Mrs Jackson as the wine service begins. "It is through the waterways, madam. By the journal of Sergeant Gass I learn the distance from the headspring of the Missouri River to the headspring of the Columbia River is not more than one mile. Sergeant Gass explore to the Pacific with the expedition of Captain Merriwether Lewis, *Gott* rest his soul."

At the middle of the table, McDougall comments to James Fairlie who sits across from him, "In the Far West, beyond the Great Lakes, there are not districts as yet. The North West Company has no charter from the Crown and, therefore, no legitimate monopoly in the manner of the Hudson's Bay Company to the north. The territory is open, sir, and the first to establish a post can lay claim."

"Then speed would be of the essence in this venture."

"Aye, that it is. We know of no post in the Oregon, but that will soon change."

Full crocks of freshly churned butter and plates of homemade biscuits are placed on the table.

Dorothea is fascinated with David Stuart. "Why would anyone come to New York to live, sir? The parties in Montreal are so much more lively than ours!" Dorothea's radiance increases as her confidence grows with the guests.

"I wouldn't know about the parties," David responds with amused gentleness, "But that is a penetrating question, Miss Astor. One reason people might leave the colonies, missie, there are restrictions which you don't have here. For example, grants held by the Crown." There is a twinkle in his eye. "That has nothing to do with lively parties, mind!"

"Grant? What is a grant?"

"Such things as…" He considers. "For example, a reservation of all pine trees. Wood used for the construction of ships is held by the King, and will be so forever unless the King's right is sold. While in the American states, you see, there is no such restriction. A man owns property and prospers from it. But you've a point about the parties, missie. There is a lot of fine dancing in Montreal among some folk!"

Dorothea suddenly fixes her gaze on Robert Stuart across the table. "What is the tartan you wear, sir?"

Robert is astonished by her directness. "Why, Royal Stuart, Miss Astor. The Stuart Clan, Loyalists!"

The wine service reaches Robert as he speaks with pride. "Aye, mistress! Me uncle's grandfather was a Gentleman Private of the Forty-Second Royal Highland Regiment."

Elizabeth who is sitting next to Robert speaks impulsively, unaware of a growing fascination with him. "Is that the Black Watch, sir?"

Robert is pleased with her reply as he notices her for the first time. "Aye, mistress!"

Mr Sullivan turns to him. "Why, you're a real Highlander, Mr Stuart!"

"Lower Highlands, sir."

"Perthshire, Mr Sullivan," David comments with nostalgia. "Aye! There a lad don't miss the sour-sweet odor of an upland tarn."

Elizabeth is intrigued by all that is said. "You must have considerable skill as a trader, Mr Stuart."

Robert replies with engaging openness, "Nay, mistress! That is a very kind thing to say, but me uncle," he gestures to David across the table, "he arranged me shares as a partner. You see, I've bided in the colonies only these three years past."

Dorothea is elated. "Then you are familiar with Highland dancing, Mr. Stuart!"

Across the table Irving turns to Mary Fairlie with mischief in his eye and speaks confidentially. "You mustn't look now, Mary, but that little assemblage of smiles and fascinations is positively luring our redoubtable Highland chieftain."

"Washington!" Mary replies, embarrassed for her young friend.

"You'll have to tell me, dear, how does one resist such a bundle of health and innocence?"

McDougall appears tired and tries to conceal boredom with James Fairlie. "The United States is a force to be considered, sir. Our Merchant Navy is second only to the British." As he listens with skepticism and no comment, he seems more at the end of an enterprise than the beginning.

At the head of the table Astor speaks with Mr Jackson. "The men I always choose carefully. The first principle of governing the Indians is to govern the men at the post. You know the German expression, *"Hans bleibt Hans?"*

"Indeed," Jackson responds. "Hans remains Hans. We say in England, *You cannot make a silk purse out of a sow's ear.* You men are enterprising, sir, and I like the way you go about it. You don't wait for fate to smile on you." He sips his wine. "Americans seem to be alike in an eagerness to do something, to be someone. Extraordinary!"

Sullivan turns and speaks intently to Jackson. "To be wealthy, sir, by forming a very lucrative business. That is the only way to be respected in this English country."

Elizabeth is more and more enthralled with her dinner companion. "You also play the bagpipes, Mr Stuart?"

"A little, mistress. But I can step to a lively jig. Mr McKay's the piper, and one of the best."

Dorothea is bursting with anticipation. "Then you must dance for me this evening, Mr Stuart!"

Astor stands and speaks to the table. "Ladies and gentlemen." The guests turn to their host. "I first like to thank the charming hostess that plan all this dinner for us, my dear Sarah." Expressions of approval come from around the table.

Astor turns to his daughter. "My Dorothea promise me faithfully that she entertain with some music," he smiles to the table, "so she can be at the party to meet all these fine gentlemen!" There is general amusement.

Astor turns to the couple seated on either side of him. "I welcome the distinguished minister from England and his charming wife who do us great honor with their presence." There is the murmur of "here-here."

"Finally." Astor turns first to David Stuart. "The four men that depart with the *Tonquin* to begin the fur trade on the West Coast of this continent."

His eyes move around the table singling out Alexander McKay, Robert Stuart and Duncan McDougall. "Gentlemen. From the time you board the ship this evening, the Pacific Fur Company is entirely in your hands. I put every confidence in you that one man put in another." He continues with feeling, "*Gott* bless you and keep you in health." He picks up his glass from the table and says with energy, "As *mein* father would say in the old country, *Man soll die feste feiern wie sie fallen*. We should celebrate the feasts as they fall." He raises his glass. "Health to everyone and *guten Appetit* (good appetite)!"

Chapter Ten

A WHOLE SIRLOIN OF BEEF is placed on the buffet. Carving begins. McDougall asks for more wine as he continues in discussion with James Fairlie. "But, sir, it is common for the savages to enslave their enemies. Ye'd insult a savage proper-like if ye refused to barter his ruddy slaves!"

Robert joins the exchange. "That is their custom. They either kill prisoners or they enslave them."

There is a gradual hush as interest in the topic of slavery spreads the length of the table. All eyes are now on the speakers. McKay leans forward and addresses the table. "Slaves are used by many nations. Aye. They build. They maintain. They are the oarsmen, for example, in large canoes that go to sea in the Pacific for whale hunting. They are very strong, mind you, for after the kill is made, it can take three days to tow one of those leviathans to the beach."

Mayor Clinton responds with interest. "Don't they prove insolent and dangerous?"

David speaks to the table. "The condition is different when they are slaves of an enemy tribe. They often are adopted and marry into the tribe. Aye, that is one way to replace those lost in battle or from sickness. Some become the head of the family when the master dies."

McDougall, feeling the wine and forgetting himself, comments, "Around the post, they cut wood and carry water. They can be of use in dragging timber and building."

"Do you mean, sir," Elizabeth exclaims, indignant, "you would have slaves at your post?"

Plates of beef are served with choice of vegetables as Astor replies, "My dear, this trading post we build is the very small colony without the Army or the protection. Condition for the escape is good, I think so. If the Indian to gather the skins, we must make the life better, not oppose the inner spirit."

Elizabeth is still smarting. "You may not know it, sir, but I am a member of the Society for the Manumission of Slavery."

"Congratulations, my dear," Astor responds warmly, "this is real honor." He continues to speak to Elizabeth as conversations around the table resume. "When I was a young man in London, I see the slaves on the ships." Elizabeth listens intently to her host. "But in Waldorf, that is a small place in Germany, I was to be putcher's apprentice, for *mein* own father. But it was like the slavery. And I run away."

Elizabeth turns to Robert, confiding with characteristic boldness. "We do a charitable work in this city, sir. We have a free school."

Dinner is in full progress. Chancellor Livingston speaks to Mr Jackson. "By all reports, your countrymen encourage the Indians to retain their ancestral hunting grounds. This wins their loyalty in trade." He continues with irony, "And it has the happy effect, sir, of inciting them against American expansion west."

Henry Brevoort comments offhandedly, "Of course the Indians remain firm friends of the British."

McDougall faces him and says pointedly, "The British trade their goods at a lower rate, sir, than your government factors." With the help of the wine, his response is aggressive. "The Crown, sir, distributes clothing each season to thousands of needy Indians. The American Government, I might add, will only give to those who have peltries for trade." Brevoort does not reply.

Mr Jackson continues to Livingston, "As you know, Chancellor, it is the French we are concerned with. The policy of Mr Perceval's Government toward your merchant shipping is consistent with the Law of Nations."

"Law of Nations! Sir!" Livingston is indignant. "Let us not play with words to the confusion of ideas."

Mrs Jackson turns with concern to the Chancellor. "But, *monsieur*, you do not recognize that *l'Empereur* Napoléon Bonaparte gathers with a great Army over the whole of Europe?"

Livingston continues to Jackson, perhaps not hearing, perhaps not wanting to hear her remark. "From first to last, sir, your British law insists upon the authority of force at the expense of reason."

Mary Fairlie leans toward Irving, having been listening to Livingston's rather loud remarks from the end of the table and confides, "I'm afraid, Washington, this is not an era when the word is mightier than the sword."

Irving replies in an undertone. "I should like to quote Pompey, who said during a dispute between two nations, "Will you never have done with citing laws and privileges to men who wear swords?"

A general hush has again fallen over the table as Chancellor Livingston speaks abrasively to Jackson. "What is the Crown's justification for Orders in Council that give your naval commanders authority to board American merchant vessels at will in order to fill crew shortages? You might as well impose a blockade on American shipping and be done with it!"

Jackson is cool, respectful in his response. "I need not point out to you that Napoleon has overturned the European balance of power and now concentrates the whole of Europe in his hands. In the present maniac state of Europe, sir, you can pray to God that England maintains her sea power."

Livingston is adamant. "But the Crown's claim of a right to interfere, to impress American sailors, is utterly obsolete and contrary to the modern form of the constitution!"

Jackson is growing impatient. "We are all aware that any person can become an American for a dollar, even after deserting a British man-o-war."

"Great God, sir!" Livingston slaps the table for emphasis. "You not only deny an American ship's captain jurisdiction over his crew, but you violate the neutrality of these seventeen states!" Livingston is completely unable to acknowledge the other man's point of view. "We are not at war with you or the French!"

Jackson will not yield. "Chancellor. Allegiance by birth to His Majesty is inalienable, not to be renounced at the will of the individual."

"Your British law, sir," Livingston answers in disgust, "exacts not a tooth for a tooth, but an eye for a tooth." He is emphatic. "You forget, we are a free and an independent people…"

"*Ja*, gentlemen, *ja*," Astor interrupts. "We are not in the equal position. We all wonder about what this time will bring."

Fanning turns to Clinton. "Precisely! If Mr Madison had only understood Nelson when he said, 'The best negotiators of Europe are ships-of-the-line.'"

"The question, Captain, is how to get this Eleventh Congress to act." Clinton is utterly serious. "Our lawmakers wear their silence too comfortable, accepting British impressment with the one hand, and French trade restrictions with the other."

Fanning throws up his hands. "I don't understand those Virginia aristocrats."

Clinton agrees. "Their passion for peace, while keeping these states without a navy, will force us to our knees."

Dinner plates are cleared as more wine is served. Mayor Clinton stands, speaking first to Mrs Astor. "With your permission, madam, I would say a few words to your fine guests," he adds with humor, "before the rattle of swords causes us to forget the reason for this gathering!"

Clinton taps his wine glass and the guests turn to him as the table grows quiet. "Ladies and gentlemen, if you will indulge me a moment." He savors the silence, building expectation with consummate skill. He is confident, relaxed. "When John Astor received a charter from this state for a company to develop the fur trade beyond the Mississippi River, he went to Washington City to seek the President's approval. Mr Jefferson assured him that it is this country's intent as well as neighborly duty not to interfere with the trade of people foreign to us, as are those nations of red men on the Pacific Coast." Livingston cups his ear in Clinton's direction. It is doubtful he hears all that is said. "Seven years ago, you will recall, Robert Livingston negotiated the treaty to purchase the whole of the Louisiana."

McDougall turns unexpectedly to Livingston. He is amazed.

Clinton speaks vigorously, "Against the will of many members of Congress, Mr Jefferson considered the vast Louisiana wilderness necessary to strengthen our Western frontier by securing that essential lifeline, the Mississippi River, for the commerce of these American states. Before leaving office, Mr Jefferson gave his blessings to John Astor, stating that he looked forward with gratification to the time when descendants of his tiny establishment should have spread themselves through the whole length of that coast…"

Mr Jackson listens with keen interest. The ramifications of Astor's project are more than he realized.

Clinton continues, "…covering it with free and independent Americans, unconnected with us but by ties of blood and interest, and employing, like us, the rights of self government."

Elizabeth rests her hand on Robert's arm in a spontaneous gesture of encouragement and interest. He responds unconsciously by resting his hand on hers, and in that moment their eyes meet and a bond forms which touches their hearts and is known only to them.

Amused curiosity colors Astor's expression as Clinton continues. "Mr Jefferson was convinced, John, that your vision has the commercial prosperity of this country at heart. Much, I might add, in the spirit of our own Chancellor who financed Mr Fulton, here," he nods to Livingston, "to design and build this country's first commercially successful steamboat, now in operation in New York, the natural emporium of this country's commerce."

Clinton gestures as he speaks, looking from one end of the table to the other. "And now we can expect from John's four distinguished partners, a vigorous commerce in furs and peltries with the nations who inhabit those thousands of miles of unknown lands. Wherever you go, gentlemen, the red men will become desirous of possessing iron, arms, useful tools, the clothes and other accommodations of civilized life, which we, in this great and growing country, will soon manufacture and supply."

Clinton lifts his wine glass. "I toast your success, gentlemen." Turning to Astor with feeling, "And to you, John, I wish to say, a man's vision is where real power lies. Once his vision becomes reality, then that power belongs to the nation."

Clinton holds his wine glass toward the guests. "Ladies and gentlemen, the Pacific Fur Company!"

There is an immediate murmur of, "Pacific Fur Company," as the guests lift their glasses.

Mrs Astor's eyes are fixed with a quiet smile on her husband as a dessert of fruits and confectionery in all shapes is served, forming a chain of fifty or sixty dishes around the table.

Astor and Jackson help themselves to dessert. "I find it curious, sir, that you have chosen men from our Canadian colonies rather than these states for your new enterprise."

"You know, your excellency, when I was young merchant, my dear friend Alexander Henry arrange the trip for me with these men on the trapping brigade to Upper Canada. For one thing, I study their technique with the Indians. I learn what these men can do."

Astor leans toward Jackson, significantly, confidentially. "To control the trading post is to control the territory. The government is for nothing."

Jackson is both interested and disturbed. "Indeed."

Mrs Astor listens intently as Mayor Clinton converses with McKay. "The Royal Geographical Society reports that your colleagues are active in the distant regions of Upper Canada."

"Aye, Mayor Clinton. The North West Company is currently mapping the rivers of Western Canada, the job Alexander McKenzie and I began seventeen years ago when we reached the Pacific Ocean."

McDougall and Fairlie speak over dessert, "Yes, sir, Napoleon acted a bit hastily for John when he sold that Louisiana wilderness to Jefferson."

"I don't know as I follow your meanin', Mr Fairlie."

"Astor had approached me in Philadelphia, and one or two others, including the Mayor, there, to form a syndicate and purchase the whole of Louisiana from Napoleon." He points down the table to Astor. "John advanced the inconceivable plan of selling the territory to the United States at two and a half percent commission. Not one of us took him seriously, of course. We couldn't imagine that Napoleon would ever sell."

Fairlie leans toward McDougall who listens from across the table. "Old John said he'd put a trading post," he lowers his voice, "every forty miles from the Great Lakes to the Pacific." He sits back laughing humorously. "And he'll do it yet!"

During conversation with Astor, Sullivan pushes his dessert plate away. "It was the vicinity of Wall Street, John, and you sold the property for something under its value."

"*Ja-ja,* my friend. I am not fond of the land unless the profit is really great."

"Your purchaser was chuckling over his bargain. He said that in just a few years time his eight thousand investment would be worth twelve thousand."

Astor is enthusiastic and evidently in complete agreement. "Your customer, he know what he is doing. But then he shall see." He pauses, amused. "With his eight thousand, I buy eighty lots tomorrow above Canal Street. By the time his lot is worth twelve thousand, my eighty lots are worth…" he considers, "eighty thousand."

Mrs Jackson pleads with Astor, almost flirting. "But *monsieur!* You must tell me the secret of your success!"

Astor teases her. "It is a matter of habit, madam. And good habits in America make any man rich."

She is puzzled. "Good habits?"

"The man who make it the habit of his life to go to bed at nine o'clock, usually get rich and is always reliable."

"Going to the bed at nine o'clock." She shakes her head. "Ah, but *monsieur*, this does not make one rich."

Astor becomes quite serious. "Such a man will be up early in the morning and do a big day's work, so his weary bones put him to bed early. Rogues do their work at night. Honest men work by day. It is a matter of habit, my dear."

Astor stands, speaking to his guests. "To the drawing room let us retire where there is served coffee and ices, and where my Dorothea prepare something nice for us!"

Chapter Eleven

Robert offers Elizabeth his arm as they walk from the dining room together. Elizabeth responds to him with feelings that are new and overwhelming. "Living on the frontier, Mr Stuart, must be dangerous. I wonder," she begins then hesitates, uncertain how to express concern and interest without giving offense. "I wonder that being so far away. So much work to do." She turns to him. "You must become lonely, sir." She breaks off, fingering a delicate handkerchief with a distinctive lace pattern and the letter "E" embroidered on it.

Robert responds to her attention. "But we will build ourselves a house. Aye, Miss Sullivan." He continues, gently. "You're not to worry yourself, lass."

He again offers his arm as they move to one side and finally stand facing one another. He continues, animated. "There was plenty of bad times in the Highlands, I can tell you. Always too much of work and not enough of food. Aye, especially the winters, when the wind comes fresh over the Grampians. We were bedeviled by hunger!" He is happy and unexpectedly confident in her presence. "Mind you, I have no hatred for sweat and shivering, 'tis a want of food I can't abide. 'Twas all sheep farming in the glens." His tone becomes reassuring and tender. "But we'll have none of that on the Columbia, me lass."

Although shy in his presence, Elizabeth is suddenly and desperately in love. She wants to reach out but uncertain how, she is in agonies to convey her feeling. "When you are so far away, sir, would you ever miss your friends? It seems you will be working with no time to consider us."

Robert's whole being is welling up with feelings of affection and tenderness he would have her know. He speaks quietly as they stand together. "There'll be a time out there to keep a journal, in the evenings. Aye. When a man has a chance to rest. To look at the stars. To think. Aye, lass." He holds her with his eyes. "In five years time, when I return, you can read me journal, if you've a mind," he struggles to confide, "and you'll know that I was a-thinkin'..." but breaks off in shyness.

Robert and Elizabeth finally enter the drawing room where coffee and ices are being served from a side table. Astor goes by them with Mr and Mrs Jackson. "It is fourteen miles around this fine city. You must accompany me on horseback, and I will show you the lovely backwoods."

Jackson responds with humor. *"Wo Fuchs und Hase sich Gute Nacht sagen?"*

Astor is pleased. *"Ja-ja!* Where the fox and the hare say good-night to each other! And where do you learn this German expression?"

"In Munich, sir, where I went to university. However, I must impose one condition on your splendid offer."

Astor is amused. *"Ja?* What is this?

"That you provide two horses, one with a sidesaddle." He nods toward his wife. "The singular pleasure of our stay in Washington City was to ride out to Georgetown, a quaint village."

"Yes, *monsieur*," Mrs Jackson comments, "we were fascinated with your farmers."

McKay and Chancellor Livingston enter the drawing room. "I meself was wed to a half-breed Cree, Chancellor. Not a savage, but still preserving many of the habits of industry and economy that characterize those women."

They sit in large, comfortable chairs by the fireplace. Coffee is served to them by a liveried servant.

"Perhaps you can explain something to me, Mr McKay. I have often wondered why men in the settlements seem to find conjugal relationships with the savages preferable to marriage with their own kind."

"They are a superstitious lot, but they are particularly well-suited to hardships which a lass," McKay gestures to the company around them, "from this society, and I've known one or two in me time, would be broken by. The labor is never ending. With the Indians as in the settlements, survival requires labor. The woman does not stop until the chores for the day are completed, whether it be sundown or at midnight.

"For example, when the man makes a kill, the woman skins the animal, removes the flesh and carries it to camp, or wolves and vultures will devour it. If the meat isn't cut and hung for drying, it spoils. Survival will brook no delays. You can be certain, sir, if the woman is neglectful, the family will starve. But before they starve, you can be equally certain a man worth his salt will cast off the woman who neglects her duty."

McKay turns toward the fire. "It is the same everywhere on the northern plains. When a tribe must move, they do not wait for one woman with a headache nor do husbands help their women to transport the baggage. It were an indignity even in the woman's eyes. She will single-handedly gather and pack and tend the animals and children, and ride until sundown, and then again, single-handedly, set up the lodge and prepare a meal. Even when there is snow on the ground, the lodge is the woman's responsibility. And she does not eat a mouthful herself until the men and children have eaten and are ready for the night's rest."

"That seems hardly just. I'm amazed they do it."

"'Tis not a matter of justice, sir. In their codes, they are direct and absolute as nature is with them. If the men were heavy laden, they could neither hunt nor travel to any considerable distance. Nor could they protect their people from attack of men or animals. Aye, they depend on the woman to carry. Women are made for labor, they say. The woman will carry on her back as much as two men will do."

"I suppose it is a melancholy truth of all savage peoples, sir, and a disgrace to the little humanity of which they are possessed, to think that in times of want, the woman always comes off short."

"In scarce times, they consider the very licking of their fingers sufficient for the woman's subsistence."

"I had no idea the men were so severe."

McKay gets up, walks to the fireplace and turns to the Chancellor. "Nay, Chancellor. 'Tis not a want of virtue in the men. They have ought to do with such that is woman's work. It is the principal wife who oversees the code, and it is now long done by tradition. The importance of the woman is regulated wholly by her capacity to be useful. And mind you,

I speak now of the migrating plains people. Every nation, as you might imagine, has its own customs."

"I have heard they take more than one wife," Livingston replies.

"Aye. As many as they can support. And they will take slaves, women captured during raids. They are kept to work, but under the other women, never under the man. And they are often adopted into the tribe. But these women are made for the hard life. They expect it and take pride in the work they do. Their great happiness is to have a husband they can boast of, a man stronger, more prosperous than another."

"But don't all women!"

"Aye. And men wed for their own reasons." He returns to his chair. "To tell the truth, Chancellor, I'd never think to ask a wee lass of proper upbringing. Too many years in the wilderness change a man. I'm no longer certain in me heart I could care properly for such a one."

Livingston stares at the fire for a moment, then turns to McKay. "We enter into marriage in this advanced society of ours with such a picture of bliss. Yet I cannot tell you how terrible and awkward the first years can be." He stares at the fire, then continues with feeling, "I have imagined, to speak plainly, sir, that the savage begets his kind with delight in the begetting, not in shame!"

"Aye, Chancellor," McKay answers gently. "There is that, those flowering years of youth—few that they are. Virginity yielded to a man of unlikely age whose heart is not hers alone. But if not divided already, she must look to divide her marriage in time with another. Certainly as she withers, which is not long to come, or not bearing male children, she will be treated as a thing unprofitable. Meanwhile, all the labor of the lodge is hers. Sweet natural love may be had for a brief moment, but you must understand, sir, when exposed to nature on all sides as these people, the demands are unending. Aye. The woman grows old quickly."

Clinton approaches an empty chair opposite the fireplace, and speaks to Irving and Van Buren who are seated nearby. "You would not have been disappointed, Washington, had you toured our Western outposts with me this past summer." He sits down facing the fire. "In the tiny settlement of Buffalo, on the edge of the frontier, your *History of New-York* made the rounds. Left there by a traveler, according to the Commandant. Everyone, even the smallest Indian trader, had a laugh from your impudent friend,

Knickerbocker. I dare say, you contribute more to their merriment than if you were present yourself."

Irving is pleased. "I am not quite certain whether that remark flatters my pen, sir, or damns its master."

Mr Jackson is standing alone in the vicinity of the side table, a cup of coffee in hand, as Mrs Astor approaches. "I have wanted to inquire, sir, if you find New York comfortable after Paris and London."

With a glint of humor in his eye, Jackson answers dryly, "The City Hotel bears a striking resemblance to the London Tavern in Bishopsgate, madam, a place I seldom frequent."

Mrs Astor is alarmed. "Oh, my, I'm so sorry."

Jackson gives her a broad grin. "For want of time, my dear, not for want of charm!"

"Oh, sir, you did give me a turn."

McKay approaches as Jackson continues, "But I do wish your streets were more convenient for foot walkers."

"I was nearly run down this very day," McKay interjects.

"The drivers shout, mind you," Jackson continues, "but in London, where, thank heaven, we have no equality, fraternity, and such hubble-bubble, the comfort of pedestrians is much more attended to."

"Forgive me, madam." McKay turns to Jackson. "Might I have a word, sir, when it is convenient?"

"Not at all," Mrs Astor replies. "I must find Dorothea."

Jackson and McKay move a couple of steps away from the table where they can talk apart from the guests. For a moment Jackson stares fixedly at the men by the fire. "You know, Mr McKay, many members of the current Parliament believe that the mob rule which prevailed to win independence in these colonies will soon bring about their collapse. It is generally thought that the new states will never unite, but instead, will drift farther apart." He pauses, considering. "But I have a strikingly different impression this evening. Is it not extraordinary what this Astor fellow is undertaking single-handedly? And others must be capable of the same." He stops, catching himself. "But you wished to speak to me, sir?"

"Yes, sir. I've been wonderin', the partners and me, that is. We've been wonderin' what would happen, sir, to us, that is, if war with England begins?"

Jackson studies McKay a moment. His words are carefully measured. "You realize, sir, that you are proceeding on a most hazardous enterprize. But I see that your object is purely commercial." He considers. "I would recommend to the Crown that you be respected as British subjects trading under the American flag. Beyond that, I can say nothing."

"There would be no accusation of treason."

"It would be treason, sir," Jackson responds with an edge of severity to his tone, "if you resisted British authority. England claims the right for her subjects to settle the North Pacific Coast as a permanent right."

John Sullivan is conversing with James Fairlie near the parlor doors. "Even if peace continues, Astor is committing commercial suicide with this enormous gamble. The Pacific is far too remote."

Fairlie eyes him skeptically. "I think old John has his nose pointed in the right direction."

"Next year we are certain to know more of what the British will do."

"It isn't the British I'm worried about, frankly, but the way our people will manage. There is a strange deficiency in Washington City of a commodity called common sense."

Astor joins them. "James! I was told you are grown as rich as you are fat, that your fortune is immense!" He embraces him warmly. "I am very glad! Bad times we have here. All the money I can muster goes for the damned business."

Sullivan looks at him earnestly. "I wish we had more decided information on prospects for peace."

Astor lowers his voice. "Between ourselves, I am told it is the opinion of Mr Gallatin that if Great Britain wishes for the peace, that peace can be maintained." He continues, confidentially, "But it is the prospects for profit, gentlemen, that we must consider!"

Chapter Twelve

Robert Fulton and Captain Fanning are seated at a table conversing over a game of backgammon. Fulton taps the ash from his cigar, throws the dice and plays. "The torpedo can be anchored to the sea bottom so as to blow up a vessel which should run against it."

Fanning rolls his dice and plays. "Certainly, sir, you do not mean that a single *torpedo*, as you call the contraption, will destroy a ship-of-the-line."

Fulton rolls his dice. "Captain, I have published certain articles on submarine projects which lead to the inevitable conclusion that torpedo war will supersede the necessity of a navy."

Fanning is amused with disbelief. "Sir!" He plays.

Fulton rolls his dice but turns to Fanning before playing. "To convince Lord Melville and Mr Pitt that one hundred pounds of gunpowder exploded underwater can destroy a frigate, a Danish brig of two hundred tons was anchored a half-mile from shore."

Fulton plays then looks Fanning squarely in the eye. "Captain Kingston, who was present, asserted that if one of my torpedoes were placed under his cabin while he was at dinner, he should feel no concern for the consequence."

Fanning rolls the dice comfortably. "I would agree with him, sir."

Fulton leans forward before Fanning has a chance to play. "Well, sir, at the expiration of eighteen minutes, the time it took to row the torpedo out and set it in place, the explosion appeared to raise the brig bodily about six feet."

Fanning is struck dumb.

"She separated in the middle and the two ends went down. In twenty seconds, nothing was to be seen of her but floating fragments. The pumps and foremast were blown out, the forechain plates with their bolts were torn from her sides. There is now no doubt."

Irving continues to talk with Van Buren and Clinton by the fire. "I am convinced that in this country, the profession of a man who knows how to write is less than nothing. That of woodcutter or barrowman is much the better."

"Not many men I know would recommend woodcutting as a profession that brings fame," Van Buren replies.

"And no income!" Irving stands suddenly. "But excuse me, gentlemen. Here, at last, is my good little girl!"

The Astor children have entered the drawing room with Dorothea. Eliza, a plain and somewhat shy nine year old with an endearing gentleness, carries a wooden transverse flute. The nineteen year old John Jacob II who is slightly overweight but handsome, stays close to his young sister. He is retarded with a mental age of nine years and carries a flower. He appears bewildered by the many strange faces. Eliza has a momentary loss of confidence and turns to her sister.

Dorothea is reassuring. "Mrs Jackson is with Mummy. She is very nice."

Irving watches the two children with affectionate and keen attention as they cross the room. Brevoort approaches Irving. He is fuming with jealousy. "Damn that Scotchman!"

Irving turns and notices Robert and Elizabeth alone on a love seat by the wall. Elizabeth is listening with fascination as Robert speaks to her.

Irving is amused. "Henry!"

"Elizabeth won't take her eyes off him!"

Suddenly Dorothea interrupts Robert and Elizabeth as she leads a reluctant Robert by the hand and takes him to the parlor. Elizabeth follows.

Irving is enjoying himself. "My dear Henry, calm yourself. You are not only the best amanuensis your uncle ever employed, but," he points in the direction of Dorothea, "observe what great friends you have in the family this evening. Your cousin seems lured by impulse and fine weather to manage the wits of Mr Stuart the younger like six-penny bits."

Irving and Brevoort follow them. "Why, our Highland chieftain will have no will of his own before the evening's out."

Astor approaches, takes Brevoort by the arm and leads him away from Irving. He speaks intensely but in an undertone. "You must write the letter to Colonel Aaron Burr that we want to purchase his property in the Eighth Ward. I receive the word from him today that he wish to sell." He stops and faces his nephew, exasperated. "Bad times we have here and he complains of the money which makes it no better."

Astor draws Brevoort closer and says confidentially, "Become friendly to Martin Van Buren, the young attorney from Albany." He nods toward the fireplace. "He is the friend of Mayor Clinton. He could be valuable to us."

Across the room the children approach Mrs Jackson. Their mother introduces them. "These are my other two, Eliza and John. They are inseparable."

Mrs Jackson extends her hand affectionately. "You are Eliza, *ma chère* (my dear). Your papa told me about the flute. You are an accomplished young lady." She turns to John. "Hello, *Jean.*" She indicates the flower. "How pretty! Is that yours?"

The boy is bewildered as Eliza leaves his side.

Mrs Astor encourages him. "Say hello, Johnny. This is the lady you picked the flower for."

John hands the flower to Mrs Jackson.

"How pretty! Thank you, *mon cher* (my dear). Let me see." She tucks it into the front of her dress. "How is that? Do you like it?" John smiles with evident pleasure. He is shy in a defenseless, child-like way.

Astor approaches and puts his arm around his son's shoulder. "This, madam," he says with real pride, "is my oldest boy. And everyone say he is most handsome member of the family! Look, he is as big as his father." He turns to the boy. "Come, Johannes, I want that you meet the men from Canada I tell you all about."

Chapter Thirteen

Astor and his son leave and soon a flute and harpsichord in the next room begin the Largo from the B Minor Flute Sonata of J.S. Bach. Mrs Jackson stands up. "Let us go listen to the children."

Other guests leave for the parlor and Mr Jackson walks alone to the fireplace. As he stands at the hearth staring thoughtfully into the flames, Astor approaches. "I take the liberty to send two small canisters of tea to your hotel which I hope you do me the honor to accept for Mrs Jackson. It is better than what is generally to be had."

"You are very kind, sir. We shall enjoy it immensely." He listens for a moment to the music coming from the other room. "Your daughter is a fine flutist."

Astor smiles. "This is Eliza. She is my eye's apple. But with the oldest boy, Johann," he shakes his head, "it is a matter with the nurse. When he is a baby, it seems to me she enjoy that he is ill and wants him only to be in bed where she can keep everybody working harder around her." He confides in a low voice, "I think she drop him. But the doctors do not know if this condition change."

Jackson studies Astor closely as he continues. "I am most of all afraid for him when we are gone." The congenial mood with this man of rank momentarily disarms Astor. "I find the best is to travel about and attend to business, to keep mind and body engaged and not reflect too much on the life. We must all suffer at some period or other." He turns to the fire. "My other son William, he is a fine young man, independent. I work for the children and wish them to have all the good of it. The more they enjoy the more pleased am I and Sarah." He catches himself. "Ah, but forgive me."

"Not at all, sir," Jackson reassures him. "If I may say so, a home is something one misses when in His Majesty's Foreign Service."

Astor takes Jackson's arm and leads him toward the parlor. "The children prepare this music for the occasion. Do you know of Johann Sebastian Bach? I regret very much there is no taste for his music in this city."

The two men enter the parlor which is more formal than the drawing room with large portraits on the walls. The guests have gathered to listen. A harpsichord is to one side with Dorothea at the keyboard and Eliza beside her with her wooden flute. Eliza reaches a high note near the end of the movement as Astor and Jackson approach their wives. Astor listens to his girls with pride.

Eliza completes the final bars and looks up from the music. She glances first at her father then stands with engaging shyness before the enthusiastic applause.

Stepping forward from the admiring guests, McKay kneels down to her height. "Faith, missie, that was lovely!" He examines the instrument with enthusiasm. "Your flute sings sweet as a bird at break of day."

Astor's young daughter quietly smiles. She is charming.

Robert and Elizabeth have remained at the back of the parlor, to one side, apart from the other guests. Her eyes search his in guileless anticipation as Robert admonishes her tenderly, "But you don't understand, me lass." He is now fully in the grip of the same overwhelming emotion that holds Elizabeth. He continues with utter conviction, "It doesn't matter where I am, lass." He indicates his heart. "It's a feelin' here. Something a man can't go back on."

Elizabeth leans toward Robert only slightly, but there is tenderness in her expression. She barely whispers, "Oh, Mr Stuart."

His eyes are gently caressing. "Aye, me lass."

She replies quietly though her tone is urgent. "But, sir, you may never return!"

"There's no way o' knowin' that, I grant ye. But I could as well return to ye a rich man."

Suddenly, a lively harpsichord begins the Anonymous "Variations on the Romanesca" from the *Dublin*.

Robert turns to her, shy but determined. "Would ye care to walk with me, lassie." He hesitates. "This evenin', down to the Battery, when we board the *Tonquin?* Mind, it will be late."

Elizabeth is overjoyed. "Oh, yes! But I shall find my father and ask him, sir. But I will walk with you! Oh, yes, I promise!"

With attention in the parlor centered on her, Dorothea plays the harpsichord with gusto.

Mrs Astor turns to her husband with concern. "Dorothea has sent Mr McKay, dear man, for his bagpipes. She is determined that young Mr Stuart will dance for her!"

Astor is amused. "They should enjoy themselves, my dear. There is plenty of time."

Dorothea watches with pleasure as Robert approaches the harpsichord. He speaks above the music. "That is an Irish ditty, Miss Astor!"

Dorothea is beside herself with excitement. "I play it for you, sir! Now you must dance for me!"

As Eliza crosses the parlor, Irving greets her, leads her to a sofa and affectionately sits her down beside him. They are great friends. "Last night, Eliza," he begins with animation, "I awoke from my sleep and I raised myself in bed and solemnly taking off my night cap with my right hand, and waving it in the air, I swore never to put it on again or to comb the feathers out of my hair until I could see you, and you would play your flute for me!" Eliza is charmed by this lovely friend of the family.

Nearby, Astor is stroking a dark, silver-tipped sea otter skin that hangs on the drawing room wall as he speaks with Mrs Jackson. "The skin should be thin and the underhair thick, madam. With the sea otter, the darker the color the better. My ships for the China market make two trips every three years." He continues, pointedly but confidentially, "They realize at least three hundred percent profit."

"So this is the way you make a big profit!"

"There are many ways, madam. He considers. "For example, with this new company I form to go to the Pacific Coast." They walk together toward the side table as he speaks with mounting excitement. "Once the men establish the overland trade with St. Louis, we give the emigrants the route to penetrate the western side of the Valley of the Mississippi. And when these people come to open the farms, they need the supplies. And then they need the protection. And where better than at our trading posts for the Army to build the forts? And the Army need the supplies. You see, there are many ways to make the profit."

The speechless Mrs Jackson is served coffee by a liveried servant and they return to the parlor.

Astor continues, "But I understand you are a splendid rider. Tell me, my dear, what do you prefer?"

McDougall approaches Dorothea in the parlor and takes a Jew's harp from his pocket. "Might I join in, Miss?"

Dorothea is very pleased. "Oh, yes, sir! Do! Please do!" She enters the final refrain and he accompanies her to the end.

Chapter Fourteen

Chancellor Livingston and Mr Jackson are conversing alone by the fire when the music from the parlor ends to enthusiastic applause. "I never cared particularly for music," Livingston comments, "and now that I don't hear well, there is no point to it. I do enjoy a good fire, however."

Suddenly, over the applause and chatter of the parlor, there is the unmistakable drone of bagpipes. Dorothea jumps up, clapping her hands with joy.

McKay enters the room wearing a glengarry and playing a set of Highland war pipes. The guests step aside to make way for him as he marches solemnly to the harpsichord and turns to face the guests.

As the rhythm of *Money Musk* goes into *Banjo Breakdown*, the two Stuarts spontaneously step forward. Their dancing is natural and filled with pleasure. The effect is heightened by the full tartan dress.

Mrs Astor's eyes are alight and her head moves in time to the music. She looks as though she will join them at any moment.

Dorothea concentrates intently on Robert's movements, imitating as best she can the rhythm of his feet. Robert takes her hand and without breaking his rhythm, guides her steps as he dances to her. She is completely overwhelmed by the excitement of the moment.

Elizabeth approaches the circle of guests surrounding the dancers and spots Dorothea dancing with her Robert. Although she is mortified, she steps bravely forward. David takes her hand and she joins them.

Astor gestures to McKay, motioning toward his daughter with gratitude and amusement.

McKay nods to his host as he plays, tapping his foot neatly to the rhythm of the final number of the set, *Glendural Highlands*.

Astor and Mayor Clinton leave the parlor for the drawing room and walk toward the fireplace. Astor speaks confidentially, "For the trade, I depend on Alexander McKay. He and David Stuart know the Indians."

"What about Lieutenant Thorn? He is a naval officer and I suppose knows nothing of trade."

"*Ja*, my friend, that is correct. But he understand the battle and the military strategy. This young man I make captain. He will not be bullied by British lieutenants who wish to board the ship and take the men. This is why I give him his first command." He continues with emphasis, "If the men do not get to the Pacific Coast, everything is lost."

Astor leaves Clinton with Jackson and Livingston at the fireplace. A liveried servant offers each a snifter of cognac. Clinton turns to the distinguished ambassador. "I am curious to know, your excellency, what strikes you as most interesting in these American states?"

Without hesitating, Jackson replies, "The astonishing number of small undertakings one sees everywhere. The American farmer, for example, never seems to settle for good upon the land he occupies. He brings land into tillage in order to sell it again."

"Exactly a democracy, sir!" Clinton replies. "Nothing is more brilliant than commerce. It attracts the imagination of the multitude."

"Quite so. Your farmer builds a farmhouse on the speculation that, with an increase of population, a good price will be gotten for it. Extraordinary!"

"Yes, yes," Livingston replies abrasively. "That we take for granted in this country. What we have fought for is our freedom." He remarks, pointedly, "You do realize, sir, that America is the only country of significance in the world today in which the life of no single person has been taken for political offense in the last twenty-five years…"

The din of applause interrupts from the parlor as the music ends.

Livingston continues, "Talk what you will, sir, you and Mr Perceval, of *the great arena of British liberty!*"

All is now quiet in the parlor as McKay speaks to the attentive guests. "In the Northern settlements, when the trapping season has ended, when the canoes are loaded with skins and the brigade prepares for the hazardous journey downriver to Montreal, then the Indians, and all their families we have worked with through the long season, will gather on the shore."

McKay looks over his audience with openness and feeling. "Then the piper begins this tune, which is the way of saying good-bye. Gradually the loaded canoes, one by one, push off into the river. And the piper is the last to leave. This is, *Farewell to the Crees*."

David Stuart watches McKay intently. As the drone of the pipes begins, there is an expression of recognition in his eyes.

Dorothea listens with great emotion, almost to tears.

Elizabeth is again at Robert's side. She takes his arm and their eyes meet. Her expression is both confident and tender.

At the fireplace in the drawing room Mr Jackson is growing impatient as the music from the parlor continues. "You would boast of freedom, sir, when your agricultural heart depends on slavery for its very life?"

"Can you name," Livingston demands in his refusal to acknowledge Jackson's point, "can you name a single European colony in the whole of the New World in which the physical condition of the blacks is less severe than in these American states?"

"It is not a question of degree, Chancellor," Jackson insists. "Freedom is absolute. Do not boast of your various freedoms, sir, when one-eighth of your population, as I understand, is owned by a handful of men who can, at will, sell them, beat them, or feed them, as the case might be."

"But, sir," Clinton replies, "we have active societies for manumission."

"I will not gainsay that manumission is a worthy cause. But, in fact, sir, I am told the black market thrives, that the resale of slaves from large plantations exceeds the profit from the crops of their exhausted soil."

Livingston is furious. "You make us sound little more than an aristocracy of landholders, sir!"

"I have no doubt, Chancellor," Jackson replies evenly, "that were the people who occupy this continent more docile, those landowners would enslave the lot of them. Eventually, societies would no doubt form to free them, and to talk of the great freedoms their country stands for."

"Sir!" Clinton responds to the sting of his words, "Call European civilization devil-driven, if you will, but history teaches that such people as make best use of the soil dispossess those who leave it uncultivated."

Jackson is quick to reply, "If ever these American states undergo a great revolution as we have seen recently in France, you will owe its origin not to equality, but to the inequality of conditions." He continues with emphasis. "There is vain mockery in a way of life and treaties in which the benefits fall all to one side."

Livingston is pleased and replies with pointed irony. "Quite so! Quite so! We do agree on that, sir!"

Jackson leans forward intently. He is piqued. "I can tell you, sir, *the great arena of British liberty*, as you scornfully call it, is the basis of British Common Law, which I need not remind so distinguished a company, is the basis for your colonial freedom, and what the French Third Estate clamored after in 1789."

"The French show us," Livingston replies, "what a people can do with the state when they take it and use it for their own purposes. They rise above all other people of Europe."

There is applause from the parlor during a momentary pause in the music as Jackson answers, "I see few advantages to a democracy whose legislation is based on the errors of temporary excitement. An aristocracy, sir, is infinitely more expert. We have the self-control to legislate with lasting design."

The drone of the pipes can be heard as another dance medley *Tulluch Gorm* begins.

Livingston responds, "Then why is Germany not a great state? I will tell you why. Because the German princes are forever squabbling with each other for control of German subjects. This is futile. Their paternalism is a disgrace before the French!" Livingston shifts his position and continues passionately, "It is political unity and national greatness the French have, and that America strives for, and will have if she uses her laws for the people and not to control them...."

Chapter Fifteen

The faithful TICK-TOCK-TICK-TOCK of the grandfather clock continued in the nearly empty tavern dining room where Franchère was intent on his narrative to Lanier at the table near the fire. "It was a full evening for them. *Monsieur* McKay reported the partners even had Mrs Astor up and dancing. Her family was from Scotland, you know, and he told me she dearly loved those old jigs and hornpipes."

Franchère motioned for more coffee. "The captain was in a foul temper that evening. There had been some disagreement over the gunpowder, and not until after dark was it stowed to Mr Fox's satisfaction." Fresh coffee was brought to the table and served. "The harbor pilot was already aboard when the partners arrived in the longboat at midnight. But there was no wind, so we sat on the East River and waited." The Westminster chimes sounded the half hour. "Man was not the master of nature he is today, *Monsieur* Lanier. We waited all that night and the next day. It was not until two days later, at four o'clock in the afternoon," the GONG-GONG of a ship's bell could be heard in the distance, "the call of eight bells, when the crew changes watch."

Part II
The *Tonquin*

Chapter Sixteen

At the *Tonquin* forecastlehead, Edward Ames is ringing the ship's bell (sounded by two rapid strokes and an interval, each pair of bells equal to one count). Although the *Tonquin* is ready to depart with captain and crew waiting for a wind to fill her sails, the deck is crowded with boxes and crates, unstowed gear, chickens and pigs and turkeys in wooden cages with bales of feed nearby. The watch is busy clearing a pathway along the deck and stowing into the main hatchway. Those crewmen not on watch spend the time with leisurely personal chores.

John Martin, a big, steady, experienced black of fifty-eight years from New Orleans, grizzled with bushy eyebrows and mutton-chop whiskers, wearing baggy pants held up by suspenders, a thick turtleneck jersey, weather-beaten suede vest, and a cap, with a clay pipe in his mouth, puffs calmly as he stitches a pair of stiff cotton duck trousers. Beside him at the rail, John White, at thirty-three a seasoned Massachusetts seaman, cuts a plug of chewing tobacco, spits, and resumes carving a small wooden figurine.

The ship rests off the corner of a small wooded island near Sandy Hook lighthouse. Beyond lies the open ocean with no apparent movement of sea or air. At the final count of eight bells the watch on deck changes but the ship remains at anchor. On the quarterdeck a bearded harbor pilot surveys the seaward horizon through his glass as Captain Thorn paces between the unattended helm and the taffrail. Thorn stops long enough to search the standing rigging for some movement of air but seeing none continues impatiently marking the short distance between the rail and the helm.

A couple of ships stand in the roadstead off Manhattan Island. With the Battery at the southern tip offering its only defense, New York City is visible as a small cluster of buildings situated on the end of the wooded island.

Fox leaves the hatchway to direct his watch, stops to scan the seaward horizon and approaches McKay who leans comfortably against the main deck rail with Alexander Ross, Gabriel Franchère, François Pillet and Donald McLennan, four clerks. There is a sense of ease and confidence among the young men as though they are setting off on a pleasure voyage. "Don't you worry none about the trade, sir," Fox comments to McKay. "We'll spin this small cargo to best advantage," he glances up at the rigging as he passes by, "if that bit o' wind on the horizon gives us a fair slant."

On the quarterdeck the pilot once again studies the horizon as Thorn approaches the rail and stops beside him. Without lowering his glass the pilot comments methodically, "We're a-goin' to 'ave a breeze shortly, Captain. It's lookin' dirty way off there to the south'ard o' east." He lowers his glass and faces Thorn. "'Pears to me to be risin'."

Thorn turns at once and bellows with energy, "Get your men together, Mr Fox! We'll be underway soon!"

"Aye, aye, Captain!" Fox calls out as he whips around with intense excitement and immediately starts forward. Near the capstan he barks, "You two, there! Heave in the slack chain!" He moves briskly as Mumford approaches from the main hatchway. "Mr Mumford! A few of your watch aloft to cast off yardarm gaskets!"

"Aye, aye, Mr Fox! Starboard watch! Mr White! Lay aloft there! Cast off!"

The *Tonquin* is instantly transformed as seamen on deck leap into the rigging and scamper up the ratlines to the yardarms. Fox watches their movements as he continues forward. "Turn to, my hearties! Turn to!" He throws open the forecastle doors and bangs three times on the hatchway. "Eight bells, there below! Do you hear the news? All hands on deck! Tumble up my hearties! Tumble up!"

The capstan, a large vertical barrel of a crank, quickly becomes a hub of activity. John Martin joins three seamen who are inserting long wooden capstan bars that extend from the drum like spokes of a wheel, in preparation to heave the capstan round and lift the heavy chain and anchor from the sea bed. "Catch a turn with the chain!" Martin commands. "Catch a turn, laddies!" The young men move with alacrity.

"Larboard watch! Stand by the weather braces!" Fox commands as he points to the ropes attached to the windward edge of the sails. "Give the old girl a chance! We'll miss our bit o' breeze if you're not quick!"

He faces the capstan crew. "Heave, Mr Martin! Heave and earn your salt, men," he commands and moves toward the bow. "Forward, there! Let go the foretack! Bear a hand, men! Come along!" He turns back to the mainmast as men position themselves to drop sails. "Mr Mumford! Be ready for sheeting home! Smartly, my hearties!"

On the quarterdeck, Aaron Slaight is now at the helm awaiting command. Thorn, with a speaking trumpet in hand, stands by watching the crew. The pilot turns to him. "Up-anchor when yer ready, Captain."

"Breeze coming, Mr Fox!" Thorn bellows through the trumpet. "Man the capstan!" He gives a quick look to the crew aloft. "I want the topsails run up smartly!"

All is astir at the forecastlehead. "Man the weather braces!" Fox booms out. "Masthead the topsail yards! Haul! Lay on your backs and haul!" He waves both arms in a gesture of command as he moves along the rail. "Fair wind! Fair wind! Let fall!"

With release of the topsails, the canvas gradually fills. "Man the weather braces, you larboard watch!" Fox barks to the men working the ropes on the windward side of the sails. "Haul, my hearties!"

He approaches the crew pushing the capstan bars where the chain winds round the vertical barrel as it turns, slowly lifting the anchor. "Come, men, can't any of you sing?" Martin is pleased and removes the pipe from his mouth as he crosses to a weather brace.

"Raise a chanty, Mr Martin! Sing now!"

"Oh! Whisky is the life o' man!" Martin's rich, full voice sings out as he heaves with the line of seamen pulling on the rope.

A chorus of hands, swaying forward on the brace, respond with gusto, "Yo-o-o-o-o-o-o…" and pulling in unison, "*ho!*" then swaying forward, "Heave the man…" again pulling in unison, "*down!*"

"Oh! I'll drink whisky while I can!" Martin sings out, and the men answer as they sway and pull in rhythm to the chanty. "Yo-o-o-o-o-o-o… *ho!* Heave the man…*down!*"

The song continues as one by one the yards are hauled up the mast and the sails sheeted home. Crewmen cross the yardarms, secure the braces on deck as the yards are trimmed, climb onto the bowsprit where the jib and flying jib are run up. The Astor flag with a red "A" on a white field is hoisted beneath the American flag.

Along the wooded horizon of islands and mainland the *Tonquin* makes way under sail. At the quarterdeck Thorn remains near the pilot who watches both the channel and the movement of wind and sails. "Bear up two points, Captain!"

"Bear up two points, Mr Slaight!" Thorn immediately commands.

"Bear up two points, sir!" Slaight repeats. Under his experienced hands the spokes of the helm move while he keeps a close eye on the compass.

Once clear of the islands of New York Harbor, the pilot leaves the ship to return to port and Thorn orders through the trumpet, "Mr Fox, send below the larboard watch!"

With stunsails set on both sides, the *Tonquin* moves large before the wind, the immense area of snow-white canvas graceful on the sea. In the distance the wooded horizon begins to fade. The quarterdeck is now quiet with Thorn by the rail scanning the southwestern horizon through his glass and Slaight at the helm.

At the ring of four bells, Stephen Weeks approaches the helm from behind. Slaight sees him and calls out, "South-by-east. Steady as you go."

Weeks takes the spokes in hand as Slaight releases the helm, steps to leeward and exits. "South-by-east!" Weeks repeats, "Steady as she goes!"

Thorn glances up at the rigging. "Keep her large before the wind!" He turns to Weeks, "Ease the helm, Mr Weeks!"

"Helm amidships, sir!"

"Steady as you go!"

"Steady as she goes, sir!"

On the bowsprit two seamen are lashing the anchor in preparation for hoisting onto the forecastlehead. "Rig out that stunsail boom!" Mumford commands as he approaches. "Bear a hand here!" He points to the rigging. "Come along! The wind is shifting!"

At the masthead John White scans the horizon from aloft. Suddenly he points ahead to the port side and shouts at the top of his voice, "Sail *ho-o-o-o-o-o-o!* Five points a-fore the lee beam! Sail *ho-o-o-o-o-o!*" He shades his eyes, straining to identify the ship. "A frigate! She's a forty-*fo-o-o-o-o-o-r!*"

On the main deck, a few of the younger seamen rush to the port rail. Some turn toward the quarterdeck, where Mumford is standing by, and repeat the sighting in great excitement. Before long a sail in the southwest coming straight toward the *Tonquin* is visible.

Thorn observes the *Constitution* under full sail with a coded signal of flags being hoisted aloft. He lowers the glass and speaks angrily as his mate joins him. "We have a man at the masthead to sing out, Mr Mumford. Do you call that rabble a watch?" He glares at his mate. "Learn to control them, man, or I'll find someone who will!"

Thorn notices Laframboise approaching from the main deck. "What the deuce!" He turns sharply to Mumford. "Keep those lubberly Frenchmen out of my sight! Clear the quarterdeck, Mr Mumford!"

"Aye, aye, sir!" Mumford moves immediately to intercept Laframboise.

Thorn watches the excited Frenchman take some papers from his pocket and shake them at Mumford, speaking unintelligibly. He turns away. "Most worthless beings that ever broke sea biscuit."

"Fore the mizzen, Frenchy!" Mumford commands.

Laframboise, who has yet to grasp anything that is said to him, is desperate and replies in a heavy accent, "I am free trappare!"

"Move when yer spoken to!"

"I am speak the English," he replies, pleading, again shaking the papers. "I am been *américain!*"

Mumford turns him roughly in the direction of a crew hauling on a brace.

Along the quarterdeck rail across from Thorn, Russell Farnham, thirty years old, a clerk in Astor's company, tall, light curly hair, conveying a quiet, natural competence, walks with Franchère, Ross, McLennan and McDougall. "That must be the escort Mr Astor mentioned," he comments.

"It has many guns," Franchère observes with surprise. The topsails of the *Constitution* are being furled as she approaches. Mumford steps up to the passengers.

"Glad to see an American flag, are ye, Mr Mumford?" McDougall greets him. "Here's one of your own countrymen, Russell Farnham, a Massachusetts lad..."

"Fore the mizzen, sir!" Mumford interrupts, excited, urgent, not having comprehended a word McDougall has spoken. "All you gentlemen. Regulations! Have to manage the ship, sir!"

"I'll be damned," McDougall replies, turning to his fellow passengers. "Our own ship freighted with our own merchandise and we're bein' ordered about!" He looks petulantly at Mumford, his blood pressure rising, "*For* the what?" He is suddenly irate. "What the bleating language are ye speakin', man? Here I'm tryin' to introduce you to as fine a young clerk…"

"Would ye move forw'rd o' that there mast, sir." Mumford is cautious but firm as he points. "Called the mizzen, sir. Regulations have it that the quarterdeck's for them that's navigatin' the ship. Our escort's approachin'…"

"Mr Mumford!" Thorn calls out. Mumford immediately crosses to the captain.

"We'll see about this!" McDougall responds as they move forward, his tone filled with resentment. "For the mizzen? Load o' rubbish! By God, that one'll never speak the King's English!"

"Mr Mumford!" Thorn barks as he paces the rail, furious, and points to the approaching frigate. "The *Constitution* is bearing down, man! There is work to be done yet this watch!" He stops pacing. "Call all hands! Furl the fore and mizzen topsails!" He stops abruptly, staring at Mumford. "At the double, man!"

Mumford springs toward the forecastle, vigorously repeating the orders to his watch.

Thorn steps to the helm. "Steady as you go, Mr Weeks!"

Weeks holds the course against the crosswind. "Steady as she goes, sir!"

Within a few minutes, the foretop and mizzentop sails are being furled on the *Tonquin* as the *Constitution* bears down, signal flags readily visible to the naked eye.

At the masthead, White and Ames hang over the foretop yard furling the sail as the *Constitution* comes alongside and assumes the same course a mere seventy-five yards away. Her twenty-two hundred tons and 204-foot length dwarf the *Tonquin*.

"See us safe to the open sea, she will," White remarks, full of self-importance but in an undertone. "Rumors have it the *Halifax* is a-waitin' us off the coast."

Ames is alarmed. "The *Halifax*?"

"Aye. A British frigate, boy."

"Oh, aye! The *Halifax* carries forty-four gun, sir!

"Nay! The *Constitution* carries forty-four gun, boy. The *Halifax* mounts fifty-four gun, and forty-two-pounders they be! Put a ball through two feet o' solid live oak, they will, at a thousand yard!"

"Mr Anderson!" Thorn calls from the helm where the *Constitution* looms prominently. He walks forward, fuming. "Where's the bo'sun?"

Peter Anderson, short, deliberate, a twenty year veteran of the sea and native of New York, approaches from the main deck. "Aye, Captain."

"Lower the longboat, Mr Anderson. Be ready to push off. At the double, man!" He is emphatic. "The *Constitution* hasn't all day to wait on us!"

Fox approaches Thorn, carrying a packet of papers and accompanied by Robert Stuart who is dressed for the crossing.

"I will expect your signal to return after dark," Thorn remarks to Fox, "when she changes course for the North."

"Aye, Captain. The papers are in good order, sir."

"The *Constitution* carries 450 men, Mr Stuart," Thorn comments. "One of the Unites States' newest frigates. Give my respects to the captain." He turns significantly to Fox. "Captain Hull was my commander in the Mediterranean seven years ago."

Thorn hands Fox two sealed envelopes.

"Personal, sir?"

"Yes, Mr Fox. Ask the first officer to post them for me in New London."

Chapter Seventeen

That evening inside the Captain's cabin, after the return of the longboat, Thorn, McKay, McDougall, David and Robert Stuart are at the captain's table finishing a dinner of chicken and dumplings. Robertson, a mulatto, enters with a plate of cheese, which he sets before Thorn, and a pitcher of ale for the partners.

"The chicken was very tasty, Captain," McDougall comments as he helps himself to the ale. "Compliments to the cook."

"You'll not eat salt beef at this table, sir." Thorn cuts a wedge of cheese. He seems relaxed and confident and savors the compliment. "More wine, Robertson."

Robertson fills the Captain's glass.

"Gentlemen," McDougall raises his mug of ale. "At the outset of our journey, let us drink together!" He is quite mellow. The partners raise their mugs, Thorn his glass. "To the King!" he vigorously offers.

"The King!" the partners respond.

Thorn, stunned, lowers his glass and sits rigidly as the toast is completed.

"Ye won't join us, Captain Thorn?" McDougall is indignant.

"Do you mean to insult me, sir?" Thorn responds sharply. "You seem to have forgotten you sail under an *American* flag for an *American* company."

"Aye, Duncan, so it is," David responds calmly. "No offense, Captain. No offense, I am sure. A matter of habit, sir."

"And right we should drink to Mr Madison, gentlemen," McKay offers with gusto.

Robert stands impulsively, raising his mug. "Good fortune to both nations, I say!"

"And especially to the men of Mr Astor's grand enterprise!" McKay adds, raising his mug.

Everyone drinks.

"You can be thankful, Mr McKay," Thorn comments pointedly, "that your men've not seen service in the King's Navy. There they'd take orders under the lash."

"And what might your meanin' be, Captain Thorn?" McDougall challenges.

"Duncan." McKay responds firmly but answers Thorn matter-of-factly. "As you say, Captain, this is an American ship."

An uncomfortable silence follows.

"There is a change of watch every four hours at eight bells," Thorn remarks, ignoring McDougall, "except for a two-hour dog watch in the afternoon from four to six followed by a second dog watch from six to eight in the evening. Each of those Frenchmen is expected to pull his weight with the rest of the crew. They stand watch under Mr Mumford."

"We are as well agreed on it as you, Captain," David responds.

"And your men are to stay off the quarterdeck at all times," Thorn continues, "All of them!"

"Aye, Captain, that they will." McKay leans forward in earnestness. "But you must look to arrangements for the lads' sleeping. They seem crowded more than ordinary in the forecastle." He turns questioningly to the table.

"Aye, the forecastle," Robert agrees.

"We've thrown a bulkhead across so your clerks have their own quarters," Thorn responds. "Every possible attention will be paid to preserve cleanliness. And I have given strict orders concerning the distribution of their food. Rice and peas are to be boiled alternately every day, salt provisions will be well steeped, and they will be given tea and sugar for breakfast."

"But, Captain," McKay continues, "the Frenchmen hardly find place to swing their hammocks."

Thorn shifts uneasily in his seat. "Are you telling me how to berth a ship's company, sir?"

"Our men are under contract, sir. They are passengers."

"Every man jack on this ship is under contract, sir!"

McKay is losing patience. "But our men are from good families. They should not be treated in this manner!"

"What the hell do you want," Thorn lashes out, "a floating hotel? Next you'll require smoked beef and pudding in the fo'c'sle and a cool spring of water in the main top!" He gets up in frustration. "Dammit, man, there's enough of room to accommodate the whole company. In Christ's name tell your men to sleep like sailors do, fore and aft! You'll be surprised at the space left over." He goes to the fireplace.

McKay responds hotly, "They are not common seamen, Captain!"

Thorn seems to ignore the remark as he knocks dead ash through the grate with a poker. Suddenly, he turns on his heel and faces the partners, poker in hand. "Who the blazes is commanding officer on this ship?" He turns directly to McKay. "Remember, my man, the captain has power of life and death over every man on board, the power to flog, the power to hang, not to mention the power to clamp you in irons! Those Frenchmen will berth and take meals with the starboard watch. They will stand watch, day or night, under Mr Mumford." He points the poker toward the men at the table. "And I will blow the brains out of the first man on this ship who dares disobey me!"

McKay turns pale and starts to rise in reflex to Thorn's challenging, contemptuous tone. Unconsciously, his hand moves for his tomahawk which is no longer on his belt.

David restrains him with a firm hand on his arm. "Aye, Captain. We are perhaps a bit crowded on the *Tonquin*. She wasn't built for so many passengers, I am sure. But I think it best we work together, gentlemen. No one will gain by our disagreement, especially the lads."

McDougall blurts out, "By God! This is our ship!"

Thorn ignores McDougall. "The starboard quarterdeck is reserved for the deck officer and myself. It is forbidden to you for the rest of the journey."

McDougall takes this as a direct challenge. "By God…"

"Aye, Duncan," David interrupts, "you cannot be telling the captain here how to run his ship."

Thorn continues, "You will see that all lamps are extinguished at eight bells."

"But Captain Thorn, you don't mean us!" McKay exclaims.

"All lamps!"

McKay is flabbergasted. "Why is that? I, for one, am given to read at night."

Thorn throws the poker into its stand and turns with irate indignation. "Mr Astor is owner of this ship, and I am her captain. You take orders from me!"

McKay maintains control with an iron grip. "Beggin' your pardon, Captain, but I am asking you as a gentleman to explain to us your reasons."

"There are two reasons." Thorn faces the partners. "The danger of fire, for one." He stands rigidly still. "And the British."

McDougall bursts from his chair, waving his fists menacingly. "By God! You'll bloody well not be tellin' me…"

"Duncan!" David speaks out with authority. "It serves no one to be breaking out angry!"

Thorn approaches the table and leans against it with both hands as he stares at the partners. He is deadly earnest. "Do you think the American Navy has nothing better to do than escort merchant ships to the open sea?" McDougall sits down as Thorn glares at him before continuing. "In fact, there is report of an armed brig off the New Jersey coast carrying fifty-four guns sent by the commander at Halifax to stop this very ship. I'll clap the whole pack of you in irons if I hear another word of contempt for my orders!"

After supper that evening, McKay descends the last step of the forward companionway carrying an oil lantern. By the dim light from its small flame he observes an enormous blacksmith's forge as he makes his way through the hold to a bulkhead forming a small compartment with hammocks staggered in two tiers. Inside a few of the clerks are reading by candlelight. The air is stuffy and there is hardly room to turn around.

Farnham is lying on the upper hammock near the door, reading. Franchère sits on a lower hammock also near the door, writing with difficulty in his journal using quill pen and ink. His candle is burned very low.

McKay leans in the doorway. "I've spoken again to Captain Thorn about the Frenchmen. He is unbending. Tell the lads there's nothing to be done but make the most of the journey."

Franchère looks up. "At least they keep the ship clean, *monsieur*."

"And we are not hungry," Farnham adds.

"Aye. But I fear hard days ahead for the lads. The captain is himself God Almighty on his ship, and to prove it he will make New Year's fall on Christmas day, if it so pleases him." He turns at the sound of eight bells. "Lights out, lads. Eight o'clock."

Farnham blows out his candle.

Franchère looks up from his journal, *"Bonne nuit, monsieur* (good night, sir)," as he begins a new paragraph:

8 septembre—Je me vis pour la première fois voguer sur mer, et les regards fixés sur cette terre que puet être je ne reverai plus... (I found myself at sea for the first time and looking anxiously at the land that I might never see again...)

Chapter Eighteen

Occasional spray from the sea blows across the *Tonquin's* bow where Basile and Ignace sit on the deck making oakum. Nearby, Martin instructs Olivier how to mix oakum with tar for caulking.

On the main deck the Belleau brothers are clearing the seams with ravehooks. Above, in the mainmast shrouds, Laframboise, slowly, precariously, makes his way down the ratlines carrying a tar bucket and swab. He gets as far as the deck near the Belleau before he drops the bucket, spilling the tar, and lurches over the windward rail, seasick.

Mumford notices Laframboise, drives home a belaying pin and says to himself, "Green as grass." He picks up his tools from the deck and walks toward the Frenchmen. "A fine time I'll have with you lot!" He notices the tar bucket and stops in his tracks. "You!" he shouts angrily. "Cabbage head!"

Laframboise turns from the rail. He is pale and shivery, obviously ill.

Mumford eyes him. There is a sympathetic undertone to his outward bluster. "Yer not to be sick at the windward rail!" He indicates the opposite rail. "Go to leeward, mate, where it'll blow to sea!" He points to the deck by Laframboise's feet. "Now you clean them scuppers, hear?"

"*Oui.*"

"Didn't I tell ye to slush down the mainmast?" Mumford points to the bucket. "Did I tell ye to dab this muck over the main deck? Blast ye! The watch spent an hour on that deck this very mornin'! Must I be all the time cleanin' up after ye?"

Tar is spreading slowly onto the deck timbers. Mumford's impatience increases the more he is unable to make himself understood. "Well?"

"No."

"No sir!"

"Sir." Laframboise bends over unsteadily and rights the tar bucket. Though he is ill, he is not intimidated by Mumford.

"Look you, cabbage head!" Mumford turns away in frustration then turns back angrily. "Don't know a girtline from a backstay! Can't even raise a pair o' whiskers!" He steps up to him. "Do what I tell ye now, or mind yer eye!"

Laframboise does not comprehend but faces him without flinching.

Mumford stares hard at him and finally yields. "Be off with ye! Out o' me sight!"

Laframboise steadies himself at the rail, staring at Mumford, uncertain of anything he has said.

"Damn me!" Mumford shouts in disgust before he stomps off in a rage of frustration.

Martin approaches and eyes Laframboise as Ames flies down the shrouds from aloft, takes up the tar bucket and begins to clean the deck. "Ye cannot flinch from it, laddie," Martin says in a slow, deliberate way and points aloft. "Ye know the wind'll be there, and the sway o' the ship."

Martin takes Laframboise from the rail and leads him toward the forecastle scuttle. "Never forget, the job's to be done. And laddie, whatever happens, don't ye look down!"

As Martin exits Olivier pulls a tiny, tattered dictionary from his pocket and awkwardly turns the pages. He says to himself as he follows his finger, searching for a word, "Dóm-mee. Dóm-mee." He turns questioningly to his brother.

Basile points to the dictionary. "*Qu'est-ce que ça veut dire, dóm-mee* (what does that mean…)?"

Olivier closes the dictionary and shrugs. "*Ça n'existe pas* (it doesn't exist)."

"*Si, ça existe* (yes, it does)!" Basile replies.

Ignace looks up from his pile of oakum. "*Ça veut dire imbecile* (that means imbecile)."

Basile and Olivier are puzzled.

"*Il dit* (he says) Laframboise ees dummy."

Olivier and Basile are pleased. They return to work as they rehearse to themselves, "Dóm-mee. Dóm-mee."

For four days the winds increase, with the sea running high as the *Tonquin* makes little headway under reefed topsails. The main deck has been cleared of cargo.

McKay braces himself with Laframboise by the lee rail. The young Frenchman appears pale and feeble as he stands bundled in a wool blanket.

"Are ye stronger today, laddie?" McKay shouts over the wind.

"*Ou...ou...oui, monsieur.*"

"There's a long way to go yet!"

As gale force winds batter the *Tonquin* the two men are covered with spray and decide to go below.

In the forecastlehead, Franchère is writing in his journal:

La mer était en feu... (the sea looked as if it were on fire...)

Later that day, with the deck awash in heavy seas and high winds, sails have been struck. White, Anderson, Mumford, and Fox, dressed in sou'westers, brace themselves by the rail near the mainmast chains. Martin and two seamen nearby maintain their balance with difficulty as they hang onto a fall from the mainmast.

Fox shouts over the wind, "We have to strike the main-topgallant mast, Mr Anderson, before she goes! Be quick, men!"

White and Anderson leap onto the ratlines and climb aloft.

Farnham approaches along the rail and shouts over the wind, "Can I be of assistance, sir?"

Fox stops momentarily, impressed with Farnham's lack of fear. He replies over the storm, "You can lend a hand on that fall, sir." He points to the rope in Martin's hands. "But mind your step!"

Fox grabs hold of the rigging. "Mr Mumford, you stay on deck! Can't risk the both of us aloft!"

"But Mr Fox, your place is on deck!"

"Never mind me, man! I must see her through! Keep a sharp eye for me signal!" He leaps into the rigging and shouts at the top of his voice, "Then haul for all your worth!"

That night below deck, a smoking oil lamp on a chain swings with the ship's movement inside the forecastlehead. There are constant dull blows of the storm against the *Tonquin's* hull causing the ship to tremble and roll without relief under the weight of the crashing seas overhead. At times the seamen's compartment rises silently, pointing up at an angle, then falls as silently until the ship's sudden impact against the water rocks the men with a dislocating shock.

The oil lamp reveals dimly lit faces of seamen in their hammocks, some sleeping, some with eyes open, and faces of the young Frenchmen, fearful, sick, uncomfortable. Water comes through the scuppers and drips onto the men each time a wave crashes overhead. All are booted and wear heavy sweaters.

Wet clothing in dark heaps on the glistening floor further crowd the compartment where a thin layer of water rushes to and fro with the ship's movement. Suits of hanging oilskins swing out and in from the bulkhead. To one side the scuttlebutt is deserted where a cold, black brazier hangs from a chain, anchored to the deck by an additional chain and surrounded by four small benches mounted to the deck. There will be no fire lit during the storm.

Laframboise lies on the floor, wrapped in a heavy wool blanket. As the deck pitches, he rolls against the bulkhead at the same time that rushing water on the floor swirls against him, soaking the already wet blanket. He awakens and gets up miserably and tries to steady himself as he feels for his hammock. Suddenly there is the sound of eight bells followed immediately by a banging on the scuttle. It is midnight.

Mumford shouts, "Eight bells, starboard watch! Fore and aft do ye hear there?"

He bangs again. "Show a leg! Turn out! Turn out!"

Laframboise moves unsteadily toward his hammock, unconsciously letting the blanket fall to the floor. He grabs a heavy sweater and starts toward the hatchway.

White pulls on a sou'wester and intercepts Laframboise. "Into your hammock, Frenchy! I'll report for ye to Mr Mumford. Can't risk ye on deck in this weather!"

Laframboise tries to push him aside as Martin intercedes.

"Ye can't fight the winds in heaven, laddie." Martin grabs him firmly. "Into yer hammock. That's a good lad. I'll send ye some hot tea!"

White flies up the hatchway followed by Martin and other seamen.

Laframboise finds his hammock and climbs in as seamen tumble into the forecastle amid a din of general grumbling, "Bloomin' wet rags!" "I'm perishin' wi' cold!" "Old man's in a temper!" and pull off their dripping oilskins while others pull on additional heavy sweaters and sou'westers and climb to the deck.

Chapter Nineteen

Five weeks later, surrounded by a dead calm sea, sails hang limp as the *Tonquin* bakes in the sun. The healthy, bare-chested Laframboise sits on the main deck in the shade of the sails, cross-legged, perspiration running down his back. Forming a circle with him, the three Lapensée brothers also sit cross-legged, two stitching moccasins, the third working on a beaver trap. Laframboise with his knife carefully shapes the blade of a paddle. All are silent.

Smoking a pipe, David approaches the Frenchmen, studies them a moment then offers his pipe to Olivier who takes a couple of puffs and passes it on. As the pipe makes the round of the three brothers, Thorn comes along the deck and notices to his disgust the pipe being shared. "Warm for middle October, Captain," David greets him.

"108 degrees, Mr Stuart. First week of a long, hot calm. Always oppressive off the coast of Africa. But we'll cross the Equator before the month's out."

"When do we take on fresh water?" he asks, and continues with a twinkle in his eye, "could do with a cool spring in the main top, Captain!"

Thorn does not appreciate the remark. "You men will have to make do. Can't risk going ashore. Too many British warships cruise this coast." He walks on. The sun beats down on a flat sea.

White and several seamen have jumped into the water. A strap from the mainmast derrick is lowered to White and he struggles to tie it onto a fifty-pound turtle. None of the men in the water will approach the turtle close enough to help.

The Frenchmen hear the commotion and spring to the rail along with idle seamen on deck. Excited instructions to the frustrated White and remarks that taunt and coax the turtle are shouted in French and English.

Laframboise dives in and manages with White to wrestle the strap on before the turtle can escape. The Frenchmen on deck are as fascinated as young children. They have never before seen a turtle.

The evening hours are balmy and still. Seamen and Frenchmen, the Stuarts and McDougall, sit together around a huge caldron of soup. A couple of oil lamps hang above the men from the rigging. Others are gathered on deck. White and Laframboise who captured the turtle slurp down the fresh broth and meat from the tortoise shell.

The crew and passengers mingle freely as some smoke, some eat. By the rail, Fox and McKay stand together watching the men. "It will be summer now," Fox comments, "most till we reach the Cape. Best part o' the journey."

"Never felt such heat as this week past," McKay responds. "But the lads needed it."

Bruslé strikes up a tune on his guitar and sings in French, "Dans Le Port De...." The Frenchmen join in the chorus.

"The breeze'll be up soon," Fox continues over the song. "Your men'll have sea legs. You'll see that." He turns to the rail and looks out toward the black horizon. "Enjoy the quiet while ye can, sir. At sea, it's a right down life o' wear an' tear, an' there's no escapin' it." He turns to McKay with feeling. "But when ye love the sea, ye grow to love the ship's routine."

Martin, with full basso, leads the second verse in French to the surprise and pleasure of all. Bruslé plays his heart out. There is an obvious rapport growing between the Frenchmen and the ship's crew as seamen join in the refrain with the same melody that would become "Camptown Races." With everyone taking part, the song reaches a crescendo of clapping and boisterous singing.

Early in November, the *Tonquin* passes the Tropic of Capricorn with a fresh wind under full sail. Thorn has hovered at the quarterdeck rail a good part of the day looking through his glass. In the distance a brig is approaching. Fox stands nearby with Weeks at the helm.

Thorn is cool and deliberate as he turns to Fox. "She's not showing her colors Mr Fox. I don't like it. She followed us all day yesterday."

"Boomin' down on us now, Captain. If she wants to speak, she'll soon show a flag."

Thorn lowers the glass. "She'd better show a flag. I don't like to be chased, Mr Fox!" He turns back to the ship. "Call all hands and the passengers. We'll make a show of men on deck, in case she's up to no good."

Later that afternoon on the main deck, Mumford approaches a group of passengers and crew mingling at the rail. "Twenty guns and won't show a flag! Keep active, men! Like yer jumpin' for a fight!" As he turns away, he comments, "Ol' man should be makin' ready the canon, if ye ask me!"

"Would she be in range afore long, Mr Mumford?" Slaight asks as he passes by.

"Aye, soon enough!"

"A half-footed gang o' bullies, that!" McDougall comments, covering a sense of real apprehension. "Bearin' down like a cloud o' midges!"

"A pirate with a good cutlass, ye mean, man," Slaight remarks cooly. "Cap'n can use them kegs o' powder!"

On the quarterdeck, Thorn with his glass and Fox beside him watch the approaching brig.

"She's having a long look at us, Captain."

"When she sees the number of men we carry," Thorn replies, "she'll have something to think about." The brig is now less than half a mile away, bearing down under full sail.

Fox takes a couple of steps toward the helm and turns back to Thorn. "I don't like the look of her, Captain. She's faster than the *Tonquin*, and the wind's freshening. Shouldn't we load the starboard canon, sir?"

Thorn watches the brig a moment longer then turns to Fox. He is confident, in his element.

"The object of this voyage is not to fight every pirate that crosses our path, but to get these men to the Pacific. When we have to fight, Mr. Fox, we'll fight!"

Thorn approaches the helm. "For now, we'll clap close by the wind. That will force her to leeward. She cannot board us, being to leeward." He turns to Fox. "Set taut the bowline, Mr Fox!"

"Aye, aye, Captain!" Fox moves forward like a shot.

Thorn turns to the helmsman. "Full and by, Mr Weeks!"

"Full and by, sir!"

Fox continues briskly toward the forecastlehead. Without breaking pace, he barks, "Now, my men! Brace 'round the yards! Mr Mumford! All hands at the halyards! Aloft top men!" he booms out to the seamen above, "Out reefs! Fore and aft, set t'-gallant sails! Sharp the bowline, Mr. Martin!"

Five seamen grab a bowline, Martin in the lead position. He veers forward, then with all his weight he hauls and shouts as he pulls, "*One!*" He veers and pulls again. "*Two!*" With his third pull, the weight of the other men is thrown in together. "*Three!*"

The bowline forces the leading edge of the lower main topsail close to the wind. As the sail just begins to luff, Martin calls out, "Belay *ho!*" The line is tied off and he moves with his crew to the next line.

Fox watches everything closely and lends a hand where needed. He moves among the men with confidence and ease.

The last bowline is hauled, and at the final "Belay ho!" Fox shouts, "Stand fast! Seems all!" He spins on his heel and booms out to the quarterdeck, "Bowlines' hauled, sir!"

Thorn watches the crew intently from his position by the helm. He is pleased with their energy and efficiency and senses their excitement. "Full and by, Mr Weeks!" He takes a step closer to the helm. "Touch the wind, man!" he insists. "Keep her to!"

"Full and by, sir!"

"It's speed we want, Mr Weeks! Look you to it sharp!" Thorn turns his glass to the approaching brig and studies it intently. "She'll not point this close to the wind."

Thorn leaves the quarterdeck and strides forward, trumpet in hand. Looking aloft, he calls out through the trumpet, "Another reef out of that foretop sail, Mr Fox! Give it to her!" He continues forward. With his first indication of pride in the crew he bellows out, "Mr Fox, she's right as a trivet!"

The *Tonquin* is moving ahead magnificently, a good slant under full sail. At the rail, Thorn observes that the brig is losing ground to the *Tonquin* as she cannot follow the *Tonquin*'s course.

From the forecastle, Fox looks aloft with real pleasure and booms out, "The girls have hold o' the tow rope now, my men!"

A brace is lowered to Laframboise who grabs it but seems unsure and turns to Fox. Fox takes the rope from him and goes toward the foremast.

"Watch me, lad!" Fox reaches the foremast and completes a tie of the brace with Laframboise beside him, observing closely. "With the belayin' pin, she's secured proper-like. An' by pullin' the pin, you release her instantly." Laframboise understands. He is finally making sense of the ship.

Fox looks aloft. "Blowin' fresher and fresher, lad!"

Thorn stops at the main deck rail by McKay. "I'll shape this merchant crew yet, sir! Mr Astor's property and you men will not be trifled with!"

"Aye, Captain, she's movin' handsomely!"

"The *Tonquin* will not be boarded while I command her!" He turns from McKay and calls through the trumpet, "Mr Mumford! Put another man at the helm! Heavy sea astern!"

Fox and Laframboise move to the bow and look back through the sails in the direction of the brig. Fox gestures toward the brig. "Can't point as close to the wind as the *Tonquin*! Ha-ha! A real man-o-war's man, our Captain! The brig's fallin' off! Look at her!" He turns to Laframboise. "You see, lad, in chasin', the idea's to make the shortest way of it you can, to come up to windward and board. But Captain Thorn has just outmaneuvered her!" He slaps the rail with pride and excitement as the *Tonquin* cuts the water at near maximum speed. "You've got the scent now, my girl! You know where you're goin'!" The brig continues to fall off as Fox moves aft. Weeks and Ames are at the helm. It is all they can do to hold the course steady.

Chapter Twenty

By noon the following day the brig has given up the chase and no longer is in sight. On the quarterdeck, Fox makes the daily observation with a sextant. Ames stands by as Thorn paces the deck.

Fox completes his reading, makes an entry in the log book, and turns to Ames. "Report twelve of the clock to the Captain."

Ames approaches Thorn. "Twelve o' the clock reported, sir!"

"Make it so!" Thorn replies.

"Aye, aye, sir!" At the forecastlehead, Ames strikes eight bells and the watch changes.

The seamen and Frenchmen now perform side by side the duties of their watch: turning in a dead-eye, clapping a seizing on a mainstay, passing a gammoning on the bowsprit, clearing a foul hawse, reeving a burton, strapping a shoe-block, or holystoning the deck. Even the names are becoming familiar as Laframboise and the Lapensée brothers climb aloft with confidence to furl the main with the top men during a sudden squall. Bruslé and the others learn the skills of the deck crew: to splice, to tie various bends and knots, to spin yarn.

With Slaight at the helm, Thorn stands by, watching the sails. As the sails begin to luff, he raises the trumpet, "Ready about, Mr Fox!"

On the main deck, Fox springs to action. "Ready about, sir!"

"Helm's-a-lee!"

Slaight repeats, "Helm's-a-lee, sir!" and spins the spokes into the wind.

The crew aloft moves with ease as commands are given, the yards trimmed, and the ship changes course.

In the evening Franchère sits near the scuttlebut, a lantern swaying overhead, writing in his journal,

Le vent se changea le 14 novembre et se fixa au S.S.O., ee qui nous obligea de Louvoyer....(the wind changed on the 14th of November and settled in the south-south-west, which obliged us to tack....)

Being seriously short of water, the *Tonquin* alters course for the Falkland Islands. The ration has been cut by half since passing the Tropic of Capricorn, and the crew and passengers are now reduced to a pint a day per man, which is very little considering that each man's daily ration of food is a pound of tough salt pork or bull-beef with nearly as much hard bread, and only half a pint of souchong tea. On Sundays they have cornmeal pudding with molasses, and the seamen are allowed to share a bottle of Teneriffe wine.

On the morning of the 4th of December, men rush on deck to feast their eyes on dry land as the *Tonquin* sails toward the larger of two rocky, apparently barren islands. Franchère joins the partners who are already gathered at the main deck rail eagerly watching the approaching islands. "What a pleasure to contemplate rocks," he exclaims.

"Sterile and terrifying, if you ask me, lad," David replies.

The sea is choppy, the wind fresh, and Thorn remains close by the helmsman. Anderson and crew prepare to lower the longboat while Mumford and crew are preparing a second boat for lowering. On the main deck where empty water casks are being rolled from the hatch toward the boats, Fox directs the watch responsible for the sails.

Thorn bellows from the helm, "Mr Mumford! Starboard quarterwatch ashore for water!"

Mumford turns from the boat and moves briskly forward. He is pleased. "D'ye hear there, fore an'aft!" he booms out, "Starboard quarterwatch ashore! Muster 'round the capstan! Jump, men! Jump!" The seamen move with excitement and purpose.

Looking aloft, Thorn paces the quarterdeck measuring the wind, the ship's movement, the distance to the larger island. Finally he whirls about, facing the main deck and barks through the trumpet, "In stunsails, Mr Fox! Down top-gallant sails! Stand by the boats!"

There is a sudden call from aloft, "Man overboard!" John White points from the masthead to a head and shoulders that bobs at the surface. "Man overboard! To leeward! Driftin' straight away!" He continues pointing. "He's tryin' to swim!"

Fox turns in alarm and rushes to the lee rail. At the top of his voice, he calls out, "Stand by the braces! Boats! Boats!"

The men on deck rush to the lee rail. Some throw benches and casks overboard, anything that will float, at the struggling figure that is drifting downwind, away from the ship.

Thorn flies to the rail where some of the boat crew are standing. They point. "Over there, sir! One of the Frenchmen!"

"Out of my way, damn you!" Thorn pushes past and the moment he catches sight of the man in the water, he turns to the helmsman and through the trumpet bellows, "Hard down the helm! Shiver her! Brace up, Mr Fox! Shorten sail! Mr Anderson, ready the boat!"

Anderson and crew throw empty casks from the boat. Thorn looks aloft and barks out, "Helm, there! Luff! Luff a point! Steady man! Steady!" and turns back to the rail and calls to Anderson, "Lower! Lower!"

"The lad can't swim, sir!" David exclaims, inadvertently coming between Thorn and Anderson.

With an intensity approaching hysteria, Thorn turns on him. "Your Frenchmen amuse themselves! No regard for the purpose of this voyage! Continually in the way!" He steps aside from Stuart. "I'll not have Mr Astor's enterprise at the mercy of fools!" Through the trumpet, he commands, "Cast off, Mr Anderson! Get that boat into the water!"

The boat is lowered and a few minutes later Anderson is at the bow as the longboat approaches the figure floating on the surface, no longer struggling. "Ease larboard oars, pull round starboard."

The men haul the body aboard. Immediately they recognize Basile who is unconscious.

Anderson holds him, pressing his ear against the boy's chest, listening for a sound of life. Suddenly he sits upright. "Lay out your oars, men! Bend your backs! He's breathing!"

Men line the lee rail as the longboat approaches. "Put about, Mr. Anderson!" Thorn commands from the quarterdeck through the trumpet. He gestures toward the casks and benches bobbing in the water. "Pick up that trumpery before you come aboard! All of it!"

Anderson is standing precariously in the bow, holding the body. "The young lad needs attention, sir! He's still breathing."

"Put about, man, or I'll clap you in irons!" Thorn storms from the rail, infuriated at his insubordination.

Chapter Twenty-One

Later that day the *Tonquin* anchors in a sheltered bay a half mile off shore. The boats are lowered and men go ashore where a spring of fresh water is located. In the evening, after carrying a boatload of casks of water aboard, Mumford, Anderson, Farnham, Franchère, the partners, the Lapensées, with Basile wrapped in a blanket between his two brothers, and seamen from Mumford's watch sit around a large campfire on the sandy beach. Five geese roast on vertical spits. Lanterns from the *Tonquin* are clearly visible where the ship is anchored. Two longboats are beached nearby.

Mumford turns to Basile with evident fondness. "There's wind and tide a-plenty on the Pacific, man. I wager you'll not be skylarkin' again." Basile looks away with embarrassment.

Anderson turns to him. "Don't take it hard, son. The best of us falls from the maintop at some time or other."

"I bring the captain ashore in the mornin'," Mumford comments. "Says he'll shoot geese for the cook."

McDougall is interested. "Fancies a bit o' sport, our Captain Thorn?"

"Aye," Mumford stokes the fire. "Told me he'd fill the longboat by sunset. Wants the crew to have fresh meat."

McDougall looks significantly at Robert. "It's a goose our captain wants, is it?"

"Should have the remaining water casks filled by noon," Mumford remarks.

Anderson turns the geese on the spits. "The starboard watch'll have a quiet time of it tomorrow, Mr Mumford. What d'ye say?"

"No tellin'. Depends on the old man's temper."

"I don't know about you lads," David remarks, "but I fancy a bit o' sport me-self tomorrow. Maybe a trek round the island."

"Aye," McKay replies. "Don't know as I can walk upright on solid land, Mr Stuart. Feels uncertain underfoot without the roll of the ship."

The men laugh and McDougall turns to Robert. "Stay with me, lad!"

The next morning before sunrise, McKay, Franchère, Farnham, and David follow the rock-bound coastline along a well-trodden footpath. There is grass but the shore is barren of bushes or other plant life. Although the open sea is beside them, they soon lose sight of the *Tonquin*.

The men approach the remains of a fisherman's cabin built of whalebone. The four rummage through the remains. "The Portuguese once occupied this island, according to Mr Fox," David comments.

Franchère picks up a dry sealskin slipper. "But why would anyone live here?"

Farnham examines a rusty hook. "A fisherman. Perhaps a deserter."

McKay eyes the hook. "You can understand that, lads."

Franchère follows the footpath a few paces inland. He comes across a small clearing marked by two flat boards, rudely carved, that are propped upright with stones. He examines the nearest board as the others join him and reads aloud, "William Stevens." He rubs dirt from the board. "Killed by fall from a rock. 21 September 1794."

Farnham scrapes the second board and reads, "Benjamin Peak. Died of the smallpox. 5th January 1803. Ship Eleonora. Cpt. Edmund Cole. Providence, Rhode Island."

With their knives Franchère and Farnham silently begin restoring the lettering on the grave markers.

A distant musket shot interrupts them. "McDougall's shootin' geese again," McKay comments. "He likes his sport."

"There'll not be space enough for us in the longboat by sunset," David comments half seriously.

"Aye," McKay responds, "but we're not to keep Captain Thorn waitin'."

At the same hour across the island, the quiet bay in which the *Tonquin* lies at anchor is lit by the rising sun. The captain's pinnace from the ship approaches shore a few yards from a beached longboat and the smoldering remains of the previous night's fire. Thorn, dressed in hunting jacket and high boots, disembarks. No sooner is he on shore than he spots a goose on the ground inland. Immediately he raises his flintlock and fires. The goose flutters about but does not fly away. Mumford, who is beside Thorn as he hastily reloads, motions the four seamen in the longboat to remain still.

Thorn is awkward in his haste. "Damn it! Out of practice, Mr Mumford."

There is a goose's HONK in the distance. "Still in range, sir. Flutterin' about like she's gone mad. Must be a broken wing."

Thorn completes reloading, aims carefully, and fires. The goose is suddenly quiet.

"Well done, Captain!"

Thorn is pleased with himself. "That's more like it!" He reloads.

As the seamen lift empty casks from the longboat to roll up the beach, Thorn turns to Mumford. "I'll expect you one hour before sunset."

"The casks'll be stowed in plenty o' time, sir." He hesitates. "Ye wouldn't want a hand, Captain. I could have Mr. Anderson…"

"I'll shoot the geese," Thorn interrupts. "There'll be time enough to gather them after the water casks are filled."

"Aye, Captain," Mumford replies, covering his disappointment.

Thorn walks eagerly to the rocks beyond the beach where the dead goose now lies. He picks up the bird to examine and finds to his horror a string tied from its leg to a rock. He looks up to see McDougall and Robert approaching with their muskets.

"Mornin' to ye, Captain Thorn!" McDougall calls out. "Good huntin' is it, this fine mornin'?"

Thorn stares at the approaching men in silent fury.

"Heard ye fire twice, Captain." McDougall indicates the dead goose then points amiably along the coastline. "Ye might want to join Mr McKay. He and the others have trekked to the far end o' the island. Plenty o' geese that direction!"

Thorn dangles the goose from the string. "This is your idea, is it, Mr. McDougall?"

"Just a bit o' sport, Captain. No offense meant." He continues with humor, "At that range, sir, we expected ye to have her down first shot."

Thorn turns away while McDougall is still speaking, drops the goose and heads back toward the longboat.

McDougall and Robert stare with disbelief after him. The joke has backfired. "No sense o' humor," McDougall remarks angrily. "The devil take him!"

"You'd better warn the others he's in a temper again. I'll return to the ship with the water casks."

"Good God, man," McDougall exclaims, "I'm tired o' this ship an' her mighty Captain Thorn!"

Chapter Twenty-Two

Late in the afternoon Mumford and crew with Robert as passenger climb aboard the *Tonquin* from the longboat loaded with water casks. Thorn is at the rail. "That's the last o' them, sir. All full," Mumford reports.

"Call Mr Weeks," Thorn replies. "Mr Mumford, keep your watch on deck."

Robert goes to the partner's cabin and climbs into the dark berth where he sleeps. He remains fully dressed as he lights a candle, takes out pen and ink, opens his journal and begins to write. He sets the pen aside, reaches for a small packet under the bedding, and carefully unties it. He removes a fine white handkerchief, with a distinct lace pattern that includes the letter "E," and admires it tenderly, savoring the aroma. He continues writing.

The creaking of the ship's timbers interrupts him. He sits bolt upright and stares silently ahead, distracted, listening with full concentration for a couple of moments then exclaims to himself, "The men are on the island!" He blows out the candle, quickly replaces the handkerchief and swings down from his berth.

Robert bounds to the main deck and rushes to the rail. The island is a good two miles in the distance. He glances at the sun which is still high above the horizon, then scans the sea, straining to locate something. Suddenly he spots the longboat with McKay, McDougall, his Uncle

David, Franchère and the others rowing out through the surf. Some of the men appear to be waving.

He turns from the islands to the quarterdeck where Thorn stands at the taffrail ordering the watch as though all were normal. "You wouldn't," he says to himself as he stares at Thorn in disbelief.

At that moment, Mumford passes by on his way to the quarterdeck. Robert stops him and points toward the islands. "The men are coming!"

Mumford is embarrassed but replies gruffly, "Cap'n's orders, sir. Won't delay no longer. Says them can catch the ship, sir."

"But it's not sunset!" Robert is desperate. "Captain said he'd up-anchor at sunset!"

"He said that, aye. But we raised the signal flag, sir. Cap'n waited half an hour." Mumford looks aloft, reaching for any excuse. "Not much wind, sir. Ship must clear them islands."

Robert immediately leaves him and goes below.

A few minutes later, Thorn remains at the taffrail watching the islands. The land is now five miles away and there is no sign of a boat. "Teach them a lesson," he says to himself. "The laggards can shift for themselves!"

"Captain Thorn!" Robert's voice accosts him from behind.

Thorn turns. "What the devil!" Robert is six feet away holding two pistols leveled at his head. For a moment the two men stand, stark still, facing each other.

"Order the ship about, Captain," Robert commands, incensed with anger.

"You take command of the *Tonquin*, do you, Mr Stuart?" Thorn replies defiantly.

"You are deserting our men!"

"Is this mutiny, Mr Stuart?"

"Order the ship about, Captain Thorn," Robert replies slowly, deliberately, "or you are a dead man this instant!"

That evening, Franchère writes by candlelight:

> *7 décembre — We boarded after rowing for nearly three hours and a half. This meanness on the part of the Captain lost him the esteem of many of the crew and all of the passengers....*

Thorn recognized at once that not one of the crew, especially the mates or boatswain, came to his assistance when compelled at gunpoint to alter the course of the ship and pick up the men. He would not forget this neglect of duty.

Eleven days later Franchère makes the entry:

> *18 décembre — The distance we have traveled since leaving New York amounts to nine thousand one hundred and sixty-six miles. Until now we have had only one man down with the scurvy....*

Chapter Twenty-Three

With the *Tonquin* under sail, the Frenchmen aloft are now the equals of the regular seamen. The partners stay together on deck. Fox is often with them. Thorn remains alone on the quarterdeck.

During mealtime, little is said at the captain's table, but among the crew, the Frenchmen teach the seamen to jig. They learn from Slaight how to repair a sail and are becoming skilled seamen in more than running up and furling sails. White is their mentor aloft, Martin and Slaight tutor them on deck. Franchère writes:

> *On the 25th, Christmas day, we had the satisfaction of learning that we were west of the Cape. We have been favored with a good wind.... Passed the Equator on the 23rd of January....At last, on the 11th of February, we glimpsed the top of a snow-capped mountain which Mr Fox, who knew these waters, told me was the summit of Mauna Loa, a high mountain on the island of Hawaii....*

Several large catamarans paddled by natives approach the *Tonquin* as she sails close to the island and into a tranquil area of coastline protected by mountains. Vegetables and coconuts are offered to eager seamen who are held in check by Captain Thorn. While the ship is moving there will be no trade.

The *Tonquin* finally anchors in Kealakekua Bay, island of Hawaii, largest of the Sandwich Island group, in clear water with a coral bottom. The Islanders have followed the ship and from their catamarans offer cabbages, yams, watermelons, live poultry, bananas, and pigs. The ship's officers trade bits of cotton cloth, beads, iron hoops for the food. The blacksmith forges an axe head for a native chieftain. Three pigs are given in trade.

On shore that evening by firelight nineteen women and one man, singing and dancing together, entertain the four partners, Franchère, Farnham, Fox, and Anderson.

The next day, after filling several loads of water casks ashore, seamen raise them one at a time with help of the mainmast derrick boom from the longboat that is tied to the *Tonquin's* side. Anderson directs the operation from the rail, shouting to the longboat, "Give way, men! Give way!" and to those on the derrick, "Bend your backs now! The last load! The last load, I say! Bend your backs!"

Fox approaches. "When the casks are stowed, Mr Anderson, your crew has leave on the island 'till eight bells. Midnight. Mr Mumford's ashore with his watch." A cask is lifted aloft, swung over the deck and lowered into the main hatch. Fox says confidentially, "Keep a weather eye on the men. Mind they all return! Captain will put a bounty on any as tries to run off. You can be certain it'll go hard for 'em."

"Aye. The men'll return to the ship. No better place for 'em, Mr Fox."

"Remember, eight bells."

After supper, McKay with three of the clerks, Franchère, Ross and Pillet stands on the main deck enjoying the evening twilight. The island is less than half a mile away where various large fires have been lit and the distinct rhythm of native drums and singing reaches them.

McKay turns to the clerks. "There's somethin' in that music, lads. Prayin' their Almighty to protect an' prosper 'em."

"My family always sings, *monsieur*," Franchère comments with nostalgia.

"Aye, a bit lonely? Many's a lad of this crew'd change places with them people. Couldn't find a better life." He gestures toward the quarterdeck. "Not like living under that bedeviled ship's master, a man surrounded by traps."

McDougall overhears as he approaches. "Aye, Mr McKay, always sneakin' about like a rat at the back of the hedge." He lowers his voice. "Wouldn't surprise me if half the crew deserted."

"It won't be long now, lads," McKay remarks. "You'll be breakin' your backs to build a post before winter sets in."

"Three weeks," McDougall adds. "Mr Mumford says we drop anchor in three weeks, says the crossing'll be a rattling gale for this great tub!"

David joins them at the rail as McKay turns back to the island where only the distant fires are visible in the fading twilight. He listens to the music for a moment then quotes, *"A correspondence fixed wi' Heav'n is sure a noble anchor!"*

"Waxin' poetic, are ye, Mr McKay?" David is pleased. "Sounds a might like young Bobby Burns, God rest his lively soul!"

"Aye, a man who made poetry and sang it." He turns to Franchère. "Bobby Burns said, *Ye'll find mankind a strange squad. Mankind are mighty weak an' little to be trusted.*"

The men listen to the distant music. "There's love in them dances," McKay remarks. "Like children. Simple, they are."

"Aye, an' too simple, sometimes, for me likin'," McDougall is quick to reply.

Chapter Twenty-Four

The following morning at daybreak, Thorn paces the quarterdeck in a frenzy of temper. Fox's eyes are riveted to him. "When were the two men last seen?" Thorn demands.

"Last night, sir."

"The bounty's been offered?"

"Aye, Captain."

"Damn their living hides!"

As Thorn paces, preoccupied with his anger, a sheepish and scruffy Edward Ames climbs aboard the main deck which is now crowded with crates of pigs and poultry, sugarcane, breadfruit and baskets of vegetables being stowed by crewmen. Mumford immediately intercepts him and calls to the quarterdeck. "Edward Ames, sir!"

Thorn stops pacing as Mumford, holding Ames by the arm, approaches. "Says he went to sleep on the island, Captain. Didn't know o' the time. Says he's back o' his own. Had no wish to delay."

"Set that man free." Thorn stands perfectly still. "Where are your clothes, Ames?"

"In me bundle on me hammock, sir."

"Mr Mumford. Fetch this man's bundle. Chuck it overboard!"

Ames is alarmed. "Them's all I have in the world, sir!"

Fox steps forward with concern. "I believe this man's honest, Captain. He's given his watch no trouble."

"Sleeping on shore, Mr Fox," Thorn responds vehemently, "is not the duty of a seaman aboard ship! Put this man off the *Tonquin*, Mr. Fox!"

"But I don't want no other ship, sir!" Ames is suddenly fearful. "I shipped to sail the *Tonquin*, sir!"

Thorn ignores Ames and whirls on Fox. "You choose to stand there to please yourself, Mr Fox?" He glares with fury at his mate. "Then you shall go to your quarters to please me, until you learn to obey orders, Mr Fox!"

Fox stares at Thorn in disbelief.

"Go below, Mr Fox!" Thorn shouts at him.

Fox reluctantly exits.

"I'll teach you, youngster, to obey orders!" Thorn immediately moves toward Ames.

Ames backs away, fearful. "Forgive me for goin' wrong, Captain!"

"Been simmering to get ashore, have you?"

"I'll keep a-movin', Captain! I'll do me duty, sir!"

"You! You hold your tongue!" Thorn grabs Ames by the neck and begins forcing him toward the rail.

Ames panics. "Take your hands off me, in the name o' God!"

"What's that you say to me?" Thorn easily overpowers Ames who struggles ineffectively.

"Don't you hit me! In the name o' God!"

Thorn's anger is fed by the younger, smaller man's fear. "By Jove, if it's a horsewhipping you want, youngster, then it's a horsewhipping you'll get!"

He grabs a sugarcane from a nearby pile and throttles Ames in a fit of passion then turns, breathless, on two seamen who are close at hand. "You! And you! Throw him overboard!"

The seamen stare at him blankly. "Overboard, I say!"

They reluctantly grab Ames and force him over the side. He is soon picked up by a pair of natives in a catamaran. Mumford appears at the rail with a small bundle and tosses it in Ames' direction.

As morning turns to midday, chickens are passed from catamarans and put into crates which are lashed to the forecastlehead. Seventeen Sandwich Islanders are brought aboard by their leader, a pompous, overweight and middle-aged native, Joshua. With one exception, Isaac, also middle-aged but slender and shy, the men are young and husky and each carries a small bundle of clothing. They are issued hammocks and shown below to the already overcrowded seamen's quarters as the watch working the congested *Tonquin* deck readies the ship to raise anchor.

The *Tonquin* sails without Ames. Franchère writes in his journal:

> *Having secured 100 pigs, a quantity of poultry, two canoe-loads of sugarcane to be used as pig feed, two canoe-loads of yams and other vegetables, our water casks all being aboard, we raised anchor on the 28th of February. Mr Anderson, the boatswain, had deserted the ship. He could not be found. After three days, Mr Fox was reinstated....*

Chapter Twenty-Five

As the *Tonquin* crosses the North Pacific Ocean on the final leg of her long journey to the Northwest Coast of the American continent, the thermometer suddenly drops. Sleet batters the ship and currents change forcing her into heavy seas. Snow flurries temporarily cover the deck including the pig pens and chicken coops that are cleaned by the Islanders. One pig gets loose causing confusion before it is recovered.

An element of uncertainty surrounds Captain Thorn who has not sailed these waters. There is defiance in his tone as though in anticipation of criticism. To add to the tension on deck, he continues to be isolated. The partners huddle together and when within earshot talk in Gaelic to maintain their privacy which only makes the good captain suspicious they are plotting against him. In fact, they ignore him completely.

Fox broods on his watch. Seamen come and go to the scuttlebutt. Some take a swallow of water from the iron pump where a tin cup is stowed. The iron brazier, coals alight, moves somewhat, restricted by its chain, with the pitching of the deck. It throws only sufficient heat to warm those immediately around it. Martin is there near the brazier making spun yarn with the Belleau brothers behind him. The young Frenchmen enjoy the unexpected drop in temperature which reminds them of home. But four husky Islanders huddle miserably together in a corner against the bulkhead. They are neither prepared for nor used to the cold.

Opposite Martin, Slaight sits near the brazier repairing a sail with Bruslé's help. He ties off a line of stitching and reaches over to check Bruslé's work. "A tighter stitch! Do as I tell 'ee now or she'll not hold when the breeze be up!"

John White completes the coveted circle around the brazier where he stitches himself a wide-brimmed cap of stiff sail canvas. To one side, a couple of seamen play checkers on a cask. Laframboise smooths the handle of his paddle which will soon be ready for use on the Columbia River. Nadeau sits beside him on the deck stitching a deerskin vest.

Slaight turns to White. "Do 'ee hear the awful silence o' the quarterdeck, Mr White?"

"Aye?" White admires his cap which is nearly completed. "Don't know o' such things in the top, Mr Slaight."

"Ye'd think conversin' be forbidden," Slaight remarks, "such a gloom hangs about."

"Cap'n don't speak to no man," Martin observes.

White leans forward. "Much the old man cares for us!"

"But Mr Fox, even," Slaight remarks.

Martin nods agreement. "His silence is full o' thought."

White completes the final stitch on his hat before looking up. "Aye. Sittin' in the lee scuppers, he is." He lowers his voice, speaking confidentially, "He'd like to bend the old man's top sails, he would!" And adds, more confidentially still, "An' right he should, I say! Cap'n has no call to treat his mate that way!"

"He'll not find a better one," Martin comments.

"Aye!" White agrees. "There be good ships an' bad ships!"

Martin looks at him squarely. "Ships are what men make of them."

Mumford overhears and approaches as White tries on his cap. He eyes White distrustfully. "And what's wantin' now, Mr White?"

White glances up. "Nothin', Mr Mumford." He continues amiably, "Just bracin' a bit for the foul weather o' the quarterdeck."

Slaight shifts his position uncomfortably. He wants to change the subject. "An' cold she be topside!"

Mumford fixes White squarely with his gaze. "Mind you, Mr White, Cap'n's a man to toe the mark. Don't like no hangin' back nor growlin'." He adds significantly, "What blows o' the quarterdeck'll flatten you plenty 'gainst the top!"

Martin looks up to Mumford. There is no banter in his tone. "Bad feelin' in the air, Mr Mumford." Mumford does not reply.

White leans forward, in an undertone, "The devil's lurkin' for a quick mistake, some say. An' there'll be no settlin' it in the Cap'n's lifetime."

Mumford takes a step toward White. "Don't you go raisin' no breeze o' your own, now!"

White looks at the others. "Don't like the silence, mates. Sulkin' about like them that won't swim w' the pack no more."

"Clap a stopper to your jaw tackle, mate!" Mumford blurts out. "Too much talk an' the whole smart lot o' you…" He is interrupted by the sound of eight bells. "Push along, you men!" He barks out angrily. "Starboard watch on deck! Ship that ladder!"

The deck is battered by sleet and ice. Frozen braces have to be chipped away from their pins. The crew works bare-handed in the top where sails are stiff with ice. They are not easily furled. The pigs and poultry, housed under canvas on the forecastlehead, are tended daily by the Islanders despite the weather.

At night a dense fog enshrouds the deck. The seamen stand watch huddled with tin cups of steaming tea.

Thorn paces alone in his cabin by lamplight. Tension marks his expression. He stops at the chart table, stares morosely at the sheet where he has plotted the *Tonquin*'s course, picks up a pair of calipers.

The calipers mark off three legs on the *North Pacific Ocean* to reach the coast of *New Georgia* where the beginning of a large river at *C. Disappointment* is indicated. "At least three days, he says to himself, if this filthy weather doesn't blow us down the coast of California." He drops the calipers and starts to turn away in disgust but notices his mother's small engraving, hesitates, then picks it up. He draws confidence from the silent, trusting eyes of the handsome figure. For the moment his sense of isolation is forgotten and his expression softens.

Chapter Twenty-Six

The next morning Fox is by the helm, Martin and Nadeau are helmsmen. The wind is near gale force, the sky dark and threatening.

Martin shouts above the storm, "Wind shifting, Mr Fox! South-southwest! Athwart the deck, sir! Can't hold this course much longer!"

Fox responds immediately, "Hard down the helm, Mr Martin!" As he springs forward to give orders to the watch, Thorn bursts from his cabin in a flurry of temper.

At the top of his voice, he calls out, "Hard up the helm, Mr Martin! You're not to change course without my order!"

Fox whirls about, coming between Thorn and the helm. He turns to Martin with authority, "Hard *down*, I say!"

Martin obeys Fox, and Thorn turns white with rage. Fox springs past Thorn to the main shrouds where he beats the trumpet violently against the shrouds and booms out, "Clew down! Clew down the yards!"

Fox whirls around in a frenzy of action. He is about to move past Thorn again but Thorn intercepts him, his fists doubled threateningly. He is unaware of anything now but disobedience. Trembling with emotion, he blurts out, "I am master of this ship!"

Fox is breathless. "Yes, sir, and I'm mate o' her! And I know my place!"

"And my place is where I choose!" Thorn retorts.

"You countermand my order, Captain Thorn, and in a few moments you'll not have sail, rigging, or sticks!" A hurricane-force gust hits them. Fox steadies himself with the roll of the ship. "The wind has veered around, sir, which you're not to know, bein' in your cabin!"

Thorn continues to ignore the crisis at hand. "I command this ship and you are mate only so long as I choose!"

Fox is unshaken. "Say the word then, Captain, and I'm done! I must obey orders, but I'm not bound to endure your insults!"

Driven by the wind, a wave hits the ship and more than half the pig and poultry crates are torn loose and swept away as the sea breaks across the bow.

Thorn sees the damage and hesitates.

Fox continues, "While I have charge of the deck, Captain, my duty is to keep the *Tonquin* under control!"

The two helmsmen are struggling. Martin calls out, desperate, "She doesn't feel the helm, Mr Fox!"

Thorn gives a sharp look to the helmsmen. Fox has already moved to the rail. "Be damned to you," Thorn utters aloud. Pale and shaking with impotent rage, he returns to the cabin.

Through the trumpet Fox barks out, "All hands take in sail! Jump, my men!" He bangs on the shrouds and shouts to the men aloft, "Let go the halyards! Fore and aft, let go!" The men fight the wind to obey Fox's orders. "Haul out to leeward! Two reefs! Two reefs, topsails! She won't blow no harder! Lay aloft there, my men!" He turns to those on deck, "Haul away, men! Bowse upon that tackle!"

Three days later the *Tonquin* reaches the Northwest Coast and Thorn stands at the bow surveying a rugged shoreline with his glass as he cautiously probes for a place to safely anchor. A high swell and gusty, variable southerly wind cause the ship to roll more than usual. Fox and Mumford are close at hand. Weeks pulls up a sounding line. "Sixteen fathoms, sir!"

Still surveying the coastline, Thorn calls out, "Lower the skiff."

The partners are silent at the main deck rail. The immense North American continent as far as can be seen is without signs of life, nothing but a succession of high, snow-capped mountains, pine forest and rock. No smoke, no fires. The *Tonquin* continues toward the coast until turbulent white water becomes visible caused by waves breaking over a bar of what could be the mouth of a wide river.

Steadying himself at the bow rail and still looking through the glass, Thorn remarks, "Can't risk getting closer." He lowers the glass. "No bay, Mr Fox. We'll have to sound for a channel through that bar. From the appearance of the shore, we are approaching Cape Disappointment. According to the chart, Point Adams is four miles to the south. Across that white water should be the Columbia River."

Suddenly the main sail begins to luff. Thorn immediately turns toward the helm and shouts, "Helm up! Helm up!" He turns to Mumford. "Run aft, Mr Mumford! See what the fool there is up to!"

Fox shouts to the watch, "Flatten in head sheets! Stand by the weather fore-braces!" Startled seamen run by repeating the orders.

The sails fill as Mumford shouts from the helm, "Going off, sir! Full again!"

"All right!" Fox booms out. "Ease off the head sheets! Coil the ropes! That will do!"

Thorn turns abruptly to Fox. He has made up his mind. "Mr Fox, you will command the skiff and sound for the channel!"

"In this weather, Captain?" Fox replies.

Thorn ignores the question. "Take Mr Martin." He points to Nadeau, "And you." He then points to Basile and Ignace who happen to be nearby, "And you two."

The Lapansée brothers are startled. They question their older brother and exchange furtive remarks in French.

Fox approaches Thorn. "Mr Martin hasn't the strength to pull half a mile, Captain. The sea is running too high and the skiff has no sail."

"Those other men are boatmen, aren't they?"

"But the Frenchmen are not experienced with the sea, Captain. You must consider…"

"Take provisions and a musket," Thorn interrupts, "in case you beach for the night. We're not more than three miles from the coast. Look for a channel north of Point Adams. No telling when the tide will flood."

McDougall and McKay approach. "Captain Thorn," McKay asks, "wouldn't you advise anchoring until the breeze drops? You can't mean to send a boat into this rough sea!"

Thorn will not tolerate being questioned. "The wind could stay up for a week. We cannot anchor here forever."

"But we cannot risk losing our men," McDougall remarks.

Thorn is indignant. "My orders are to land you at the Columbia River. We must cross that bar where the sea is breaking in order to find safe anchorage!"

McKay approaches the mate. "What do you say, Mr Fox?"

"This sea is too high for any boat to live in, sir."

Thorn replies sharply, "Mr Fox, if you're fearful of the sea, you should have remained in New York Harbor!"

Fox, stung by this, motions to Martin and the Frenchmen. "You men! Into the skiff!"

The Lapensée brothers embrace and Ignace and Basile follow Martin as they lower themselves to the bobbing open boat. McKay goes to the passengers' cabin and returns with a sheet which he hands to Fox. "This might do for a sail."

Fox takes the sheet and remarks confidentially to McKay, "My uncle was drowned here not many years ago. Now I am to lay my bones with his."

"If you can't manage it, man, return to the *Tonquin*. I'll take it up with Captain Thorn."

"Once we're out there, sir, there's no turnin' back in this sea." He motions to the seamen who stand nearby. "Farewell, my hearties!"

As Fox descends to the skiff, Slaight shouts in response, "Ye've a soul to be saved, sir!"

The seamen and partners gather tensely at the rail as the small boat pulls away from the *Tonquin* and almost immediately sinks from view in the heavy swell, momentarily rises as the men row desperately toward the rolling white water, then plunges again from view.

Mumford watches from the rail. As he loses sight of the skiff, he turns away distressed and shakes his head with pessimism.

Olivier sees his brothers disappear in utter disbelief, then approaches the Captain as though he would speak with him.

Thorn ignores him completely and returns to the quarterdeck. "Up helm, Mr Mumford!"

Mumford booms out to the watch on deck, "Stand by the weather braces!" and to the men aloft, "Flatten in head sheets!"

Throughout the remainder of the day the *Tonquin* beats into the wind and toward evening again approaches the bar without catching sight of the skiff. That night with the wind still blowing, seamen and Islanders stand watch at the rail the full perimeter of the ship. Every second or third man holds a lantern which he occasionally swings outward, trying to see into the black, stormy night.

Mumford approaches White at the bow where he stands watch. White remarks above the storm, "Nothin' left o' the universe but darkness an' fury!" He swings the lantern out over the rail and searches for the skiff.

Mumford remains silent for a moment, then comments, "No sign o' Mr Fox! No fire ashore, even!" He stares at White. "Cap'n's worried! Can see it in 'is face!"

"What's done can't be undone, Mr Mumford! The sea will 'ave 'er own! We'll all end w' Davy Jones if the ol' man don't come to 'is senses. There's no gettin' this bottom across that bar. An you's the man to tell 'im!"

Mumford backs away. "Nasty night, mate! Nasty night!"

"There are ships where nothin' ever goes right!" White looks hard at Mumford. "Who'll the Cap'n be rid o' next, Mr Mumford?"

Eight bells suddenly tolls loudly nearby. Mumford is momentarily unnerved and moves away from White toward the main deck but by the final bell he has recovered and shouts vigorously, "Keep handy the watch!"

Chapter Twenty-Seven

The next morning, with the wind somewhat less, the *Tonquin* probes closer to shore. Below Cape Disappointment an angry sea of white water appears as impenetrable as ever where waves break over the bar. There is no sign of a passage and nothing of Mr Fox or the skiff is seen during the day. As daylight fades with the approach of evening, the *Tonquin* again moves out to sea.

The wind drops during the night, clouds disperse and the skies clear. With first light the following morning the watch discovers that wind and current have caused the *Tonquin* to drift north and toward the coast. Above Cape Disappointment the ship anchors in fourteen fathoms.

The wind remains calm at sunrise and Mumford is sent to take soundings but finds the breakers too strong and returns to the ship about noon. Again the sea appears impenetrable across the entire four-mile stretch of white water between Cape Disappointment and Point Adams. McKay and David accompanied by a number of the young *voyageurs* volunteer to go ashore to look for Fox and the men but are unable to find a place to land and return to the ship late in the afternoon, as eight bells is being rung.

With the first dog watch from four to six, a light wind comes from the northwest and the *Tonquin* raises anchor and stands just beyond the white water. Stephen Weeks prepares to lower himself to the pinnace which is tied up beside the *Tonquin*. Two seamen and two Islanders are already aboard.

"Stay to the north under Cape Disappointment, Mr Weeks!" Thorn's voice rings with authority though tension and uncertainty are plainly written in his expression. "When you find not less than four fathoms, hoist a flag!" Weeks hesitates at the rail as he leaves his shipmates. "At the double, man!" Thorn commands abruptly. "Pull while the wind is calm! Pull to the north, Mr Weeks!"

On the masthead of the *Tonquin*, a seaman is assigned to keep the boat in sight and signal the channel once it is found. The lookout scans the distant shore but on the agitated sea loses sight of the boat. While the wind remains light, there is no letup in the turbulence across the entire bar, and the shoreline to either side is rugged and forbidding, offering no place for safe anchorage.

Two hours pass and the second dog watch begins at four bells. Shadows lengthen as the sun approaches the horizon. Another seaman takes the lookout's position and scans the shore. He stops suddenly, his gaze fixed. He squints. Then he points and shouts, "Signal *ho-o-o-o-o-o-o!*"

The *Tonquin* changes course and begins to close the gap to the small boat, with its flag hoisted, where the men can be seen rowing with effort against the current. On the quarterdeck, Thorn directs the *Tonquin* to follow the pinnace under easy sail. "Four fathoms. Good," he remarks as they appear to enter a channel and orders the helmsman, "Steady as you go!"

"Steady as she goes, sir!"

Mumford rushes to Thorn in alarm. "Night is coming on, Cap'n. The wind is dying down. We should anchor 'till morning, sir!"

Thorn points to the pinnace with its flag hoisted which the *Tonquin* is overtaking. "Mr Mumford, at least four fathoms. Go to the masthead and point out the channel!" Mumford stares at him blankly. "At the double, man!"

McKay and David confront Thorn with urgency as the *Tonquin* enters the rolling white water. The vast turbulence is frightening. "The longboat can't pull alongside, Captain!" McKay shouts over the roar of the sea. "*Tonquin*'s movin' too fast, tide's too strong!"

Thorn does not reply.

McKay is nearly frantic. "But we've got to help 'em get in reach of a tow line, sir!"

Thorn walks toward the helm, half-ignoring the plea. "I'll not risk the *Tonquin* for five men, Mr McKay."

"But the tide!" David interjects.

Thorn whirls on the partners. "I command the *Tonquin*, Mr Stuart!" He points toward the pinnace. "The wind is dropping. They'll have to row ashore!"

McKay steps forward. "To back a sail and throw a rope would not be the work of a minute!"

Thorn shakes with anger and seems half mad. "Are you deaf, man?" he bellows. "I will not endanger this ship! Clear the quarterdeck! The both of you!" His order is no sooner given than the *Tonquin* strikes bottom and is held for nearly a full minute while the sea crashes against her stern. Finally she breaks free but then bumps bottom again and again as the rolling waves pound the stern, forcing her onto the bar and out of control as the sun sinks below the horizon.

The men in the longboat wave frantically as they are pushed by the current beyond the *Tonquin*. In the open ocean they are left to cope with sea, wind and tide.

The *Tonquin* eventually clears the bar, passing from less than three fathoms into seven fathoms of water, but is then obliged to anchor, the wind failing completely. Though anchored, she remains in constant danger of being swept back over the bar and out to sea by the receding tide. The crew works feverishly into the night preparing an extra anchor. However the flood tide comes again and with it an ocean breeze. The men are then able to raise anchor and despite the darkness of night the *Tonquin* sails into the mouth of the river and reaches Baker's Bay, sheltered by Cape Disappointment, where good anchorage is found. There is no sign of the pinnace though it is near midnight when the crew finally retires to rest. The wind having once risen blows violently the remainder of the night.

Part III
Fort Astoria

Chapter Twenty-Eight

Six weeks later shortly before sunrise the stark, snow-bound silhouette of the Cascade Range throws long, distinct shadows across the dawn sky. Far below, a river traces the narrow valley within a dark, forbidding, forest-covered canyon where wind carries the piercing call of a bald eagle as it glides with ease over the treetops of this mountainous country, reaches a nest and alights. The power of an enormous, seven-foot wingspan is immediately apparent.

On the river below a second eagle's call from a young aboriginal chief cuts the chilling wind. With eyes fixed ahead and body painted black, he is poised flat against the prow of a six-man, solid cedar war canoe. Black feathers as headdress and a polished dentalium shell through the nasal septum give him a wild, frightening appearance. A skin loincloth and thick fur shoulder-covering are his only clothing, a short flint-tipped spear the only weapon. His lean black body glistens from a coat of oil. The canyon is silent as the canoe glides effortlessly downriver in the dawn light.

Nineteen war canoes with high, carved prows carrying 120 armed Cowlitz Indians follow the chief silently through the morning mist. The forward canoes are mastered by five headmen in the prime of life, also painted black for war, who lie flat against the prows, surveying the river.

With a slight movement from the lead canoe, all paddles stop. For a moment the chief's gaze is fixed on the horizon beyond the bend of the still, silent, 150-yard-wide river. The canoe continues to glide with the deep, invisible current that courses a dense stand of fir.

Again the silence is broken by the chief's shrill call. Proud, alert eyes reflect the first rays of sunlight that glow in the eastern sky as he confidently watches for a sign from the water ahead. A distant call answers when an eagle somewhere high in the canyon leaves its perch.

Three miles below the Cowlitz war party two Skilloot Indians in a small solid cedar canoe lead a tiny brigade against the current upriver. They watch the horizon apprehensively in the direction of the distant eagle's call. Both are bare-chested and wear a polished strip of bone through the nasal septum.

Six Indians in a second, larger cedar canoe follow silently, cautiously. They wear new but familiar plain cotton shirts received in trade from the *Tonquin* and no facial ornament. Coalpo, their leader, is a tall, strikingly handsome chief of the Clatsop tribe that occupies the south bank at the mouth of the Columbia River where men from the *Tonquin* have landed and a post is being built.

A third solid cedar canoe appears in the mist with Alexander McKay standing in the stern and steering with a long, hand-hewn paddle. He too is bare-chested and wears the buckskin leggings, long knife and felt hat we saw on the Hudson River. Laframboise paddles the lead position. Franchère and Bruslé paddle amidships. The rhythmic lapping of water against the paddles is the only sound as the canoe moves upriver. McKay's eyes are fixed on the horizon ahead where the rising sun penetrates with bright sunlight that gradually moves down the distant mountainside.

Once more the silence is broken by the piercing call of an eagle. McKay continues to search the still landscape ahead as the lead canoe approaches a bend in the river. All remains quiet in the misty morning light but something unseen alerts the Skilloots and McKay notices their reaction. "Steady lads," he warns in an undertone.

The Skilloots move cautiously as they near the bend. The eagle's call again tears the silence. It is closer now. The men stop paddling and Franchère points to the agitated Indians. *"Monsieur."*

McKay's attention is riveted ahead. "Aye." He and the Frenchmen hold their distance as the Skilloots chatter uneasily with the Clatsops before continuing to lead the party upriver. They are troubled and appear indecisive.

Without warning one of the Skilloots lets out a terrifying shriek. He points ahead to the war canoes that fill the river as they drift around the bend. The Cowlitz chief quickly springs to his feet, brandishing the short, sturdy spear and begins to move rhythmically behind the prow, as though dancing, all the time howling and shrieking with menace.

The headmen follow his example while their oarsmen backwater and the war canoes pull abreast into a formation six wide and three deep across the river behind two lead canoes. The Cowlitz begin an impressive war chant, paddling together downriver with increasing speed as they approach.

The Skilloot and Clatsop canoes have turned away and seek McKay for protection. The compelling war chant grows louder as the Clatsops reach McKay's canoe babbling in terror. Using sign language, Coalpo insists that McKay shoot his flintlock at the enemy.

McKay watches the approaching Indians, ignoring the pleas of his guides. Without flinching or losing his grasp of the situation, he motions in sign language to the Cowlitz to land ashore and parley.

The paddles of the war party stop. There is apparent amazement and confusion as the Cowlitz suddenly comprehend a man of white skin speaking to them.

McKay continues to ignore the frantic Coalpo and repeats his invitation in sign language. "Paddle ashore, lads! Steady now! They are not enemy to us, and they shall not be!" McKay's canoe moves toward a nearby strip of beach in front of a broad meadow with the Clatsops close behind and lands. The men jump ashore.

All at once McKay turns with concern. The small canoe is fast-disappearing downriver as the two Skilloots paddle with all their strength to escape.

McKay yanks off his cap and shouts furiously, *"Mit-lite* (stay)! *Mit-lite!"*

He slaps the cap against his leg in angry frustration. "Fools! You know better!" He turns from them in disgust. "They'll not see another sunrise!"

Two large canoes leave the pack to begin the chase. The primitive war chant builds in tempo as they move swiftly side by side, past McKay and his party in pursuit of the fleeing Skilloots. They overtake the small canoe out of sight downriver where the Cowlitz separate, pulling abreast on either side. One Skilloot dives for the river as the Cowlitz leader releases his short spear with a terrific lunge. The headman of the second canoe is poised to throw. The first Skilloot strikes the water with a flintheaded shaft through the base of the neck. The second Skilloot hits the water nearby. He is gripping a spear that has impaled his trunk from behind. The blood of the two tribesmen stains the water as they drift with the current, lifeless.

In the meantime, Franchère has not taken his eyes from the Indians upriver. There is a wildness to these men, something unpredictable he has never before witnessed. They terrify him as they disembark and assemble on shore. While Bruslé and Laframboise beach the canoe, McKay steps from the water's edge and, using sign language, again invites the war party to parley. As the Cowlitz assemble not far above them along the same meadow, he turns to his men. They must be prepared to meet these strangers. "Michel. Fetch the pipe and a carrot of tobacco. They will smoke with us. Make that two carrots of tobacco!" McKay moves quickly, surveying the clearing. "Louis. Gather some driftwood for a fire. We make camp here this day."

The Cowlitz appear fascinated by the white men but at the same time suspicious and uncharacteristically shy. Coalpo and McKay talk together using some words but primarily sign language. McKay sends him as messenger to the Cowlitz. He turns to Franchère and quickly recognizes that the young clerk is not himself.

McKay takes Franchère a couple of steps upriver. "These people exchange slaves and skins and deer meat with the Skilloot village on the Columbia, where we slept last night." He speaks reassuringly and gestures downriver. "Our Clatsops tell me those two would warn their people of the war party. Something's happened between the tribes."

McKay turns to the Cowlitz as they prepare to meet his party. "This is a daylight raid, lad, when the Skilloot are away from their village, fishing downriver. If the war party continues, ambushes, assassinations, the capture of women and children will be everyday occurrences."

He turns back to Franchère as he says pointedly, "A year could pass before they trade again." His expression is set with determination. "We will find a way to stop them. Prime Ol' Duchess," he says confidently, "and keep her at hand. She is our medicine."

Coalpo returns at a run and again speaks with McKay. They watch the Cowlitz spread in a line from the forest to the river. There is some agitation amongst the main group where the headmen are gathered.

Despite McKay's assurances, Franchère does not take his eyes from the wild men. "*Monsieur*," he utters, nearly paralysed with uncertainty, "they plan the attack!"

McKay dismisses Coalpo. "No, lad. They've not seen white men before. They're consulting what they should make a present of." There is a glint of humor in his tone. "The stranger, if he is strong, must have a present made to him."

Franchère is not listening. He is slipping into a state of mind in which everything becomes a threat. "But they form the line, *monsieur!*"

McKay is quick to respond. "If our medicine is strong, lad, they will be our friends."

"But it is five days to the post the men build on the Columbia!"

McKay turns from the Cowlitz. "Aye, five days. We have no choice now." He holds Franchère with a steady gaze. "We have entered their territory. We are obliged to prove ourselves. And mind you, the Indian never considers himself the aggressor. No mistakes, or we are dead men."

Further agitation upriver among the milling Cowlitz distracts Franchère. He turns to the river and gasps in horror. *"Nom de Dieu!"* (In the name of God!) He is momentarily speechless as he points to the river behind McKay.

The two war canoes are returning from the chase. The head of a dead Skilloot is held by the chief on the high prow of each canoe. The decapitated bodies overhang the bows. There is a simple chant from the warriors as the Cowlitz paddle upriver to their tribesmen.

McKay watches the canoes with keen interest. He speaks confidently to Franchère. "Now we can stop them. The chant tells they have avenged the wrong against their people." He listens intently. "Do you hear it, lad? The calm. There is no rage."

Franchère does not comprehend the song. He is momentarily overwhelmed as he struggles for self control. The war canoes pass by. "But, *monsieur...*"

"Come, lad," McKay insists, "we've no time to lose."

Franchère approaches Laframboise who is measuring and cutting two carrots of tobacco. "Do you ever see such a thing? Michel, we must make no mistake!"

"Oui." Laframboise has seen the canoes go by but continues with his business. Franchère, in his agitated state, is further confused and angered by Laframboise's apparent indifference.

Suddenly frantic, Franchère explodes with nervous tension. *"Oui?* Is that all?" He steps forward in an aggressive gesture of complete frustration. *"Sacré enfant de Grace* (Holy Christ)! You no understand!" He grabs Laframboise, continuing hysterically, "That could be your head! *Là!"*

Laframboise drops the tobacco and turns on Franchère in exasperation. He, too, is suddenly angry. *"Va te faire fiche* (be damned to you)! He shakes Franchère sharply and shoves him back. "You think I am amuse? *Mordieu* (God's death)!"

The two are ready to come to blows as McKay steps between them. He is emphatic but even. "There is but one way to get what we want of these people." He faces Franchère. "Don't be a fool. The Cowlitz must come downriver for trade, not for war." Then to Laframboise. "Michel, fetch a looking glass, some beads, extra tobacco for gifts. And a flag!"

Franchère's attention is again distracted as he notices the triumphant savages land their canoes and join the others. McKay turns back to him. "Courage, lad. And be quick!"

Franchère steps immediately to the canoe, struggling to master the fear that has him in its grip. "I can no understand such a thing!"

Laframboise speaks with feeling. "You suppose this vengeance is bad for us. But *Monsieur* McKay, he understand. You see, *mon ami*. You see!"

"*Oui*, Michel. *Oui*." Franchère locates McKay's flintlock. His hands are shaking slightly as he takes the heavy weapon from the canoe but his every move is deliberate as he tries desperately to get hold of himself.

He removes the long buckskin cover. There is heightened concentration in his expression as his hands respond and become steady. He opens his own pouch, loads and primes the gun. He is growing aware, despite his fear, what it means to enter an inhabited wilderness.

McKay studies the Cowlitz every move. "Come, lads." He turns to the men at the canoe. "Michel. Gabriel. The headmen will be stepping forward."

Bruslé drops an armload of driftwood near a dead log. "Louis, keep guard on all that is passing. We are utterly unknown to these people. A trifling accident might produce serious effects."

McKay and Coalpo move off toward the Cowlitz. Laframboise follows with a long pipe, small skin bundle, and a stick wrapped in the American flag. Franchère shoulders McKay's flintlock.

As they draw steadily closer, the six headmen stand forward of the line. The war party which is armed and uneasy watches the white men approach.

McKay studies the headmen then speaks to Franchère and Laframboise. "They are purposely ugly and menacing, lads. You understand they want to put fear in their enemy's heart with that grotesque garb of war paint, skins, and feathers."

Franchère cannot shake the sense of apprehension. He glances at Laframboise who walks toward the Cowlitz with no outward emotion. His gaze merely shifts between McKay and the war party.

The chief at the center, the largest of the men, makes a slight motion with one hand.

McKay sees the gesture and stops abruptly. A spear suddenly flies toward them and lodges in the ground a couple of paces ahead.

McKay surveys the Cowlitz less than a dozen yards away. The line of 120 armed men is restless, suspicious, and alert. Coalpo is uneasy.

McKay turns to his men. "Step back, lads!" He gestures to the ground just behind them. "Sit there. The flag, Michel!"

He takes the small flag and pushes the stick into the ground. The familiar banner unfurls in the breeze. "We make our flag a mark of friendship. It will suggest many tales to their tongues to fill the empty hours. Next spring when we come to establish a second post, our flag will be known through this entire valley."

McKay turns to the Cowlitz and invites them in sign language. He sits at the center between his men. "Now, we smoke!"

The Cowlitz approach and completely surround McKay's small party though they remain a few paces away on all sides. The headmen sit on their haunches in a semicircle before McKay and his men and each in turn puffs on the pipe. The tobacco is agreeable to them. When the last man finishes, he hands the pipe back to McKay.

McKay motions to Laframboise for more tobacco as he taps the ash from the bowl.

Laframboise cuts a piece from one of the carrots and inadvertently drops his knife as he hands the tobacco to McKay. The Cowlitz chief snatches it up and examines the blade curiously.

Laframboise turns impetuously to the chief and reaches for the knife. "*Le couteau* (the knife)!"

The chief ignores him, but there is a stir among the surrounding warriors.

Laframboise gestures again. He is ready to fight. The chief looks at him coolly, betraying no emotion. His concentration is that of a cat ready to pounce. There is no longer restlessness or curiosity among the war party. They are alert and poised with weapons in hand.

McKay rises to his feet and steps with authority in front of Laframboise, facing him squarely. "Stop Michel," he utters in an intense undertone, "unless ye want your teeth strung out on a necklace for the chief, here, to wear." He turns immediately to the chief. His every word and movement are deliberate and vigorous.

He gestures in sign language as he speaks, "That is not a chief's knife." He removes his own ornate long knife and offers it to the chief. "Here. A chief's knife for you."

The chief takes McKay's knife and drops Laframboise's with indifference. He examines the shiny blade and jewelled handle with curiosity.

McKay recognizes his interest and seizes the moment. He yanks up the flag and hands it to the chief.

The chief is impressed. He stands up, McKay's knife in one hand, American flag in the other, and begins haranguing his men.

The war party relaxes as the men lower their weapons, gather closer and begin to touch the white strangers, to pull up trouser legs, feel feet and legs to be sure they are men like themselves, and to open their shirts to see that the skin of their bodies is like that of their faces and hands.

Laframboise has learned a lesson as he removes his wool toque and puts it on a savage who is admiring it. The Indian is pleased.

The warrior takes one of the ornaments from his fur shoulder covering, a shrunken scalp among several, and gives it to Laframboise who accepts the gift. They are now brothers.

The two parties separate. A group of the Cowlitz walk with the men downriver to their campsite and watch Bruslé intently as he cuts and splits driftwood with his axe. They do not take their eyes off him as he scrapes dry inner bark from a log of dead spruce, rubs it out to loosen the fibers, forms a pouch of tinder, showers it with the sparks of a flint and steel and soon has a flame started.

That night McKay and the Frenchmen sit quietly around a campfire. Less than a hundred yards upriver by the light of two bonfires dark figures dance, and the men listen uneasily to the rhythm of their chant.

Franchère remains apprehensive. In the uncertainty that dominates their situation he treads, unwittingly, a tenuous line between confidence and fear as he reclines by the campfire trying to concentrate on what McKay is saying.

"They believe that when the world was young, all life, birds, human beings, animals, all spoke the same language. The wind, for them, is the breath of the universe." McKay stirs the fire. "You see, lads, they understand the signs among the animals so well that through them they predict changes in weather, or the coming of strangers, even. The gift of a scalp, the ears, a dried scrotum, any part of man or beast, is not to be refused." He speaks to Laframboise. "Aye, to be given a portion of a warrior's medicine, what he depends upon when called to the hunt or to make war, is an honor, indeed, Michel."

"But, *monsieur*, why do these people make the war?" Franchère asks.

McKay sips from a mug of tea as he watches the neighboring camp. Though outwardly at ease, he is fully alert to all that is passing with the Cowlitz. "Vengeance, lad. A family feud. Our Clatsops talk of a Cowlitz woman who married a Skilloot. Evidently she spoke harshly to her husband. The Skilloot chief was so enraged by her bad temper that he beat her on the head with a club and terminated her life."

"Monsieur!"

"Aye, lad." He continues, quietly. "The other women disposed of her in the forest with no more notice than if a dog had been killed. But her relations got word."

"Oui," Laframboise agrees. "The Skilloot don't want to come up the river."

"Aye, and from the sound of that chant, the poor devils will be roasted by their slayers."

Coalpo approaches the camp in agitation. He urges McKay to shoot the flintlock to impress the dancing Cowlitz.

McKay refuses in sign language and sends the guide back to his campsite downriver.

Franchère is wide-eyed and nearly speechless. "They eat the body of a man?" He is utterly bewildered.

"Not to satisfy hunger, lad. The eating of human flesh is a sacred ritual, a privilege for those born to rank such as a chief, or initiated warrior. A common Indian would never be granted that distinction."

"Sacré enfant de Grace (Holy Christ)!" Franchère exclaims.

"The chief will feast on the heart to receive any supernatural power his enemy possesses." He continues matter-of-factly. "The bones are burnt before they decay and cause corruption in those who have touched them. You must remember that among these people, blood alone atones for blood."

Franchère is agitated. "But even the Eskimo…"

"Understand, lad," McKay insists, "every tribe has its own customs and its own superstitions. But the result is the same: their vengeance is to cause the enemy to mourn for the dead as they have done. Listen to them. There is no aggression, no anger. The people who killed their woman have been punished. Now they are free to trade."

Coalpo returns and again urges McKay to fire the flintlock.

McKay dismisses him as before then grabs a stick of driftwood and again stirs the fire. He is thoughtful. "Coalpo wants me to fire Ol' Duchess, to impress them we are on guard." He throws the stick onto the fire. "I refused. We must not appear fearful in their eyes. Tomorrow, lads, we journey to their village."

Chapter Twenty-Nine

The following day Franchère and Bruslé make their way cautiously through a large, oblong, Cowlitz lodge, each carrying a bundle of gifts. They are joining McKay and Laframboise whom they left earlier. The walls of the lodge are of rush matting with mud at the base. The roof is of split cedar resting on heavy support poles, and open fires in shallow pits mark the cooking area and place for gathering. Dried heads and bunches of two or three scalps hang from the main support poles. Near the entrance, an upright cedar log carved into figures of birds and animals stands like a shrine in a space close to the wall that is completely cleared of all implements. Rush is piled to one side drying beside large baskets of acorns. Dried salmon hangs from racks overhead in the dense, smokey air.

A shelf of cedar boards along one end of the large, open room contains primitive tools and implements such as a stone pestle, elk horn chisels, flint cutting pieces, wooden scrapers and bowls. They pass by a hungry dog that sniffs around a wooden pot near one of the open fires. A stick flies across its path and the dog cowers and moves off.

All is silent. Beside another fire a slave, partially covering her nakedness with a cedarbark skirt of her own weaving, uses a pair of antlers to lift heavy, red-hot stones from the fire and drop into a solid cedar cauldron filled with boiling water and venison. On the ground near the cauldron, another woman cuts flesh from a joint of venison and drops it into the same container. A sharp piece of flint is her cutting tool. Sniffing for scraps, another hungry dog wanders near and she smacks it soundly with a stick that lies at hand. The dog yelps and slinks away past two babies who play naked in the dirt.

An old male slave kneeling on the ground patiently works a split board of ash back and forth against a large, flat rock, half buried in the earth and convex at the center, shaping one end of the board into a paddle with two points. Experience and calm are written in his wrinkled face.

Across from him, on a flat section of the same rock, a woman with two deep scars across one bosom, sits on the ground and pounds smoked salmon with a stone pestle. A basket of the salmon is to one side, a basket of acorn meal to the other. As the flesh breaks apart, she mixes in the acorn meal forming a mash she shapes into a ball before tossing the ball into a third basket. She moves quickly, skillfully, and does not look up from her task.

As they draw closer to the center of the lodge, Franchère and Bruslé pass by two proud women who sit on grass mats beside a pile of rush, weaving baskets. They too wear cedarbark skirts of their own making and well-dressed deerskin capes decorated with porcupine quills that half cover torsos saturated with oil. Each richly displays a long dentalium shell through the nasal septum.

Three naked boys with small dentalium shells worn like the adults, stare with fascination as they move unconsciously toward the center of the lodge where white men and tribal members have gathered. A sharp command from one of the basket weavers stops them. They step back.

The two Frenchmen reach the gathering place of the lodge where rows of young warriors sit on their haunches forming semicircles behind the headmen who are opposite their guests. Each warrior wears a dentalium shell across the nose, an ornamented collar of porcupine quills skillfully stitched on deerskin, and deerskin leggings. They stare toward the approaching Frenchmen with confident fascination. There is no formality in their bearing, and there is no mistaking they are primitive aborigines. Behind them a low fire burns in a shallow pit.

Franchère and Bruslé join McKay and Laframboise who sit at the center of the lodge on mats across from the chief and headmen. Their bundles are added to another bundle of gifts the men have brought. A fire burns beside them. After inhaling the white man's tobacco, the principal Cowlitz chief stares at McKay with unusual intensity. McKay's pipe continues around the circle of headmen opposite him. They wear their hair loose and thinly covered with strips of skin to which dentalium shells are stitched. Each wears an eagle feather or two in the hair, a well-dressed deerskin shirt and leggings. With the white men, the Cowlitz chief and five headmen form the innermost circle of the lodge.

On the ground before McKay lies a 40-pound smoke-dried salmon. After the last headman has smoked, McKay accepts the pipe that is passed to him and solemnly points the bowl first to the sky, then to the earth, then to east and to west. He takes four deep puffs and passes the pipe to Franchère who is now beside him.

As Franchère repeats the ceremony of the pipe, McKay quietly removes a small phial of gunpowder from his buckskin pouch and rests it on the ground inconspicuously beside him. Franchère passes the pipe to Laframboise who puffs once and passes it to Bruslé. Laframboise cannot hide his dislike of tobacco. The warriors stare at the white men, their expressions a mixture of cockiness and intense curiosity.

McKay opens the two bundles beside him which contain a wool blanket, tin kettle, brass axe, and five red-handled scalping knives. The additional bundle contains a skin cloth of enameled glass beads with a mirror. He stands with the small phial concealed in one hand and gestures in sign language as he speaks slowly in a deliberate tone of authority. "We come over the stinking waters in great canoes with sails like clouds. We come to you from a land of white people, a people of many canoes and much powerful medicine." He waves over the shallow pit beside him and the fire flares high.

Immediately he turns with sternness to the startled warriors and continues, "We build a large house where the big river that flows toward the setting sun touches the stinking waters, and many white people wait there for a strong party of our brothers who follow the sun across the mountains. We watch for them each day, and when they reach our house, we will sing and dance!"

The young warriors are flabbergasted. They cannot take their eyes from McKay. "Our white father has many gifts and sends gifts for you and your women. He desires his people to be your brothers." He places the blanket and axe on the ground before the chief. "In the house we build, there are many gifts of powerful medicine for your strong hunters. Our white father, who lives beyond the mountains in a great village of many canoes, knows your skill in hunting the beaver and the red-tailed deer. He sends his people to trade for beaver!"

The Cowlitz watch McKay with piercing scrutiny. "The strong hunters grow powerful with white man's medicine. Our white father looks with favor upon those who trade beaver pelts, which he greatly desires!" He sets the kettle and mirror before the chief. He then places a scalping knife and a small pile of beads before each of the other headmen, returns to his place and sits.

The chief motions to the basket weavers. They join the circle between McKay's party and the headmen and exclaim, *"Oy-oy!"* as they sit on the ground. The chief motions for the pipe. McKay takes a burning stick from the fire, puffs deeply to kindle the tobacco then hands it to the nearest woman. Each of the wives puffs once.

After the women have smoked, the chief stands and uses sign language as he speaks in a round, formal tone. *"Hwul-i-tum hla-ktlk!"*

McKay leans to Franchère and whispers, "He says, white people wish beaver."

Without examining the goods, the chief hands one woman the blanket, the other the kettle and mirror. The basket weaver handles the blanket with admiration. *"Oy-oy!"* she exclaims.

The second woman does not know what to do with the kettle and mirror. As she turns the kettle upside down the lid drops off, startling her. She notices it is hollow, puts her hand inside, turns it upright, discovers the spout and use of the lid, and suddenly her expression changes to surprise and wonder. *"Oy-oy!"* she too exclaims.

She then picks up the mirror, looks curiously at it and is startled at the face looking at her. She turns the mirror and cranes her head to see if it is still there. She then turns to McKay in awe.

The chief addresses his warriors who sit behind McKay, then he turns to his wives. He uses sign language as he speaks with gravity. *"Skoh mukp shlta-lahw…"* he points upward and continues, *"stoq qus-su-wun!"*

McKay nods toward Franchère and whispers, "Smoke of our fires rises to high earth…where dwells the thunder and darkness."

The basket weavers watch their husband with obvious pride and express conviction in the rightness of his words with an occasional *"Oy-oy!"*

The chief turns to the headmen beside him. *"Hwul-i-tum shoh stoq qa-la-mihltn. Hwul-i-tum…"*

McKay whispers, "White people come as the wind with long thunder stick. White people…"

The headmen nod agreement as their chief continues, *"…qa-le-mihltn, kwa-homn hla-ktlk. Slaqs-ma-ni-chu pa-nikshl-tumh hla-ktlk!"*

McKay whispers, "…trade tobacco, knife, for beaver. Snow peak contain many beaver!"

He addresses McKay, continuing with both words and sign language. *"I-limh pa-nikshl-tumh sil-ken. Ske-wuhl-ku. Hla-ktlk. I-limh hwul-i-tum a-tush-tqulh!"*

McKay whispers to Franchère, "Cowlitz people strong with many slaves. Follow river. Catch beaver. Cowlitz people desire white man's medicine!"

There is a stir among the young warriors as a very old chief, plainly dressed but with three eagle feathers in his snow-white hair, appears before the circle with a young slave boy.

The chief who has been speaking steps back to the headmen and sits in deference to the old patriarch who, bent and deeply lined, walks with difficulty using both the boy and a thick, stubby stick for support. This ancient one stops at the fire and squints long at McKay, leaning slightly forward, eyeing him from head to foot, his expression marked with strong curiosity.

Finally with the help of the boy the old chief sits on the ground in front of McKay. He feels McKay's feet and legs as he continues to stare penetratingly at him. At last he seems convinced that McKay is a man and gives a hearty grunt and faces the circle.

"Qa-la-mihltn (the pipe)!" he exclaims, and the long pipe is immediately lit and offered to him by McKay.

He takes four deep puffs, swallowing the smoke between each. He exhales to the sky, to the earth, to the east and to the west. He enjoys each puff more than the last, then speaks to McKay using both words and sign language. *"Hwul-i-tum qa-le-mihltn a-hest. I-limh hash hwul-i-tum hash."*

McKay turns to Franchère with a confident glimmer in his eye. "He thanks us that he has the pleasure to smoke good tobacco before he dies."

The old chief motions toward the women. *"Skoh kumk* (smoked salmon)!"

One of the chief's wives brings a second large smoked salmon and lays it before McKay. McKay immediately picks up a two-foot roll of tobacco and places it before the revered figure.

There is a general stir as the men lift their hands and arms to the sky in a spontaneous gesture of approval, now convinced the white people they have met come as friends.

Chapter Thirty

Except for McKay, Franchère, Laframboise, Bruslé, Thorn, and three or four seamen, the entire company of seamen and passengers from the *Tonquin*, including a gaunt Stephen Weeks, is gathered around a rude graveyard to one side of a rough, one-acre clearing that borders a two-mile wide river. The day is overcast and windy, the soil wet from continuous rain, and the site littered with fallen trees, stripped logs, tree stumps, and holes where stumps have been blown out by gunpowder. After more than a month of unremitting, backbreaking toil, less than a single acre of forest has been cleared.

Inland, dense forest stands on all sides and, except for a narrow strip of beach where a small pier has been constructed into the river, the shoreline is rocky and uninviting. Near the pier stands the partly-assembled frame for a thirty-ton schooner. Across the river in the deep channel the *Tonquin* lies quietly at anchor. No Indian canoes are present.

Near the center of the clearing behind the gathering of men a log storehouse is under construction. Next to it stands a makeshift blacksmith's shed with the forge from the *Tonquin* set under a lean-to roof. Smoke rises from the chimney above the forge. Half a dozen eight-man white tents used by the men for sleeping are scattered in the yard. Between the storehouse and graveyard, an American flag flies atop a stripped pole, the trunk of a young fir left standing.

The graveyard, bordered on three sides by large, split logs, contains three mounds of earth, one fresh, each with its own marker of split cedar. To one side a sizeable wooden plaque mounted on two posts offers a grim reminder. The hand-carved lettering reads,

AT THE ENTRANCE OF THE RIVER

PERISHED EIGHT BRAVE MEN:

March 22nd 1811	March 23rd 1811
J.C. Fox	J. Coles
J. Martin	J. Aiken
B. Lapensée	Sandwich Islander
I. Lapensée	
J. Nadeau	

JONATHAN THORN, MASTER, SHIP *TONQUIN*

Three of the subdued company that has gathered show signs of serious injury: a bandaged head, a homemade crutch, stump where a hand once functioned.

There is no break to the overcast and occasional light rain. David Stuart, standing nearest the graveside, a Bible in hand, looks from the men to the fresh mound of earth where the plaque reads,

SANDWICH ISLANDER — KILLED BY INDIANS

May 12th 1811

He opens the Bible and reads aloud, "The Lord shall judge among many people, and rebuke strong nations afar off. And they shall beat their swords into plowshares, and their spears into pruning hooks. He hath shewed thee, O man, what is good!"

David glances at the other two mounds where the hand-carved grave markers read,

SANDWICH ISLANDER — KILLED BY INDIANS
March 28th 1811

SANDWICH ISLANDER — KILLED BY INDIANS
April 15th 1811

He continues from the Bible, "And what doth the Lord require of thee, but to do justly, and to love mercy and to walk humbly with thy God?" He looks up at the men and all at once bursts out urgent, personal, "A naked people, lads, fierce in habit, with subsistence of game and wild fruit, do not amuse themselves with the building of a trading post."

Stress and fatigue are written in his expression as he turns some pages of the Bible and continues to read. "And the angel thrust in his sickle into the earth and gathered the vine of the earth, and cast it into the great winepress of the wrath of God. And I saw, as it were, a sea of glass mingled with fire: and them that had gotten the victory over the beast, and over his image, and over his mark, and over the number of his name, stand on the sea of glass, having the harps of God!"

There is silence as he stares at the grave and then turns to the men. He closes the Bible. "And let us ask that Mr McKay and the lads return with a good report from inland."

He turns from the grave. "Back to work, lads! We're obliged to complete the storehouse before we unload the *Tonquin*. Only then a proper trade can begin!"

Near the edge of the forest where the clearing is being extended, Robert swings a crude, homemade ladder against a rough scaffold of split boards his crew has built around an old fir, six-feet above the forest floor and past the massive base of the tree, where the trunk rises straight and even. Antoine Belleau and two of the clerks, Ross and McLennan, each carrying a five-foot, double-bitted felling axe, rest their flintlocks conveniently near the base of the ladder and silently mount the scaffold. Robert picks up an axe and follows.

The four men survey the forest uneasily as they take positions equidistant around the trunk. The clearing is less than a hundred feet away, yet the forest is dark and forbidding around them. Some roll up sleeves and tie on a headband for the labor ahead. Robert makes eye contact with each, studies the height and lean of the tree, checks the positions of the nearest big trees. "Right," he shouts confidently and points. "We want her to fall there!"

The men exchange quick glances of reassurance mixed with amusement. They know by now that the tree will fall where it will, but Robert's confident tone is welcome in this unrelenting wilderness they are determined to tame.

Robert makes the first cut. The men follow, one by one, around the tree. After swinging, each turns and surveys the forest until his turn again to chop. Bit by bit flies from the giant trunk. From the nearby clearing, sounds reach them of chopping, shouts, an occasional explosion as tree stumps are blown up to clear the ground.

While routinely surveying the forest, Antoine's attention is suddenly riveted. *"Le Sauvage* (a savage)!" he shouts and drops to his haunches as a flint-headed arrow pierces the tree trunk above him.

The men instantly drop to the soft ground six feet below, grab their flintlocks, turn to confront their assailant but all is silent. There is no movement in the forest as they search cautiously in pairs in the vicinity of the giant tree. "Enough of bloody savages!" Robert shouts in anger at the still forest around them. "Show yourself, damn you!"

In another part of the forest beyond the clearing, Olivier Lapensée, mumbling to himself in frustration, climbs impatiently onto a scaffold which surrounds a second large Douglas fir. The trunk has been chopped nearly through. Jean Baptiste Belleau awaits him on the scaffold with two felling axes.

François Pillet and an Islander on the ground have hold of a heavy rope that is tied around a limb high on the trunk. Lapensée grabs his axe from his partner and shouts impatiently, *"Puul da* rope!"

They chop with a vengeance as the two men pull. *"Merde de merde* (Shit)! *Puul*, by *gar!*" he shouts again, *"Puul! Puul!"* The tree stands firmly.

The men shift the direction of their pull and the Frenchmen move opposite and chop. *"Puul! Par le sang de Dieu, puul* (for the blood of God…)!"

Lapensée climbs down from the scaffold in disgust and stares helplessly at the large tree. He raises his voice, gesturing in frustration, *"Je renie Dieu* (I deny God)!"

The Islander steps back to survey the tree. He points to the top and waves to Belleau on the scaffold, "Missi Bell! Missi Bell!"

Belleau jumps off the scaffold and joins the others. They stare at the treetop. The upper branches are entangled with the tree next to it, holding it in place. Belleau glares at the elated Islander with extreme aggravation. *"Bougre* (bugger)!"

Lapensée turns to them with fierce determination. *"Très bien, mes amis* (very well, my friends). They come together!"

Chapter Thirty-One

At the storehouse construction site, David notches the end of a squared, twenty-foot log that sits on top of a wall he is constructing. Without his noticing, five Islanders approach carrying a thirty-foot log suspended between them by log tongs with Russell Farnham in the lead position, a flintlock slung over his shoulder. They dump the log beside others for his use and return on the muddy ground to the forest.

Two seamen work a frame pit saw. As they complete one board they add it to a pile beside them. In the vicinity, two additional seamen are removing cedar bark strips with peeling spud and draw knife.

David completes the notch, wipes his brow, and turns to two Islanders who work behind him, squaring the next log with draw knife, mallet, and chisel. "Right, James Cook! You and Patrick!" He points to a large pile of moss beside one half-completed wall. "That moss, now! Make a good job of it before the rain comes again!"

The Islanders grab handfuls and begin spreading the moss evenly over the top log of the wall he is building.

Throughout the morning and into the afternoon, Robert and crew swing their heavy axes into the enormous Douglas fir. They have stripped off shirts and are well-lathered with perspiration and bits of wood from the exertion and terrible repetition of their labor. The circumference of the trunk is now fully wedged. Suddenly an arrow strikes the trunk and the men again jump down and search without effect for the hostile party.

Later the same day in the clearing near the forest, two Islanders chop and dig beneath the base of a massive six-foot diameter tree stump. Stephen Weeks approaches with a quart-sized canister of black powder and examines the shelf the men have been hacking beneath the stump. He puts the canister down and turns to the Islanders. "Move back now, and clear the area." He motions them toward a fallen tree. "Behind that big log!"

Weeks again climbs beneath the stump and sets the canister well into the shelf and then unrolls a long fuse. He carefully runs the fuse out of the trench and along the ground for several yards. "All clear for blasting!" he shouts.

A few men in the vicinity move away. Weeks lights the fuse and runs. He dives behind the fallen tree where his crew waits. Cautiously he peers around the end of the log and spots an Islander carrying a felling axe, limping in the direction of the stump from the forest.

Weeks jumps up, waving desperately. "Get ba…" The explosion rocks the massive stump and drowns his voice. Dirt, bits of wood, and white smoke engulf them. The Islander is thrown back.

Weeks and his crew reach the fallen man and turn him over. He is unconscious with blood on his head. The two Islanders who dug the shelf pick up their countryman and carry him off toward the tents.

Weeks examines the tree stump. Two-thirds of it is still intact. He is puzzled.

In the forest two of the young Islanders pick up a large hunk of moss cut from the mulch beneath the trees and stuff it into the top of a high pack. Isaac and Joshua watch them closely. The boys lift the towering pack and place it against Joshua's shoulders. They dutifully hold it in place as Joshua ties the two shoulder straps before marching off toward the clearing.

The day continues overcast and windy as David, with help from James and Patrick, adds to the storehouse with another twenty-foot log set onto a log well-layered with moss. David drives a log dog with a wooden mallet into the fresh log to anchor it in place. He then begins working a draw knife over the inside half of the log as Joshua, with the full pack of moss, approaches. James and Patrick immediately drop their work and respectfully remove his pack. With formal and pompous gestures, part of a seemingly private ritual, Joshua empties the pack. David notices but does not acknowledge this imperious routine between the senior and younger Islanders.

Nearby a second building of the same dimensions is being laid out. With the blacksmith's shed between the two, it will form the third wall of a quadrangle. The work of clearing and building progresses despite the weather.

The next morning between showers of light rain, McDougall plants seeds along an evenly-furrowed plot of ground. Isaac is hoeing ahead of him on the same furrow. Nearby are pens containing two sheep, four goats, and fourteen pigs landed from the ship.

McDougall stands upright, straightening his back with difficulty. With a wool scarf around his neck, he is not well. "Bring that sack o' potatoes." He coughs and points. "Isaac! Them that's survived the voyage!"

Isaac drops his hoe and obeys promptly. McDougall opens the cloth sack and dumps the potatoes onto the ground. "Only twelve?" He picks one up and mutters to himself, "By God! I fancy ye for me supper this day." He glances furtively toward the storehouse site. "Can't live forever on dry fish," he gasps, breathing heavily, but notices Isaac watching him and bellows out, "Grow like weeds, ye will, in this bloody wet soil!" He turns to the sky, bursting with pent up frustration. "Bloody clouds! Bloody rain…" He breaks off in a fit of coughing. "Bloody hell!" he utters as he gathers up the potatoes and moves along the furrow, dropping them one at a time. He scolds Isaac as he moves. "Along this furrow. Do 'em as I tell ye! Be quick, man!"

The benign Isaac seems puzzled and hesitates.

McDougall bellows, "By God, Isaac, don't give me none o' them prickly looks!" He stops and faces Isaac squarely. "Full moon's the time to plant, man! And, mind ye, space 'em out proper!"

Chapter Thirty-Two

At the edge of the forest, moving toward the clearing, Olivier, harnessed to one side of a heavy trunk, pulls at the lead position, ahead of Jean Baptiste, Pillet and the Islander. Mumford, at the head of three husky Islanders, pulls opposite them on the same trunk.

Two Islanders place a short log used as a roller at the front of the huge trunk, as it moves slowly forward, then run to the rear, pick up a log roller that has been left behind, and return to the front and place it in position, thereby keeping the large trunk on "wheels." The two crews in harness, with quick reflex and sheer main, prevent the log from rolling sideways off the makeshift rollers as they doggedly approach a wooden track in the clearing that leads to the storehouse.

As the trunk shifts dangerously close to Mumford's crew, Olivier, hollers out to his men, "*Puul! Puul!* Jean Baptiste, *puul!*" With strength beyond their sizes, they keep the log from rolling sideways out of control.

The trunk shifts back to center and begins to roll toward Olivier's crew. He shouts, breathless, "The feet, Mumford! Dig the feet! *Puul! Puul!*" Mumford and crew pull with all their strength but Mumford loses his footing and falls. The trunk slides off the rollers.

Olivier slips out of the harness and points to Mumford's position. "Jean Baptiste, you take the place or we no make the track!" He points to Jean

Baptiste's position behind him. "Mumford! I give you the chance. Now you *puul* this place!"

"Lost my footing, dammit!" Mumford complains, breathless. "I can damn well pull here."

Olivier, who is nearly Mumford's height, becomes angry and aggressive. "Mumford! You my crew! You do that I tell you!" Humiliated and resentful, Mumford reluctantly changes places with the Frenchman. Though the load is more than he can handle, the tall second mate will not admit it.

Back in harness, the men of the two crews strain against the enormous weight to keep it on the rollers. The massive trunk moves, but slowly. Mumford remains silent and sullen. The tables are completely turned from ship-board days. At the end of the track, the trunk rolls off nearly jerking the men off their feet. *"Mauvais bougre* (ugly bugger)! We make the stop!"

Mumford immediately slips out of the harness and goes to a rain barrel near the tents, raises the lid and drinks from a common tin cup. David who is hand-drilling a hole at the end of a partially stripped log notices him at the rain barrel. He sets the augur aside. "Mr Mumford. Could I have a word with ye?" Mumford is silent as he approaches. "What do ye think now of them French boatmen? Strongest devils on two feet," he comments. "Pull a loaded flatboat all day against the current. Aye! And sing all night, they will, when the rest of us would sleep!" There is resentment in Mumford's eye but he says nothing.

David turns toward the storehouse. "Have a look inside, would ye, laddie? Them Islanders say they've completed digging the cellar. Ye know better than any of us the storage kegs of powder require."

Mumford leaves David without comment and walks over to the storehouse. Within the partially completed structure, a pit five-feet deep that runs about a third the length of the building and covers nearly the full width is completed. The sides are cut straight with a dirt ramp at one side that leads to the bottom. Two Islanders are carrying buckets full of loose earth out of the pit. A third stands proudly at the head of the ramp.

The angry second mate stops at the edge of the ramp, turns silently from the Islander and walks a couple of paces along the edge of the pit before he whirls about suddenly and faces the startled man at the top of the ramp. Bursting with pent up indignation he bellows, "It's to be eight-feet deep!" He gestures as high as he can reach. "I swear by liver an' lungs, it's to be eight feet! Dunderhead! Jackass!" He turns on the flabbergasted men with the buckets who face him from the far edge of the pit. "Ye have to dig more, blast ye! Dig!"

Mumford swells with rage and self-importance before the bewildered Islanders. He leans toward them as he speaks. "Now didn't I tell ye to dig a powder magazine, blast ye? A powder magazine, I say!" He gestures with his arms, "It's the *cool* earth we want to surround them kegs o' powder! They must all lay beneath the cool, dry earth!" He points to the lead Islander. "Do as I tell ye now! Dig! I can't be standin' here all day to watch ye! Dig!"

In the meantime, at the blacksmith's forge in the shed, a red-hot bar is placed on an anvil and pounded into a long strap hinge. The blacksmith, a big man wearing a leather apron, shapes the end of the hinge into a loop to fit over the pin of a doorjamb. Weeks, unshaven and gaunt, approaches the forge with a broken iron pick axe. He holds it up to the blacksmith with a shrug, slips on his leather apron and goes to work opposite the smith to repair the tool.

At the edge of the forest, Olivier, Jean Baptiste and crews carry their harness off toward the forest to pull another giant trunk. Mumford stands sullenly to one side as Olivier and Jean Baptiste separate the harnesses. Nearby is the second of the two firs Olivier's crew has cut down. Olivier walks up to Mumford and drops one harness in front of him. "Mumford, you put harness this side. I put the other side."

Mumford kicks the harness toward him. "Make a hand o' it yourself, Frenchy!"

Both men glow with resentment as their eyes meet. "You my crew, Mumford," Olivier replies in a quiet but intense voice. "You not on the *Tonquin*. You put harness this side."

Mumford stands his ground. "Heart alive, man, have done!" he replies aggressively. "Me orders is to pull, and that's all!"

Olivier steps up to him. "Mumford, you do that I tell you!"

In reply Mumford lunges for him but Olivier springs aside with lightning speed and sends the bigger man sprawling. Mumford leaps to his feet, a knife in hand.

With instantaneous reflex, Olivier lets his long knife fly. Before Mumford has time to look up, Olivier's knife impales his forearm to the hilt. Mumford is knocked back into a sitting position, his own knife falling to the ground in front of him. He looks up at Olivier in disbelief then reaches with his uninjured arm for his weapon.

Olivier is on him before he can grasp it, drags the injured man to his feet and smacks him squarely on the jaw. Mumford drops.

The Frenchman leans close to the unconscious mate and utters with burning rage, "If you the captain, *Monsieur* Mumford, you be dead man!" He jerks his knife from the injured forearm, pulls a scarf from Mumford's neck, ties it firmly around the wound, and stands up. He motions to two of the husky Islanders. "Put this man on the *Tonquin*!"

Chapter Thirty-Three

Early the next morning the *Tonquin* lies at anchor with a boarding net securing the entire deck while ten Cowichan sea canoes, with twenty men and a pile of furs in each, await a turn to board and trade. The largest and most ornate of the sea canoes glides silently around the ship with only ten men aboard. The gunwales from stem to stern are studded with small marine shells, which, from a slight distance, appear to be teeth.

On board the *Tonquin*, the main deck is piled with wool blankets, bales of blue and green and scarlet cotton cloth, piles of colorful Indian calicos, madras prints and cotton bandannas, an open case of small, green-handled knives. There is a cask of light blue glass beads and one of brass coat buttons of various sizes and figures, a case of fishhooks, an open hogshead of Brazilian twisted leaf tobacco. A case of familiar red-handled scalping knives with "LONDON L" stamped on the blade also lies open.

Occasional grunts are uttered by nine Cowichan Indians who inspect the goods on deck. On the rail, McDougall faces a fantastically ornamented chief who stares silently at him with considerable native pride. With black teeth and blood-red lips, his face is streaked with red and white paint. Characters in red and white are painted on his body and a cap embellished with wavy plumes of rooster feathers sits atop his pate. Before him lies a pile of sea otter skins and behind along the rail nine piles of seal and otter peltry unattended.

Captain Thorn leans against the taffrail watching McDougall who stares intently at the chief. With wool scarf around his neck, he turns, chagrined, picks up two blankets, one of the red-handled knives, and again faces the chief holding his thumb upright. *"Ikt* skin!" He holds the goods out to the chief who glances cursorily and waves them away.

The chief replies, *"Itk t'kope ten-as!"*

Thorn calls out from the quarterdeck, "What's holding up the trade, Mr McDougall?" He approaches and eyes the chief disdainfully. "What does this barbarian want?"

"A Cowichan chief, Captain. He's come by sea from north along the coast to trade…" He breaks off, coughing heavily.

Thorn steps forward, irritated. "Of course he's come to trade, man! Name your price and be done with him!"

"Beggin' your pardon, Captain, but that's not how it's done! A refusal to trade will be considered an open declaration o' war, even if the goods are inferior."

Thorn is indignant. "In the meantime, they'll try to steal everything they lay hands on!"

"But, Captain, the chief here has as fine otter skins as I've laid me eyes on."

Thorn studies the chief. He is incredulous and begins pacing in exasperation as McDougall bargains.

Thorn finally turns on McDougall, interrupting his apparent long-windedness. "For mercy sake, man, have done! Make him a trade! Others are waiting to come aboard!"

McDougall is losing patience with Thorn. "But, Captain, he is unwilling to receive anything we can conveniently spare." He indicates the others. "And this lot won't trade unless he does. He sets the price."

Thorn turns to the chief. He takes up the end of one well-dressed skin. "What have we here? How much, chief?" He holds it up bruskly to the chief.

The chief eyes Thorn silently, evenly.

Thorn shakes the skin. "Trade! How much?"

McDougall interjects, *"Ikta mika tumtum* (what do you think)?"

The chief replies, *"Ikt t'kope ten-as."*

Thorn looks at McDougall. "Well? What is it? What does he want?"

"That's the problem, Captain." McDougall looks Thorn in the eye. "He insists upon a young white lad, to roast."

Thorn is stunned. He turns on the chief with sudden indignation. "You confounded rascal! The devil take you! I've a mind to spread you across a thirty-pounder and cut your ugly hide with a cat-o'-nine tails! Teach you to respect an American!"

"Nay, Captain! Nay!" McDougall bursts out. "Ye mustn't insult the chief! A slave would be a customary gift. But he don't believe me that we have none. 'Tis their custom."

"A pack of impudent knaves!" Thorn replies hotly. "Mr McDougall, at eight bells I want the *Tonquin* cleared of these barbarians." He strides angrily forward. "Worthless beggars. Mr Mumford!"

Chapter Thirty-Four

CONSTRUCTION OF THE POST continues. The month of May is nearly half over when one afternoon as Weeks and the blacksmith work at their anvils under the low roof of the log shed there is a sudden cry of alarm from the edge of the clearing. Various voices shout, "Savages! Indian attack!" There is the sound of a musket shot. Weeks drops his hammer, grabs a nearby flintlock and runs toward the disturbance. The blacksmith follows. They join others who rush to the edge of the forest. Two Islanders scramble down from the roof of the storehouse which appears nearly completed.

As the men begin to converge, Joshua rushes helter-skelter from the forest into the clearing, a full pack of moss impaled to his back by an arrow. He screams for help all the time gesticulating wildly.

Robert and crew emerge from the forest carrying flintlocks. Farnham and crew appear as well as Olivier and crew and David with his two Islanders from the construction site. There is chaos as the men gather around the frantic Joshua, all talking at once. "Steady, lads!" David shouts. "Steady now! Did any of ye see 'em?" A confusion of excited voices respond as David reaches Joshua, motions to the men for calm and immediately spots the arrow.

He turns Joshua to face away from him. "Right Chief!" Without ceremony, David reaches around the pack of moss. "Ye don't want that wound festering before your very men's eyes. No dignity in that, me good man!" He takes hold of the shaft. "Steady, chief!" With a quick pull, David removes the arrow from Joshua's back.

Joshua shrieks when he sees the shaft tipped with fresh blood. "Only a flesh wound," David comments and touches the arrow tip. "Unless this flint is poisoned, ye'll be right as rain. We'll know by sunset."

He closely examines the shaft and feathers. "I'll have a word with Coalpo when he returns. He is our friend." He turns to the men. "Someone wants us off this side of the river."

McDougall steps forward. He is agitated. "It's the want o' trade, I tell ye! There can be no trade on this river so long as the *Tonquin* is here. Every day is the same!"

"But there is reason they fear us," David replies. "Some of them Clatsops are terrified we bring evil medicine."

"Whatever have we done to them?" Weeks responds with resentment. "We trade fish hooks and sewing twine and tobacco leaf for food."

The men are restive and angry. David again motions for calm. "Now listen, you men. It is not many years since a ship anchored here which spread the small-pox." He looks evenly but firmly over the crowd. "Four chiefs and several hundreds of the Clatsop nation were destroyed. Aye! An' that according to our Chinook friends across the river who speak the same language. That is why the Chinooks are today a larger, more powerful tribe. Many of them Clatsops remember."

David turns toward the construction site while the men continue to mumble together in groups. "Back to work, lads! Keep a sharp eye, now. We can't be losing no more men!" He motions to his nephew and they walk a few steps together. David puts his arm on Robert's shoulder. "What Mr McDougall says of the trade here is on me mind. Ye'll be with the *Tonquin*, lad, when she goes north for the summer. Even if the trade goes poorly, keep a close record of what skins ye see so we know which places to return to."

Robert is concerned. "You mean, sir, another ship might make a better trade?"

"'Tis not the ship, but the captain," David replies and Robert nods agreement.

As they separate, David points to the forest "When will that fir be down, lad?"

"It's taken a bit longer, sir."

"Warn the lads before she goes. We want no one hurt."

Robert responds with confidence. "Aye, sir, tomorrow. Tomorrow she'll be down!"

The clearing returns to normal activity. At the riverbank the carpenter and two seamen drive wooden pegs with large mallets into thwarts of the frame that is now taking on the shape of a schooner. Two Islanders hoist an additional thwart into position. Arosss the river, not far from the north shore, the *Tonquin* rests quietly. The boarding net is up. There are no canoes visible.

On top of the storehouse, two Islanders lay cedar bark on the roof. A seaman works with mallet and chisel to even out the doorjamb while a second seaman with a cant hook works a cedar log into position for splitting. Weeks, with David's help, measures the shutters of windows for hinges.

Late in the day Robert, Antoine, Ross and McLennan continue to swing their felling axes at the giant fir. Their endurance is mule-like, sure. Each man surveys the forest between strokes. There appears no letup in their rhythm or earnestness. They are now three-quarters through the massive trunk.

The GONG-GONG-GONG of the supper bell interrupts their work. Robert shoulders his axe, breathless. "Right!" He surveys the deep cut surrounding the trunk. "Tomorrow she falls!"

Antoine rubs his dirty brow. He too is breathless. "I believe it, *monsieur*, when I see it."

The four men drop their axes from the scaffold and jump to the soft floor of the forest below. Robert steps back and surveys the tree, measuring its height, lean and girth with his mind's eye. "She'll fall, all right, an' she's going where I said," he points away from the clearing, "there!"

"No, *monsieur*," Antoine responds. "The wind, she blow to the north." He gestures toward the clearing. "She go this way, with the wind." The other two nod in agreement.

They pick up their flintlocks, axes and shirts and start toward the clearing together. All at once there is a sharp cracking sound. They all turn and gasp in one voice, momentarily paralyzed. The giant fir has begun to fall towards them. They cannot believe their eyes. "Run for it!" Robert shouts, his head suddenly exploding in terror.

The enormous fir falling, falling, falling, hits with earth-shaking force, smashing all in its path to oblivion. As the dust clears, Robert, Ross and McLennan face each other. Antoine is missing.

In utter panic, Robert runs along the branches of the huge fallen trunk that is nearly his height in diameter. "Antoine! Antoine!" he shouts out desperately, races back and stops in front of Ross.

"We can do nothing, sir!" Ross insists.

Half mad with fear, Robert again bolts toward the butt end of the giant trunk. He reaches the huge splintered stump that remains upright in the ground, turns the corner and runs straight into Antoine who appears, axe on shoulder, walking unconcerned around the fallen tree to meet him. Robert stops in his tracks, startled as though seeing a ghost.

"I tell you, she fall with the wind," Antoine reminds him matter-of-factly. Robert throws his arms around Antoine's neck in an impulse of overwhelming gratitude.

The four men, suddenly realizing their task is complete, join arms together with a great "Hurrah!" of spontaneous relief and run jubilantly toward the dinner gong.

Chapter Thirty-Five

That evening, between the tents, blacksmith's shed, and storehouse, the men lounge in the yard around the communal fire. They eat, smoke, repair clothing, sharpen tools. Robert writes in his journal. Two quarters of elk roast and a big brass kettle steams nearby. Occasionally one of the men slices off a piece of meat for himself or fills his mug with tea. There is a feeling of friendship among them, whether seaman, Scotsman, American, Frenchman or Islander.

David, Mumford, Weeks, Olivier and McDougall sit together on the ground. Mumford gnaws with relish on a rib nearly as long as his arm. A scruffy piece of cloth is tied carelessly around his injured forearm. "Haven't seen ye about our table, Mr Mumford," McDougall comments offhandedly, "since ye did that injury to yourself."

Farnham joins them as Mumford glances a bit sheepishly at Olivier who is now his comrade. "Aye, that." With forced bravado, he complains, "Cap'n forbid it! Says a mate's place is aboard ship." He licks his fingers. "Should have meat more often, Mr Stuart!"

"Feelin' a bit peckish, are ye?" McDougall asks.

"Can't spare men for hunting," David replies. "Must rely on the natives for food."

"Aye," McDougall comments sarcastically. "Obliged to get our Captain Thorn on his way. God preserve his cheerful bones!"

David nods in agreement. "Tomorrow we can discharge cargo from the *Tonquin*. The storehouse roof is complete."

"Aye," McDougall remarks, "and it won't be soon enough for our captain."

Mumford looks significantly at the men. "Cap'n says he'll sail before the month's out."

David is surprised. "Aye?"

Mumford leans toward him, confiding. "Says he'll land only part o' the cargo now." He lowers his voice. "Says he's waited long enough for the likes o' you to build a storehouse. Them was his very words, sir!"

Weeks is embarrassed. "He wishes to sail this coast while the weather's good, sir."

David puffs thoughtfully on his pipe. "Anxious for a bit of trade, our captain?"

Farnham turns to David. "We could lay in enough supplies for summer. They'll be back before the end of August, sir."

"Aye," Mumford agrees. "We'll bend our course here by the middle o' August. It's only a coastin' excursion Mr Astor's ordered, as far as Cook's River."

"The lads have work enough for the present," David responds. "Better to discharge the trade goods, I'm thinking, when ye return."

Mumford settles himself comfortably. He turns to Weeks. "Enjoy the fire while ye can, mate. There'll be none aboard ship."

On the other side of the fire, Antoine begins to sing "Alouette" and the men join in the song. The two injured Islanders sing with them.

All at once a distant gunshot reaches them from the river. The men are instantly silent. They turn to one another in uncertainty. The tension builds for a couple of moments before a second gunshot is heard.

David listens intently, staring away from the fire. There is a glint of expectation in his expression. The tension continues to build among the men and some reach for their flintlocks.

A third gunshot at last cleaves the air and David breaks into a broad grin. He jumps to his feet, grabbing his flintlock. "That's Mr McKay, lads! Let's return his signal!"

The whole camp explodes with a cannonade of wild musket fire. The men are momentarily enveloped in white smoke but that does not stop some from grabbing a burning stake and rushing off, torch in hand, to the river.

As McKay's canoe followed closely by their Indian guides appears on the expanse of dark water, the men burst into spontaneous and raucous cheers. The canoe lands at the pier and McKay, Franchère, Bruslé and Laframboise are overwhelmed with affectionate embraces.

The Clatsop canoe lands nearby and Coalpo disembarks. McKay breaks away from the men and approaches him, full of robust spirit. "Come to me after the *Tonquin* departs," he says with some sign language. "I will give you each a smoke. And I'll shave you again, Coalpo!"

Coalpo responds in broken speech. "Mac-kay talk paper. King George!" He is pleased with himself. "Mac-kay talk," indicating himself, "Coalpo!" The Clatsops depart.

McKay and David walk together along the riverbank. "They are exceedingly fond of all white chiefs who come from King George," McKay offers wryly.

"They believe every white man who visits this river comes from King George," David responds with humor.

"For a trifling present we had a guide from every tribe upon the way which prevents any hostile encounter with his own tribesmen. Aye, and better guides you'll never find, Mr Stuart!"

McDougall joins them as they head toward the bonfire. "And the trade, Mr McKay? Any sign of Simon Fraser or John Stuart?"

"The river is ours!" McKay's enthusiasm is catching. "No sign of the North West Company. The higher we ascended, the more eager and friendly toward us were the natives."

"I say well done, lad!" David points ahead to the new structure lit by the open fire. "Come. This evening we're feasting on a side of elk, and it's roasted to a turn. Completed the storehouse today, we did." He gestures to McDougall, "Break out a cag of rum, Mr McDougall." He shouts to the men, "A dram all around to welcome the lads!"

The men respond with noisy cheers. McKay can hardly contain his optimism and the good feeling at their safe return. He turns to his friend of many years as they walk toward the storehouse, "A six-penny worth o' rum, Mr Stuart," he requests with a twinkle in his eye, "and warm, if you please!" The two comrades laugh heartily.

Chapter Thirty-Six

Later that evening inside the storehouse the walls of squared logs are dimly lit by lanterns. Shutters are open, and through the doorway can be seen the remains of the fire in the yard. The cellar is concealed by rough wooden planks with a trap door to one side. At the end of the room is a fireplace and stone hearth. While some of the men gather in familiar camaraderie on the floor, the Frenchmen sing "A la Claire Fontaine" to Bruslé's accompaniment. The Scotchmen, Weeks, Mumford, Farnham, and Franchère sit on benches around a long, hand-hewn table.

In front of McKay, a lantern spreads its thin glow onto scraps of notes kept on the journey inland. He holds a crude, pencil-sketched map of the Columbia River valley and indicates the territory from the mouth. "The whole of the country abounds in beaver and other kinds of fur. There's seal aplenty at the falls. And the people of this valley were numerous and well disposed." McKay sets the map aside and sits down.

Franchère adds, "Many tribes do not see the white man before."

McKay looks up significantly to the men at the table. "Some of the people imagine the whole world to live on a river running through a mountain wilderness like their own. Having inquired of me in which part lay the lodge of the white people, they bid me tell how many were the canoes of our village. Small is their horizon, lads, but these people still follow the old custom. While in their lodge, a guest wants for nothing. They have not yet learned to give only to those who can pay."

"They'll learn soon enough!" McDougall responds.

The men listen intently as McKay continues. "Aye, through the whole of the tribes, I have seen no flintlocks or weapons of war. Rarely bow and arrow. They use lances fit for antelope. But as ye know, lads, flint tips break and many a fine buck is lost."

"They depend on the river for food?" David asks.

"When they can. But inland, it is roots and berries, and what few salmon they get in trade. They would follow the deer throughout the winter if their weapons were shod with iron. They greatly desire iron spear tips and knives."

Robert responds with enthusiasm, "The more the better!"

"Nay, lad," David responds, "the fewer goods they require, the better."

McDougall adds ominously, "They want but little at first, that is certain. But the more they obtain of our manufacture, the more unhappy will they be, as the possession of one article creates a desire for another and so they are never satisfied."

The singing ends and the men turn to the conversation at the table.

"Remember, lads," McKay remarks, "this is new territory. We do not want the people jealous and quarreling among themselves. When people are at war, they do not trade."

"But let us finish the business, Mr McKay," David intercedes.

"Captain Thorn comes ashore in the morning. Our lads have a long day ahead.

McKay stands and speaks to the room. "The Americans here are a very different people from those near our settlements on the great prairies. Not a single insult or aggression was attempted on us. I told them we would supply trade for peltry. These Americans appear anxious to possess everything they saw with us."

He moves away from the table as he speaks with increasing intensity. "As far as we traveled, this is a virgin land. At some grand rapids we found a gathering of many tribes for trade among themselves. Those who live near the Rocky Mountains assured us that no white men inhabit their territory. But men from the north spoke of a party last spring approaching the upper Columbia." He looks at David. "I assume this is Mr McKenzie and Mr Hunt with our men from St. Louis." He can hardly contain his optimism. "Aye, lads, we've beat the North West Company! You've built the first trading establishment on the Great River of the West, and you've put the flag of the Unites States of America above her." He turns to Mumford with ironic good humor. "That makes us *Americans*, lads! Right, Mr Mumford?"

Mumford agrees. He has grown fond of the men despite himself. Laframboise is especially pleased.

McKay continues, "Aye, this isn't Fort William, but the Columbia River is ours! Lads, ye've made a day to remember!" The men respond with hearty approval. "Next spring when the winter snows have melted and our overland party is here, Mr Stuart and I will take some of you upriver to build a second post. But." He pauses, thoughtfully. "Let us think of Mr Astor this day, and be thankful, lads, for this, for God's country!"

Laframboise speaks up impulsively, "It is our coon-trae, *monsieur*!" which brings on laughter among the men.

McKay is amused. "Aye, lad, and a grand country she is!"

David hands McKay a roll of cloth and McKay unrolls a flag with a red "A" on a white field. "To honor Mr Astor, the partners agreed before we left New York that we name this establishment *Fort Astoria*. Tomorrow we raise Mr Astor's flag beneath the Stars and Stripes."

McKay turns to McDougall vigorously, with a twinkle in his eye. "Now, Mr McDougall, we can't have these *Americans* sitting here dry o' throat when we're celebrating our new establishment!"

Boisterous agreement erupts from the men but McDougall is peevish. "Should have small beer for this lot, Mr McKay. Drink like Christians, they do!"

During the general merriment, David leans over to his nephew. "Better ready your chest, lad. Get it aboard ship. Ye'll soon be leaving us."

David stands and gets the attention of the men. "There's work to be done, lads! Tomorrow we discharge cargo from the *Tonquin*." He turns to Bruslé. "Louis, strike up a song to end this day. That's a good lad!"

A momentary commotion follows before Bruslé stands. He turns from the men as though there has been some agreement between them. "*Monsieur* McKay," he says. "*Monsieur*, the men want that you play the bagpipe!"

Enthusiastic agreement from the floor both pleases and surprises McKay. "Aye, lads, if that is your wish." He goes to a chest by the wall and lifts out his pipes and tunes them. "Now then!"

He turns and stands proudly before the men. "There's an old ditty some of you know me to play. Recalls to mind the earliest event of me life I distinctly remember." He grows serious. "Was but a wee lad when Scotland was a-changin', with woolen mills in Glasgow and Greenock. Bad days when the Highlands were cleared for sheep. Aye, lads!" He speaks with feeling. "Not a time of meal and milk and plenty. No place me old father could earn the bread. From Berwick to Cape Wrath, a Scot was no longer a Scot."

He and David share a knowing glance. "It was during the middle of summer we left. I know the time of year because I recall the small berries were ripe."

He continues with emotion he cannot fully suppress. "Aye. They shipped us away, and these pipes were all me father kept in the world."

He positions the pipes and speaks to the men with spirit. "Now, lads! I'll give you *Three Brave, Loyal Fellows*, which father, who was Alexander McKay, taught me during the long sea voyage to the continent of America."

Chapter Thirty-Seven

With main deck hatches of the *Tonquin* open, seamen and Islanders move barrels and supplies into position for unloading. The pinnace and longboat are tied off alongside the ship to receive the goods and Mumford directs men from the rail as they lower a load of iron bars to the longboat. "Ease 'er down! A bit more, now! Aye! She's on!"

Before the load is tied off Thorn calls out, "What the deuce are you loading?" Mumford turns speechless to his captain who is fast approaching from the quarterdeck. "Essential items, Mr Mumford! What did I tell you? Only essential items!"

"But, sir, Mr McDougall there," he points to McDougall, "he ordered 'em, sir! Wants the whole lot."

"*Ordered* them, you say?" Thorn stops before his mate. He is furious. "While you are officer aboard this ship, Mr Mumford, you take orders from me!"

Forward of the main hatch, McDougall, dressed warmly as usual, confers aloud with Weeks from a list. "Forty-three New York steel traps, two brass swivels on carriages." He looks up to Weeks. "And ye can take them four barrels o' coarse salt."

Thorn immediately crosses the deck and speaks sharply as he makes his way by the hatchway to boldly confront McDougall. "You are to discharge essential items only, Mr McDougall!"

McDougall turns aggressively to Thorn. "An' what do ye think I'm takin' for the present, Captain Thorn?"

"What in the devil is that boatload of iron? You plan to construct a drawbridge, sir?"

"To be sure, them are axe bars o' iron, Captain Thorn. One o' the chief items o' trade, as ye're no doubt aware, is axe heads for the natives." He continues pointedly, "The smith will make 'em by the hundreds." He coughs. "Kindly permit me, if ye'll be so gracious, Captain, to get our goods discharged so ye can depart!"

Thorn turns away, seething. McDougall mumbles to himself, "An' good riddance."

Later that day Mumford and three sailors row Thorn ashore. He is wearing a hunting jacket and carries a musket and leather pouch. Robert waits with a large wooden trunk near the pier. The *Tonquin* lies quietly at anchor across the river.

Mumford holds the pinnace at the pier as Thorn completes instructions. "The mainmast is to be rigged shipshape while I'm hunting, Mr Mumford." He disembarks. "I want that unsightly forward hatch trim before supper!"

Robert approaches the pier. Thorn turns and nearly bumps into him.

"Captain Thorn, would ye allow me trunk to be carried aboard the *Tonquin* in your longboat?"

Thorn stares at Robert with more than annoyance. He has not forgotten the Falkland Islands incident. "Mr Stuart, the Captain's dinghy is not a freight barge." He turns pointedly to Mumford.

Robert is flabbergasted and turns to Mumford who at first seems willing to help but under Thorn's eye quickly throws the rope to the seamen and pushes off.

"Get your own trunk on board the best way you can!" Thorn remarks and walks past him toward the forest.

Robert returns to the storehouse with his trunk. He summons the other partners and the four meet at the table. "If ye take me advice," he urges angrily, "ye'll clap the ruddy bugger in irons. Refused to carry me trunk aboard the *Tonquin*!"

McKay is concerned. "The Captain has no experience of trade."

"Aye." McDougall responds. "But what damn fool would go with him?" He leans forward, confidentially. "Even Mr Mumford told me he don't want to continue aboard the *Tonquin*.

"Captain don't care for nothing but the importance o' his rank!" Robert insists. "I'll not set foot aboard the *Tonquin*!"

McKay gets up from the table and paces the floor in agitation. After a moment, he comes to a decision. "I'd sooner go in the ship than run the risk of losing the coastal trade."

"I am not agreed with ye, lad!" David replies. "We need ye here! There's lodgings to complete. We're obliged not only to prepare for winter," he adds with emphasis, "but we've a second post inland to consider."

"Then there's them Chinooks," McDougall observes. "Our numbers will be greatly reduced, and no telling what they will proclaim to all the tribes around."

McKay is not convinced. "But we must consider the coastal trade. I've seen otter and seal aplenty to the north. And the *Tonquin* will return in no more than three months time."

Early the next morning the thirty-two men of the post gather at the pier. The *Tonquin*, fully rigged for departure, remains anchored across the river in the deep channel near the north shore. The longboat with Bruslé and a large chest in the bow and two sailors aboard awaits McKay. A subdued Stephen Weeks, dressed for the sea as an officer, is on the pier ready to cast off.

Nearby, Mumford, wearing clothes like the men at the post, stands beside a wooden chest. McKay and McDougall approach from the storehouse. McKay, in gentleman's attire, greets the men but is intercepted by an agitated Franchère. "*Monsieur* Mumford has quarrelled with the captain. He is to remain here at the post!"

McKay is momentarily startled but continues outwardly calm. "You're not to be concerned, lad. We'll be gone but a short time."

David approaches McKay from the pier. Conflict is written in his expression. He is not reconciled to McKay's leaving. "Louis Bruslé agreed to travel with ye. He's put your kit aboard."

"The captain has now discharged the only officer on board," McKay comments.

"Aye," David responds. "Another of his frantic fits, and the *Tonquin* already short of crew. Keep your wits about ye, lad!" David grips McKay's shoulders with restrained but real feeling and addresses him in the mother tongue of their native Scotland. "*Beannachd leat!*" (Blessings on you!)

"*Beannachd leat!*" McKay replies and adds impulsively, "If you ever see us safe back, it will be a miracle." He steps aboard the longboat followed by Weeks. The sailors push off with their oars. The longboat reaches the *Tonquin* and McKay takes a last look across the river at the tiny post before climbing aboard.

On the first day of June although there is no breeze, the *Tonquin's* crew begins a chanty and topsails are set for departure. The ship weighs anchor and drifts with the river's current down the deep channel to Baker's Bay, in expectation of departing for the voyage north along the coast.

Day after day after day the crew wait for a favorable wind to cross the bar. Finally on the evening of the fifth day, Franchère sits on the hearth of the storehouse in front of the fire with his journal. By the flickering firelight he writes:

> *Le 5 juin le navire sortit de la riviére...* (On the fifth of June the ship left the river...)

Chapter Thirty-Eight

The natives begin to visit the post more often and a fairly large camp of transients grows up. The demand for food at the post is constant, and before the salmon begin running, the women trade fruit which is beginning to ripen: small sweet white strawberries and red and yellow raspberries. The men of the post find blueberries, red currants, cherries, wild pears, black currants and wild apples, very sour unless cooked. Villagers from inland along the river supply blackberries, hazelnuts and acorns in exchange for fish hooks and glass beads.

The walls of the second log building, the lodging beside the blacksmith's shed and opposite the storehouse, are complete and roof girders are being put in place by a crew of sturdy Islanders. Into the clearing between the lodging and storehouse, Olivier and Jean Baptiste, flintlocks hanging from their shoulders, each lead a crew of Chinook Indians carrying twenty-five-foot stripped logs from the forest.

In the patch of field between the post and the river, McDougall, with wool scarf around his neck, drags a sack of seed along one furrow of the tilled ground toward Isaac and a small crew of Islanders who are extending the field.

The furrowed ground now surrounds the grave site and covers the area between the post and the river except for a broad pathway between the pier and storehouse. A stake fence partly surrounds the field.

McDougall pulls the sack abreast of Isaac and stops, breathless. "All the way to them bushes!" he orders. "Do ye hear me, Isaac? Keep the lads workin' now!" He reaches into the sack and lifts a handful of wheat kernels as he watches the men and lets them run through his fingers back into the sack. "Drill this lot from here."

The sound of a musket shot from the river interrupts McDougall and rivets his attention beyond Isaac. He stares with a mixture of surprise and alarm. "What have we here?"

Black powder smoke is rising from the first among a fleet of thirty-odd canoes filled with Indians. A second puff of smoke rises from the lead canoe followed by the sound of the distant musket shot. He begins to make out the sounds of Indians whooping and yelling.

McDougall bolts in alarm across the freshly planted field. Mumford joins him, wooden mallet in hand, from the schooner frame where he was working. "Where are them two-pounders, Mr Mumford!" he ejaculates as the two men rush together toward the others who are quickly gathering. David has climbed to the top of a wall of the lodging for a full view of the river as they reach the clearing. There is confusion everywhere.

McDougall is breathless and beside himself with urgency. "Can ye see the end of 'em, Mr Stuart?"

Calm and deliberate, David takes in everything at a glance. "There are not over one hundred and fifty. One musket. A chief leading the party."

The men press tightly around David. Mumford bursts out, "Can stop 'em easy, sir! Keep 'em from landing! Where's the brass swivel?"

McDougall is aflutter with instructions. "Someone call the men from the forest! Quick now!"

David climbs down and turns to the men, raising his hands to calm them. "You men! Mr McDougall, will ye steady the lads!"

Franchère and some men from the storehouse approach with flintlocks. McDougall's confidence returns as David takes charge. "Gather round! Listen to what ye're told now!"

David points up the river toward the approaching canoes. "Two of you lads give 'em a welcoming volley!"

The men are confused, Olivier incredulous. "But they plan the attack, *monsieur!*"

David is insistent. "You two." He points to Franchère and Olivier. "Fire in the air, one at a time. Do as I tell ye!" Franchère fires followed by Olivier.

McDougall and the men stare at David in disbelief.

"There is nothing to fear," David responds. "They come to introduce themselves, perhaps to trade."

"But they bring the gun, monsieur," Laframboise observes.

"Aye," David replies emphatically. "And they bring their women and children. Now, Mr McDougall, you're the chief factor at this trading post. I suggest you prepare gifts and be ready to smoke with the headman and his relatives in the customary way. Some of you lads come with me to pay respects and bring 'em to the post when their camp is made."

That night, David and Mumford, who carries a torch of split cedar, lead the principal chief, his head held high, toward the storehouse. They are preceded by chanting warriors who also hold torches. Behind them follow the chief's five teenage sons, various headmen and a number of the band who rhythmically chant and clap. No women are present but the men appear happy and confident.

The chief, with black piercing eyes, wears a coolie hat and American trousers torn off at the knee. As tall as Mumford with ears slit and ornamented with strings of small sea shells, the chief proudly marches along. A piece of polished bone held by a slit in the nasal cartlidge protrudes at both sides of his nose. Fish oil moistens his skin. With the help of sign language he speaks to David. *"Na-di-da-nuit i-qa-qa ie-ka-nok, posh-tun!"*

David nods significantly to Mumford. "They bring bear skins and beaver to trade."

The chief stops and removes a dog-eared scrap of paper from his trouser pocket and gives it to David. He breaks into a child-like grin and points with pride to the paper and himself. *"Posh-tun!"* He points again to the paper but David is puzzled and not sure what to make of it. *"Posh-tun!"* the chief insists.

Mumford responds, "Poshtun. Aye. Heard it before, sir, on the Pacific. This lot no doubt trades among the coasting ships. Likely where that old musket come from."

David unfolds the paper. The chief again insists, *"Posh-tun!"*

David turns with some annoyance to Mumford. "What is he saying, man?"

Mumford replies with a chuckle, "They've not heard o' New York, sir. The trading ships they think of as belonging to the same tribe. Each year along the coast they see them. He means to say, *Boston.*"

The chief recognizes the sound and is pleased and repeats it. *"Posh-tun!"*

"That is their name for all American traders, sir."

Mumford holds the torch close to David as he reads aloud with difficulty from the paper. "The bearer of this says he's a Wishram chief." David glances at the chief who watches him with fascination. "That he's… the best friend the whites ever had… but I believe he is… a damned rascal…" David's eyes light with humor, "so watch out for him. Nathan Winship, Captain, Ship Albatross, Boston, 20th June eighteen hundred and ten."

"To have a message come out of those marks," Mumford observes, indicating the paper, "he thinks is magic."

David folds the note with care and hands it back to the chief with an air of deference. "No doubt the magic in this letter gives him special power."

The chief puts the folded paper into his pocket and points to himself with self-importance. *"Posh-tun!"*

"Aye, chief," David responds with a significant nod, *"Poshtun!"*

Chapter Thirty-Nine

Inside the storehouse that evening, the table and benches are pushed aside and the men gather on the wood floor for the ritual smoking of the pipe. McDougall sits opposite the chief who sits on his haunches with his sons beside him forming half a circle. David and Farnham on one side of McDougall with Robert and Franchère on the other, complete the circle. Half a dozen headmen sit on their haunches behind the chief. The warriors with the torches remain outside chanting and clapping.

After the chief's final deep puff of the pipe, Laframboise removes it from the circle.

The chief fixes his eyes on the ground for a moment then addresses McDougall solemnly, both verbally and with sign language. *"Na-di-da-nuit i-qa-qa ie-ka-nok, posh-tun!"*

David translates for the men. "They bring bear skins and beaver to trade with us."

The chief stares at McDougall across the circle and grins. McDougall studies him, impassive. The chief points to himself, insistent, *"Posh-tun!"*

David leans over to McDougall, "They think white traders are all members of a tribe called *Boston*."

McDougall is nonplussed, but he nods gravely to the chief and uses sign language as he responds. "We welcome the Wishram people who live on the upper reaches of the great river that follows the setting sun. In our house there is good medicine for trade, and aplenty. We give fair exchange for skins. We desire to see all your skins!" He motions to Laframboise. "We have special gifts for the great chief of the Wishram people!"

Laframboise brings a bundle of clothes forward and places it before McDougall who picks up the garments one at a time, holds them out for inspection, gives an exaggerated nod of approval for each item, and then returns them to Laframboise. When the final item is shown, McDougall commands, "For the chief!"

Laframboise crosses to the chief and, beginning with a check shirt, helps him to dress, putting on breeches over his trousers, a waistcoat of baize, stockings of yarn, one red and one blue. Laframboise ties the stockings below the knee with worsted gaiters. The chief refuses a pair of leather moccasins and insists on remaining in his stocking feet. He is then helped into a bright red coat of coarse cloth with regimental cuffs. The suit is ornamented with orris lace. In place of the coolie hat, he is bedecked with three ostrich feathers of bright colors and a worsted sash is wrapped and tucked around his crown. Laframboise finally ties a small silk handkerchief around the chief's neck.

As the chief takes the first tentative steps swaddled in his new finery, the sons are each helped into a plain blue coat and ordinary mariner's cap.

McDougall rises with effort and speaks with the help of sign language. "Before ye return to your lodge, chief, we wish to carry a bit o' refreshment to your warriors. The morning sun will signal the beginning o' trade. Until then, your people are me guests!" Again he motions to Laframboise who, with Olivier, brings forward large wooden bowls piled high with prunes and biscuit and sets them before the chief.

The chief samples a prune and then, with a grunt of unabashed approval, fills his pockets before the men take them away.

At a signal from McDougall, Franchère raises an Astor flag that is attached to a short staff. Robert tunes a set of pipes and begins a slow march out of the storehouse and into the yard. Farnham, carrying a lantern, joins Franchère and David as the four men lead the procession. Behind them, the Belleau brothers, Laframboise, and Olivier carry the biscuit, prunes, several pipes, tobacco, and a two-gallon keg of brandy. McDougall lights a pipe and, handing it to the chief, steers him into line behind the Frenchmen. The Indians follow.

The chief walks in stocking feet, erect and stately, smoking the pipe and responding to McDougall's sign language with lofty grunts. The procession moves toward the Indian encampment near the edge of the forest. Franchère, Farnham, and David stand aside as the chief, followed by McDougall, enters the largest of the skin lodges.

Clean pine bows line the floor with beaver skins as carpet placed near a small fire at the center for the white men to sit on. Six Wishram women wait on the ground to one side. The chief motions McDougall to sit opposite him. With a wave of the chief's hand, the women move to the back of the lodge, away from the gathering place near the fire, and come forward with shallow, carved wooden bowls of their own making.

The chief motions to his sons who enter followed by David, Franchère, and Farnham. They sit opposite each other behind their leaders. The Frenchmen set the food and keg before the chief.

The chief gestures again and the youngest of the six women comes forward and, to the astonishment of the white men, turns the spigot on the keg and fills one bowl with liquor.

McDougall is not happy. "So ye've drunk with white men before." He turns to David. "Drive a hard bargain, he will. Can see it in his eyes."

The chief hands the bowl to McDougall. That he is offered the first taste of his own liquor is an ill omen, but not wanting to offend the chief on his initial visit to the post, McDougall raises the bowl to the sky. "A successful trade, me man!" Obviously thirsty, he downs it in one gulp. The woman refills the bowl and hands it back to him. McDougall in turn offers the refreshment to the chief.

The chief refuses. He has had liquor before and does not like the white people's drink. Outside the lodge the Indians begin a rhythmic drumbeat and chant.

McDougall is again nonplussed. Suppressing impatience, he signs to the chief as he speaks, "Now, *tye-yea*, why do ye refuse to drink with me?"

The chief is amused by the question but firm in his reply. "*Nika muck-a-muck* bloody rum!"

David whispers to Franchère and Farnham, "I drink bloody rum!"

"*Nika paht-lum* bloody dlunk!"

David continues, "I get bloody drunk!"

The chief gestures that he was tied hand and foot as he continues, "*Tenas pight til-li-kum mamook cow!*"

"Young warriors tie me like captive!"

The chief gestures "no." "*Wake* bloody rum!"

David whispers, "No rum!"

The chief gestures "no" a second time. "*Wake* bloody dlunk!"

"No drunk!" David translates.

McDougall turns to David with a nod of respect for the chief. "Aye. Just as well."

McDougall rises stiffly from the ground. With sign language he addresses the chief, "Now then, *tye-yea*, we'll leave ye to your pleasure." He signs "good-bye" to the other Indians.

The chief motions McDougall to stop and, standing with ease, gestures to his wives who immediately pick up the bowls of food and exit. His sons follow. The keg is removed by the Frenchmen.

The chief leads McDougall outside to a gathering of Wishram warriors and women around a communal fire near the river where they have begun to celebrate in anticipation of a favorable trade. The biscuit and prunes are distributed by the women while the tobacco and pipes are hoarded by the old warriors who smoke constantly throughout the evening.

The Frenchmen, partners, and clerks mingle together amidst the tribal members. Two men, painted and masked, begin to dance in the clearing around the fire.

McDougall gives David a long-suffering glance as he passes with the chief and his six wives to mats near the fire where he sits. A pipe and tobacco are offered to McDougall who lights the pipe and hands it to the chief.

Across the fire, in the shadows beside a group of warriors, two Indians dressed as tribes east of the Rockies stare directly at the white men. David notices them and leans toward Franchère and his nephew. "Look over there, lads. Them two dressed in buckskin."

"They could be men we used to employ around Grand Portage, sir," Robert responds with concern.

David is clearly puzzled. "Aye, lad. My very thought. What in the devil are Cree or Iroquois doing on this side of the mountains, and traveling with this lot from upriver?"

Robert is indignant. "Traveling for the North West Company. Come here as spies!"

"Don't jump to no conclusions, lad. We'll find out soon enough."

The chanting grows in intensity as the dance continues and those facing the circle feast and sing. The chief is full of self-importance as he sits on his haunches and smokes the white man's tobacco with an uncomfortable McDougall at his side.

The chief's younger wife who poured the brandy suddenly enters the clearing. Her arms are now draped with bracelets of copper. She begins to dance. The male dancers retire in deference to her. The chanting and rhythmic drumbeat continue without a break.

She stops suddenly with a frantic scream of pain and throws her arms out. The chanting and drumbeat stop. All is silent. With great intensity her eyes move deliberately around the circle. She begins to sing and to shake the bracelets on her arms in rhythm to her song. She moves around the edge of the clearing. With wild, frenzied gestures, she pulls off one bracelet at a time and gives it to the nearest person, whether tribal member or white man.

She approaches the Frenchmen and offers a bracelet to Laframboise. He refuses it, backing away from her. She becomes hysterical, throws her arms wildly about as she chants and moves away from Laframboise and toward the fire.

The chief watches her silently, gravely.

As she nears the center of the clearing, she jerks herself violently about, dancing to the fire as if it had consciousness of her presence, all the time removing her bracelets, one by one, and throwing them individually to the flames. She continues dancing, arms bare, as she crosses to her husband. Panting and perspiring, she snatches a sharp piece of flint from his hair behind one ear. The chief remains totally passive, his eyes fixed on her with grave concern.

The other wives are held by the hysterical woman as if in a trance. She stops momentarily, then begins to dance again as in the beginning, but instead of removing bracelets, she now slashes her arms, one gash at a time, with the flint knife. The Indians around the fire begin a steady, low chant of mourning in rhythm to her movements.

David is alarmed by her behavior and glances around at the warriors. They are quiet. They, too, watch the dancing woman.

The dancer's arms are now bloody, and she rubs the blood onto her hands and wildly smears it about her face. She seems possessed beyond her control and finally gives herself up to a complete frenzy before collapsing unconscious on the ground by the fire. Women rush to the fallen figure, chanting still with their tribesmen, and gently straighten her body where she lies.

David crosses to Laframboise and the Frenchmen. He speaks in a low, intense tone. "Don't ever do that again, lad! You give them reason to consider us the cause of her madness. We might all pay with our lives for such an insult!"

Laframboise is mortified. "But, *monsieur*..."

"You men stay together here." David cuts him off. There is urgency in his tone. "Remain quiet now, and do exactly as you are bid." He glances around to see Franchère approach the wives surrounding the collapsed figure and offer help. The women wave him away.

The drumbeat begins again and various warriors, with no masks or makeup, take up the dance. Others join as the entire village chants rhythmically for the chief's wife.

Apprehension is building among the men from the fort. David is concerned. McDougall emerges from amidst the shadowy figures in the clearing. "Get the men to the post, quick! No tellin' what this lot will do now."

"We must offer the chief a handsome present," David responds.

"Nay, Mr Stuart. He admitted to me she's possessed. But she is his favorite."

"She is mad!" David replies.

"She's called, `One-that-speaks-with-the-stars.'"

"Did you see them two in buckskin?"

"Aye, that!" McDougall replies curtly. "But this is no time for us to be pryin'!"

He turns to the Frenchmen. "You men return to the post with Mr Stuart!" He coughs heavily. "Stay together! And stay clear of them women, do ye hear me? Don't want none of them in the tents tonight. We don't know this lot!" He glares significantly at the men.

The buckskinned Indians approach McDougall with the chief. *"Poshtun!"* the chief calls out. *"Moqsht na-di-da-nuit* (two Indian people)!"

The taller of the two steps up to McDougall and hands him a white envelope.

McDougall takes the letter and stares at it in utter disbelief.

Chapter Forty

That night inside the storehouse the three partners, Franchère, and Farnham are gathered around the table where a lantern burns. McDougall faces them with real concern. "They don't speak the Iroquois dialect," he exclaims in complete frustration. "Couldn't understand a single word they said!"

"They might be Algonquin stock," David remarks.

"Aye," McDougall responds. "They've come from the north. Tomorrow ye have a try, lad." He gets up in agitation, letter in hand, and begins pacing in the dim light. He shakes the letter as he talks. "This proves it, lads. The North West wants our ground." He stops at the table and holds the letter to the light, reading, "To John Stuart, Fort Estekatedene, New Caledonia."

McDougall throws the letter on the table and sits down in angry desperation. "Where the devil are Hunt and McKenzie with the men from St. Louis? We can't meet this challenge without more men!"

David remains calm. He points to the letter. "This simply indicates the North West Company has at least one post farther west than we supposed. Never heard of Fort Estekatedene. But three years ago after an expedition with Simon Fraser to the Pacific, John Stuart became a partner and was posted to Fort William. He is my cousin. Last I knew, he was in charge of trade throughout New Caledonia. The question is, how far south will they come?"

McDougall stands up. "They will move, by God, down the valleys that feed this river," he exclaims emphatically, "and we'll lose the trade!"

David picks up the letter. "This could be a deception, if their purpose is to spy on us. But I do not consider it so. They would send one of the factors, or one of the partners, if they wanted information about us. 'Tis a bit of good fortune, lads, this has fallen to our hands." He gestures toward the Indian encampment. "Those messengers traveling uncharted rivers are most likely lost and believe they are at Fort Estekatedene."

He rises from the table and looks decisively at the men. "We will meet this challenge! Mr McDougall, how many men can ye spare? We have no choice but to mount a brigade inland this season and establish a trade."

McDougall is stunned. "Ye can't be thinkin' to mount a brigade upriver before the *Tonquin* returns!" He faces David, incredulous. "Now? Aye, an' short o' supplies that we are?" He slaps the table. "T'will be winter an' ye'll not have lodgin's built nor game enough put aside!"

"Tomorrow I'll talk to those two with François Pillet. He speaks the Algonquin tongue. We must learn their motives, and if the country is rich in beaver. I want to know which river they were working before they picked up the Columbia." He sits down at the table. "We have to establish ourselves inland to convince the North West Company to abandon any posts they have west of the mountains. In exchange, we will not interfere with their trade east of the mountains." He considers. "Three small canoes will do it, lads. And six or eight men. Never mind the winter!"

Chapter Forty-One

For several days the Wishram remain camped near the fort where their stock of furs is gradually traded off. All the while David prepares the expedition to the interior and the routine at the post continues. Under the roof of the open blacksmith's shed a beaver pelt is branded. Smoke rises as the hot iron burns the skin and when removed the small Astor symbol (IA) is clearly visible. While Laframboise ties a pile of branded skins into a bundle, the blacksmith works a hot iron bar at the anvil. Soon a completed axe head is reheated until a reddish glow appears along the cutting edge. It is then dunked in the nearby rain barrel before the steaming piece is broken from the bar and tossed to the floor of packed dirt. Laframboise carries the bundle of skins to the cooper's bench nearby where a wooden balance is held by a crude tripod. He checks the bundle's weight before packing it in a seventy-gallon puncheon. The cooper fits a lid into the top of the full cask and seals it by driving home an iron stave. He returns to his bench where he is constructing new casks from pieces of green oak.

Laframboise rolls the sealed cask to the blacksmith's forge and the smith burns the Astor symbol into the lid and side of the cask. He then rolls the cask to one side where others marked with the Astor symbol are stored under cover of the shed until they are put in the storehouse.

Outside the shed with wind and rain, the yard of the fort is a sea of mud. Islanders dressed in oilskins, under the disgruntled direction of the Belleau brothers, carry a twenty-foot log into the slushy clearing outside the shed and dump it in the mud with others beside the incomplete second building.

As they do so, Farnham leaves the storehouse and runs to the shed carrying an armload of fresh skins. He throws the skins down for Laframboise and, without uttering a word, runs back through the rain and mud to the storehouse where Wishram are gathered on one side of the long table with furs ready to trade.

An occasional Wishram enters with a bundle of pelts. Those few who depart carry trade goods rolled in a blanket and, occasionally, a kettle. Franchère and Pillet negotiate with the Indians, weigh the skins on a tripod scale, hand out beads, fish hooks, pipe and tobacco, knives and blankets. Farnham assists.

Those who have traded and remain in the storehouse are grouped into two clusters on the elm-covered floor and are separated by a small clearing where a solitary Indian sits between them. There is a considerable store of blankets, knives, tobacco, and kettles beside this gambler who opposes the group before him in a game of chance.

The gambler holds up a small piece of bone which he then conceals in one hand, singing and crossing his hands back and forth over one another. With speed and dexterity, he transfers the bone back and forth between his hands until he suddenly stops.

There is animated discussion as the group before the gambler argues and individuals insist on which side the bone is held. Their choices are indicated by placing a stick, one for each man, into the ground on the appropriate side. All sticks must be on the correct side for one team to win the entire pot.

One Indian puts his stick on the side opposite his team's choice. Heated debate follows but he will not yield. The bone is revealed. The solitary Indian was correct. The losing team gives up another share of its trade goods as the game of shifting the bone begins again.

At the trading table, an Indian with a fine sea otter robe refuses one, two, then three blankets that Franchère offers him. He refuses a fourth and a fifth. The Indian gestures, *"Dap-tash* (blue), *posh-tun!"*

Franchère is puzzled. He holds up a knife, a kettle, different items of trade to be added to the blankets as Farnham enters the room. Finally he is exasperated and exclaims, "But we have no blue beads!" and pulls out a handful of yellow buttons. "Plenty of yellow."

The Indian refuses with a wave. *"Dap-tash, posh-tun!"* He is insistent.

"We left all the blue beads on the *Tonquin*," Pillet laments and turns to replace the goods in their respective casks and crates. The Indian with the robe sees Farnham approach the table and goes over to him. He touches Farnham's belt. "Your belt, Russell," Pillet remarks with a chuckle. "He wants your belt!"

Farnham is at first puzzled but looks down and sees he is wearing a belt made with small blue beads. He goes behind the table, at first refuses to negotiate but finally removes his old belt and with feigned reluctance gives it up in even trade for a splendid sea otter coat. The Indian fingers the blue beads with wonder and taking this new treasure in hand leaves the storehouse.

At a small table by the wall of the storehouse, McDougall and David sit with a lantern between them in close consultation. McKay's map and the North West Company letter are on the table. Both men are oblivious to the chatter of gambling and trade that fills the room.

"Fifteen days those two descended looking for Fort Estekatedene," David comments, "from a river they call the Spokane. They were uncertain of their way but followed the course of the Columbia to the Falls and learning from the tribes there of white men at the mouth, they never doubted we were the people for whom the letter was addressed. Seven to eight hundred miles they must have traveled." He indicates the map. "'Twill be very unlucky if we don't pitch on a place where the North West Company will be certain to take notice. If they abandon their post rather than compete with us, of course, we will not interfere with their trade to the east."

"So those two confirmed the richness of the interior as Mr McKay predicted."

"Aye. Pillet understood them perfectly. And in exchange for safe passage upriver with us, they are to put me in the way of the Spokane where I will establish a small post and begin a trade with the local people."

That morning before the noon muster, when trade for the day is nearly complete and most of the men are involved in construction around the post, McDougall speaks with two Chinook hunters who have brought a fresh carcass of venison to trade. The hunters each carry a musket. There appears to be some disagreement and David joins them from the nearby lodging that is under construction.

"This great fool demands half a pound o' tobacco, powder, shot, a blanket, and a knife for a single carcass!"

"We're short of food, Mr McDougall. Ye have no choice. Can't spare men for hunting. There is dried fish aplenty, which the Islanders relish, but some of the men are sick from it. Too rich. We need the deer meat."

McDougall turns to the second hunter. "Where is your meat? One isn't enough! *Me-si-ha mow-itch* (your deer)?"

"*Wake mow-itch* (no deer). *Skoo-kum* (ghost)!" the hunter answers.

McDougall walks with David a few steps away. "By God, Mr Stuart, suspicious devils. That one tells me a ghost haunts him. Hasn't shot a deer this season. When the salmon begin to run, they will not trade without the heart removed. And it must be consumed before sunset. And it cannot be boiled, but only roasted, or the salmon will not return to the river. We'll jolly well starve!"

"Pay him, man. But have them gut and hang it with the rest. I can spare no men today."

McDougall turns to enter the storehouse as the door flies open and a Chinook bursts through and runs directly into his arms. The young man tries to escape, but McDougall holds him firmly. Franchère appears at the door. "He take the tobacco, *monsieur*!" Franchère is breathless. "I give him the knife and the pipe for his skin, and he take the tobacco and run!"

Late that day, the Chinook has been tied up and put into a seven-foot deep, open pit where a stump has been blown clear. Antoine, a musket in hand, listens to McDougall. "Keep him there for the night. Teach the savage a lesson. We're not bloody sheep, after all!"

Two Chinooks who work with the men at the post approach McDougall, eyeing him with displeasure. He spots them and cries out harshly. "Back to work, you two!" He waves them away. "*Mam-ook!* (To work!...) *Mam-ook!*"

Chapter Forty-Two

The following morning at dawn, smoke rises from the chimney of the storehouse. A shutter is thrown open and by the lantern light within, a disheveled figure appears and heaves the content of a bedpan through the open window. Another shutter opens and McDougall reaches outside with a hammer and strikes a metal bar that hangs from above. Soon a Frenchman from the tents, pulling on his coat, walks through the mud to the storehouse. Then a second, rubbing his hands, his breath steaming, as the men begin another day.

At the open pit surrounded by the morning mist, Antoine is sitting against a log fast asleep. Franchère approaches and shakes him. *"Bonjour, Antoine."* (Good morning...)

Startled by the greeting, Antoine reaches for the musket before he realizes what is happening. It is not beside him and at once he sits bolt upright. *"Le mousquet!"* He springs to his feet without thinking and stares bewildered over the edge of the pit. It is empty. In exasperation he throws his hands up and utters, *"Sacré imbécile* (damned fool)!" He turns to Franchère. *"Sale individu...* (rotter...) *Foutriquet* (little fucker)!"

Franchère acknowledges the grey, overcast sky and shakes his head. *"Bougre de temps, mon ami* (it's an ugly day, my friend)." Together they walk to the storehouse.

The fireplace is alight with a large kettle of tea steaming on the hearth. McDougall is shaking Isaac. "What d'ye mean, the meat is gone? By God, I saw them hang venison yesterday forenoon with me own eyes!"

David approaches and McDougall turns to him in complete exasperation. "Paid a price to 'em, and now they've stolen it all! And today, on the very birthday o' Saint John the Baptist. A Godless people, Mr Stuart!"

David turns to the men nearby. "Jean Baptiste. This is your saints day. Find your brother. The two of you take muskets and hunt. Don't come back 'till you have fresh meat for the kettle." He is emphatic. "And pray for a Godsend, lad!"

Franchère and Antoine enter as David turns to the others. Jean Baptiste spots Antoine, motions to him, and the two men leave. David continues, "Now, you men! Be jugging down some tea. 'Tis all the same, saints day or no. That's all the fresh food you'll have 'til our hunters return and the salmon starts to run." The men are deadly still. Hunger is written in their silent faces. "There's mischief in them woods today. You men stay together. Don't no one go wandering alone!"

By late morning, when trade for the day is complete, the sky has cleared and David instructs Olivier and half a dozen Islanders who carry felling axes. "Twenty feet long and so big around." He indicates a diameter of eighteen inches. "We have to secure the post. No choice now that our numbers will be reduced. Get them Chinooks to drag in what ye cut."

"But the Indians do not like the fence, *monsieur*." Olivier protests.

McDougall approaches. "Tell them it's for another lodge."

David walks over to Laframboise who is squaring the mantle for the front door of the new lodging. Laframboise is expecting him. "We will need three canoes," David remarks, "but small, mind you. There'll be nine of us, and what goods Mr McDougall can spare."

Laframboise is concerned. "Only nine men, *monsieur? Sacrebleu* (damn it)!"

"We must plant post for post with the North West Company and use what resources we have, or they'll take the territory from us. Now see to it, lad. And get your own kit in order."

As David turns away, the two Chinook hunters tentatively approach leading a half dozen skinny, agitated dogs tied together with a piece of rawhide.

One of the Chinooks steps forward. David recognizes him as the hunter who had no meat the day before. *"Wake mow-tish,"* the Chinook declares and points to the dogs. *"Kam-ooks muck-a-muck. Kloshe muck-a-muck!"*

McDougall crosses the yard with his pipe which he lights using his spectacles to magnify the sun's light onto the tobacco. "They have no deer," David comments, "but he has brought dogs. Probably all he has in his lodge. He claims dogs are good eating."

The two hunters react to McDougall's pipe lighting without fire. McDougall waves the dogs away in disgust. *"Wake* (to work)! *Wake!"* He continues on his way toward the field.

The hunter offering the dogs becomes apprehensive and humble before David. *"Ol-la-pishka,"* he says.

David is amused and calls out to McDougall. "He says you are *The-man-who-makes-fire*." He motions to McDougall to return as he speaks to the hunter. *"Ik-tah shoo-kum?"*

"T'kope man... mokst cole Il-la-hie..." the Indian replies, then hesitates. *"Ni-ka... mam-ook poo!"*

David studies the man with interest and comments to McDougall, "He wants to know if you have medicine to cure him." He turns from the Indian.

"A couple of years ago it seems he killed two white men from a ship. Now he sees their faces and cannot shoot straight. He asks if your medicine can cure him."

McDougall looks at the hunter with interest. "Aye," he answers, calculating, "I've got powerful *mes-tin* for ye," and gestures in sign language as he speaks. "So it's white men's spirits have ye in their grip, aye?" He stares intently into the eyes of the frightened man. "Only one thing I know can drive them from ye." He starts toward the storehouse and motions for the Chinook hunter to leave the dogs and follow.

Inside the empty storehouse, McDougall leads the hunter to the table and motions for him to put both hands on the tabletop, bending over as he does so. David remains at the door to prevent others from entering.

McDougall removes his coat and rolls up his sleeves. The man with hands flat on the table watches him as he walks over to the fireplace and selects two wooden switches with good resilience, then a third and a fourth.

He returns and suddenly smacks the table with a sharp, stinging blow. The man jerks upright with a start.

McDougall is grave. He patiently sets down the switches, moves over beside him and with both palms smacks the table, indicating that he must keep his hands flat on the tabletop.

No sooner does he resume the position than McDougall again smacks the table sharply. He flinches slightly but, in real fear of the "spirits" who possess him, holds his position.

David is at the door watching. When McDougall moves into position to give a beating, David unlatches the door and exits.

Chapter Forty-Three

THE NEXT DAY, THE 15th of July, is chosen for the departure of David's brigade. There is considerable activity as three small canoes, tied up at the pier, are loaded by the Frenchmen with bundles of gear.

About midday in the yard outside the storehouse, the partners and clerks have gathered around McDougall, laughing at his story. "Ye should o' seen the bugger's face! I convinced him, a'right, that no spirit would again enter his ugly hide."

An unexpected interruption stops him when the guard calls out that a large canoe flying a flag is rounding the point upriver. The group moves down to the riverfront. "That can't be our men," David remarks with concern as she approaches. "They were to winter on the upper Missouri." A Union Jack becomes visible and eight people aboard, five of whom they recognize as Canadian *voyageurs*. Two are buckskinned Indians.

"What have we here?" McDougall utters in complete surprise as the canoe draws up to the pier opposite the small canoes and a well dressed man who appears to be the commander leaps ashore.

Without formality, he walks directly to the group and introduces himself, "David Thompson, partner in the North West Company."

David steps forward followed closely by McDougall and Robert. "Welcome to Fort Astoria, sir. Pacific Fur Company."

The men exchange greetings and walk together up the embankment toward the post. "We have no residence as yet," McDougall explains, pointing ahead. "As you can see, it is under construction. But you and your men are welcome to the storehouse which acts as warehouse and dwelling for the present."

That evening the partners and clerks are gathered in the storehouse listening to Thompson's account of his journey to the Pacific. "After three months enforced encampment because of heavy snow last winter at the extreme northerly bend of the Columbia River, several of the men deserted so we could not proceed down the Columbia. I went to the headwaters before we made our way back to Spokane House in April.

"We crossed from the Pend d'Oreille to *Ilthkoyape* Falls on the Columbia in June and laid up. Two weeks were required to find suitable cedar timber and build a canoe. We set off on July 3rd. Our purpose, as you might guess, is to survey the river to open out a passage for the interior trade with the Pacific Ocean. I travel as a geographer not a fur trader. You should know that the wintering partners think it best to abandon the posts west of the mountains rather than compete with you, on condition that you do not interfere with their trade east of the mountains."

"In that case," David responds, "perhaps it will interest you to know we have here two Cree messengers carrying a letter addressed to John Stuart at Fort Estekatedene. They seem to have lost their way and hearing from Indians at the falls that there were white men building a post at the mouth of the Columbia, came here believing they were at Fort Estekatedene."

Thompson seems genuinely puzzled. "Fort Estekatedene? There is no such place." The men stare silently at one another. "It seems to me this letter could be a hoax," Thompson continues after an awkward moment, "that these two were somehow troublesome to the factor and sent away to be gotten rid of. All the factors know John Stuart is one of the wintering partners at Fort William."

"You can meet them for yourself tomorrow," McDougall replies skeptically.

"Sir," Thompson answers with great earnestness, "I carry a letter addressed to William McGillivray, chief of their house in Canada, from the wintering partners supporting what I say about the trade."

"Aye," David responds, "no doubt. Then we are in agreement. In fact, when you arrived today we were about to send a small brigade inland to open trade in the interior. We can assure you we have no intention of trading east of the mountains."

Over the next few days, Thompson with his men explores to Cape Disappointment and makes several observations with sextant and compass which he enters into a journal and thereby completes a survey of the major rivers of Canada from Lake Winnipeg to the mouth of the Columbia.

Before departure, McDougall again invites Thompson and his men to the post to resupply as needed for their return trip. He is eager to please Thompson while at the same time desiring information about the interior. However Thompson describes the interior to them in the most unfavorable terms. "Though there are meadows, this country shows much rock and large stone near the water's edge, and the banks steep with loose earth and stones. For long stretches there are no woods but a chance tree, and then a straggling fir. The whole may be said to be a vast low mountain of meadow showing much rock, irrigated into valleys that come down to the river. Of course there can be no beaver."

"No beaver, ye say," McDougall concedes and gives a quick sidelong wink to David.

"The Indians have bear and rat skins with a few sheep and black tailed deer. Horses they have many and the country appears good for them."

"We shall travel upriver in company," David remarks. "Them Cree messengers will join us for safety."

The 23rd of July is chosen for departure. Packs of axe heads and spear tips, bundles of personal kit, pieces containing beads, cotton cloth, hooks, pipes and tobacco and other gear for the trade including muskets, powder and ball, are stowed and the men of the post cluster near the pier to see the party off. David waves a salute and boards his canoe. He is accompanied by Laframboise and an Islander. The other canoes are occupied by Olivier, Ross and an Islander, and McLennan, Pillet and an Islander.

McDougall gives a pre-arranged signal and two muskets are fired into the air in salute. The three canoes move away against the current with David Thompson and his men and the Cree strangers in their own canoes close behind.

As the men return to the fort, McDougall comments to Franchère and Farnham, "No doubt Thompson was sent by the North West Company. He would take possession at the mouth of the Columbia, display the Union Jack to gain protection from the British navy. They would block Mr Astor."

"And no beaver inland!" Farnham exclaims with irony.

"He was describing the Columbia basin itself as if it were the whole of the countryside. Clever lad, that!"

"He would have been here before us, *monsieur*, but some of his men deserted."

"Aye," McDougall agrees, "but he found himself too late. The Stars and Stripes fly over Fort Astoria."

Chapter Forty-Four

Near the end of September, the lodging for the men is completed and tents removed from the yard. The new lodging has a dining room and sitting room with a fireplace and small apartments for sleeping plus a work room for the cooper and carpenter, all under a single roof. As the fall season progresses, women of the Chinook tribe work in the open outside the gates winnowing the first meager crop of grain. Farnham and some Islanders delve and grub and drill in the field. Three men are hitched to a plow. Two pull a harrow.

McDougall supervises a submissive Joshua as the abundant and unexpected first crop of 192 potatoes is harvested to McDougall's great relish. A couple of potatoes disappear into his pocket. The rest will be planted for next year's crop. Inside the yard two Chinook saw planking under Jean Baptiste's supervision.

Early in October, the men gather at the completed schooner for its launching. McDougall performs the ritual christening with a bottle of Teneriffe wine and names her *Dolly* after Astor's daughter Dorothea, a favorite with the partners. Mumford is appointed master and, with a crew of two Islanders, he and Robert set off upriver to cut oak for the cooper and obtain as much food as possible.

On the 5th, Pillet and McLennan accompanied by two Islanders surprise the men at the post with their unexpected return. They report the country inland is most encouraging with many signs of beaver. The inhabitants caused no trouble, the climate was healthy and, true to Mr Thompson's report, large numbers of horses were available from which they were able to obtain a supply at a low price. After going up the Columbia as far as a pretty little river the local people called the Okanagan, a post was established on its bank. Having built a house, Mr Stuart thought it wise to send back the extra men.

By November at Fort Astoria, with no salmon or sturgeon running, food is continually running short. Antoine and Jean Baptiste are again sent out to hunt. After being away three days with no word from them, McDougall accosts Robert in the dining room where the men gather before setting out to work. "Have ye heard report o' them Belleau brothers among the savages?"

"None, sir. No sign at all."

He is concerned. "They're in trouble then. Should have been back yesterday." He motions to Franchère. "Tomorrow you and Farnham go upriver. Get word of 'em." He stops suddenly, troubled, a new thought occurring to him. "And what's to prevent them running off?" But he quickly dismisses the idea. "No. Too risky. Take muskets and a brace o' pistols and some dry fish. Ye might be a few days on the trail. Pray God they're alive!"

McDougall turns abruptly to the men. "Time to relieve the guard! Keep a sharp eye for stag elk or grizzly bear. An extra dram to the man who brings meat for the kettle!" No one responds. "There'll be no meat 'til our hunters return, if ye don't liven up a bit. Can't depend no more on them Chinooks. Many families have gone inland for the winter." The men turn away dissatisfied, subdued, and grumble privately amongst themselves.

Robert watches them. He does not like what he sees. "They don't want any more dry fish and biscuit," he comments to McDougall. "Antoine and Jean Baptiste should have been back."

Chapter Forty-Five

On the Columbia River four days after leaving the post, Farnham and Franchère beach their canoe within sight of a small village. Farnham crosses the embankment and walks as far as a river emptying into the Columbia beyond the village. After a few minutes he returns to Franchère at the canoe. "They slept here three days ago. Left the Columbia and followed this river." He points north. "They went into the mountains. The old chief says they will return to the Columbia."

Before sunrise the next morning the two men paddle their canoe upriver into the mountains. The air is cool with a layer of fog rolling up the canyon from the big river below. As the morning brightens, the forest is alive with birds' singing and the vegetation drips from the night's moisture. The rising sun quickly dissipates the fog except on the shaded side where fog clings to the sheltered clefts of the canyon wall.

As they move slowly against the current a white-headed eagle makes a long, graceful arc from high in the canyon, glides overhead, skims silently above the river and lifts off gripping a large salmon trout in its talons. As it gains elevation, the struggling fish breaks free and falls to an open stretch of embankment. Farnham steers the canoe toward shore. "There's our breakfast! And we check for footprints."

The men land and while Franchère works his way inland searching the ground for evidence of the Belleau, Farnham gathers sticks for a fire. He showers some tinder with flint and steel but has difficulty nursing the embers into flame. Franchère returns following the underbrush that lines the embankment. "Everything is damp," he declares. "I can see nothing."

Franchère settles beside Farnham, opens his buckskin pouch to remove a knife when he at once freezes. Cautiously he takes hold of Farnham's arm and intones quietly, "Russell, do not move."

Farnham turns slowly to the river. A canoe of four aborigines approaches. They carry hunting spears.

Farnham whispers, "I have a pistol in my pocket."

Franchère is desperate. "I have nothing!"

The Indians land at the edge of the embankment, upriver from their beached canoe. Without paying attention to the white men, they set about their business.

Farnham quietly removes the pistol from his pocket. "Where is the horn and pouch?"

"In the canoe."

"Damn! Only one shot. Ignore them!" He leans over the smoking twigs and continues blowing to nurse the tiny embers into flame.

Franchère opens and cleans the fish as he watches the Indians' every move.

Two of the natives gather sticks while one wades into the river and climbs onto a rock. The fourth takes a short piece of split cedar from their canoe and sits on his haunches beside the pile of sticks the others have gathered. He places the end of a round stick against the flat underside of the cedar board. With a pinch of sand at the point of contact and a few deft whirls of the stick, smoke rises, and soon a small fire is ablaze.

The Indian on the rock pulls two or three long hairs from his head and ties them together to make a line. He takes a familiar red-handled knife obtained in trade and cuts a tiny piece of buckskin from his shoulder covering and attaches it to the end of the line in place of a hook. He then throws the bit of buckskin into the river. Almost immediately he pulls a small fish four or five inches long from the water.

Farnham continues to blow at the smoking twigs.

As Franchère carefully separates the pinkish-white meat from the backbone, he notices the fisherman pull fish after fish from the river, and toss them ashore. They are immediately impaled on green sticks and set upright in a circle around the fire to roast.

Farnham is finally nursing a small flame as the four aborigines sit together around their fire and eat the entire catch of fish, head, fins and all. Finally, they kick the embers into the sand and embark.

Franchère watches in amazement. One of the departing men makes a friendly gesture. Franchère waves.

Farnham carefully adds a couple of sticks to their small fire, and the two turn to each other and burst into nervous laughter.

Later in the day they come upon tracks they suspect were made by the Belleau brothers' moccasins. They follow them along a trail that leads into a thick stand of spruce and pine. The trail is broken by a wide, gentle creek that wends through a forest too dense to penetrate. They must cross the creek.

Farnham cuts and strips a long sapling and tests the depth. The water is shoulder deep a couple of feet from the side. They glance at each other and without speaking set to work. Farnham strips a fallen log that lies nearby. In the lengthening afternoon shadows, Franchère locates a fallen tree, strips it and drags it to the creek. They locate another dead tree and join the three logs with creeper vines to make a crude raft.

After preparing a second pole to help guide and steady them on the water, Farnham gathers up the muskets while Franchère holds the raft against the bank using a piece of vine. With musket, powder horn and bedroll over his shoulder and long pole in hand, Farnham mounts the raft. It immediately sinks below the water line and is highly unstable. Franchère begins to mount but jumps back as the raft will not support them both.

With Farnham balanced at the center, Franchère releases the raft which begins to drift, guided by Farnham's use of the long pole. Farnham lands and both men realize they have not provided a means of returning the raft to the other side. Nonetheless, with all his strength Farnham shoves the raft into the creek and back toward Franchère.

Almost immediately the loosely tied logs come to a peaceful stop and begin drifting quietly downstream beyond the reach of the two men. Farnham heaves his pole after them in complete exasperation. He is furious with himself as the raft slowly drifts away.

Not to be long delayed, however, with moccasins and bedroll and powder horn around his musket and held high overhead with one hand, and using his pole for support with the other, Franchère wades shoulder-deep into the icy creek. When nearly across, he suddenly disappears underwater. After a moment, he comes up with a splash and tosses his wet musket with soaked bundle to Farnham. He reaches the shore and with the help of the pole, Farnham pulls him out.

That night Franchère, wrapped in Farnham's blanket before a blazing fire, is shivering violently as he attempts to drink from a mug of steaming liquid. His clothes and blanket hang nearby, drying by the fire's heat. Farnham sits opposite, watching him with concern.

Suddenly Franchère's eyes widen as his gaze fixes on the shadows behind Farnham. His spasms of shaking cease instantly. At first there is nothing, then with the slightest movement a pair of eyes seem to be staring in at the fire.

Farnham reads Franchère's expression and without turning reaches slowly for his musket. Quietly, he loads the barrel with the ramrod and primes the piece. He rests the musket on his lap and takes a pistol from his pocket, primes and cocks it. Farnham calmly hands the musket to Franchère. With the weapon ready on his lap, Franchère again surveys the flickering darkness behind Farnham. There is forest and shadows.

With pistol in hand, Farnham grabs a burning branch from the fire, swings around and with the torch held high takes a few steps away from the fire. There is no sign of life.

Farnham adds fuel to the fire and settles himself with the pistol on his lap. The men agree to take turns sleeping.

At midnight Farnham is asleep before the fire. Franchère struggles to keep awake. Four hours later, the fire has burned low. The two men sit side by side sleeping. The night is misty and black.

At dawn, only embers remain. The two men are sound asleep. Opposite them in the small clearing, four aborigines sit. One of them is smoking a familiar pipe which would have been received in trade at the post or from natives who traded at the post.

The man with the pipe picks up a twig and breaks it in two with a snap. The sleeping men spring upright, alarmed, and on their feet in an instant. The native taps the ash from the pipe he is smoking and calmly motions the startled white men to follow. "They have the Belleau," Farnham speculates, half asleep, as he falls in line with the natives.

A quarter of an hour later they approach a cluster of low, cedar-board lodges which stand in a clearing near the wide creek. Each has an overhanging eve that holds racks of small fish which are being smoked. With the coming of daylight the settlement is fully active. Dogs and children have the run of the place. Here and there an old person or a woman sits by a lodge repairing a fish net, weaving a basket, or pounding roots. Franchère and Farnham pass by an elderly dandy who sits on his haunches with a sprig of bracken extending from each side of his nose in place of the usual dentalium shell. They are led to the largest of the lodges at the center of the village.

Farnham is taken to one side as the Indian leader motions Franchère to enter through the low opening. At first he sees nothing in the solitary room except a small fire at the center. All is silent as an opaque object moves in front of the fire blocking his way. Suddenly a torch flares behind the object, is whirled up and thrust at him, revealing a medicine man's grotesque, feathered and painted, wood-carved mask. At the same moment, the figure behind the mask lets out a piercing shriek.

Franchère goes rigid as the medicine man begins chanting and dancing, whirling the torch, thrusting it here and there as though it were a wand of magical power.

With the torch's irregular movement, Franchère begins to see snatches of the lodge interior: wooden totem poles carved to represent birds and animals considered friendly, dark figures huddled on either side of a very young, very naked and pregnant female, lying on her back near the fire, her knees elevated in position for delivery.

Franchère is transfixed by the movement of the flaming torch. A rhythm of clapping sticks begins in time with the medicine man's chant. Franchère glances left and right with heightened alarm as the masked figure dances and chants around the pregnant girl. He now sees by the constantly moving torchlight that her skin is well oiled. She cannot be over thirteen years old and her eyes are riveted to the dancing figure as she hardly dares draw breath in his presence.

As he chants, the medicine man weaves a pattern of jumps and contortions around the helpless child, holding an eagle feather in his free hand with which he often touches her. He moves toward Franchère and seems to construct an imaginary wall between him and the pregnant girl.

Suddenly the child shrieks over the rhythmic chant and stick-clapping as she begins labor.

Franchère is as suddenly pulled back toward the entrance where he finds himself thrust beside Farnham in the darkness. Farnham leans inconspicuously toward him without taking his eyes from the moving torch. He whispers intently, "We're in some trouble, Gabriel. Pray the Mother of Life answers those prayers. If that baby does not arrive healthy, or the mother dies, they will kill us. They believe our presence near this village prevents the child's birth." He turns to Franchère significantly. "*White man bring evil medicine!* I understood that much of what they said to me!"

"But we do nothing," Franchère whispers helplessly.

The moving torchlight and occasional shrieks of pain from the pregnant child continue as the chant grows louder with those present joining in the medicine man's rhythmic prayer. The uncertainty is nearly unbearable as Farnham and Franchère strain to see what is going on. Anxiety and fatigue line their faces.

The chant and rhythmic stick-clapping are suddenly broken by an agonized and prolonged shriek from the girl. Franchère's expression fills with dread.

In the dim torchlight he senses rather than sees the beginning of delivery. The painful cries drown all other sound. Finally the baby's hips and legs pass from the mother. The lodge is suddenly silent. The baby's first cry is heard and Franchère's expression relaxes. Moisture fills his eyes with the hint of a smile.

The medicine man receives the umbilical cord and dances, wrapping it on his forearm and chanting wildly. He is full of confidence. The child and mother will live.

Chapter Forty-Six

At the back of Fort Astoria a row of pickets forming a palisade closing out the dense forest has been completed between the storehouse and lodging thus securing one side of the post. During the early morning hours, smoke rises from the chimneys of the post. The blacksmith in the shed between the two buildings is busy at his forge. Axe heads are piling up on the floor as he shapes, cuts and hardens the iron bars brought from the ship.

At the front of the post overlooking the river, two Islanders dig a four-foot deep trench across the opening between the two log buildings. The first half-dozen, pointed pickets have been raised by the storehouse. Another picket is being wrestled into place by a pair of Islanders working from a crude scaffold. Robert helps the men get the log into position then shouts, "That's straight! Fill it!" and they pack dirt in the trench at the base of the log.

Robert then goes to a scanty pile of twenty-five-foot stripped logs, grabs the end of one with a cant hook and, single handedly, drags it a few yards to an x-shaped horse where he sets the end of the log. His strength is more than his sinewy, almost slight, frame would suggest. Using a broad axe he hacks a wedge with sure strokes to form a point at one end of the piece that will soon be part of the palisade at the front of the fort.

Four Islanders enter the clearing, carrying a twenty-five-foot stripped log with log tongs and drop it beside the couple of others that lie on the ground. Robert completes the first wedge and turns to them. "Joshua!" he shouts. Joshua quickly comes forward. He no longer is pompous. "Your men must work faster." He indicates the few remaining logs on the ground. "We will be short of pickets before the sundial indicates midday."

He buries the axe in the log, steps up to Joshua and lowers his voice. "We must complete this palisade to the gate by supper time. The Indians. None come to trade these last days." He glances around at the nearby forest. "Can hear them buggers roamin' about at night." He turns back to Joshua. "Step lively, man! Remember, eighteen-inches thick. She must hold once she's up." As Joshua sets off, he rotates the log with the cant hook and cuts a second wedge.

In the vegetable garden which is now surrounded by crude wooden fence posts, McDougall wearing a heavy jacket and wool scarf walks between furrows toward the fort examining a healthy growth of greens. He inspects the plants for infestation. All are thriving.

Something distracts him and he stops abruptly, scowling at the forest, his face thin and drawn with tension. He is both unwell and burdened with concern. "Too damn quiet!" he suddenly ejaculates, coughs, moves in the direction of the fort and waves toward Mumford who is on the *Dolly* tied off at the pier. "Mr Mumford!" he shouts and motions to him to come up to the fort. He then passes by the Islanders digging the trench and stops beside Robert who is cutting the final wedge. "Mr Stuart, I'd like ye inside for a meeting."

A few minutes later, McDougall, Robert, and Mumford are at the table in the storehouse with a pencil sketch of the fort on the table before them. McDougall speaks to Robert. "The blacksmith should have straps for the gates ready by the end o' the week. In the meantime, ye begin a bastion," he indicates on the sketch, "here, at the corner, where ye'll have a clear shot across the front and the eastern side by the forest." He looks significantly at the two men. "Too quiet out there. Don't like it!"

He turns to Mumford. "Ye drag out them four two-pounders, Mr Mumford. Clean 'em up an' fire 'em this noon after the midday hour is struck."

Mumford is uneasy. "Since Mr Stuart took his brigade inland, we've had no Indians for trade but them Chinooks."

"Aye," Robert agrees. "They want all the trade, what little we can offer."

McDougall adds ominously, "Aye, that. An' they'll report we're short o' men!" He gets up and paces back and forth. He is troubled. "They talk among themselves of a gathering o' tribes across the river, savages who come from the north by sea to fish for sturgeon, more fierce and warlike than those of this neighborhood. Them savages don't come to trade!" He coughs heavily. "And them Clatsops tell o' rumor among 'em of a trading ship destroyed on the coast." He turns back to the table. "Wish to hell the *Tonquin* would return. Something's not right."

There is a sharp banging at the door. The men look up as James Cook enters, bursting with excitement. "Indians on water! Them be comin', Missa Dougal!"

The men rush outside. Two ten-man Chinook solid cedar canoes are beached near the pier with a crowd of Chinook clustered near a tribesman reclining uncomfortably on a cedar plank. McDougall approaches a young Chinook woman who stands at the water's edge earnestly watching the man on the plank.

At the same time Robert kneels beside the injured man whom he recognizes as Calpo, Chief Comcomly's son. Calpo cannot move his left arm which is in considerable pain. An abrasion on the left shoulder is the only apparent injury but with no sign of blood. Robert carefully runs his fingers over the shoulder and arm, feeling for a broken bone. Both are sensitive to his touch.

Robert turns to McDougall. "There's a small bump on his collar bone, sir. It might be broken. Otherwise, he seems fit."

"Are ye certain?" McDougall replies. "This is his sister. He's Chief Comcomly's oldest son, lad."

"Aye. If we put his arm in a sling and tie it off so he won't use it, it should mend. Tell his sister our medicine is strong. We can help him."

McDougall speaks and gestures with sign language to the young woman. "Before the sun has traveled half its journey to the horizon, your brother will be ready to return with ye." She gives approval.

Robert motions to four of the men from the fort. "Steady now! Into the storehouse by the fire. Put him on the table."

"Did this in a game with one o' them visiting tribes," McDougall comments to Robert as they follow the men to the storehouse. "They play rough! Wasn't he the young lad who pulled David from the river when we capsized crossing from the *Tonquin*?"

"Aye. He is a good friend to us."

The men enter the storehouse and two bottles of Teneriffe wine are brought out. Robert heats a large mug full and helps Calpo to drink it down. Calpo remains flat on the plank which is now on the table. He grows quieter. McDougall, sleeves rolled up and wool scarf around his neck, soaks some lint in a bowl of wine. "James Cook, heat another mug o' wine for our friend here."

Robert stands beside Calpo. Cook takes a hot iron from the fire and dunks it into a pewter mug of wine. The liquor sizzles as it warms. "Hasn't he had enough?" Robert asks.

"When he goes to sleep, then he's had enough!"

Robert gently pours the wine on Calpo's lips and Calpo swallows. His eyes indicate he wishes to say something.

Robert leans over him as he speaks just above a whisper. "*Smoke. Hy-in si-wash chah-ko.* (Many Indians come.) *Si-wash mam-ook!* (Indians fight!) *Is-hum ik-tan!*" (Take goods!) He searches the room with his eyes before continuing. "*Skoo-kum* house!" (Strong house!) He momentarily closes his eyes.

McDougall and Robert exchange significant glances as they prepare for the operation. "Better bleed him before we tie up the arm," McDougall suggests. "Need to purge the blood." Beads of perspiration stand on Calpo's brow. He is now panting with quick, short breaths. The wine is taking effect. He is drowsy, impassive to his surroundings.

McDougall takes the lint from the bowl of wine, rolls and squeezes it. He then removes a knife from his belt and wipes it on his shirt. "Are ye ready, lads? *E-lip, chief, tl'ko-pe!* (First, chief, we cut you!) *Hy-ak! Kloshe!*" (Quick! Good!) Calpo's expression is now fully relaxed. He seems about to go to sleep. "Bring that pan here to catch the blood."

"Right, chief, *Al-ta*! (Now!) That's it." McDougall shifts his position and shouts at Calpo, "*Skoo-kum* chief!" (Strong chief!)

McDougall pierces the vein inside the right elbow and blood starts to flow. He holds the shallow pan below the elbow. Calpo's muscles relax as he blacks out. "Well done, lads!"

McDougall again wipes the knife blade on his shirt and returns it to his belt. "Now hand me that roll o' lint, Mr Stuart. Quick, lad! Stop bleedin', damn ye!"

McDougall presses the roll against the cut and hands the pan to Robert. "Tie this lint on the arm with a piece o' cloth. We must fix that arm in a sling and wrap it before he awakens. And we wrap it firmly, so it don't come unwrapped!"

McDougall and Stuart work efficiently, silently together. They have done this before.

An hour later, Calpo remains sound asleep on the cedar slab, his left arm in a sling and firmly wrapped to his chest. McDougall slaps his right hand. "All right, chief! Come, lad, wake up!"

Robert replies, "He's dead drunk."

"Aye, that he is." He turns to the men. "Carry him out to his sister. That should heal proper, now!"

Chapter Forty-Seven

The next day with the GONG-GONG-GONG of the iron bar that marks the noon hour, men approach from the forest while the guard watches casually from the gallery, a flintlock resting over the top of the palisade. The men gather in the yard near the gap where the gate will be fitted and bunch into two irregular corps, one near Robert and one near Mumford. A trench for the bastion at the front corner of the post, beside the vegetable garden, is already being dug.

McDougall walks from the storehouse and stops before the men. "Anyone missing?" he calls out officiously.

Robert and Mumford reply together, "All here, sir!"

"Half-rations until the hunters return. Meat supply low! Tonight ye rotate the guard. Mr Stuart, your crew takes first watch. Mr Mumford, ye take the final watch. Any word o' Franchère and Farnham?" He stares first at one group, then at the second. No one replies.

That evening inside the lodging, the Frenchmen, Islanders and clerks sit quietly after supper in the dining room or on the sitting room floor. They repair clothing and tools with no signs of merriment.

Robert, Mumford, and McDougall are alone at a table by the fire. "Before Calpo passed out," Robert confides, "I heard him say smoke would signal a-gatherin' of many tribes."

"What smoke?" Mumford asks uneasily.

"We don't know, do we?" Robert replies, an edge to his voice. The uncertainty is wearing on him as well. "All we can do is wait." He turns to McDougall. "He said the Indians take our goods. That's all. Then he referred to the storehouse and mumbled something about *strong house*."

McDougall is agitated. "Devil's own work afoot! Obliged to put fear in them savages! Prove our strength!" He leaves the table impulsively and stirs the fire, paces a moment then returns to the table and sits down. "Mr Stuart, you take your men and accustom them to the use o' firearms. Do ye hear me?"

"Aye. But I'll want ball and powder from the magazine."

"Ye'll have it!" McDougall replies emphatically. "And everyday now, when we make it midday and the men gather to be counted, ye stop work for one hour an' drill!"

McDougall again gets up and nervously paces beside the table as he speaks. "Mr Mumford! Ye pick a crew for each o' them two-pounders." He slaps the table for emphasis. "And ye train 'em, man! Every midday ye fire them canons for practice. And ye do it in the open where the savages'll take notice, by God!" He paces to the fireplace and back. "Beginnin' tomorrow, we post a double guard. An' train 'em to march with them muskets, Mr Stuart! And ye do it in the open!"

McDougall finally sits down. "Any word o' Franchère or Farnham?" The two men are ominously silent. "Pray God we lose no more, or I fear for the life o' every man." He stares into the fire. Fatigue is written in his expression. "Should o' waited for the *Tonquin* before sendin' Mr Stuart inland."

Chapter Forty-Eight

Farnham and Franchère, both with a week's growth of beard, stay close to shore as they paddle upriver into the mountains. The current is strong and, with a head wind, the going difficult. They approach a small village set back from the water. A few natives are visible and smoke rises from huts of cedar mat. The men guide their canoe to the embankment. "Maybe the Belleau stop for food," Franchère comments. "Maybe their track on the sand." Farnham leaves the canoe.

Gradually the villagers gather around Franchère in open but silent curiosity. As he awaits Farnham, one of the men, bolder than the others, approaches and Franchère lets him touch his white skin to confirm that he too is a man.

Farnham returns from an examination of the ground accompanied by the village elder. "I don't understand," he remarks, puzzled. "These people haven't seen them. There is no sign for three days now. They must be following this river!"

"Maybe they travel at night," Franchère suggests.

"Too slow and too risky. And they would not see any game. We'll find signs of them soon."

The villagers silently fall back, opening a path to a young couple that is walking from the village. The woman, dressed in a full-length otter skin robe, approaches slowly, silently. She carries a bundle wrapped in cedar mats in her arms and is gaunt and pale, a desolate expression dominating her appearance. Her husband carries a slightly larger bundle but remains back, apparently shy before the white men.

The woman sets her bundle on the ground and gestures to Franchère as she speaks. Farnham translates. "Her two children are possessed of evil spirits. She begs you to restore life to them." The woman removes the robe she is wearing, exposing a frail body. She lays the fur garment before him. "She will reward you with her own coat. It is all she has to offer."

Franchère returns the robe to her before quietly bending down and unwrapping the bundle. The child appears asleep. He touches the cheek with the back of his fingers and immediately withdraws his hand. "Dead," he comments to Farnham and stands. "No sign of the small-pox."

He turns to the mother and looking into her eyes gently takes her two small hands. "Tell her, Russell, that the child's spirit is with the Mother of Life. Now she must give the body back to the earth." Farnham gestures to her with sign language. The young pair walk back to the village.

Together in grief they sit on the dirt before their lodge, astonished, and begin a low chant without complaint. Their song asks that the day returning from the east be fortunate for them, that they see not the evil. While the two children are no longer with them, all is ruled, they seem to acknowledge, by the Great Will above.

The next day Farnham and Franchère continue their journey into the mountains in search of the Belleau brothers. Late in the morning they carry their canoe over a long portage. Both men wear heavy packs. "They can't disappear!" Farnham shouts from his lead position. He watches the track closely for signs of a footprint.

The men stop and Franchère rests his end of the canoe to adjust his pack. "They cannot pass through this forest. They have to travel on the water!" The two resume walking. "I think they look for the North West Company post," Franchère observes. "They are hungry, *mon ami*. (my friend.) The Belleau want food. They do not come to this river to hunt!"

"They must be mad to travel this far inland alone," Farnham comments as he watches the portage trail the few yards ahead that he can see from under the bow of the canoe. Suddenly, bare legs appear on the pathway. He stops and looks out from under the canoe. Eight aborigines, nearly naked, face him blocking their way. The leader, taller than the rest, stands at the front holding his spear across the path.

The two men set the canoe down and Farnham unsheaths his flintlock in the same motion. Franchère reaches for his own flintlock but freezes as he glances back where a dozen aborigines stand a few yards away blocking the portage trail from behind. They are also armed.

Momentary confusion turns to resolve as Franchère surveys the group behind then turns to the group ahead. "The chief is the tall one at the front," he observes calmly. "Invite the chief to smoke with us, Russell." Franchère removes a tobacco pouch and pipe from the canoe. "If we put ourselves in his care, maybe he protect us."

Soon Franchère and Farnham sit on the trail surrounded by the Indians. The chief sits on his haunches opposite and puffs on Franchère's pipe. "Tell him we have a gift for him when his men carry our canoe to the river at the end of the portage."

Farnham gestures in sign language. The chief stops smoking long enough to reply in sign language.

"What does he tell you?" Franchère asks.

"He wants to know what he is to receive if his men carry the canoe."

Franchère thinks for a moment then points to the buttons on his coat, one by one, indicating they will all be the chief's.

The chief seems unsure. He gestures to Farnham in sign language, a disapproving expression on his face.

Farnham turns to Franchère with a significant look in his eyes. "He says the Wasco people pay better for two white men."

Franchère studies the chief. Farnham gestures in sign language as Franchère speaks. "We come from our great father across the mountains," he points to the east, "who knows of your strength."

Franchère eyes the chief steadily as he speaks. There is no longer fear or hesitation in his expression. "We seek our brothers, and we pay with strong medicine. We are content with the great chief who smoke with us. Your enemies fear you. No one harms the men you protect."

The chief listens to the speech and agrees. Soon two Indians carry the canoe and two pick up the packs. Farnham walks at the head with his musket. Franchère, coat open and buttons conspicuously missing, walks at the rear. The chief follows the last bearer and holds Franchère's tobacco pouch. He continues smoking as they walk and gradually lags farther behind.

Farnham reaches the high point of the portage and starts down the last leg to the river. The Indians with the canoe stop on the trail. Farnham indicates they must carry the canoe to the river, but they gesture they will go no further. Farnham again indicates they must carry the canoe to the river.

Franchère and the chief approach with the two pack bearers. Farnham shouts, "They refuse to carry the canoe to the river." He gestures in sign language to the chief.

The chief points to the river below. In a loud, mocking voice he demands and signs, *"Cul-tus pot-latch!"* (A gift!)

The bearers unexpectedly throw off their packs which roll over the side of the embankment and tumble into the underbrush by the river. With a loud "Whoop" from the chief, the others drop the canoe and all run off into the forest.

Franchère waves desperately and shouts, "The tobacco!" At the same moment, Farnham levels his musket with cool deliberateness and fires. A limb above the chief is broken by the ball and falls in front of him. The chief, momentarily overcome with fright, looks back at the white men in disbelief, drops the pipe and tobacco pouch and disappears in the trees.

Farnham grabs Franchère, breathless with excitement. "He said the Wasco people pay better for two men! That means the Belleau are alive! They have been sold as slaves. It also means they are not injured!"

"Pray they are kept for work and not for sacrifice!" Franchère exclaims. "We return to the post for more men."

"There is no time." Farnham is emphatic. "We must locate them while they're alive." He disappears over the embankment to recover a pack.

Alone for the moment, Franchère is suddenly aware of the endless quiet of the forest. The soughing breeze, pushing through pine and fir, creates a subdued, continuous sound of flowing water while the floor of the valley, with a thick covering of dry needles, is everywhere silent underfoot. The complete stillness, surrounded as he is with mountains in all directions, seems to enclose him and he is momentarily bewildered. To the returning Farnham he utters in a voice fraught with uncertainty, "How do we find them here, *mon ami?*"

"By looking," Farnham responds, breathless, pack in hand, as he approaches from the underbrush on the steep embankment.

That afternoon, the two men paddle their canoe near to the bank searching for signs as they pursue the way north against the current. They are hungry but observe neither game nor signs of the Belleau.

Late in the day, both men are fatigued as they round a bend in the river and come upon several aborigines sitting on their haunches at the riverbank. Nearby is a small cluster of low cedar huts. Franchère and Farnham paddle toward the group though some of the men retreat up the riverbank, eyeing the strangers suspiciously.

"Cheerful bunch," Farnham comments from his lead position in the canoe. "Maybe they've seen our men. Trade for dried fish, if they have any. It's a mighty long day without food!"

"But we stop above the village, Russell!"

Farnham takes his musket and pouch from the canoe and speaks with five men who remain near the shore. He soon returns. "They know nothing of the Belleau."

"We come too far up the river, Russell. I think so."

"We look for signs as far as the next rapids. If there is nothing, we return. But today we trade for smoked fish." Farnham takes a handful of glass beads from his pack and returns to the small group and spreads the beads on the dirt before them. He gestures toward the river raising his thumb. "Salmon. *Equanna!*" (Food!) Again he gestures to them as though putting food in his mouth. *"Equanna. Muck-a-muck!"* (Food. Eat!)

The men scowl with complete indifference. Farnham calls to Franchère, "What if they have no fish! God, I'm hungry!"

Other men approach as he speaks and signs again to them with no response. Exasperated, he picks up the beads and again calls to Franchère. "They refuse the beads. I even offered two blankets and tobacco!" He turns back to the natives. "Suspicious rascals! Don't know what's good for you!"

There are now fifteen men gathered about him. They stare with unpredictable, surly looks. With growing agitation Franchère urges, "Russell, they do not have fish! They do not trade fish for nothing! I think we go before they make the attack!"

Farnham pulls his flintlock from its buckskin cover and grabs an axe from the pouch he carries. He is cool and certain. "Stay in the canoe while I amuse them!" He strides confidently through the gathered men to a tree near the edge of the clearing a dozen steps away. He buries the axe conspicuously into the trunk so as to be in silhouette from their point of view and, as boldly, returns to the midst of the villagers.

They fall back in uncertainty before the stranger's actions. Farnham loads and primes the flintlock, glances back at Franchère who is waiting to shove off, turns to the distant tree, levels his piece and fires.

The villagers leap back in terror from the report and smoke. At the same time, they hear the ball strike the axe and see it fall to the ground by the tree. Several of the men run toward the axe. Farnham slips back to the canoe unnoticed as the men cluster in the direction of the fallen axe.

One bold individual approaches and cautiously circles, then finally picks up the axe and immediately races back to the group displaying the trophy prominently before him. They examine the hole in the blade, jabbering amongst themselves. Suddenly the man with the axe raises it over his head and lets out a loud war whoop. The villagers dance triumphantly about the new prize while the Franchère and Farnham continue the search upriver.

Chapter Forty-Nine

That night, Franchère and Farnham sit under a tree smoking. A windbreak of large rocks and cedar matting protects their campfire. The wind gusts occasionally and big drops of water sizzle when they land on the rocks that surround the fire. The men have now been without food for two days. Franchère pulls his blanket around him. Farnham adds a dead limb to the fire and looks at the sky. "The clouds will burst any minute."

"Tomorrow we must hunt for meat. Damn Belleau! I shoot them both with my own hand!" The wind is rising and begins to threaten the cedar windbreak and disturb the fire.

Farnham leans forward to steady the windbreak. "You'll have to find them first. I wish you'd be quick about it!" He reinforces the windbreak and then wraps himself in a heavy wool blanket as a peel of thunder rolls overhead.

Franchère searches the sky as the rain increases. "The savage don't bother us tonight, *mon ami*."

"Superstitious devils. Give food to their gods but let the white man starve."

The next morning under a large cedar where they are protected from the rain and beside a fire partially sheltered from the wind by the tree trunk, Franchère and Farnham, wrapped in blankets, each gnaw voraciously on a tough leg of roasted porcupine.

Farnham throws the bones into the fire and pulls his knife to cut from the carcass that is upright by the fire. Franchère's hand stops him. He is staring toward the river. Farnham looks in the same direction where a half dozen aborigines stand at a canoe that is beached beside theirs. Approaching from the river, a man and woman guide an old man toward their fire. The natives are protected from the rain by woven conical-shaped caps and capes of woven cedar bark. Franchère drops his repast. "Your pistol dry?"

Farnham reaches under the blanket. "Primed and dry." The two stare intently at the advancing Indians.

"He is blind!" Franchère suddenly exclaims and points. "Look!"

"The one at the center," Farnham observes. "He must be a chief. The slaves bring him to us." He removes his hand from under the blanket. "Come, we give him tobacco."

After cordial but formal greeting and inquiry, the blind chief sits on his haunches under the tree across from Franchère and Farnham and puffs on Franchère's pipe. His two slaves wait quietly behind. They do not smoke.

Finally the chief sets the pipe on the ground and gestures in sign language to the white men.

"Our brothers have been sold to his neighbor," Farnham translates. "He says his neighbor is weak. They will not make war on white people."

"The village. How far is the village, Russell?"

"*Kah, tye-yea* (where, chief)?"

The old chief gestures and speaks to the male slave. "*Ikt o-te-lagh. Ick-hol.*" The slave points toward mountains to the east.

"One sun," Farnham translates. "That's a full day by canoe on the river that joins this one from the east. Thank God they're alive!"

Two days later at daybreak on a damp, misty morning, Franchère and Farnham disembark with their muskets in hand near a cluster of cedar lodges set back from the river. They survey the riverbank where all is quiet. The village appears deserted.

Farnham suddenly stops and points toward the largest lodge. "Look," he whispers and points. From a carved post near the entrance, two familiar muskets hang along with the scalps and articles of "medicine" of this warrior's lodge. They glance at each other in recognition then proceed cautiously, not moving far from their canoe, inspecting what they can from the riverbank.

Farnham spots a heavily tarnished brass ship's bell hanging from a tree near one of the bigger lodges. He points it out to Franchère and whispers, "Not so lucky crossing the bar as the *Tonquin*."

They turn back along the riverbank toward the other end of the settlement. All at once Antoine appears, ragged and gaunt, walking up from a creek behind the village carrying two large baskets of water. The moment he sees them, he stops dead in his tracks and bursts into tears.

Franchère cannot believe his eyes. Forgetting himself, he runs up to his countryman. *"Mon ami,"* he whispers and embraces him. "Jean Baptiste, *il est toujours en vie* (he is still alive)?"

Antoine is speechless but nods "yes."

Farnham motions Franchère to join him and walks toward the ship's bell. With Franchère at his side, Farnham rings the bell loudly and continuously.

Instantly, the entire village is alive with the shrieks and confused movement of women, children and old men. "Where are the warriors?" Farnham comments as the people cluster around an elder who approaches and leads them to a low roofed, cedar hut that is dark and smokey and quickly crowded with villagers. Franchère and Farnham sit opposite the elder, a low fire in a shallow pit between them.

With single-minded determination, the old man refuses the pipe proffered by Farnham. He will not smoke. Franchère and Farnham remain stern and attentive though aware of the helplessness of their situation. Finally he gestures to them in sign language. Farnham translates. "Six winters pass since white people follow the great river from the mountains to the stinking waters. My people strong in life! White people return to the mountains. My people strong to live!"

Farnham turns to Franchère. "He must mean Lewis and Clark going to the Pacific."

The man's expression grows particularly grave as he continues. Farnham reads his sign language. "White people come from the stinking waters. White people bring small-pox. Indian people say white man destroy village, take lodge!" He does not flinch as he stares fiercely at the two strangers.

"He seems to believe that traders on the coast intend to harm his people," Farnham remarks.

Franchère studies the man for a moment then stands, confident in his expression. Farnham gestures in sign language while Franchère speaks with gravity. "White people build a great lodge on the big river that follows the setting sun. My people fill their lodge with strong medicine for our Indian brothers and for their women. We see that our Indian brothers are strong to live, that every day they sing and dance."

He gestures to the sky and continues. "White people know that the Great Spirit is the only master of the ground, that it was so in the day of your grandfathers, as it is now, and it continues to be for your grandsons!"

The elder stares intently at Franchère. After a few moments he picks up the pipe and gestures to the white men that he will smoke.

Later that day, the head man and his relatives sit on their haunches on cedar mats in front of the lodge. Franchère sets a copper kettle and an axe on a pile of eight blankets that lies before him. He steps back to Farnham who has the two muskets that were taken from the Belleau brothers. They await the decision.

The two brothers stand opposite watching the negotiations in suspense. The entire village of twenty to thirty children and adults is gathered behind them.

Franchère speaks. "Tell him, Russell, that this is payment for our brothers." Farnham conveys the message in sign language.

The old man, obviously displeased, consults his relatives. One of them points to the bell. He turns to Franchère and gestures in sign language as he speaks. *"Posh-tun tin-tin!"*

"He seems to want another bell," Farnham replies, puzzled. "I don't understand him." He gestures in sign language.

The elder picks up the pipe and points it awkwardly at the bell as though it were a fowling piece. "Boom!" He points to the bell. *"Tin-tin!"*

Franchère turns to Farnham. "He wants one of the muskets. Tell him we do not trade musket."

Farnham gestures but the elder rejects the answer. "He'll not let the men free. We have to give him something!" Farnham has an idea and pulls a pistol from his pocket. "This one's in poor condition. The lock will soon break."

He steps forward with the pistol in hand, beckons to the head man who follows him before the gathered Indians.

With gravity Farnham points to the bell which is hanging a few paces away and then to the pistol. He demonstrates how to cock the piece, then takes aim and fires. There is a puff of smoke and the familiar ring as the brass bell rocks with the impact of the ball.

The elder is ecstatic and reaches eagerly for the pistol. Farnham removes his powder horn and indicates that he will instruct the old man how to load.

Late that afternoon Franchère and Farnham paddle downriver followed by the Belleau brothers in their canoe. Franchère calls out from the lead position, "We must reach the portage before the sunset, Russell! We cannot trust the people on this part of the river!"

Farnham's reply is emphatic. "We must clear the portage before dark! Those men will be bolder the second time." They round a bend and approach a likely stopping place.

Jean Baptiste shouts from his canoe, "Gabriel! We are hungry, *mon fils* (my brother)! We do not eat for three days!" He points to the shore indicating a place to land.

"We have no food!" Franchère shouts back. "We do not stop! *Le sauvage!*" They finally reach the portage and both canoes are beached and unloaded. The Belleau brothers prepare to carry their canoe.

Farnham, wearing a brace of pistols in his belt, is checking his flintlock primer as Franchère, with pack and flintlock, steps up to him and whispers, "They are not strong enough to carry the pack and the canoe. I go with them and you stay here with the packs. We return in one hour, Russell."

Instead of something to eat, Farnham gives each of the brothers one of the pistols. "We have no food," he repeats. "Keep a sharp eye, especially when everything is quiet."

As the two men set off, canoe overhead, following Franchère along the portage trail, Farnham goes to his pack and removes another brace of pistols. With bullet pouch and powder horn, he loads the pistols then checks the surrounding forest, the trail and river. He is tense, alert, expecting trouble any moment.

He tucks both pistols into his belt. The silence is suddenly broken by the discharge of a musket. Farnham grabs his flintlock and bolts up the trail leaving the canoe and packs.

He rounds a bend of the trail at a dead run to find Antoine, an arrow through his leg, on the ground beside the canoe. A tall aborigine is about to club him. Franchère is a few yards down the trail keeping three aborigines at bay with the butt of his flintlock. Jean Baptiste is scuffling desperately with four men in an effort to get to his brother.

Farnham raises the flintlock while still running and fires from his waist. The Indian with the club is thrown back by the ball. Farnham leaps over the fallen body, draws a pistol and immediately fires at one of the savages trying to overpower Jean Baptiste.

As the second Indian falls, Farnham breaks the stock of his flintlock over the head of another Indian, throws down the piece and, waving his arms wildly, lets out a full-blooded, plains-Indian-style war whoop. He passes between Jean Baptiste and the Indians, pulls the second pistol and fires at one of Franchère's attackers.

The man falls while the others, panic stricken, run in terror as Farnham, whooping and swinging his discharged pistols, bolts down the trail and into the forest after them.

He stops abruptly and turns breathless to Jean Baptiste who has followed him at a run. "Pull that arrow from your brother's leg! We must get away while there's fear in their hearts!"

Chapter Fifty

Three nights later at Fort Astoria, the Belleau brothers, haggard and downcast, sit on a bench along the wall of the sitting room beside Franchère and Farnham. Robert, Mumford and McDougall face them from the table in front of the fireplace. Indian drums and chanting in the distance are heard distinctly over Farnham's report to McDougall. "They worked without food, sir, forced to do slaves' work, like gather wood and carry water. No doubt before the clan moved inland for the winter, they would be sacrificed. Fewer hungry mouths to feed." Antoine reaches for his older brother's arm as tears involuntarily fill his eyes. McDougall watches the brothers closely.

"They believe we bring the small-pox," Franchère adds significantly. "They understand we are white men but not that we could be other than a tribe ourselves. The chief say Indian people believe white man come to destroy the village and take the lodges."

McDougall is puzzled but interested. "Now who in the devil would give 'em that idea?"

Farnham leans forward intently. "We assured the chief of our friendly intentions and paid him all our blankets, the copper kettle and an axe for the Belleau. Fortunately, the warriors and young men were away on an expedition to gather food, otherwise we would not have gotten them so cheaply. But the chief was not satisfied without a pistol and some shot, and my jacket, sir!"

"Your jacket gives him status with his people."

"They tell us the beaver is plenty in their valley," Farnham relates. "But they won't leave the territory and visit our post. They're as shy a clan as I've yet seen. We will have to go to them to collect skins."

By now McDougall is staring hard at the brothers. "Ye might open a post among 'em and have a good return for your trade. But, no! Ye have to run off! Goin' to cross the continent afoot, are ye? Back to Montreal? And I go to bloody Boston!" He gets up and paces in agitation. "As God is my witness, this is a vast wilderness! Seventy men been travelin' more than one year to reach this post from St. Louis. And they're not here yet!" He stops before the fireplace. "And now there's fresh rumor among them Clatsops." He breaks off and again paces.

"What rumor, sir?" Farnham asks.

"A load o' rubbish, lad," he replies. "A ship's been taken, they say."

"But, *Monsieur* McKay!" Franchère responds, shaken by this news.

McDougall approaches the table. His reply is quick, off-handed, but defensive. "A load o' rubbish, I say! Tryin' to scare us. Some o' them Clatsops want us off this side o' the river." He turns on the Belleau brothers. "So ye'd rather have your teeth decorate the prow of a savage canoe than earn an honest meal with your own kind?" He continues pacing, his anger rising. "Destroy me confidence in ye, aye?"

Jean Baptiste is mortified. "No, *monsieur*."

"An' to rescue ye, with them savages everyday increasin' their numbers around this post, I risk two good men." He stares directly at Jean Baptiste. "Two men that last night I thought were lost forever!" He turns to Franchère. "And well ye might o' been from the sound o' that dancin' and singin'. All night! Night after bloody night!"

"We do not go again, *monsieur*," Antoine replies.

McDougall returns to the table and sits down heavily. He looks over at Franchère. "Ye deduct the cost o' the ransom from their wages, and ye put 'em both on half wages for one month." He points to Antoine's wrapped leg. "And no wages for you, lad, while you're on the sick list." He bangs his fist fiercely on the table. "Run off again, by God, and the devil take ye! We'll leave ye to them savages!" He speaks to the room with desperate determination. "Until the *Tonquin* returns, not another man leaves this post but to hunt or to gather food!"

McDougall turns suddenly to Farnham. "It's them Chinooks!" he bursts out with decision. "Spreadin' bad reports upriver. Say the white man brings small-pox. Keep them other tribes away. Can't be trusted. Chinooks want the trade for themselves, by God!"

Chapter Fifty-One

The next morning in the shed, the blacksmith removes a partially formed piece of iron bar from the forge and works it into a spear tip. After heating the tip to a red glow and dipping it into the rain barrel, he knocks the steaming piece onto the floor which is littered with spear tips. He replaces the bar in the coals, mops his brow and shakes his head with wonder as he pulls out another glowing bar and begins again in a cycle that seems to have no end.

Except for the gate opening, the post is fully enclosed. The front bastion has been completed. Construction on the rear bastion and a gallery on the rear palisade continues. From the busy yard, Robert enters the shed and accosts the blacksmith. "The gate posts are complete. Have you the straps ready?"

The smith looks up from the anvil with surprise. "No, sir." He puts the iron bar into the burning coal and presses on the bellows a couple of times.

Robert steps forward, trying to control his temper. "We're obliged to complete the gate. It's the safety of the post we're considering!"

Without rushing, the smith removes the bar and pounds a couple of strokes. "When I'm done with Indians' work." He tosses the piece back into the coals. "Mr McDougall's orders, sir. Wants these for trade." He indicates the floor. "Every time a savage comes to this post he brings some old rusty scrap resurrected from God knows where!"

He grabs another iron bar from the coals and pounds intermittently as he talks. "And he comes a-beggin' for all his friends and relations. My orders is to give 'em what they want. They never cease beggin', sir. And they never go away satisfied. Indians are all alike. Want to be men of great significance with *Posh-tun*, but they are only troublesome."

Robert is angry. "Beggars! I'll see to this!" He crosses the yard where Chinook are involved in all the activities of the post. In addition, there are idle ones in groups who hang about the post out of curiosity while some sit together gambling. He enters the storehouse which is full of noisy Indians waiting to trade.

McDougall works at the table weighing individual pelts on a crude balance with Franchère's and Pillet's assistance. Robert crosses the room and is about to speak when McDougall spots him. He is desperate. "Good God, man, where the devil have ye been? The entire Chinook tribe is here! They demand three times the value of each pelt!" He throws down a skin in frustration and turns on Robert. "I can't keep order! Get Farnham in here and a couple o' them Islanders. Be quick! They'll steal all we have!" McDougall grabs Robert and pulls him closer. He speaks in an intense undertone. "And ye get a message to Comcomly. He must send a guard o' his Chinooks to keep order! Tell him I have a handsome gift for him. We must have protection!"

Farnham bursts through the door in excitement and announces, "Chief Comcomly's coming. He's bringing six women and several canoes of warriors!" McDougall is momentarily speechless. But immediately on the mention of Comcomly's name, the Indians begin to exit, mumbling among themselves.

McDougall eyes the departing men with suspicion. As the last one leaves, he reaches under the table and uncovers a blunderbuss which he sets to one side on a barrel. "Franchère, you greet Comcomly. Usher him here, and then stay with me. Farnham, you find Mumford and post the guard with canon. Mr Stuart, you and Pillet issue musket pieces, but remain quiet. And keep the men together until I see what the beggar's up to." He glares hard at the astonished men. "Mind ye, we want no trouble!"

At the riverfront, a half-dozen ten-man canoes follow one still larger to the narrow strip of sand by the pier. The canoes beach stern first, as is their custom. Comcomly, who is about forty, disembarks and stands proudly surveying the new post. With one eye lost years before, he remains a strong, well-made man wearing a kilt-like skin around his waist under a full-length sea otter robe. His hair is cut short and he carries a musket.

Among the women in Comcomly's canoe is the daughter who accompanied the injured Calpo. The women do not disembark. Comcomly steps forward while slaves and warriors gather on the shore behind him.

Franchère leaves the post and walks to the riverbank to greet the chief. "MAC-dugal!" Comcomly demands, his tone indignant, his English picked up over many years from trading vessels.

"*Monsieur* McDougall is very glad you visit the post," Franchère responds. "He greet you inside, *Monsieur* Chief."

Comcomly eyes Franchère. "I come," he replies sternly. Franchère and Comcomly, followed by the warriors, walk to the post.

Inside the storehouse, McDougall stands as Comcomly enters and moves around the table to greet the chief. Before he can say a word, Comcomly stops, holding his head high and pointing at him. "MAC-dugal give rum Comcomly son!"

"We give wine," McDougall replies, flustered. "Wine good, chief."

"Calpo laugh!" Comcomly is irate. "Slaves see Calpo! Calpo damn fool! Warrior no laugh! Woman laugh!"

"Wine for sleep." McDougall responds.

Comcomly ignores him. "Chinook warrior strong! Good hunter! Chinook drink rum, no strong! Laugh like woman!" He is emphatic. "MAC-dugal no give rum!"

McDougall scowls formidably. "Calpo sleep for white man's medicine. Wine powerful medicine!"

"Sleep two day! No move!"

"Fix bone! Good sleep!" McDougall ignores Comcomly's indignation and walks back to the table where Franchère remains at the far end quietly sorting skins. McDougall is now relaxed, amiable. "Come, *Tye-yea*, let us smoke. What can I do for ye?" He pulls the bench out and Comcomly sits opposite him by the fire.

McDougall lights a pipe and Comcomly smokes as McDougall examines the chief's old flintlock. "It wants a screw flattened, *Tye-yea*, so as to catch here. The blacksmith can put it right." He lays the piece on the table. "I've something to show ye!" He picks up the blunderbuss.

McDougall is full of self-importance as he approaches the chief with the short, sturdy weapon. "Have a look at this, will ye. A blunderbuss,

Tye-yea. A blunderbuss of Mortimer's make, carrying balls of eighteen to the pound." He hands the weapon to Comcomly who handles it gingerly. "Used close up. When there's no time to aim. Sends out a spray o' balls. Deadly!"

McDougall takes back the piece. "Works like your flintlock. Look here." McDougall pulls back the lock. "It cocks in the same manner." He releases the lock and the weapon discharges with an ear-shattering concussion. The two men are instantly enveloped in white smoke.

Suddenly all is confusion as Comcomly bursts through the storehouse door wearing only his kilt and carrying no weapon. At the sight of the chief running, there is a cry of "murder!" and "treason!" from the sentinels. Robert moves forward, his flintlock at the ready as the startled Indians in the yard look around with uncertainty and the men along the perimeter of the post suddenly show their weapons. At the same moment, Franchère and McDougall bolt through the door following Comcomly with both hands in the air gesturing "peace." McDougall bellows out, "Nobody's hurt! Hold your fire! 'Twas an accident! An accident!"

The Indians gather around Comcomly who makes his way directly to the beached canoes. All the Indians depart before McDougall can offer the chief a gift.

Chapter Fifty-Two

Construction on the post continues without the Chinooks. A strong rear bastion is completed, two stories high like the front, in which men on guard sleep each night with the two-pound cannon and muskets at hand. The two bastions command the four sides of the post. The palisade is fifteen feet high and a gallery around the inside with holes pierced large enough for musketry gives a heightened sense of security. The men continue drill practice at noon with their muskets.

At the end of each week the sound of the dinner bell brings the company together outside for supper around a communal fire lit to consume debris and remnants from construction. With gate straps mounted, the gates are closed for the night.

Mumford and Franchère enter the yard from the storehouse and walk together toward the fire. "Damn savages," Mumford complains. "No way o' tellin' what's in their head when they won't come about the place. Not one of me crew worked this week."

"Indians now camp on both sides of the river."

Robert and McDougall join them and the four leisurely walk to join the others. Robert is concerned. "Indians increasin' their numbers daily."

"The sturgeon should be running again," Franchère remarks. "The people come from the north to gather food."

Mumford stops abruptly and turns to Franchère with an air of authority. "Don't ye believe them stories!" He points confidently to the gates. "What do ye think them pickets is for? Savages are greedy, I tell ye! No different from human kind. They're waitin' their chance. That's all."

"Mr Mumford," McDougall responds with irritation, "there ye go again, half-cocked, spreadin' rumors."

Suddenly from the bastion a guard calls out, "Savages! A-landin' at the river!"

The men stop dead in their tracks and turn as one. Nobody moves. All eyes are riveted to the guard. "How many?" McDougall shouts.

"Eight!" the guard responds, "One canoe!"

The men look at each other with relief. "Must be them Chinooks," McDougall remarks. "Mr Stuart, you see to them."

"Maybe Comcomly's sendin' a peace offering," Mumford quips sarcastically.

A few minutes later, Robert returns through the gate and approaches McDougall who is now at the fire with the other men. "Comcomly's sick. Asks for Franchère to bring him medicine."

McDougall is interested. "What's wrong?"

"Sore throat. Sounds like tonsillitis."

McDougall is pleased. "A chance to make it up to him. Aye! You and Franchère take some medicine. Ye can cross at daybreak and return in the evening. And ye take his newest wife a gift o' cloth from me."

At first light the next day Robert and Franchère leave the post and walk toward the riverfront, each carrying a small bundle. As they pass the corner of the fort there is a noise from beside the palisade. They stop. "Who's there?" Robert asks. They move cautiously into the shadows in the direction of the sound.

"Calpo's sister!" Franchère blurts out. She is waiting for them with two of her brothers and motions for them to approach. They speak briefly together then the men return to the post.

Before sunrise inside the storehouse, Franchère and Robert meet with McDougall, Farnham, and Mumford. Robert is shaken. "She took up a handful of sand and threw it into the air and, pointing along both shores, said the Indians are as numerous as the grains of sand." There is real concern on all their faces. "'The Indians have bad hearts,' she said. 'I can no longer speak with my father. He will not listen to me.'"

McDougall is irate. "Another o' them Chinook tricks!" He begins pacing in front of the fire then stops, facing Franchère. "Sore throat! He wanted you in his power!" He resumes pacing and suddenly bellows with frustration, "An' where the devil is the *Tonquin*? Short o' supplies! Short o' men! By God, we'll be destroyed one by one before our mighty captain decides to return!"

All eyes are riveted to McDougall. "What can we do, *monsieur*?" Franchère asks.

"Ye can do nothin', lad. It's up to me now." He stops pacing, considering. "It's up to me. Fool! Should o' never allowed the *Tonquin* to sail with half our supplies an' trade goods still aboard." He starts pacing again, desperate, searching. "We must convince them savages we have power. Or the tribes will come together to starve us and steal what goods we have." An idea occurs to him.

He approaches the table with sudden decision. "All right! I have a plan, lads. Now listen carefully. Every man must do exactly as he is bid."

Chapter Fifty-Three

A FEW DAYS LATER, McDOUGALL sits quietly alone inside the storehouse watching the far door. He is neat and polished, wearing his best traveling clothes. The outside shutters of the storehouse are closed. The room is lit by the fire in the grate and a solitary lantern on the table before him. All is silent except for an occasional crackle from the fireplace.

Franchère enters the room. "They come, *monsieur.*"

"How many?"

"Seven."

"Good. And Comcomly?"

"He leads them, *monsieur.*"

McDougall leans forward intently. "Only the chiefs are to enter. Their men must remain outside."

"*Oui, monsieur.*"

Franchère exits and waves to Robert who stands at the gate where about one hundred warriors have gathered silently outside. At a signal from Robert, six chiefs and Comcomly, each ornately dressed and painted with black and red, their heads highly ornamented with feathers and marked with a bearing of confident, severe dignity, enter with a small retinue of men who follow behind them. The gate is closed and they are led to the storehouse by Robert.

Inside the yard the men of the post work at their usual chores. Weapons are at the ready but concealed from the Indians. As the procession of solemn aborigines, led by Comcomly, passes by, the men glance up with no indication of alarm. Rather, there is an atmosphere of calm which gives a sense of confidence. The motley procession approaches Franchère at the door. He directs the followers to wait in the yard.

Once inside the storehouse, the chiefs cross to where McDougall awaits them and, following Comcomly's example, they sit with some uncertainty on the long benches at each side of the table. Except for Comcomly, most have never sat on a chair or bench before. Their custom is to sit on their haunches.

McDougall is at the head of the table with the fire at his back causing him to appear as a black specter in silhouette. The dim orange light of the lantern partially reveals the features of the different savage chieftains. There is a long silence as McDougall eyes each man, sternly, individually. Comcomly is to his right, the Wishram chief to his left. All eyes are riveted to him.

Finally he reaches forward and draws the lantern across the table slowly closer to him so that it lights his face. He stares directly at Comcomly and speaks evenly, with commanding authority. "I have heard the treachery of your brothers in the north toward a trading ship. A ship destroyed on the coast!"

Comcomly is startled. *"Al-ah."* He turns to the other chiefs, translating. *"Al-ta posh-tun an-ah si-wash."*

The Wishram chief turns to Comcomly. *"Ik-tah?"*

Comcomly speaks to McDougall. "What MAC-dugal want?"

McDougall again looks around the table at the chiefs. "I am determined to revenge them!"

"Hyas sol-leks," Comcomly translates.

The Wishram chief stares hard at McDougall, curious but puzzled, trying to get inside McDougall's head. *"Kah-ta?"* He asks.

"What the matter MAC-dugal?" Comcomly translates.

McDougall leans forward, almost over the lamp, talking, apparently, to the Indian farthest away. His demeanor is stern and he makes use of sign language as he speaks. "White man few in number. That is true! But white man medicine strong!" He stares around the table, angry, unflinching. Finally, he takes out his spectacles and puts them on.

The chiefs draw back in astonishment.

McDougall stares hard at them as though he is about to cast a spell. "Now! See here!" He suddenly produces a small glass bottle and carefully places it on the table in full view of the chiefs and well under the lantern's light. Pressing it to the table with a finger on the cork stopper, McDougall turns the phial slowly. The label reads "OIL OF QUININE."

The chiefs are clearly bewildered. Expressions of distrust and fear are apparent.

McDougall nods "yes" in full confidence and stops rotating the phial but keeps his finger resting on the cork as though it would open of its own will were he to allow it. He stares significantly at the small glass container. "In this phial," he raises his eyes to the chiefs, looking deliberately around the table, "the small-pox!"

At mention of the dread disease, there is an immediate stir of alarm. Eyes widen in terror as the men realize what he has said. All arrogance and sense of self-importance vanish. Several shift their positions noticeably back from the table but no one has the temerity to challenge McDougall.

Comcomly is shaken. *"Al-ah! Small-pox lam!"*

Outside in the yard, various Indians wait quietly near the gates. Farnham and Antoine, walking with a slight limp, both wearing a brace of pistols tucked in their belts, feign indifference as they proceed together across the yard. Everywhere work appears normal. On the forward bastion, Mumford and crew watch quietly from beside the canon.

Franchère stands alone outside the storehouse door. Robert and Jean Baptiste, both carrying flintlocks, approach Franchère. "Any word yet?" Robert asks.

Franchère is surveying the yard. He replies in an undertone, "They are quiet. Nothing." His gaze stops. Farnham and Antoine are arguing. Antoine starts to walk toward a group of Indians but Farnham restrains him.

Robert notices them and turns with concern to Franchère. "I'd better see what is wrong there."

As Robert and Jean Baptiste approach the two men, Antoine appears agitated and continues to argue with Farnham. "But I tell you, this is the one! He take my gun! He is the same!" The Indians appear indifferent toward the small excitement. "I cut off his ears, by gar!"

Inside the storehouse, McDougall sits motionless, holding his finger firmly on the phial. "The small-pox is safely corked!" Suddenly McDougall snatches the small bottle from the table and holds it out dramatically, close to the lantern.

The chiefs pull back in terror, their gazes held in hypnotic fear by the tiny vial.

McDougall stares with a vengeance at the small container as though he has full power over it. He again sets it under the lantern's light and signs as he speaks slowly, deliberately. "But. If I draw this cork. The small-pox will spread over the land. Your brothers and their children. You and your wives. All will vanish from the earth!" Again he snatches the phial from the table.

The chiefs all speak at once in complete confusion. Comcomly is struck with awe. "*Kakh-tsaik-ta small-pox* (a bad thing…)! *MAC-dugal posh-tun kap-ho* (McDougall Boston brother)! *Chinook posh-tun kap-ho* (Chinook Boston brother)!" He turns to the chiefs, "*Posh-tun sikhs* (Boston friends)!"

The chiefs nod in agreement. "*Ah-ha* (yes)! *Ah-ha!*"

Comcomly turns to McDougall with real earnestness. "Small-pox fire! *Ma-sa-tchi* (bad)! *Posh-tun* no kill! Chinook *posh-tun* brother!

McDougall leans back as though considering the chief's argument. He is now fully confident. "Aye, chief, ye make a strong point." He signs as he speaks. "No good, ye say, to kill friends." He looks over the group. "The Chinook people don't like the notion o' killin' friends. Well, then."

McDougall stands and faces the chiefs, again holding the vial before them in plain view. "The small-pox will remain here, sealed up, so long as no man o' this post is hurt by the Chinooks and these your friends! But let one of ye injure a white man," he warns with intensity, "I will draw this cork an' put an end to ye!"

At the same time in the yard, a commotion is developing around Antoine. He is agitated and angry. "*Le sauvage! Merdeux* (dirty dog)! He must pay for the gun!"

The Indians outside the gate continue to mill about but the few in the yard now watch the white men with uneasy suspicion. The man who escaped with Antoine's gun quietly slips from view behind members of his tribe.

Suddenly the storehouse door is thrown open and one by one the seven chiefs, stern, rigid, shaken to the core, exit solemnly. McDougall and Franchère follow them. McDougall is equally solemn but shows no lack of self-importance. In an undertone, he confides to Franchère, "Heaven bless 'em! An' keep 'em ignorant, lad!"

The Indians in the yard wait quietly. Mumford and crew remain at the canon in the bastion along with men on the gallery who watch both the Indians in the yard and those outside.

Antoine, unaware of anything but his concern over the stolen gun, rushes up to McDougall with Farnham and Robert close behind. Before they can stop him, Antoine comes between McDougall and the procession. *"Monsieur! Le sauvage!* He steal the gun! The very..."

"What the devil!" McDougall exclaims, taken aback. He is forced to stop as Antoine moves closer still, crowding him. "The gun, *monsieur!*" He points toward a group of Indians in the yard. "I see *le sauvage!*"

McDougall is irate. "Out o' me way, blast ye! Can't ye see I've business?"

"But, *monsieur*, the gun!"

The others have gathered around. McDougall turns to Robert. "What's gotten into him?"

"The Indian who ran off," Robert replies, "the one we put in the pit overnight who stole the gun. Antoine spotted him."

McDougall's expression changes. He is interested and turns to the excited Frenchman. "Ye recognized the very identical?"

"Oui, monsieur!"

McDougall is firm. "No mistake, now!"

"No, *monsieur*. I cut off his ears, by *gar!*"

"Ye'll do no such thing." He turns to Franchère. "Bring them two benches. From inside. Be quick, man!" He turns to Antoine. "Point the rascal out to me."

McDougall speaks to Comcomly and there is a commotion around him before his tribal members disperse. The gate is thrown open and the suspected man leaves the fort at a run. The benches are set up and McDougall sits on one flanked by Antoine, Franchère, Robert, and Farnham. Comcomly and the chiefs occupy the second bench.

McDougall eyes the chiefs sternly and gestures in sign language as he speaks. "No white man will let a stranger be injured while in his house, under his protection. White man has good spirit!"

There is a disturbance outside the post. McDougall turns toward the gate as the suspected warrior enters the fort with the missing musket.

Comcomly stands, pulls off his otter skin robe and spreads it on the ground before McDougall. He takes the flintlock from the breathless warrior and lays it on the robe.

McDougall is pleased. "Ye can trust to white man's honor, *Tye-yea!* But white men have laws, and one law is that a thief must be punished!"

Comcomly consults with the chiefs before turning to McDougall. "Chinook *posh-tun* brother! Chinook give *posh-tun* gun!" He turns to the accused. *"Ecu-toch* (bad spirit)! *Al-choya* (go away)! *I-ake* (be quick)!"

McDougall gestures to the accused savage. *"Mit-lite* (stay)!" The Indian obeys him and remains. McDougall turns to Robert. "It seems to be their custom that to return stolen goods pardons the thief."

"Aye. Fair enough. We don't require no more trouble."

"Oui, monsieur," Franchère agrees.

McDougall turns to Antoine. "Are ye satisfied?"

Antoine is reluctant. "But, *monsieur,* the lock is broken!"

McDougall is impatient, almost sarcastic. "Beggin' your pardon, lad, but I somehow don't like the notion o' punishment today. 'Twould be unfortunate indeed if it got in the way o' good tradin' relations!"

"Oui, monsieur," Antoine responds quietly.

McDougall turns to the chiefs and gestures in sign language as he speaks with intense conviction. "White man's law says that a thief must be punished. And white man never breaks his word, *Tye-yea!*" He stands and indicates Antoine. "But this man is as well agreed as I. He has a good heart for the Chinook people. He tells me he is satisfied. The thief should not be punished!"

He picks up the flintlock and fingers the broken lock with exaggerated disgust. An idea occurs to him. McDougall glances at the chiefs before handing the broken weapon to Antoine. "But now, *Tye-yea*, I will show you the effect of a gun in the hands of a white man!"

He turns to Farnham with a hint of bravado. "Mr Russell Farnham. From the hills o' Massachusetts, aren't ye?"

"Yes, sir."

"One of the first shots in the company, I hear."

Farnham is embarrassed. "Not as good as some, sir."

"But good enough!" McDougall points toward the river. "Set up a mark through the gate. Demonstrate your skill, lad, so them chiefs will be sure to take notice. 'Twould be a very good thing!"

A few minutes later Robert walks through the gate toward the river carrying a rough plank with a two-inch white spot near one end. Jean Baptiste accompanies him carrying a large wooden mallet. The Indians separate forming a clearing to the river. At about eighty yards distance, Farnham signals. "Bloody rascal!" Robert remarks, amazed. He sets the plank in position and comments, "I couldn't find the board from there, let alone see this mark!"

"He don't see only the mark, *monsieur*," Jean Baptiste replies, "he see the grain in the wood, by *gar*!"

Farnham watches intently as Jean Baptiste in the distance pounds the board into the muddy turf. The Indians are silent. They have no idea what to expect.

He quickly checks the priming of his piece then measures with his eye the distance to the board and waves. The two men at the target step aside. Farnham holds up three fingers for all to see and shouts, "Three shots!"

With ease he cocks the piece, rests it firmly against his shoulder, aims and fires. There is a stir among the Indians as they react to the smoke and the double sound of the report followed immediately by the ball smashing through the plank.

Farnham skillfully reloads and in less than twenty seconds, he raises his piece and fires a second shot. Again the Indians react to the double sound. Farnham is now in his stride. Without wasted movement, the piece is reloaded and leveled to fire.

Robert watches the board closely from not ten feet away. The splinters on the back-side of the plank, where the two previous shots have penetrated, are prominent. He sees the puff of smoke as Farnham pulls the trigger. Almost immediately the board splinters with a third hole followed by the sound of the report. He shakes his head in disbelief as he approaches the plank. All three shots have hit the mark forming a tight group. He pulls up the board and returns to the post. As Robert passes with the board held prominently before the eager warriors, they react with excitement and astonishment.

Farnham takes the board from Robert. He barely glances at the target before turning to McDougall. He is fully intent on showing the accuracy of his piece. The matter of his own skill does not occur to him. Indicating the musket, he declares, "Now she's warmed up, sir, she'll do some real shooting!"

McDougall is immensely pleased. He turns to Comcomly. "Watch the lad, now, *Tye-yea!*"

Farnham puts a dark hazelnut into one of the holes.

Robert again carries the plank to the target site and Jean Baptiste pounds it into place. He waves to Farnham in the distance and the two men step aside.

The dark hazelnut is suddenly cracked by a hole that is punched through contiguous with its hole followed immediately by the report.

As the smoke clears, Farnham sees that he did not smash the nut. Quickly he reloads and aims his piece.

The hazelnut is completely shattered by a ball that rips through half its hole. Robert yanks up the plank and runs toward Farnham. As the warriors see the shattered hazelnut pass by in Robert's hands, they erupt with excitement.

One young tribesman lets out a blood-curdling shriek and heaves a small grass hoop high into the air. Before the hoop begins to fall to earth, half a dozen arrows and spears fly spontaneously from the hands of the surrounding warriors and pass through the hoop without affecting its movement. McDougall is struck dumb in amazement at the skill of these wild men who have made the very weapons they depend on for survival.

Chapter Fifty-Four

A WEEK PASSES QUIETLY AT the post with Indian relations returning to calm and order. On a blustery afternoon, once trade for the day is completed, a woman carrying a child wrapped in a woven, cedar-bark blanket walks through the yard toward the storehouse door. She passes by Frenchmen and Islanders beating furs spread over crude vertical racks for airing. A distant rumble of thunder accompanies her.

In the shed the blacksmith is fueling the forge with charcoal from an open bin. Furs are brought to the cooper's workroom nearby where they are branded with Astor's mark before being put into casks. The cooper seals the casks and the blacksmith burns Astor's mark onto each cask. Chinook Indians assist in stretching bear and elk skins with stakes on the muddy ground while a detail of Frenchmen and Islanders cut oak and make charcoal for the blacksmith.

Inside the storehouse, an old Clatsop, lame and nearly blind, limps away from the table near the fire where McDougall sits. The table is spread over with tins and phials of medicine. Local people, both Clatsop and Chinook, wait quietly in the room. They are all ages but noticeably injured, ill, or crippled.

Across the table, Robert washes the red and swollen eyes of a woman who is speaking to him. He does not understand and glances questioningly at McDougall. Their eyes meet and the older man shrugs. Robert gives the Indian a small tin of salve, gesturing that it must be applied each day as the sun rises.

The woman who crossed the yard earlier uncovers her child for McDougall. There is an abscess on the lower back. He studies the affected area then gives her a tin of the same salve Robert has just prescribed.

The afternoon remains windy and overcast as Farnham and a crew of Islanders dig up enormous turnips from the rich, muddy dark soil of the cultivated garden. Turnips and potatoes are all that survive the mice.

Women carrying large bundles of sticks make their way past them to the fort. Others haul grass from the forest as fodder for the animals that endured the voyage. The pens house a lone sheep, three goats, and thirty hogs which thrive at the post. Hunters salt a side of elk for storage.

Near the end of daylight, driftwood and sticks along the shoreline in front of the fort are gathered into two huge piles by Chinook women. McDougall lights the first pile and then the second. The cheerful, inviting flames rise high.

Comcomly arrives with his six wives and two daughters and joins McDougall. Chinook warriors and their families follow including slaves carrying wooden platters piled high with strips of salmon and sturgeon, both dried by fire.

Comcomly and McDougall together watch the gathering from the post and from the Chinook village across the river to share an evening meal around the warm communal fires. There now appears an easy but formal bond between the two men. They are pleased at the gathering of their people.

With the setting of the sun the Frenchmen dance and sing in the firelight accompanied by bagpipes or guitar. The Indians clap in rhythm to the men's songs and try to join in their dances. They are enchanted with the white man's music. McDougall, full of wine, boldly singles out Comcomly's elder daughter and teaches her to jig. He is enchanted with her.

As night comes on, the Indians form a huge circle around both fires. Men, women, and children dance to their own rhythms and keep time well together. Some of the Frenchmen and Islanders join in. McDougall cannot take his eyes from Comcomly's daughter.

Three weeks later at the pier, Mumford supervises a crew of Islanders who unload a few bundles of skins from the *Dolly*, oak for the cooper and dried salmon and sturgeon from the Chinook village for the post. Rain continues nearly every day, and the distant mountains are turning white with snow.

Inside the lodging, sprigs of hemlock with cones and clusters of bracken and hawthorn give the dining room a festive air. Year's end brings singing and drinking among the entire company. After two months of fish dried by fire, fowl is now roasting by the fire. Large succulent mussels traded by the Clatsops are boiled in soup. McDougall offers a toast. The spirit of revelry pervades the post.

Chapter Fifty-Five

A few days later across the river, McDougall, dressed in his best, walks with Comcomly from a large cedar lodge at the center of the Chinook village. The two in evident agreement are now the best of friends. McDougall signals to the men at the schooner, which is tied up at the riverbank, to begin unloading. He fusses nervously as Islanders carry a considerable quantity of blankets and colored cloth, spear tips and beads and axe heads to Comcomly's lodge.

Near the Astoria pier the following day, Comcomly and his suite disembark. McDougall, again neatly dressed, meets the chief with great attentiveness and is presented with a fine robe of otter skins. Comcomly's slaves with baskets of smoked fish for the post follow the two leaders into the stockade. The day is cold, the ground dusted with snow.

At the full moon, a ruddy cheeked and happy McDougall, wearing his handsome otter robe and carrying a new flintlock, horn and pouch, dispatches a train of Islanders to the schooner. Among other items, the Islanders transport a fifty-gallon iron kettle.

The day after, Comcomly's lodge is the scene of a festive gathering, the crowded interior a mixture of comfort, dignity, and filth. At one end of the lodging, McDougall and his bride, Comcomly's daughter in all her finery of porcupine quills, scarlet paint, and otter skins, sit in front of a fire in a sunken pit on a clean white doe skin, eating. Comcomly, with his sons beside him, Calpo proudly wearing a blue regimental coat, is opposite McDougall and overlooks the feast. The chief wears a red officer's coat awkwardly but with a bearing of self-importance. A few men from the post are on McDougall's side of the fire with a considerable number of Comcomly's relatives across from them.

Over the general din there are occasional "thuds" against a wooden tray as the six wives and younger daughter, gathered behind Comcomly and his sons and animated with excitement, gamble with large seeds. They throw them like dice into a tray.

Women slaves serve the guests. Others are busy in the smokey cooking area amidst several small fires which burn beside large watertight vessels made of woven bark. Hot stones from the fires are dropped into the boiling contents of fish soup. The women pound salmon and take down tiny smoked fish that hang in the rafters. An enormous tree, rudely carved to represent animals and birds and colored with red ochre and black, supports the roof in their quarter.

Old men along the side of the lodge, with charcoal rubbed on their faces, keep up a rhythmic chant with shafts of elk horn they clap together. A couple of thin but elusive dogs prowl for scraps of dried fish among the baskets of beads, bolts of cloth and blankets that have been recently deposited from the post.

A wooden tray of marrow bones passes amongst the guests and villagers. The marrow, a favorite food among the villagers, is pushed out with a stick and eaten heartily.

A gigantic totem, carved from a huge block of timber that supports a part of the roof, stands behind McDougall. Smaller totems nearby are draped with Comcomly's medicine bundles which include feathers and many scalps, ears, bits of shrunken skin and skulls from different animals and men.

The Belleau brothers appear at the festive lodge during the day with a message from the post for McDougall. He at first refuses to be interrupted and dismisses the urgency of their news but, as the afternoon progresses he has second thoughts and decides finally to leave his bride in comfort with her parents. Full of wine and self-importance, McDougall insists that he return with his men to the post to take care of business. He sends the Belleau brothers to alert those at the post that he is coming alone and should be met at the riverbank. Proudly and with no small degree of recklessness, he refuses all assistance from his hosts in crossing the river. The

Belleau brothers deliver his message and by evening, as the weather turns more and more blustery with the threat of rain, arrive back at the Chinook village to assist the men in returning to the post.

Across the river with the coming of darkness, Robert, Farnham and two Islanders, all holding lanterns and bracing themselves against the oncoming storm, search the riverfront outside the post. There is an occasional flash of lightning followed by peels of thunder. Robert shouts over the wind, "I told the Belleau not to go back tonight! Fools!"

"They want to prove themselves after running away!" Farnham shouts in reply.

"Aye! It's suicide to cross this river when a storm is coming!"

"Jean Baptiste is the best canoeman in the company, sir!"

"That's right! He should know better! McDougall could wait!"

Franchère intercepts them at a run carrying a lantern. "The men arrive! Quick!" He indicates upriver. "The messenger say they land on the point!"

The five men immediately set out for the point. Franchère again shouts, "McDougall is ill!"

"By God! Serves him proper!" Robert exclaims with anger. "Had the nerve to take from stores to buy himself that wife! Claimed credit against earnings!"

Ahead at the point there is confusion and movement in the darkness as two six-man canoes are unloaded. The Belleau brothers, each wearing a large pack, try to confer despite the filthy weather.

McDougall joins them, wrapped in a great skin coat and wool scarf. He is coughing. "Where's the post, you two? Get a move on!" He coughs again. "Lead the way!" The brothers immediately trudge off as Jean Baptiste shouts, "Follow us, *monsieur*!"

McDougall labors after the Frenchmen in the darkness, breathing with difficulty as the rain begins to knife down, driven by a howling wind. He shouts with effort, "Did ye send that messenger ahead as I told ye?"

Unable to hear in the storm, Jean Baptiste turns to McDougall. *"Monsieur?"*

McDougall again shouts, breathless, "Did ye send a messenger, blast ye?" He coughs and begins to shake with chill, tucks the wet scarf into his greatcoat. Not hearing him, Jean Baptiste drops back with concern and takes his arm. They move together through the wind and rain. "By God," McDougall shouts with impatience, "if they don't meet us, we'll make our own way!" He has another fit of coughing and the two men stop. He soon recovers and turns abruptly to Jean Baptiste. "Of a sudden have ye lost your wits? Don't just stand there, man!" The small party, led by the two brothers, continues through the woods in the direction of the post.

Later that night, McDougall, flushed with fever and shaking with chill, enters the crowded sitting room and moves toward the fire. His clothing is fresh and dry, and he holds a blanket around himself for extra warmth. Between the dining room and sitting room the entire company is assembled. The men are tense and silent, watching McDougall, waiting. Something is in the air.

Robert approaches with a mug of wine. He warms it with a hot poker from the fire.

McDougall stops at a chair by the fire and turns to Robert, hoarse and nearly spent. "Worst bloody night I've seen in me damnable life," he confides and sits down heavily.

Robert hands him the wine but his hands are too unsteady to hold the mug for drinking. Robert helps him take a long swallow and comments in an undertone, "A few grains of Dover's powder in this, sir. Will relieve your headache."

McDougall scowls as he wipes perspiration from his face with his bare hand. He is breathing heavily and makes no effort to reply.

Suddenly McDougall looks sharply at Robert. "Well? You call me back," he says with effort, "and this me wedding night! Ye have good reason, Mr Stuart?"

"We have word of the *Tonquin*, sir," Robert replies as McDougall eyes him closely. "A half-breed come here with a band o' Clatsops. Says he traveled aboard as interpreter. Calls himself Lamazee."

McDougall turns away and stares across the room. "Thinks he can trade this coast, our mighty Captain Thorn? And not a single officer aboard!" He glances accusingly at Robert. "Where is the *Tonquin* now? Captain Thorn make his own damn orders, aye?" He coughs. "And low on supplies and trade goods that we are!" He turns back to the fire. "Will she be long delayed?" McDougall reaches for the mug and manages a good draw without help. He seems utterly spent.

"I'd like you to hear for yourself, sir."

"More rumors!" He fidgets nervously with the blanket. "Never worth a badger's hide!" Again he coughs. "Well?" McDougall turns to him. "Where's the bloody half-breed?"

Robert motions to Franchère who is across in the dining room. Franchère approaches through the company followed closely by a man about thirty years of age who walks with evident uncertainty in the interior of the trading establishment. Lamazee is slender, a little shorter than usual but well built and dressed in buckskin trousers. He resembles the local people in manner and appearance except for the trousers, red hair and a light, freckled complexion. Although he understands English, he speaks with an accent and an unconscious admixture of French. The right forearm is tattooed *JACK RAMSAY*. Men from the dining room crowd into the sitting room as the two cross to McDougall.

Robert comments, "Says his father was an English sailor who survived shipwreck." He points out the tattooed arm. "It seems he wanted to be remembered. Did that before he died."

"Or was killed!" McDougall interjects. He watches Lamazee approach and continues, sarcastic. "We know he lived long enough to teach his lad the use of trousers." He takes another long draw of wine then eyes Lamazee suspiciously but with keen concentration as the half-breed stops before him. McDougall is no longer shivery.

"Well, Jack Ramsay," he comments vigorously, "take to the sea like your own father, aye?" The blanket falls from his shoulders as he leans forward. "And where did ye board the *Tonquin*? And where the devil is she with our winter supplies?" He coughs. "Captain Thorn trade it all, did he?" With anger rising, he continues, "Set sail for the East Indies without botherin' to again cross the bar o' this river?" Once more coughing stops him and McDougall turns away and stares hard at the fire. "Great fool of a ship's master," he pants breathlessly.

He takes another draw of wine before again turning to Lamazee. "Well? Have ye nothin' to say, man?"

The half-breed is confused by McDougall. Franchère moves forward and encourages him to speak.

Taking a step toward McDougall, Lamazee's open expression and frequent gestures reflect intense inner emotion. He relives what he tells and begins by pointing to himself. "Lamazee be goin' eighteen days *Tonquin* ship. Cap'n Torn. Mac-kay. Good English, by *gar!*" He removes a small pocket knife from under his waistband. "Mac-kay. Give Lamazee."

McDougall's expression changes. With sight of the pocket knife, he is at once deadly earnest. "Let me see that!"

Lamazee hands the knife to Robert who examines it with McDougall. There are hand-carved letters, *A M'KAY* on the wooden handle. McDougall leans toward the half-breed shaken but convinced. There is an ominous questioning in his expression. "Tell everything, Jack Ramsay," he says in a low, intense voice. "Everything, do ye hear me?"

Lamazee replaces the knife under his waistband. Nervous but animated, he continues. "*Tonquin* ship. Be goin' nord. Many village. Many skin. Good skin, by *gar*!" His expression is troubled. "No trade!" He turns to Franchère. "Cap'n Torn. He no make present! Mac-kay. He say English make present. Good trade!" He points to himself as he glances around at the company. "Lamazee say make present. Good trade! Cap'n Torn. He say no present, by *gar*!"

Fearful of retribution, he turns uneasily to McDougall. "Many skin. No trade! Chief no like *Tonquin* ship. Cap'n Torn. He no make present!"

McDougall is growing impatient. "Aye! They made no present. And where might ye say the *Tonquin* is now?"

He responds as though McDougall had not spoken. "*Tonquin* ship be goin' big village." He holds up both hands for emphasis. "Two chief. Many skin! Indian want trade! Indian cut net!" He looks again with concern at McDougall.

"Aye, the boarding net." McDougall nods impatiently. "Go on, Jack Ramsay!"

Lamazee turns with uncertainty from McDougall to Franchère. He does not want to be blamed for the ship's fate.

McDougall watches him intently. There is no longer sarcasm in his tone. "Tell everything, Jack Ramsay. I'll make ye a handsome present!"

The half-breed takes a step closer to McDougall. His red hair glowing in the firelight, he speaks as though McDougall were the only person in the room. "Cap'n Torn. He see Indian cut net. He be angry, by *gar*! Indian. He be goin' in canoe. Cap'n Torn. He take chief. Make prisoner! Next day Indian no be goin' *Tonquin* ship. Indian no trade. Mac-kay. He watch village." Lamazee gestures with both hands. "Mac-kay. He say village be angry. Give present. Village want chief. Cap'n Torn. He make present. Chief. He no want present. Chief. He be goin' village. Indian no trade!"

The amber firelight plays on Lamazee's expressive face. "Mac-kay. He say Cap'n Torn we quick be goin', by *gar*. Village be angry! Chief be angry!" He pauses, eyes wide with anticipation. "*Tonquin* ship be goin' nord. *Tonquin* ship need water." He stares past McDougall into the fire. "Woody Point. Big village. Nootka people. Strong people!"

Chapter Fifty-Six

In the vicinity of Woody Point on Clayoquot Sound overlooking a flat sandy beach at low tide, the flicker of firelight plays on a lone raven totem. The sun has set and the only sounds are of the wind and rhythm of surf that accompanies the incoming tide. In the dim evening twilight blubber from the exposed, partially stripped carcass of a gray whale, towed in and beached at high tide, is being rendered by Nootka slaves.

Stones heated by large fires are dropped into huge cedar chests and strips of blubber added to the boiling contents. One of the slaves is distracted when he glances out to sea and unexpectedly lets go his tools and runs off into the forest. A ship's lanterns soon become visible in the approaching darkness to reveal a brig under sail that has entered their protected waters.

Before long out of the forest the tall figure of Maquinna appears, a full bear skin over his shoulders. He stands alone, silently studying the ship.

At sea on the *Tonquin* quarterdeck, two sailors pay out a sounding line. By lantern light, they mark the depth. Thorn approaches, nods acknowledgement, and turns away. McKay and Lamazee stand together at the rail.

Thorn's expression is black with gloom as he surveys the forest and firelit beach in the distance through his glass then orders the anchor dropped in what appears to be a snug harbor. There is confusion on deck as Weeks supervises. McKay lends a hand with the cable.

Crewmen rush to the rail when a brightly-lit canoe is spotted approaching the *Tonquin* from shore. A few minutes later a twenty-man, solid cedar, ocean-going canoe with a high prow and fire burning on a bed of stones amidships pulls alongside the *Tonquin*. Sixteen men paddle, a big man wearing a thick fur cape stands in the bow. Other canoes from shore, also with fires burning amidships and a chief in the bow, approach the *Tonquin*. Soon seven large canoes form a tight circle around the brig which is now brightly lit.

The next afternoon, seven Nootka chiefs sit on their haunches on the quarterdeck, their faces painted in the form of a shark's jaw with red and black ochre. Their only covering is a mantle of woven bark, and each wears a small piece of jewelry, polished copper, through the nasal septum and a high cap, woven of cedar bark and dog hair, pointed at the crown and ornamented at the top with a tuft of feathers. Robertson, the steward, passes small tin cups of rum among them.

Each chief, with a surly expression, snatches the proffered gift and immediately drinks. They like the spirits. Maquinna stands before them eyeing Thorn with a stern air of natural, unaffected curiosity. His face is completely black and covered with glittering sand, his long hair oiled, tied at the top of his head and powdered with white down. A full mustache and goatee complete the imposing facial ornament. He wears a cloak of black sea otter skins which reaches to his knees. Tiny bone ornaments decorate his ears as do bracelets of bone on both arms.

Thorn raises his cup to the formidable figure without looking him in the eye, not realizing that Maquinna's eyes are riveted to his. The two men drink. McKay watches their every move from the rail.

Thorn sits and gestures to McKay and Lamazee to join him at the same time he offers a chair to Maquinna. The chief refuses and sits on his haunches as the other chiefs have done. He motions and one of them rises. At the same time a slave comes forward carrying a brace of live, wild ducks.

The chief presents the ducks to Thorn who accepts, hands them to McKay and, in return, offers the chief a blanket of wool. The chief snatches the blanket from Thorn with a surly expression. Thorn is taken aback, becomes agitated toward the chief but Lamazee quickly says something to Thorn and he nods and appears to relax.

A second chief rises and approaches Thorn. He carries a small bark parcel. The chief opens the parcel and holds it out to Thorn who starts at the gift and, momentarily stunned, stares in utter disbelief. A dried human hand rests on the bark covering. Thorn's eyes shift venomously to the chief as he abruptly rises from his chair and, shaking with disgust, walks away, leaving the chief holding the parcel.

The chief steps back at the insult, sudden anger in his eyes. He puts his hand to his throat as he stares, unflinching, after Thorn. Lamazee is concerned and speaks to McKay who steps forward and accepts the parcel.

The following morning all is quiet along the densely forested shoreline. Blubber continues to be rendered from the beached whale but the lodges of a sprawling village along the sound are not visible from the sea. Although the boarding net to control access to the deck has been set, when, to everyone's puzzlement, no Indians show for trade, the net is taken down and empty water casks are lowered into a longboat. McKay consults with Lamazee before both swing over the rail to join the men going ashore. McKay will seek out a chief who invited him to his lodge the day before.

A reluctant Robertson and a sailor lower themselves into the Captain's pinnace where two seamen await them with Thorn's linen which is to be washed in fresh water ashore. Thorn gives final instructions, but the stark reception from the villagers is evident in the crew's uneasiness to go ashore. Such unexpected behavior augurs an evil omen to which their suggestive imaginations play. As a precaution, Robertson is ordered to carry a musket.

The next day, McKay, sitting on a stump inside a lodge, is fully at ease with the chief's family after spending the night on a bed of sea otter skins. The chief who presented the ducks onboard ship and his four young sons surround McKay in fascination while he holds a compass before them and, with movement of his pocket knife, causes the needle to turn at will without touching the compass.

The oldest of the boys is especially impressed and remains before McKay captivated in admiration. McKay reaches out to the boy and puts him on his knee. With his pocket knife, he removes the metal buttons from his coat, strings them, and hangs them around the boy's neck. The child immediately takes hold of his new treasure. McKay's attention to his son pleases the chief.

By midafternoon, the main deck of the *Tonquin* becomes crowded with villagers who come aboard to trade but they also mill about, endlessly curious, and take up whatever is not fastened down. On the main deck a brisk trade is in progress. As Thorn paces along the rail, a villager removes a hand spike to examine. Thorn grabs the spike and returns toward the quarterdeck. But a chief stops him holding out a musket with a broken lock. Thorn hands the piece to Weeks in a temper and orders the deck cleared.

Later that afternoon on shore, Robertson gives a handful of glass beads each to a couple of slaves whose only covering is a cedar bark skirt. The women have finished washing a portion of Thorn's linen and he dismisses them and then directs two of the sailors with arm loads of clean linen toward the longboat. The third sailor is to await his return with a slave who is completing her portion of the wash. The three men board the longboat, push off into the sound and almost at once are accosted by native canoes.

Painted in red and black, these young tribesmen carry spears tipped with pointed mussel shell. Their canoes draw confidently close to the longboat forcing the two seamen to stop rowing. One canoe comes alongside as if to challenge them and the young warriors bang pointed paddles aggressively against the gunwale of the longboat. When Robertson brandishes the musket, the canoes withdraw and the seamen continue toward the *Tonquin* which is anchored in the sound less than half a mile distant.

The sailor on shore is aroused by the nearly naked woman as she bends over Thorn's linen. He approaches, roughly fumbles with her pendulous bosoms and would maneuver to mount her from behind but she rejects his crude, lazy sensuality, pushes him off and continues the washing.

Late in the afternoon with no boarding net in place, a large canoe carrying twenty Indians appears alongside with skins to trade. The men on watch let them board. Soon a second and a third canoe appear, also with furs to trade. Thorn is in his cabin as the *Tonquin* main deck becomes thronged with men desiring to trade. Weeks attempts to supervise although trade goods are in growing disarray. Thorn appears on the quarterdeck, paces indecisively, scans the shoreline with his glass, and giving a look of disgust at the crowded and disorderly main deck, leaves Weeks to cope and returns to his cabin.

Inside the Nootka lodge, McKay sits cross-legged on the ground beside the chief and his principal wife. Before them is a long wooden tray of steaming herring spawn. They eat with their fingers. Lamazee eats at a separate tray with the chief's four sons. A fine raven totem is prominent in the dense, smokey atmosphere of the lodge.

To one side, mats are removed from clams that have been steaming on leaves over hot rocks and served. When the tray is taken away, the chief's oldest son approaches McKay with a bag of white down. The boy sprinkles down over his new friend in a manner to represent the falling of snow. McKay is flattered, the chief and his wife amused. Lamazee is pleased. They have been accepted into the family.

At sunset, and still with no boarding net in place, McKay and Lamazee climb aboard the *Tonquin*. McKay is alarmed at the disorder and recognizes that the villagers on deck more than outnumber the ship's crew. Immediately he sends Lamazee aft to alert the captain. Bruslé joins McKay and the two move quickly to assist Weeks. The sailors hoist the longboat.

From the quarterdeck, Thorn spots McKay and starts toward him but the chief who gave him the broken musket earlier in the day seeks the musket. Thorn motions the man to move aside but instead, the chief holds out an otter skin. Thorn ignores him and tries to pass, but the chief refuses to yield, insisting on the musket in exchange for the otter skin. Thorn suddenly grabs the skin and roughly shoves it into the man's face as he again attempts to pass. The chief grabs Thorn's arm in a vice-like grip at the same instant raising a piercing shriek.

At once, turmoil breaks out over the entire deck. Villagers drop their skins. Clubs and tomahawks are drawn and the sailors set upon. A few of the crew manage to leap into the rigging.

Onshore the washing is completed. The sailor continues to eye the woman as she bends over gathering clean linen. A violent urge to bed down with her drives him and he moves behind, without ceremony drops his pants and holding her naked back forward presses his legs between hers, pulls the voluptuous thighs toward him and grasping her, enters from behind. He copulates hard and fast and almost at once is finished. Rid of the sudden rush and without acknowledging the object of his pleasure, he sits back on the ground and leans against a tree to catch his breath.

The *Tonquin* is now surrounded by canoes as natives freely climb aboard and numbers of canoes from shore approach. Villagers shriek with triumph when Bruslé's lifeless body is flung from the deck overboard.

On the quarterdeck, Thorn, with jacket ripped and face bleeding, holds three natives at bay with a pocket knife. He is fighting for his life.

McKay defends himself against two men but is clubbed from behind by a third. He falls unconscious to the deck and is immediately set upon. Lamazee jumps over the rail into the sea. He is picked up by a canoe of women and offers himself as a slave. They hide him under cedar mats as villagers freely swarm up the side and onto the *Tonquin* deck. Another sailor's body is flung to the sea as the natives completely overrun the ship.

On shore, the woman has moved away from the clean linen and positions herself behind the sailor. Facing the sea she listens intently to a rising chant in the distance. The sun is below the horizon as she removes a piece of flint from her hair, silently approaches the man and without warning strikes a deep gash across his throat. This slave of the Nootka people begins to chant and completely ignores the gasping seaman who struggles to rise, reaches out and sways unsteadily then falls over, bleeding profusely on the ground. Immediately she crosses to the village of cedar plank lodges where women are scampering to the roofs to join other women who chant and beat the roof planks rhythmically with sticks.

Still chanting, the slave walks past the village to the beach, joins other women in a canoe and pushes off into the sound. Many women from the village take canoes through the light surf toward the ship. They paddle with energy, keeping rhythm to their chant of triumph. Except for some movement of torches on deck, the ship appears quiet where it is anchored.

Inside the hold, villagers with torches swarm through the hatchways unopposed. They ransack the hold, breaking open casks to remove beads and knives and everything they lay hands on. One villager sets a burning torch on a large keg marked in red, *LG POWDER — DANGER*, and begins hacking into an identical keg next to it with his tomahawk.

The women continue to chant as they paddle toward the *Tonquin*, the movement of torches on deck clearly visible. Without warning, the ship suddenly explodes, disintegrating in an enormous ball of flame and smoke, throwing body parts and pieces of timber and metal in every direction.

All is silent as the water settles and the smoke clears. Where the ship once floated, a few bits of burning timber bob on the sea.

Epilogue

LATE THE SAME DAY we left Franchère and Lanier in the tavern, they walked together down Wall Street toward the New York waterfront with the sun descending to the west and bare masts of tall ships extended above the buildings and filling the horizon ahead. It was 1848 and Lanier took notes as Franchère continued his narrative.

"The Nootka tribe lost over two hundred of its people in that unforgettable massacre. Not one of the twenty-three men aboard the *Tonquin* escaped, only the half-breed, Jack Ramsay."

As they approached the waterfront, vendors with loaded handcarts, hawkers with horse and cart and drays heavy with supplies and pulled by mules and horses crowded the roadway. "As for the overland expedition of the enterprise," Franchère said, turning to Lanier, "the plan was to meet at the mouth of the Columbia to build the post."

"The overland group was led by a Mr Hunt of St. Louis?"

"Wilson Price Hunt was a fur trader. He headed the overland expedition and was to be in charge of the post on the Columbia. *Monsieur* Astor put great confidence in him, but until he agreed to join the enterprise in 1809 at the age of twenty-six, he had almost no experience of wilderness travel and little knowledge of Indians. Ramsay Crooks, Donald McKenzie, Robert McClellan, also partners, and John Reed, a clerk, all men of great experience in the trade, traveled with him overland. John Day, a Virginian, met the party on the Missouri River and joined the expedition as a hunter."

"They followed the route of Lewis and Clark?"

"They did not proceed along the upper Missouri where the buffalo range as Lewis and Clark had done. Instead, to avoid the Indians north of the Yellowstone River who had been so troublesome to Lewis and Clark, sixty-two well-armed men left the Missouri River, which they had followed from their encampment above St. Louis, and headed west across the Big Horn Mountains into unexplored country. Too late in the season to turn back, they discovered there was not game enough to support so many together on the route they had chosen. Eventually they divided into three smaller groups along the Snake River midway through the Rocky Mountains and arrived separately at Fort Astoria during the winter and spring of 1812. The journey involved considerable suffering and some loss of life. A few of the men immediately gave up their shares and wished to return to St. Louis."

A black, nine hundred-ton clipper ship loomed large as the two men entered South Street on the East River and passed near the ship's immense, gilded Chinese dragon figurehead.

Franchère continued. "The end of June that year, in 1812, Robert Stuart, carrying important papers informing *Monsieur* Astor of the arrival of both expeditions, their success in the inland trade, and the loss of the *Tonquin*, led a small group of men overland through the Louisiana back to St. Louis. They went even further south to avoid the Indians of the Yellowstone and discovered the South Pass in the Rocky Mountains. Their route is now the *Oregon Trail* followed by wagon trains that travel westward to the Willamette Valley."

"Didn't young Stuart marry the daughter of one of Astor's associates?"

"He married Elizabeth Sullivan shortly after his return to New York."

"In the meantime," Lanier comments, "the War of 1812 broke out with England."

"After Robert Stuart had set out for St. Louis, during that summer of 1812, we received word of the war when David Stuart made contact with North West Company traders inland. He brought to Astoria news of President Madison's proclamation along with his winter packs of furs. The following year, with American ports blockaded, making it unlikely that *Monsieur* Astor would be able to send supplies to the Columbia River, Duncan McDougall, assuming that all would be lost if the British captured Astoria, sold the fort and its stock of furs to the North West Company for one-fifth its value. One of the terms of sale was that he be made a partner. The North West Company sent an overland brigade of seventy-five men led by John Stuart and Joseph McGillivray to Fort Astoria at the mouth of the Columbia in October 1813 to complete the sale.

"Before that year had ended, the British sloop *Raccoon* anchored in the river with orders to seize and destroy the American establishment. But since it had become the property of the North West Company, her captain instead raised a Union Jack to the top of the staff and taking a bottle of Madeira wine, smashed it against the pole. He proclaimed in a loud voice that he took possession of the establishment and the country in the name of His Britannic Majesty and named the post Fort George."

Franchère stopped and faced Lanier. "I vividly recall the day, *monsieur*. I was present, and in that moment all our hopes were dashed. Three cheers were given and three rounds of musketry fired by the British on shore and three rounds of artillery answered by the ship. Of course, there was no American naval vessel to oppose them."

They continued along the waterfront as Franchère spoke. "Duncan McDougall acted contrary to the wish of David Stuart and *Monsieur* Hunt who were against the sale. By then, with additional men from the overland expedition, we had not only two inland posts on the Okanagan River, but a post on the Willamette and one on the Spokane, all of which yielded a rich return in furs, far more than we expected. Over the first winter, for example, with trade goods worth thirty-five pounds sterling, Alexander Ross on the Okanagan procured more than fifteen hundred prime beaver pelts with a value of over two thousand pounds sterling on the China market. David Stuart saw no difficulty in storing our furs inland until after the war."

"Why did Hunt allow the sale?"

"He was away from Astoria on the *Beaver*, one of *Monsieur* Astor's ships to supply the post. In fact, it was the *Beaver* that confirmed the loss of the *Tonquin*. Trading ships from the Northwest Coast had brought word of her destruction to the Sandwich Islands before the *Beaver*'s arrival. The partners agreed that *Monsieur* Hunt should sail north to identify places for coastal trade and to establish contact with the Russians at Sitka. You must keep in mind, Fort Astoria was to be a depot for trade not only across the continent but on the coast as well. When the *Tonquin* was lost, with her went all our knowledge of the Northwest Coast.

"*Monsieur* Hunt was deeply troubled and extremely critical when he returned to find Fort Astoria under the British flag and in foreign hands. He called all the clerks before him and expressed his regret that so much talent and effort had been employed to no purpose and `thrown to the winds,' as he put it. I recall those very words."

Lanier looked up from his pad. "I wonder what Astor thought."

The two men stopped and Franchère again turned to Lanier. "He received forty thousand dollars in bills payable at Montreal for approximately two hundred thousand dollars worth of furs. He told me, *monsieur*, he would have rather the fort surrendered to a British frigate than have the confidence he placed in his own partner misused. But he did not regret the enterprise. Had it not been for his partner selling out, he believed he would have been most richly rewarded.

"David Stuart and many of us remained loyal to *Monsieur* Astor and we left Fort George together in the spring of 1814. On the return trip to Montreal one of our canoes struck a rock in the Athabasca River and broke up. The men had to swim to save themselves and unfortunately Olivier Lapensée drowned."

"How many were killed in the enterprise?"

"In all, sixty-three men lost their lives."

They continued walking. "Michel Laframboise stayed on at the fort as guide and trapper. A few years ago, he bought a farm in the Willamette Valley where he has settled."

"There was that other clerk you mentioned, Russell Farnham."

"Farnham," Franchère smiled, responding with feeling. "He was an extraordinary man! After the sale of the fort, he left by ship with *Monsieur* Hunt in 1814 carrying a satchel of money and papers for *Monsieur* Astor. To avoid capture by the British he was landed on the coast of Russia, at Kamchatka. We were still at war. That young man accomplished something to my knowledge no other man has done: he walked *alone* across Siberia, across the heart of the Russian continent, to Copenhagen. He suffered terribly from hunger, more than any of us on the expedition could imagine. In fact, to stay alive, he had to eat his own shoe leather. The journey required over two years, but he safely delivered the satchel to *Monsieur* Astor in New York."

Lanier's response was a blank stare. He had not been listening but, rather, was absorbed in his own thoughts. He stopped walking and looked down at his note pad, again scribbling. "The War of 1812 must have cost Astor a fortune," he threw out, half to himself.

"He lost probably one-half million of dollars with the Pacific Fur Company," Franchère replied. "The success of Fort Astoria was within our grasp and we could not hold it. But he was lucky, *monsieur*. Not one of his ships was captured during the war, and the price of tea doubled. In fact, he made an immense fortune."

"Where did Astor's plan for a post on the West Coast and trade with China come from, I wonder."

"He told me he got the idea from his old friend in Montreal, Alexander Henry." Franchère weighed the point. "I believe *Monsieur* Astor was at his best when carrying out the ideas of other men. He always learned from their successes and failures."

The two men resumed walking. "I'm convinced the Pacific Fur Company was a dead loss, sir," Lanier suddenly declared with confidence.

"No, *monsieur*," Franchère disagreed. "Fort Astoria was the only American settlement on the Pacific Coast. We were overcome by circumstances, that is true, but *Monsieur* Astor's enterprise strengthened America's claim for the Oregon. All the region we occupied on the Columbia, Willamette, Spokane and Okanagan rivers was restored by the British under the Treaty of Ghent after the War of 1812. It would become the Oregon Territory. The United States otherwise had little claim to the West Coast of this continent."

Franchère pondered for a moment then continued. "One of life's prizes is to gain the respect of our peers. *Monsieur* Astor achieved that with his bold plan."

"But Astoria lost money," Lanier repeated. "Duncan McDougall was the only one to profit from Astor's gamble. He became a partner in the North West Company."

"We all were disappointed. The risks we understood too late. But to be frank, *monsieur*, I shudder to think I might have missed that enterprise."

"Are you serious?" Lanier was uncomprehending.

"Not every man is appointed by Providence to traverse the wild regions of America. The unknown was compelling to us, a challenge to our youth. We were fearless, after all, and eager to reach out. We believed we would make our fortunes. But experience forces one to learn one's place. This is not easy to explain, *monsieur*."

They stopped at a busy wharf beside a poster advertising the voyage of the clipper ship *Sea Witch* to the port of Valparaiso. Franchère reflected a moment then spoke from deep within himself. "When you face the unknown, you seek the measure of the world in which you live, but most important, you find the measure of yourself."

Lanier closed his note pad. The story was his and he no longer listened. Instead, the men scampering up the ratlines and onto yardarms to cast off gaskets aboard the immense vessel fascinated him. Forward and aft gangways were being removed and lines cast off with preparations for departure underway. She was wholly under canvas and the braces, yardarms and sails were worked by muscle alone. A sea chanty began as the *Sea Witch* eased from the wharf and slowly turned before the wind.

Yardarms were hoisted, sheets fell and the chanty faded with the distance as the two men watched her embark on the voyage ahead. While the sun rested near the horizon, the four-masted clipper, unmatched in symmetry and magnificence, left the roadstead going full before the wind. The chanty could no longer be heard but the young seamen vigorously set sail as they began their journey beyond the great water.

The End

CPSIA information can be obtained
at www.ICGtesting.com
Printed in the USA
FSOW01n0238290415
6789FS